Hickory Flat Public Library
2740 East Cherokee Drive
Canton, Georgia 30115

MRS. LEE
AND
MRS. GRAY

Center Point
Large Print

Also by Dorothy Love and available from
Center Point Large Print:

A Respectable Actress
The Bracelet

MRS. LEE
AND
MRS. GRAY

DOROTHY
LOVE

CENTER POINT LARGE PRINT
THORNDIKE, MAINE

Library of Congress Cataloging-in-Publication Data

Names: Love, Dorothy, 1949– author.
Title: Mrs. Lee and Mrs. Gray / Dorothy Love.
Description: Center Point Large Print edition. | Thorndike, Maine :
Center Point Large Print, 2016.
Identifiers: LCCN 2016018556 | ISBN 9781683240662
    (hardcover : alk. paper)
Subjects: LCSH: Lee, Mary Randolph Custis, 1807-1873—Fiction. |
African American women—Fiction. | Slaves—United States—Fiction. |
Female friendship—Fiction. | United States—History—19th century—
Fiction. | Large type books. | GSAFD: Historical fiction. | Biographical
fiction.
Classification: LCC PS3562.O8387 M77 2016b | DDC 813/.54—dc23
LC record available at https://lccn.loc.gov/2016018556

For Mary and Selina.
You are not forgotten.

True friendship is a plant of slow growth
and must undergo and withstand
the shocks of adversity before
it is entitled to the appellation.

—George Washington

★ 1 ★

MARY CUSTIS LEE

1873

There was a time when Arlington was a magical place, enchanted and inviolate, the place where all that was beautiful in my world began.

I grew up amid its thousand acres of rolling green hills and pleasant shades, my hands stained with the rust-brown soil of Virginia and branded by the oil of roses from hot summer days working in the gardens with my mother.

A great-granddaughter of Martha Washington, I learned reverence for my family's storied history as soon as I could talk. By the age of eight, I could recite the particulars of the Battle of Trenton and recount details of the bitter winter at Valley Forge. By twelve, I had committed to memory substantial portions of General Washington's writings, and I delighted in showing off my knowledge to the constant stream of politicians, poets, and artists who arrived by carriage or boat or horseback to dine at my father's table. A man of wide interests and legendary hospitality, he enjoyed entertaining the obscure and the famous in equal measure, so long as they were interesting. By the age of seventeen, I had broken bread with horse traders, newspapermen, soldiers, and tobacco farmers—and with such public figures as Sam Houston, Washington Irving, and Lafayette.

After my daily lessons in French, Greek, and Latin, I was free to plunder my father's studio, a thrilling and amusing hodgepodge of books, maps, mementos, and half-finished paintings and plays. I spent hours poring over his volumes of botany, history, and poetry while General Washington kept watch from his portrait above the fireplace mantel. On rainy afternoons I sprawled on the floor with paints and canvas, making sketches of flowers and people and the cats that roamed the house.

My father, George Washington Parke Custis, inherited a number of slaves from his father's estate, sixty of whom lived at Arlington in quarters that stretched from the backyard and along the river to the fields of corn and winter wheat. I knew each of them by name, and they would pause in their various occupations to exchange a greeting whenever I happened by. I spent hours on horseback roaming the silent loveliness of the woods and fields, which were full of foxes, rabbits, and deer. I waded in the cold streams that meandered through dense thickets. I captured butterflies and studied the beetles inching their way along the forest floor. When I grew tired I stopped to rest at our little chapel nestled in a grove of trees. Even now, it is pleasant to recall the sound of voices lifted in song that lingered in the evening air like a benediction.

How long ago it seems. How innocent I was of the ways in which life could wind. I couldn't have imagined that one day this dear old house, the scene of so many happy hours, would be stolen from me, trampled by a lawless foe, never again to shelter me and mine.

★ 2 ★
MARY

1827

The forty-mile journey from Arlington to the home of my mother's cousins in Fauquier consumed an entire day. My mother usually accompanied me on visits to her cousin Thomas Turner's family, but she was fighting a cough that spring. I was nineteen, old enough to make the trip without her, so it was Eleanor, affectionately called Old Nurse because she had looked after Papa and then me from our earliest childhoods, who sat with me in the carriage, her sewing on her lap, our lunch basket at her feet.

We left Arlington before sunrise, crossing the dark river that shimmered beneath a waxing moon, meandering eastward past the sleeping farms of Fairfax and Chantilly before turning north to

Kinloch, every mile punctuated by Eleanor's complaints about the bumpy ride, her aching bones, and the gathering heat. It was quite a relief when through the deepening twilight the house came into view.

Though the Turner place was not to my eye as lovely as Arlington, it was pleasantly situated on a rise that afforded a view of meadows that in spring were thick with wildflowers, and beyond, acres of rich green fields that spread out in all directions.

My cousins spilled from the house to greet me. Old Nurse climbed stiffly from the carriage and trailed me up the steps and onto the porch while Daniel began unloading my trunks.

"Mary Anna." Cousin Elizabeth, Thomas's wife, squeezed my hands. "Welcome, child. We've missed you."

I kissed her cheek. "Mother sends her love. She said to tell you she hopes to come out later on, when she feels better."

Thomas, tall and spare, consulted his watch. "It's nearly seven. You must be famished by now."

Caroline, who had recently turned eight years old, said, "Papa, we are all famished." She turned her dark eyes on me. "We have been waiting forever, Mary. We thought you would never get here."

"It was a long trip." I smiled and embraced my frank young cousin. "Goodness, you've grown so much since last summer."

"I know it. Almost two inches."

"Mary!" Eliza, two years younger than Caroline, launched herself into my arms. "Guess what?"

"What?"

"No, you have to guess."

"Well, you must give me some clue."

"We have a new animal in the barn. Guess what it is."

"A kitten?"

"Bigger."

"A puppy?"

"Bigger."

"Bigger than a puppy? Let's see. Do you have an elephant hiding in your barn, Eliza Turner?"

She giggled. "It's a foal. Papa says he's a real beauty and I get to name him."

I set her on her feet and we all went inside. Daniel carried my trunks up to my usual room. Old Nurse went with him to unpack my dresses.

Elizabeth herded us to the table and rang for Wilhelmina, who had presided over Kinloch's dining room for as long as I could remember, and supper was served.

After asking for the news from home, Thomas described a series of agricultural talks he had heard at last year's lyceum in Massachusetts. Elizabeth asked after Mother and Papa. Caroline and Eliza finally nodded off and were taken up to bed by their nurse. The boys, Edward and Henry, badgered their father to continue his reading of *The Last of the Mohicans*.

"I'm afraid my sons have nothing but Indians on their minds these days," Elizabeth said when Wilhelmina had removed the last of the dishes.

"It's the best book there ever was," Edward said. At eleven years old, he was the younger of the two boys and, like his father, tall and thin, with a shock of brown hair and lively eyes. "Have you read it, Cousin Mary?"

"I have not. But you can tell me about it later, when I am not so sleepy. Right now I don't think I can stay awake for another minute."

"Go on up to bed, Mary," Elizabeth said. "Let me know if there is anything you need."

Old Nurse had prepared my bed and taken out my nightdress and hairbrush before retiring to the little alcove off my bedroom. I washed my face and hands, brushed my hair, and climbed into bed, where I slept like the dead until the crowing of the rooster woke me at sunrise. Old Nurse was still asleep.

I dressed quietly and went downstairs. No one was stirring except Thomas, who was in his library surrounded by crates of books.

"Mary. There you are." He picked up a book, glanced at it, and set it aside. "The boys are off somewhere, and Elizabeth has taken the girls down to the stables to see the new foal. They shouldn't be long. Are you hungry?"

"Not a bit. I ate too much at supper last night."

He nodded in that quiet way of his and poked through another crate.

I looked over his shoulder. "A new shipment of books?"

"Just the opposite, I'm afraid. The shelves are overflowing, and I need to make room for newer works. Some of these are headed for the trash heap, sorry to say."

"Oh, may I have them?"

He looked up, surprised. "I suppose so. But I don't think you will find much that interests you. Elizabeth tells me you and your mother are very fond of novels."

"Yes, but there might be something I can use for my schoolroom."

He frowned. "So the two of you are still teaching your servants to read?"

I ignored the disapproval in his eyes. "We are. I have seven pupils at present, five girls and two boys." I peered into the crates. "Maybe there is something in here to hold their attention. The girls are very keen to master their lessons, but the boys are harder to impress."

"A dangerous business, educating slaves when nothing good can come of it." He set down the book he was holding, a large volume bound in mustard-yellow leather. "The more they know, the more discontented they become."

"Papa says the same thing, but then he admits that slavery will end one day. Maybe sooner than we think. Mother and I want the children of Arlington to be prepared for it."

He nodded, tight-lipped. "I'll leave you to it then."

I rolled up my sleeves and poked through the crates. Most of the books were boring tomes: instruction on agricultural practices, collections of sermons, political treatises. Some were so moldered they fell apart in my hands. Some were missing pages. I was about to give up on finding anything useful when I opened a thick book bound in red leather and found beautiful illustrations of flowers and wildlife. Another book contained poems for children, and a third was a book about sailing ships. These three I set aside for my schoolroom.

I was looking through another crate in search of more treasures when I heard the sound of a horse approaching. I looked out the window, then quickly brushed the dust from my skirt and ran out to the porch just as the rider dismounted and handed his reins to the stable boy.

"Robert Edward Lee, what a happy sight!" I couldn't hide my joy at seeing my favorite cousin. We had been childhood playmates and the closest of confidants before he left for his studies at West Point. Cadets were allowed only a single leave at the end of their second year, and the separation seemed interminable.

"Hello, Molly," he said, using my old childhood

nickname. He came up the steps and clasped my hands tightly. "I cannot tell you how long I have waited for this day."

We went into the house together. Except for the servants, we were alone.

"I went first to Arlington, and your mother told me you were here," he said. "I came as soon as I could."

"I'm glad you did," I said. "Have you had any breakfast?"

"No, but I don't want anything." He set his leather hat on the table in the parlor. "All I could think about these past weeks was how much I wanted to walk with you and read with you and ride with you."

"So you said in your letters."

Robert had been an extraordinarily handsome boy, and in his two-year absence he had matured into a strong and handsome man.

"I missed you, Cousin."

"Splendid. Perhaps I can make you forget those other beaux who danced attendance on you while I was away."

"I wouldn't call them beaux, exactly. And anyway, they have all absconded now."

He smiled, seemingly relieved. "What have you been doing?"

I told him about my book-sorting project and led him into the library to see for himself.

"You've grown up since I've been gone," he

said. "You seem so much more serious now."

"Maybe I am." I was not very good at sharing my innermost thoughts, but there in the Turners' library with dust motes swirling in the beams of sunlight streaming through the tall windows, I told Robert how very badly I wanted to make a contribution to something that mattered. "After all, what is life worth if you can't accomplish in it something for the benefit of others? Especially those who are so entirely dependent upon our will and pleasure."

"Your mother mentioned that you two are still working on behalf of the colonization society."

"Yes, but progress is difficult when we are obliged to *purchase* slaves in order to free them. And then there is the cost of their passage to Liberia."

I nattered on, because suddenly it had become important to me that he understand. I leaned on the corner of Thomas's desk. "The children have nothing that's only theirs, and the fact of it is truly shameful. An education, however rudimentary, is something that no one can take away from them, whether they choose to go to Liberia or not. And one day when—"

He smiled then.

"Are you laughing at me?"

"Of course not. I was thinking how pretty you look in that green dress."

16

"Oh." For the first time in my life I felt shy around him.

"And you have changed your hair too. It's very becoming."

"Mother says ringlets are all the rage these days. I take her word for it."

"So you are still not interested in fashion."

"Not in the least."

Elizabeth and her girls returned from their visit to the foal then, exclaiming over Robert and asking a thousand questions about his life at West Point. By the time Thomas and the boys returned, it was too late for breakfast, but presently an early dinner was set before us, during which Robert described his studies and his plans to become a member of the U.S. Army Corps of Engineers.

Wilhelmina came in with dessert—a strawberry cake with boiled icing. Robert ate two pieces, and after a polite interval in the parlor he caught my eye.

"What do you say, Mary? Shall we go riding?"

We set out across the meadow at a smart canter, giving the horses their lead. We forded a shallow stream and passed through a forest thick with old oaks clothed in summer green.

I was so happy to see Robert I could have ridden with him all day, listening to his tales of life at West Point, but after an hour the sun disappeared and black clouds boiled up in the distance.

"We ought to head back," Robert said, and we turned our mounts for home.

But the sky suddenly opened and we were caught in a downpour. We sheltered beneath a stand of old oaks. Raindrops glittered in the gusts of warm, humid air that blew against our faces. A low rumble of thunder startled my little mare, and Robert reached for my reins.

Our fingers touched. His eyes met mine and held, and all at once everything changed, and I *knew*.

The storm slackened and we rode home. Leaving our horses to the stable boy, we went inside, laughing together and shaking off the rain.

Supper that night was a feast to welcome Robert home. Everything was delicious, but I was too jittery, remembering the touch of his hand on mine. I pushed my food around on my plate, listening to the Turner clan chatter on about the new foal, all the while wondering how on earth I could continue to breathe if Robert did not return my tender feelings.

Thomas said something that made everyone laugh. Robert caught my eye across the candlelit table and smiled. And I saw then—to my great delight—that he too understood we were meant for each other.

I knew he couldn't declare himself for a long while yet. He still had two more years at West Point, and after that the challenge of his first posting as an army engineer. But on that warm May evening at Kinloch, I was as happy as I had ever been. One day Robert Lee would be mine.

Three years later

He proposed marriage over a plate of fruitcake.

It was summer and Arlington was in its full beauty. The broad green lawn sloped gently toward the shimmering Potomac. The gardens brimmed with myrtle and roses and lilac. Children and dogs played among the trees. A family of orange cats lay sunning themselves on the front steps.

Robert was visiting, and we had spent every moment since his arrival walking by the river or talking politics with my father. Following Sunday services, Papa read to us from the new play he was writing. After that we enjoyed an hour of listening to Robert reading aloud a novel by Sir Walter Scott.

When he reached the end of the chapter, Mother caught my eye and said in that sweet, gentle way of hers, "Mary dear, perhaps Cousin Robert could use some refreshments after such a long reading."

Her smile was an unspoken apology for the disagreement we'd had earlier that morning after church. I had changed into an old yellow calico dress with a frayed hem instead of the new apricot silk she had recently made for me. To keep the peace I'd donned the silk, but during dinner I treated her with cool detachment to underscore my displeasure.

Then Robert had arrived, impeccably attired as always, and Mother had sent me a look that plainly said, *See, I have saved you from embarrassment.*

Now I returned her smile, for it was impossible to remain at odds with someone of such refinement and gentleness. Mother was a quiet-spoken woman whom nothing ever defeated, a model of piety and parental love. I despaired of ever becoming her equal.

"I could do with something to eat." Robert set his book on the empty chair next to mine.

I went into the dining room to see what was available, and he soon followed. As I finished cutting the fruitcake I'd found on the sideboard, I felt his arm slide around my waist. Drawing me close, he said without preamble, "Molly, will you be my wife?"

My hand trembled so terribly I feared I'd drop the knife. I set it down and turned to face him and was struck anew by his beauty. He was nearly six feet tall, broad shouldered, with a military bearing that made him seem important whenever he entered a room. His hair was thick and dark. His eyes were deep brown and shining with the love that had been slowly growing between us nearly all our lives. I had dreamed of this moment since that magical summer at Kinloch, for I was drawn to him as sunflowers turn toward the sun.

But I had been told all too often that I was too unrestrained in my speech and too unconventional in my conduct. Also, plain and dull. Although I was not completely without male attention, my mother, when she thought I was out of earshot, confided to my aunts and her friends that she as worried about my matrimonial prospects. "Wherever will we find someone suitable for Mary?" was her constant refrain.

Now the perfect suitor was standing in my dining room holding a plate of fruitcake, waiting for an answer.

Yet as deeply as I cared for Robert, I wondered how I could keep faith with the promise I'd made to improve myself while learning to be a wife to an army officer and a mother to the children who were sure to come.

And I worried about my little scholars, particularly Selina Norris. She was only eight years old, whip smart and eager to learn. Each week she came faithfully to my schoolroom, her stubby fingers clutching her book, her eyes blazing with curiosity and excitement. How could I disappoint such a willing pupil?

And then there was Papa. While my relieved mother would be delighted to welcome Robert into our family, I worried that my father might not approve the match. Though Robert was from a fine old Virginia family, his father had been involved in scandalous brawls and shady financial schemes, and had gone to debtors' prison before abandoning his family for good. Everyone in our vast and far-flung clan of aunts, uncles, and cousins knew all about Lighthorse Harry Lee.

I was the sole heir to Arlington and its treasures from President Washington's Mount Vernon estate. All of my father's other holdings—houses, fields, mills, and slaves—would one day pass to my children. Papa would not allow my future and the future of my inheritance to fall into the wrong hands.

"Well, Molly?" Robert was still waiting, an expectant smile on his face. "Will you have me?"

Looking into his warm and hopeful eyes on that balmy June afternoon, I knew—despite my worries—what my answer must be. "Yes, Robert. I will."

★ 3 ★

SELINA NORRIS GRAY

1831

It was freezing cold in the barn, and I leaned upside Lottie as I milked her. Seemed like she enjoyed the warmth her own self. She stood still while I squirted milk into the pail. Ever' so often she'd look back over her shoulder and blink her eyes like she was asking me how much longer did she have to stand there. I just laughed at her. I had loved Lottie since she was a calf. Milking her twice a day was the chore I liked best. It smelled good inside the barn. Like milk and straw and leather mixed together.

I finished the milking and patted Lottie's sides and let myself out. I was careful not to spill the milk. Mister Custis never paid too much attention to us unless we broke one of his rules. One of them was don't spill anything. Another one was don't break anything. Don't steal. Don't sass the missus. It was a lot to remember even for grown folks, and I wasn't even nine years old yet.

I started up the path and there was Ephraim. He helped Missus Custis in her gardens, but now it was winter. Too early for planting flowers, so he was working with Luther in the smokehouse tending to hams and bacon and such. He was tall as a tree and so thin you'd miss him if he was to be walking toward you sideways. When the weather was warm he would go up to the house of an evening and sit on the porch with Mister Custis, and they would smoke their pipes and talk about this and that until ten o'clock. Then Peter would come up to shut the front door for the night and send Ephraim home. If you couldn't see Ephraim, you still knew he was close by just from the tobacco smell.

He bobbed his head at me, and I went on up the path. The leaves were off the trees, and I could see the house and the smoke coming out the chimneys and Daniel taking the carriage around to the front door. The horses were stamping and shaking their heads, and their breath made white clouds in the cold air.

I hoped Daniel was there to drive Miss Mary into town. Last week at my lessons she promised me a new book, something called a primer that you had to send away for. In the schoolroom there were books with pictures in them. There was chalk and slates and pens and paper for practicing writing my name. There was a Bible and a spelling book with a blue cover on it and a map of Virginia tacked to the wall.

I liked words. The shape of them on the page. Some were long and skinny like *grasshopper* and *strawberry,* and some were short and round like *pump* and *bulb* and *bowl.*

But Miss Mary was busy from morning till night getting ready to marry Mister Lee, and the house was all aflutter. Ladies mostly, coming and going for parties and such. They had to be careful where they stepped, because Mister Custis had hired some men to help fix up old Arlington. Making it shine for the big day. Paint buckets and ladders and wheelbarrows were scattered everywhere.

All the other young ladies were jealous of Miss Mary because of how handsome Mister Lee was. My daddy saw him riding up to the house one day and said they wasn't another man in all of

Virginia who looked as good in the saddle as Mister Lee. He was always bringing little presents for Miss Mary and making her laugh. He was helpful to Missus. Last fall he helped her with the planting, digging with a shovel and a pick just like Ephraim.

My milk pail was getting heavy, so I switched it to my other arm and hurried on past the chicken coops and into the cabin where Althea and Thursday were busy making our breakfast. George, the head cook, was fixing breakfast for the Custises in the winter kitchen down in the basement. I smelled the bacon and woodsmoke and cinnamon from clear across the yard. I set down the milk bucket and scooped up a handful of Althea's biscuits. She popped my hand right smart and told me to get busy with the churn, and then she took a sip of the rusty-nail water that was supposed to cure her warts.

Althea picked up her broom. I hoped she would tell me a story. She knew stories about the tortoise and the spider, and the woman with two skins, and why the sun and moon lived in the sky. One time she told me she was a princess because her grandmother was a queen back in Africa, snatched off her throne and fetched up on the shores of Virginia. Althea could read the future in coffee grounds, and one time she told me I would be famous someday. I asked her how, and she said the coffee didn't say.

Althea was old as dirt, and her back pained her some. She took ahold of the broom and her face folded up into a frown, and I knew better than to ask for a story. She grunted a little ever' time she moved the broom. I started to laugh, and she straightened up and frowned at me.

"What you laughing at, girl?"

"Nothing."

"You 'bout finished churning the butter?"

I lifted the paddle and checked. "Not yet."

She pointed a bony finger at me. "More churnin', then, and less foolishness."

The door opened and my own mauma came inside.

"Mornin', Sally." Althea spoke to Mauma without even looking up from her sweeping.

Mauma nodded her head at Althea and grabbed my arm. "Leave that churn and come on home."

She never fetched me home before the chores got done, so I knew something had happened. First I thought my daddy was sick. Or maybe they was a new colt in the stables. Something like that. But when we got outside Mauma said, "The missus has sent for you."

Never in my whole life had I received such a fearful summons. "I done nothing wrong, Mauma. I swear it."

"Not supposed to swear." Mauma was hurrying toward our cabin so fast I had to run to keep up with her. We got home and went inside.

We lived in one room with a mattress for her and my daddy. A ladder led up to a loft where my mattress was. There was a window where I could look out at the moon and stars at night before I went off to sleep. We had a table and some chairs and a fireplace to keep us warm in the wintertime.

Mauma had set the tub we used for washing in the middle of the room, and it was full of water so hot I could see the steam rising up off it. My best dress, a pink calico with little white flowers on it, was spread out on her chair.

She pulled my dress over my head and handed me a sliver of soap. "Get in."

"Who died?" Anytime a slave passed at Arlington, it was my mauma who helped lay them out, and we Norrises dressed up for the burying. Otherwise nobody took a bath unless it was truly necessary.

"Nobody died. Now hold still." Mauma picked up a rag and scrubbed me so hard, head to foot, till my skin was just about rubbed all the way off. I let out a sigh and squeezed my eyes shut to keep the soap from stinging. I was burning with curiosity, but wasn't no use in asking more questions. Mauma wouldn't tell you a thing till she got good and ready.

She lifted me out of the water, dried me off, and helped me into my pink dress. Finally she said, "Miss Mary gettin' married come summer. Missus

Custis need some girls to help with sewing Miss Mary some new clothes."

"But I don't know how to sew."

"She figures on teaching you how. She's gone teach Kitty and Liza too."

It was just about the worst news I'd ever had in my life so far. I belonged outside, taking care of the chickens and milking Lottie and helping pick vegetables in the summer garden and churning butter while Althea told me a story. The thought of sitting inside all day, stitching new drawers and whatnot for Miss Mary, knocked the breath right out of me.

"I don't want to."

"Girl? Since when do slaves get a say in what we want?" Mauma stepped back to look me over, then swatted my bottom and told me to get on up to the house. Missus was waiting for me. "And pick up your hem so's you don't go tracking dirt into the house."

"But, Mauma, what if I can't learn it? What if—"

She put her hands on my shoulders. "Now listen to me. This your chance to learn something useful that might can help you make a way in the world someday."

Someday meant when slavery times were over. Freedom was the thing all the Custis slaves talked about, sitting around the cook fires in the evening, the sweet hope of liberation lighting up their faces.

In the Bible it tells of all the ones God delivered.

Moses, for instance, and Samson, and Jonah who got swallowed by a whale. Daddy said one day God would deliver us too. Didn't any of us know when that day was going to come, though.

Mauma gave me a little push. "You go on now. And don't you be dawdling on the way up there either."

I hiked my skirt and headed up the path to the house, my stomach full of bees. Why did my whole life have to change just because Miss Mary and her sweetheart decided to jump the broom?

MARY

Robert was confident that getting Papa's permission to marry was a mere formality, but months passed and my father had not given us his blessing. I decided to extract it from him myself or know the reason why.

I found him in his studio one morning, his pipe clenched in his teeth, working on a landscape picture, though December rendered the scene outside the window in drab shades of brown and gray. An old cat lay napping in Papa's chair. The entire room smelled of tobacco and turpentine.

"Mary Anna." He set down his pipe and wiped his hands on an old rag. "You're up early."

"I want to talk to you." I shooed the cat away and plopped down in the chair. "It has been six months since Robert's proposal and we're still waiting for your blessing. I cannot understand such a long delay. Mother has agreed to our match. Why won't you?"

"Your mother is thinking with her heart and not her head. I am the one who must guard your inheritance."

"I see. You think Robert is only after my money. I cannot even express to you how offensive that is. For both of us. He is no opportunist. And I would like to think he finds *something* in me to admire. If not my looks, at least my mind and my heart."

"That was not at all the point."

"Then what is the point? He has a small inheritance from his mother, and Shirley Plantation is still in his family. And you cannot deny that his character is exemplary. Four years at West Point without receiving a single demerit ought to count for something in your estimation."

"He is a fine man. I am satisfied as to his character and prospects. But I worry about how you will fare, living on some army post, far from the shelter of your family and home. You and your mother are so very entwined, I can't imagine how either of you will manage without the other."

"I will miss her terribly. But I'm twenty-three years old. Old enough to know my own mind."

He sighed. "You are quite certain, then."

"Yes. Robert will be coming for Christmas in a few weeks. It would be the best present of all to have your blessing." I got up and threw my arms around him. "It's the only present I really want, Papa."

"Very well. I shall write to Robert this evening."

I wrote to Robert too, that very afternoon, and by spring letters about our coming bridal were traveling back and forth between Arlington and Cockspur Island near Savannah where Robert, now Lieutenant Lee, was involved in building a fort to protect that city.

His missives were filled with sweet declarations of his affections, but also with descriptions of canals, embankments, barracks, and wharfs. He wrote observations of his men as well—which ones had a cough and which ones had escorted the ladies to a ball. Often he alluded to his great loneliness at being apart from me. *I have arrived in the land of corn bread and ice milk,* he wrote last fall. *I hope it will keep me alive while I am apart from you.*

His letters pleased me, as they were proof he considered me his intellectual equal, someone who would understand his work and appreciate the challenges involved. Most men of my acquaintance preferred women to be seen and not heard, pretty but not necessarily educated.

Robert and I exchanged our ideas for how the

wedding should commence without setting a firm date. Finally, exasperated at his stubbornness and after deliberately delaying my reply, I told him to have everything his own way.

The morning his reply reached Arlington, Mother and the girls were already assembled downstairs, sewing dozens of undergarments to see me through the first year of marriage. I was still in my room, having been late for breakfast, finishing a letter to my cousins at Kinloch. When Eleanor plodded upstairs to say that Daniel was back from town with a letter for me, I ran downstairs without waiting to do up my hair or change my dress.

I sat on the porch steps in a patch of early spring sunlight and opened the letter.

So now, my own sweet Mary, since you allow me to have everything my own way, let it be this. I expect operations here to be suspended on the first day of July. I will therefore have some fast-sailing vessel bound for some Port in the Chesapeake pass down the Savannah the evening previous. Aboard of which I will place myself and my trunk. And after a short passage of two days will enter Hampton Roads just as the S. Boat is passing for Washington. I will—

"Miss Mary?"

I looked up to find Kitty, one of my mother's

personal maids, standing in the doorway holding a silk dressing gown. "Missus says to come inside and try this on. Make sure it fits."

I slipped Robert's letter into my pocket and went into the unfurnished ballroom opposite the parlor, which had been converted into a veritable garment factory. Liza was busy sewing pale blue satin ribbons to the sleeve of another dressing gown and didn't look up as I crossed the room. Selina glanced at me and smiled. She was my favorite even then. She was curious about everything and not at all shy about asking whatever questions came into her head.

I returned her smile and began unbuttoning the wrinkled calico dress I always wore for mornings painting in the garden. Too late I noticed a smear of red paint from yesterday running from knee to floor and bits of black dirt clinging to the hem. I tried brushing it away before my mother saw it, but her sharp inspection of my person missed nothing.

"It is nearly noon, Mary Anna, and here you are, running about looking rumpled as a pauper's child."

"Papa is liable to be one by the time he finishes paying for this wedding."

She pursed her lips. "That is not in the least amusing."

"It wasn't meant to be." I handed her my dress and slipped into the new dressing gown. "Honestly, I wish he didn't feel he had to spend so much. Robert and I will be just as married without all the expense and fuss. I wish—"

Mother stopped my words with a shake of her head and a sharp glance at the servants. I clamped my mouth shut and stood still while she arranged the folds of the dressing gown and marked the location of buttonholes with pins. She pinned the hem and adjusted the bodice. "You've gained weight."

"I know it. Three pounds at least."

She was worried that in another two months my wedding dress wouldn't fit, but the dress was the last thing on my mind. For almost a year, my forthcoming marriage had existed for me only in the abstract. Now everything was becoming vividly real. My mind filled with the worries of any young woman embarking upon the uncharted waters of matrimony. Could I learn to run a household, to manage servants, to keep my own accounts? And what of the requirements of the marriage bed? When I contemplated this question my feelings veered wildly between apprehension, curiosity, and the sweet anticipation of any woman in love with her intended.

Mother held the sleeves while I shucked out of the dressing gown. "Don't forget we have the society meeting this afternoon."

"Oh dear. Is that today? I was hoping to finish the landscape sketches I started last week."

"Your artistic endeavors will have to wait upon

our more important pursuits." Mother cupped my chin in her hands. "And please, child, humor me and wear a decent dress for the occasion."

Impatient to escape her critical eye, and to finish reading Robert's letter, I slipped back into my old dress and returned to my sunny spot on the porch.

> I will arrive at Washington anytime on the night of the 3rd. At daylight the next morning I will be landed at Arlington as the sun is rising and you are coming out to walk. And then you will be deprived of your walk, Miss Molly. I am sure there can be no objection to this Plan.

His fanciful imaginings of such a wedding, so romantic and so utterly impossible, made me laugh out loud. Robert knew very well that a proper Virginia wedding required months of preparation, tons of satin and lace, and enough food to satisfy an army. There could be no clandestine arrival, no early-morning nuptials on the dewy grasses of Arlington. But I loved the beauty of his daydream all the same.

A flash of pink caught my eye, and I looked up to see Selina running from the house.

"Selina!" I caught up with her and found her trembling, one finger dripping blood. "What on earth happened?"

She was crying so hard I could barely make out

her story. Finally I understood that my mother had given her the cream silk dressing gown with orders to hem it. The needle had slipped and stabbed the poor child's finger, and blood had smeared the hem. The dressing gown was ruined.

"Now Missus will beat me." Selina threw herself onto the ground in another fit of tears.

I took her by the arms and hauled her to her feet. "Don't be silly. She may be angry, but she won't beat you."

"But your fancy new gown got blood on the hem. And Liza said it was real silk and cost a fortune."

"It was expensive, but it's hardly worth a fortune." I pulled my handkerchief from my pocket and handed it to her. "Dry your face and let's go back to the house."

"I can't go back."

"What will you do, then? Hide in the garden forever?"

She wiped her nose on the sleeve of her dress, an unfortunate habit that made me wince. "Got to hide somewhere."

"Whatever mistakes we make in life, Selina, we must own up to them. Running away won't solve anything."

We started for the house.

"Miss Mary, you gone to stop teaching me now?" Her round little face puckered with worry.

"Of course not. Why would I?"

"I just wondered." Selina peered up at me, her eyelashes spiked with tears. "Wisht I could learn everything I want to know before you go away."

"After I'm married to Mr. Robert, Mother will continue your lessons. She mentioned just the other day that we need more books for all our young scholars."

"Oh." Selina smiled at last and skipped along beside me. "When you get married you get babies. That's what Thursday said. You gone get you some babies?"

"That's up to our heavenly Father. Such things are not for me to say."

"When you get married you gone kiss Mr. Robert?"

Even though she was a child, such intimate questions made me blush. "No more questions. Let's go inside. I have things to do."

I returned to my room and dashed off the remainder of my letter to my cousins. A reply to Robert would have to wait. To please Mother I arranged my hair and dressed in a pale blue frock trimmed in white lace.

She had sent Ephraim to cut baskets of roses for us to sell in Washington before we attended the meeting of the American Colonization Society. Our flower sales had raised a modest sum directed toward training bondsmen for useful occupations and for purchasing their freedom in preparation for their relocation to Liberia. Several thousand families had already made the journey to a new life. But I was impatient for faster progress.

Presently Mother joined me, and we set off for the city.

Our flowers sold briskly, and when the hour of the meeting drew near, we left Daniel with the carriage and walked the short distance to the society's offices, dodging loose cattle wandering about and mud-caked pigs rooting for garbage in the gutter.

Outside on the street, a small but vocal crowd had gathered, and soon it was clear that they had come to disrupt the proceedings. An angular man dressed in the garb of a minor aristocrat stood in the doorway, blocking our path. His sunken cheeks and piercing eyes gave him a slightly feral look.

"Please excuse us," Mother said. "We don't wish to be late."

He glowered at us. "You're the Custis women. I recognize you from the last picnic at Arlington Spring."

"Since you have availed yourself of my father's hospitality, surely you won't wish to disrupt our afternoon," I said. "Kindly step aside, sir."

"So you can make plans to send the Negroes packing."

"It is not my first choice, but so long as they cannot be fully accepted as free persons in America, their best hope is a new homeland."

Another man, with reddish-gold hair and a

gingery beard, elbowed his way to the front of the small gathering. "It's people like you who are making the slaves restless. They have taken up this talk of freedom, and most of 'em aren't educated enough to even know the meaning of the word."

"And whose fault is that?" Mother asked.

"Certainly not yours. Everybody knows you are breaking the law, teaching your slaves how to read, lettin' them come and go as they please."

"What we do with our servants is no concern of yours," Mother said.

"Yes, it is. Increasing the desire for freedom only gives them false confidence and incites rebellion." He spat a stream of tobacco, barely missing the toe of my shoe. "The trouble with the black man is that he don't know how good a life he's got. He don't have to worry about food or shelter. He gets doctored when he's sick and he's got his church meetings on Sundays." The interloper fixed me with his snakelike eyes. "They's plenty of white folks in Virginia worse off than your slaves."

A team of oxen pulled a creaking dray down the street. Somewhere in the distance a church bell pealed.

"Come along, Mary Anna." Mother took my arm and attempted to press through the gathering.

But I could not let the man's comments pass unchallenged. "It's easy for you to stand there and declare the advantages of the slaves' lives. They may not be educated, but I can assure you they cherish the prospect of liberty, no matter how faint that hope may be."

The door opened and Mr. Pierce, who chaired our meetings, came out. He glared at the men and offered an arm to Mother and me. "I do apologize for the disturbance. Please allow me."

We went inside, and the meeting commenced at the appointed hour. The discussion was the usual mix of reports on the progress of fund-raising and the applications of freedmen hoping to emigrate. My mind wandered to Robert's letter and plans for our wedding. Dozens of my friends and cousins were expecting to be bridesmaids. It would take the skills of a diplomat to make the final choices.

When the meeting ended, Mother and I went out to our waiting carriage. The sun had disappeared and now a rainstorm threatened. Daniel urged the horses on, and we got home just as the first raindrops fell.

Mother went upstairs for a nap, and I hurried along the back hall to the schoolroom where my scholars waited. Today only the Burke sisters and my two boys were waiting at the table where I kept slates and primers and the cast-off books I had brought from Kinloch three years before. The old volumes were well thumbed and falling apart, but the children loved the colorful illustrations and the stories I invented to go along with them.

Selina peeked in, her eyes still swollen from the morning's ordeal. I waved her to a seat and began the lesson. I was not trained as a teacher, but having suffered through years of dull recitations with my own tutors, I made up games to amuse the children while they learned to read and cipher. Today I asked them to write words that rhymed with *bat*. Chalk clicked on the slates as they bent to their task. Afterward they read the words aloud, then took turns reading from the primers I had obtained in the city.

Just as we were closing the lesson with a song, I glimpsed the face of a young boy at the window. I sang louder, hoping to entice him inside, for I wanted to encourage more boys to learn to read. But by the time we finished and I went to the door, he had vanished into the woods, his blue flannel shirt flying out behind him.

Mother met me in the hallway.

"Was that Selina Norris I saw leaving just now?"

"Yes. Why?"

"I banned her from her lessons for the week as a consequence for ruining your dressing gown."

"Oh, Mother. You didn't! It's the very thing she looks forward to most."

"It's only a token punishment, Mary. To impress upon her the need for caution when she's handling other people's things." She patted my arm. "Don't be cross. There's tea waiting in the parlor. Come along before it gets cold."

★ 5 ★
SELINA

The first day when Mauma sent me up to the missus, I was shaking so hard I thought she would hear my bones rattling. She took me into the room with Kitty and Liza and two white girls I never saw before. Turns out they was Miss Mary's cousins, come to stay for a while and help with the sewing. The house had wide, open doors that went from one big room to another. They had rounded openings at the top, like doors on churches in one of Miss Mary's books. There was a fire going, and the room smelled like paint.

Outside was Thursday's boy, Nathaniel, painting the window frames. He put his face up to the glass and stuck his tongue out at me. I didn't pay him any mind. He thinks he's funny, but I don't. Nathaniel's aunt Judah makes up bags filled with strange things supposed to ward off evil spells. She calls them jacks. You supposed to wear the jack around your neck. Judah sells the jacks to black folks, and some whites too, but Mauma says they are foolishness, so I never had one and do not know if they work.

Missus set me down at a table. In the middle was a sewing basket the size of a wheelbarrow,

42

and in it was everything you would ever need to make clothes. A purple needle case, scissors in the shape of a swan. Thimbles, pincushions, and some other things I hadn't ever laid my eyes on before. Missus named them and told us what they was for: bodkin for drawing cord through a hem, seam ripper in case you make a mistake and have to start over, spool caddy for holding different colors of thread, a strip of cloth with numbers painted on it for measuring out the cloth. Missus gave us gloves to wear so we wouldn't get any dirt on the cloth, and we unrolled the bolts of silk and satin and white linen and pressed out the wrinkles with a hot iron.

The two white girls, Emily and Harriett, pinned a pattern to one of the pieces of linen, and Missus cut it up. Missus said it was gone be a pair of drawers, which made Kitty giggle until Missus frowned at her. Sure enough, that stopped her cold. Missus showed us how to thread a needle and made us practice stitching on an old piece of blue cloth she took from a bag of rags. I about poked my fingers full of holes until Missus showed me how to use a thimble, and how the needle would slide through the cloth easier if you pushed it through a cake of beeswax first. Why she didn't say so in the first place is a big mystery.

The first several days, Missus wouldn't let me and Kitty do anything but practice. Then she started us on finishing the legs of the drawers and then Harriett sewed the legs onto a waistband. We made a dozen pairs.

Next was petticoats. Missus tried to teach me how to make tucks in the cloth, but I never could make the rows come out even and she gave up. Instead, she showed me how to do embroidery. It was the same motion with the needle over and over, and after a while I was making little blue flowers all over the bottom of Miss Mary's new petticoat, which seemed silly. Who's gone see the flowers anyway, hid under Miss Mary's skirts? But then again, white folks have lots of notions that don't make hardly a lick of sense when you stop to think about it.

Every day along about dinnertime Missus sent us out to the porch where there was a table set up, and we had bread and butter and milk. If the sun was out we could walk to the garden to see if anything was blooming yet, and then Missus would clap her hands and bring us back to our work.

Afternoons, with a full belly and the sound of the cousins chattering back and forth, it was hard to stay awake. I practiced spelling words in my head. I thought about Thursday and Althea down in the kitchen, and I wondered if Lottie forgot about me already and if she would remember me when the sewing was done and I got back to the dairy again.

After a while we had filled a trunk with chemises, drawers, and petticoats. Daniel brought the carriage around one morning and took the white girls home. Then it was me and Liza and Kitty left to help Missus finish the dressing gowns.

Missus told us over and over to be careful because the silk was dear as gold, and the more times she reminded me of it, the more nervous I got. One day somehow the needle slipped and stuck my finger. Blood dripped onto the hem.

Missus was busy folding another petticoat Kitty had just finished, so she didn't see me when I jumped up and ran out the door with no safe place to go. I didn't dare face the missus, even though she would find out soon enough that I had ruined her finest creation.

I ran as fast as I could, my head filling up with all sorts of terrible things. Every slave at Arlington knew about folks from other plantations who had been sold South for things like breaking a crystal butter dish or leaving the field too soon or talking back. Althea said once you was sold South you wasn't never heard of again. What if Missus sent me South? I'd never see Mauma or my daddy again. No more helping Ephraim in the garden. No more of Althea's stories. No more Lottie. No more lessons with Miss Mary.

I couldn't go home to Mauma either. She wouldn't send me away, but she would whip me so hard I'd wish for the next boat to anywhere. I was crying so hard I was blinded.

Then Miss Mary called my name. I cried even harder because I had ruined something special that was hers, and even if I survived whatever punishment was coming to me, Miss Mary never would speak to me again. That was the worst part of it.

She gave me her own handkerchief, which smelled sweet. Like flowers or spices or something. "Now, dry your eyes and go back inside," she said.

"I can't go by myself. You got to come with me."

She bent down to look me straight in the eye and told me I had to have courage for whatever things happened in life. Then she held my hand and we went back inside.

I wasn't anybody's fool. Mister Robert was bound to take up most of the room in Miss Mary's heart. But I hoped she would save a little spot for me.

★ 6 ★
MARY

Robert wrote that he was unwilling to wait any longer and would arrive at the end of June. At which time we would become husband and wife and then proceed to his new posting at Fortress Monroe. I chose half a dozen bridesmaids. Robert rounded up an equal number of men to stand as groomsmen and chose his brother Smith to be best man. Papa conferred with our minister, the Reverend Dr. Keith, and the ceremony was set for the evening of June thirtieth.

Servants, both ours and borrowed, were dispatched to ready the house for the guests and our wedding party. Food was prepared, beds made up, silver polished. The china and silver that had once belonged to my great-grandmother graced table and sideboard. The carpets were beaten and aired, the curtains washed and pressed, the woodwork polished to a high gleam. Mother prevailed upon friends and family to lend us mattresses, candlesticks, punch bowls, and cake baskets, and by the eve of the wedding all was in readiness.

Except for the bride. Unable to sleep and seized by a strange melancholy, I wandered through the rooms of the only home I had ever known, pausing at the touchstones of my childhood. The portrait of President Washington when he served as colonel in the Virginia Militia. My great-grandmother's tea table in the parlor, and her silver service on the sideboard in the dining room where Robert proposed. The chair where I often sat on Papa's lap while he read to me from the newspapers. Porcelain cups on the mantel. Shelves of books I had read over and over.

My new life, fraught with uncertainty, was about to commence.

I went to bed after midnight and slept fitfully until Mother woke me and sent me down to breakfast. I managed to eat a biscuit with a cup of tea and was on my way upstairs when Papa intercepted me in the hallway.

"Mary Anna, you are pale as milk, my girl. Are you sorry now that you prevailed upon me to approve this match? If that be the case, it is not too late to change your mind."

"Don't tease me, Papa. I am already a ball of nerves."

"I would be worried if you weren't. Marriage is a serious business."

"Robert says the wedding service has all the charm of a death warrant."

He chuckled and tucked my arm through his. "Walk with me awhile."

We went out into a June morning heavy with clouds. In the garden, Ephraim and Selina were busy cutting roses for the vases in the parlor. Daniel was readying our carriage for the first trip of the day, ferrying family and guests from the river landing to the house for the ceremony.

"I want to speak to you about the matter of your allowance," Papa said. "I'm thinking that a sum of—"

"You are quite generous, Papa, but no. Robert and I must live only on his military pay if we are to forge a true partnership."

48

His brows rose. "Do you know how little a lieutenant earns?"

"It isn't much, but we will be living at Fort Monroe, and our expenses will be few." I watched the boats plying the glassy Potomac. "Besides, you have many other financial obligations to consider. Repairs to the house and this wedding have cost a—"

"That's my business, not yours."

"Anything that worries you worries me. And I know you've spent far more on this bridal than we can afford."

"My only child deserves the best." He patted my hand. "At least you won't be completely without comfort and assistance. Your mother insists upon your taking a servant with you."

"Yes. She's sending Cassie, though I don't know why. Robert says we will be living in officers' quarters. In so small a space there won't be much for Cassie to do."

The rattle of harness and the creak of carriage wheels announced the arrival of my bridesmaids. "I must go, Papa."

"I know." He caught both my hands in his. "I have loved you desperately all my life, and that won't change, Mary Anna, when I am compelled to share your affections with Lieutenant Lee. Wherever you must go, be assured of your father's tender affections, and never forget that Arlington will always be your home."

He headed toward the garden, and I went back to the house in time to see my cousin Marietta and my friend Angela exiting the carriage.

"Dear Mary!" Marietta dropped her hatbox to embrace me. "Are you not excited beyond words?"

Excited? Yes. But lacking the inner peace I so desperately needed. Everything was moving too fast. Angela embraced me in turn and we went inside. Daniel followed with their trunks. There was scarcely time to get Marietta and Angela settled into their rooms before my other attendants arrived. Mother served a light luncheon, after which a small army of servants appeared to drape flower garlands in the doorways to the dining room and the parlor.

Robert arrived, bearing six extravagant bouquets for my bridesmaids and looking so resplendent in his dress uniform that my heart seized. The bouquets were a gallant and charming gesture, so typical of him. But I couldn't help thinking that surely those flowers had cost him a month's pay.

"Shall we help you with your dress?" Angela asked.

"In a little while." I felt dizzy, and my skin had gone hot. I retreated to my room and stood at the window, watching as the sky darkened and rain began to fall. Guests arrived, hurrying along beneath black umbrellas. Our old servant Peter manned the door. The sound of his greetings wafted up the stairs.

I pressed my fingers to my temples. Papa was still worried about my transition from the ease of life at Arlington to the trials of a nomadic army existence, but I had complete faith and trust in Robert. Still, as the hour of our marriage drew near, my faith in my own adaptability faltered. I doubted my ability to be selfless where my husband's happiness was concerned. I was, as I have said, accustomed to getting my own way. Renowned among my friends and family for my disregard of convention. Admittedly, I had fallen into a terrible habit of arriving late to important engagements. And more than once I had turned up somewhere important without the proper attire, much to my mother's dismay.

Such things mattered little to me, but Robert was a military officer, an engineer accustomed to precision, order, and punctuality. He was a delightful suitor—charming and affectionate— but what if we were too different to live together for the rest of our lives?

Someone knocked at my door, and then Angela burst in, her eyes bright with amusement. "Mary! Your preacher has arrived soaked to the skin, and there are no clothes but your father's to dress him in!"

Three of my other attendants crowded into my room, all of them stifling laughter.

"I caught a glimpse of the poor half-drowned reverend, and I must say he looks quite comical,"

Angela said. "But don't worry, his robes will cover the fact that your father's breeches come barely to his ankles."

Then Mother arrived to help me get dressed. My gown was exquisitely made and perfectly fitted to my small frame, but compared to my beautiful and vivacious bridesmaids I felt like a wren among a flock of exotic birds.

Mother finished doing up the buttons and turned me around. "What's the matter, child?"

"Nothing. It's just that Robert is so handsome and I'm so plain. I fear I won't be a credit to him tonight."

Mother patted my cheek. "Stop your fretting. Whatever a girl may be the day before her wedding, or however she may appear on the day after, on her wedding day she is always beautiful. Now don't keep Robert waiting."

The bridesmaids assembled in the upper hallway. We walked down the stairs single file and into the candlelit parlor where Robert stood next to Smith. His groomsmen were lined up behind him, their faces solemn in the candlelight.

Robert winked and reached for my hand, and Dr. Keith began the service. Later I could recall nothing of it except the reading of scripture and Robert's chaste kiss after we said our vows.

Our friends crowded around us, offering kisses and congratulations. Supper was served, after which Aunt Nelly took her place at the piano and the dancing commenced.

Robert swept me into his arms. "Well, Molly, the deed is done. How does it feel to be Mrs. Lee?"

He was a head taller than I, and I had to pull away to look up into his eyes. "Why, it feels just fine, Lieutenant."

"You're not sorry you didn't marry Sam Houston? I heard he was quite taken with you."

"Heavens! Sam Houston is nearly forty. And anyway, he married someone else."

"I heard she left him right after their I-dos, poor devil." Robert twirled me around. "Promise never to leave me, Molly. I could not bear it."

"I never wanted anyone but you."

"I never expected you would be mine, and see how it turned out. Your parents have given us a lovely celebration," he murmured. "Our wedding is certain to be long remembered."

Smith tapped my husband's shoulder. "Mind if I dance with your bride, Robert?"

Smith took me in his arms. "You make a lovely bride, Mary."

"Thank you. You make a handsome best man."

He smiled. "Aren't you just a wee bit sorry you married my little brother when you could have had me?"

"You never were serious about marriage, Smith Lee, and you know it."

The song ended and our guests gathered hats and shawls, summoned their carriages, and went home. Papa and Mother and our wedding attendants made themselves scarce as the evening waned.

Robert took my hand. "Shall we retire for the evening, Mrs. Lee?"

We went upstairs to the room that had been prepared for us. The lamps were lit, and the yellow flames guttered softly in the rain-cooled breeze that stirred the lace curtains at the open window. Vases of lilacs perfumed the air.

Robert scooped me up and carried me into the room. "There," he said softly. "We are safely over the threshold. No evil can come to us now, Mary."

It was nothing more than a lovely old superstition, but that night, safe in my new husband's arms, I believed it was true.

Each night was filled with an abundance of food and drink, dancing, and good-natured teasing. The men played card games and billiards, raising such a commotion that at times our quiet home seemed more like a barracks. My bridesmaids danced and flirted with Robert's groomsmen, and everyone admired our wedding gifts displayed on a table in the parlor. The frolicking reached all the way to the servants' quarters, where Papa had seen to it that our servants had plenty to eat and drink.

On Sunday night, tired and overwrought from the constant press of warm bodies and the smells of powder, wine, and lavender wafting through the rooms, I retreated to the back hallway for a breath of air and a moment of solitude.

"There you are, my dear." Papa came down the stairs and kissed my cheek. "I've been waiting for a moment to get you alone so I could give you this." From his pocket he took a small box carved of ivory and set with emeralds and rubies. "I saw this in New York and wanted you to have it as a remembrance of your wedding."

"It's exquisite, Papa, and I'll cherish it forever. But you have done so much for us already, I—"

"Mr. Custis?" Smith Lee came into the hallway holding a glass of punch. "Mrs. Custis is looking for you."

Papa excused himself. Smith bowed to me and followed him.

Before I could reach the back door, Mrs. Pinckney, a large woman with a florid complexion and a mass of jet-black curls, wandered in from the conservatory. She was related to one of Robert's groomsmen—I wasn't certain exactly how. Her eyes went immediately to the ivory box in my hand.

"Oh, what a dear little thing! And so unusual. I have never seen anything like it." Mrs. Pinckney held out her hand. "May I hold it?"

Reluctantly I handed it to her.

She said, "I don't suppose you'd consider selling it."

I gaped at her. "Of course not. It's a wedding gift from my father."

She handed it back, then opened her reticule and pressed a calling card into my hand. "If you should ever change your mind—"

"I can't imagine I ever will."

She went back to join the ladies, and I escaped into the cool June evening.

By Tuesday most of our guests had left. Mother went with Robert and me to visit kin at Ravensworth, where she and I fell ill with fever and ague. I was mortified, but Robert was an attentive husband, forever asking how I was feeling, always ready to bring a glass of water or an extra blanket whenever I needed it.

After I had been abed for several days, he came into the room and laid half a dozen white rosebuds on my counterpane. "Dear Mrs. Lee," he said gravely, "I do hope you are feeling better today."

Who could not feel cheered by such charming gallantry? I smiled up at him. "I am much improved, thank you. Have you seen Mother yet this morning?"

"I have, and she seems better as well. She is having tea and toast as we speak. Shall I bring you some?"

"I don't think so. I'm well enough to get dressed and go down." I threw back the covers and got to my feet, feeling weaker than I was willing to admit.

Robert came up behind me and kissed the back of my neck. "I'll leave you to your ablutions then, dear wife, and wait breakfast for you downstairs."

I took fresh underthings from my trunk and poured water into the washbasin. "I won't be long."

At the door he paused, a mischievous gleam in his eye. "Are you certain I can't help you dress? Although I would much rather help you *out* of those lacy fripperies than into them."

The next morning we left Ravensworth for visits with cousins at Woodlawn and Kinloch. It was my first visit to my Turner cousins in over a year. Thomas and Elizabeth fussed over us, showering us with food and gifts and good wishes. Their girls dragged me to the stable to see the colt Eliza had named Fauquier, now a handsome three-year-old. They peppered me with questions, wanting to know every detail of the wedding.

"Did Cousin Robert bring you flowers?" Caroline wanted to know.

"Yes, and he brought bouquets for all my bridesmaids as well. You should have seen our parlor. It looked as if all the flowers in the world had escaped their gardens and come inside."

Eliza squeezed onto the settee between her sister and me. "Mary, did you have a ball, like in *Cinderella*?"

I laughed. "All that was missing was the glass slipper."

Henry and Edward came in then, teasing Robert and me so mercilessly that I felt an emotion akin to panic. To please Papa I had tried to master every task set before me, but mastering three languages seemed much easier than mastering the responsibilities of married life.

I was relieved when the visit ended and Mother returned to Arlington, leaving Robert and me to continue our journey to Fortress Monroe. As our carriage bowled eastward over the narrow road, I slipped my hand into Robert's. He regarded me with a mixture of worry and tenderness.

"Is something wrong, Robert? If you're concerned about our accommodations at the fort, you needn't be. I am quite resigned to living in two rooms."

"One of them is the size of a piece of chalk. It's more like a closet with a window in it."

"I know. I heard you telling Papa about it. Something else is bothering you."

The clatter of the carriage wheels over a wooden bridge forestalled further comment until we reached the other side.

"I am worried for you, Mary," he said at last. "You have been so much at home and have seen so little of mankind. I'm afraid the change from Arlington to a garrison of wicked and blasphemous soldiers will be greater and more shocking than you anticipate."

"Don't worry about me. I will get used to it."

As our journey neared its end, I could only pray my words were true.

SELINA

The day Miss Mary sent me back to the house to face Missus after I bled on Miss Mary's dressing gown, Missus looked at me like I was a worm nibbling on her prized roses. She didn't whup me or sell me South. But she had promised all of us some candy when we finished the sewing, and she gave my part of it to Kitty and Liza. And she told me I couldn't come to reading lessons that week, which was worse than missing out on the sweets.

Then sewing time was over and it was Miss Mary's big day. I wanted to watch the ladies arriving in their fancy dresses and feathered hats, but Mauma sent me to help George and Thursday with the refreshments. We had to tote everything up to the house in covered boxes because it was raining hard, like the seam of the sky had been ripped open and all the water in heaven spilled out. But later on that night the rain stopped.

Mister Custis sent down cakes and hams and

such, also some spirits, and told us to eat whatever we wanted. We fell on the food like the
locusts from Bible times. The menfolks emptied
the bottles of spirits and the grown-ups danced
until the last light in the house went out.

While everyone was eating I slipped away and
ran up the path to the house. There was people
everywhere, talking and dancing and carrying
on. I stood at the back door hoping to see Miss
Mary in her fancy dress. I had worked for weeks
helping sew her wedding things, and I wanted to
see how the big day had turned out.

Mister Robert came into the conservatory. I
ducked down so he wouldn't see me and counted
to fifty before I raised my head again. And there
was Miss Mary standing beside him in a dress
the color of fresh-churned butter. It had lace on
the top and a skirt the same shape as the bell
Missus uses for calling us up for prayers. Her
hair was all in long curls and she was laughing.

I stood on my tiptoes so I could see better, and
just then she turned her head and saw me. I froze
in my tracks and my heart was galloping.

Miss Mary whispered in Mister Robert's ear,
and he put his arms around her and twirled her
around. It was the finest sight I had seen in my
life so far. When they stopped, she winked at
me and then they went back to the parlor and I
couldn't see them anymore.

I thought the next day things would go back to

the way they used to be, but the celebrating went on for days, with company coming and going at all hours. One morning I was coming back from the garden toting a basket of squash, and I saw Miss Mary sitting outside the conservatory with her paint box. It was early. The gardens were still wet with dew. The sun had come up butter-soft and hazy.

She waved to me, so I went over to her and set down my basket. "What are you painting?"

She showed me a piece of heavy paper no bigger than a page from my primer. The picture showed a brown-skinned girl just about my size, barefooted and carrying a brown basket on her head. She was wearing a white apron, and behind her was a fence like the one that ran along the winter wheat fields at Arlington.

"Is that me, Miss Mary?"

Before she could say yes or no, Missus appeared at the door and told Miss Mary it was time to come inside and get dressed. Still being the boss, even though Miss Mary was grown up and was now Missus Lee.

Missus Lee packed up her paints and went in the back door. I went on home with my basket of squash, and in a little while the carriage pulled up and Miss Mary and Mister Robert got in. Also Missus Custis. I reckon she wasn't ready to let go of her only baby girl just yet. Mauma told me they were going visiting to the relatives that hadn't come to the wedding. Off they went and I got a empty feeling in my chest, thinking I might not see Miss Mary again.

But I was too busy to study for very long on how lonesome it seemed without her. In the mornings, after I milked Lottie, I went to the garden with Mauma to pick what was ready and take it to Thursday—greens and squash and beans, melons and corn. She could make any of it into a feast. When Thursday was cooking, the quarters smelled good any time of day.

Thursday was short and round, with skin the color of cinnamon. She had only one front tooth, and one arm had a shiny pink scar on it where she burned it when she was a girl. Sometimes when my own chores were done, she would put me to work shelling peas or shucking corn, and she taught me songs learned from her mauma a long time ago. Liza said Thursday was ugly as a mud fence, but how that woman could sing. Althea told the best stories, but nobody could sing like Thursday.

One Sunday Ephraim come back from his usual stay acrost the river in Washington City and brought a letter from Miss Mary. First time I had a letter of my own. It was short and sweet.

Dear Selina,

We are settled in at Fortress Monroe. It is quite different from Arlington. But I suppose I

62

will get used to it. This morning as I changed into a fresh petticoat I saw the blue flowers you sewed, and they made me think so fondly of home. What would I give for one stroll on the hills of Arlington on this bright day.

Say your prayers, learn your lessons, and give my love to everyone there.

MC Lee

I read it two times and put it in my pocket. I fed the chickens and then it was time for church. On Sunday nights everybody at Arlington walked through the woods to the chapel for preaching and singing. A white preacher read to us from the Bible. Mostly it was about how slaves supposed to obey their masters, and then there was singing. Some of the songs were long and full of words I didn't know. *Firmament, foundation, omnipotent.* But then came the children's hymns. My favorite was "Old Ralph in the Wood." Like Miss Mary's letter, it was short and sweet.

After all the amens we headed for home.

One Sunday Mauma and my daddy were in the clearing talking to George, who cooked for the Custises, and Lawrence, the market man. Kitty was standing next to Missus, waiting on her. Liza and Rose, the laundry girl, were whispering about something. The boys all ran off into the woods.

I started up the path to the quarters. It was a hot summer night, and lightning bugs drifted around my head. When I got near to our cabin, I stopped to check on my baby wrens. I had been watching the nest for a while. I knew by and by the babies would leave the nest, but when I got there that night and saw it was empty I busted out bawling.

Mauma caught up with me and put her arm on my shoulder. "What on earth has got into you, girl?"

"I don't know. The birds flew away."

"Well, of course they did. A nest is warm and sturdy while the birds are growin', but it ain't nothing but a temporary stopping-off place. Come on home now. Thursday brought us a slice of pie."

I ate the pie and it was good, but I couldn't stop thinking about my wrens and wondering where they had gone. If they were safe. If they missed their home.

★ 8 ★

MARY

Robert held open the door for me. "Welcome to the Tuileries, dearest," he joked. "It's nothing so grand as Arlington, but we'll be fine, won't we, Miss Molly?"

I could see how important it was to him that I not be disappointed. He had warned me that we would be sharing quarters with his commanding officer, Captain Talcott, but I hadn't realized that the captain's sister, Abigail Hale, her husband, Horace, and their two little girls were also in residence.

Our two rooms had small windows and a dirt floor. A far cry from the French imperial palace. Living in such close quarters with five other people was not the ideal arrangement for a couple married for only a month. But this was the life I had chosen, and I would not repine of it now.

I summoned as much enthusiasm as I could and stood on tiptoe to kiss my handsome husband. "We will indeed be fine."

While Robert took up his duties with Captain Talcott, I arranged a few furnishings Mother had sent from Arlington. I placed a small table near the window where I might sit to write. I unpacked an oilcloth for the dining table and a small gilt-framed picture Papa had painted when he was a boy. Beside our narrow bed I placed the oil lamp and a crystal vase.

With Cassie to see to the daily chores and Robert attending to his engineering duties, I read and sewed and took short walks with the captain's young nieces, Rebecca and Catherine. The children were as besotted with my new husband as I was and would run to greet him with shouts of "Lee, Lee!" when he returned home in the evenings. He basked in their attentions and would often bring them a handful of wildflowers or a particularly pretty stone or a clump of red moss, accepting their squeals of delight with his customary courtly grace.

As the summer wore on I took to early-morning walks on the beach and to saltwater bathing with some of the other wives at the fort. We ventured forth by midmorning with children and servants in tow, and remained until late afternoon, sharing news of home and exchanging recipes for pudding or soup while the children splashed in the water.

A Sunday school had been established at the fort, and a chapel that was off-limits to the Negroes, so I was obliged to conduct services for Cassie at home. I took pains with my lessons for her and prayed that my words might fall on a fertile heart.

I missed my newspapers, my daily political discussions with Papa, and most of all reading with my mother. I was delighted when Mrs. Hale suggested we read together. We chose a book about the life of Luther, but the children and servants and the constant racket of the busy fort interrupted so often it was hard to make much progress. Too, we were much occupied with news of the death of President Monroe, who had expired on the Fourth of July. There were many recollections among the ladies of the July Fourth just five years before, when the souls of President Jefferson and President Adams had taken flight within hours of one another.

One afternoon near the end of August I had just returned from Mrs. Hale's when my husband arrived, clearly agitated.

"Robert? What's the matter?"

He tossed his hat onto the table and sank heavily into his chair. "Where is Cassie?"

"Outside with Rebecca and Catherine. They're attempting to tame a white cat that appeared here this morning. Luring him out of hiding with a saucer of milk."

He blew out a long breath. "Two nights ago a deranged slave called Nat Turner gathered a number of his friends, and together they have slaughtered more than fifty whites. The militia is out looking for them."

"Dear Lord. Where?"

"In Southampton County. Near Jerusalem." He passed a hand over his face. "The abolitionists are being blamed for stirring up the Negroes and inciting rebellion."

I must have looked stricken, for Robert chafed my hands and told me not to worry. "Turner and his murderous band won't get anywhere near Arlington. Or here either. They'll be apprehended soon enough. In the meantime, Colonel Eustis has ordered that no Negroes of either sex can be harbored or tolerated inside the fort."

"What about Cassie? What does he expect me to do with her?"

"Servants of officers are exempt from the rule.

So are those working in the hospital and the Quarter Masters Department."

I stood and began assembling things for tea. Robert and I often dined with the Talcott family, but I liked having tea alone with him in the quiet of the afternoon, when we might speak privately. "That's sensible, I suppose."

"Yes, but the rest of his order is not at all sensible. My work crews must come here to procure water and mortar, and my draftsmen own slaves who must enter the fort now and then."

I sliced some bread and set out butter and the jar of currant jelly Mother had sent from home. "What can you do?"

"I've voiced my objections to Colonel Eustis, and to Washington too, but I don't expect his orders will be countermanded."

Despite Robert's assurances as to my safety and that of my home and family, the news of such a murderous rebellion left me feeling unsettled, and more certain than ever that eventually slavery must end. "The sooner the country is rid of human servitude, the better."

Robert joined me at the small table. I poured tea, and he helped himself to bread and butter.

"Slavery is a terrible legacy. But the problem is one that can be resolved only gradually, and with God's help."

"I am pleased you acknowledge the need for Providence." I didn't intend to sound so self-righteous. But I was worried. Despite Robert's early exposure to his mother's religious teaching, he had not yet seen the need to be confirmed. It was the one thing I found lacking in him.

"So we are back to the subject of my immortal soul, are we?" Robert set down his cup. "Despite what you might think, I am not unacquainted with my Creator, Mary. My mother saw to that when I was a boy."

"Then why won't you be confirmed? Then I should have nothing more to wish for on this earth with regard to you."

"I thought we were discussing the gradual emancipation of the Negroes. At least we are agreed on that point. Though at present they are unfit to make their own way in the world. As to the future, who can say?"

"You say that as if you care little for how long it may take."

He frowned. "What would you have me do, Mary?"

"Perhaps it would hasten the day if men of influence were more forceful in their support of the Colonization Society. Especially now that President Monroe and your uncle Richard have died. Mother says the value of their wisdom cannot be overstated."

"You still have Henry Clay and Daniel Webster on your side."

"Yes, but we women can do little more than

write letters and sell flowers to support the cause."

"I know how passionate you are about this, Mary, but shipping the freedmen off to Liberia is hardly the answer." Robert finished his first slice of bread and buttered another. "This morning Talcott and I were discussing the possibility that Virginia may outlaw slavery in the wake of this Nat Turner business. I'm sure there will be calls for something to be done, but I can't imagine enough votes can be mustered to make a two-hundred-year-old institution illegal." He sipped his tea. "Talcott agrees with you, by the way."

"About?"

"He is of the opinion that colonization is the only means—short of war—for ending slavery."

"Then perhaps I can persuade the captain to lend his support to the cause when he is next in Washington City."

Robert studied me over the rim of his cup. "I have known your feelings on this matter for a long time, but I did not think you were such an abolitionist. After all, you are dependent upon the slaves at Arlington to see to your every need. Are you ready to take on the preparing of meals, the laundering of clothes? The scrubbing of floors and the emptying of chamber pots?"

"How dare you include me in the group being blamed for this man Turner's rampage? I am no rabid abolitionist, but I am a realist. You know as well as I do that slavery cannot endure forever.

We have a moral obligation to prepare our servants for that day when they are emancipated. Even if my father doesn't share my—"

The door burst open, and the Hale children rushed inside. Catherine was holding a squirming white cat. "Lee! Look what we got."

Robert scooted his chair away from the table and took both child and feline onto his lap. "What a fine specimen he is, Miss Catherine. Have you thought of a name for him?"

"I want to call him Frosty because he's white as frost. But Rebecca thinks we should call him Lucky."

"Because it's lucky we found him before he got sick or something." Rebecca climbed into Robert's lap with her sister. "Lee, did you bring me anything today?"

"I'm afraid not today."

"But you will tomorrow," Catherine said, turning on her most beguiling smile.

Rebecca took his face between her two small hands. "Promise to bring us something special."

Robert laughed. "Go along, you little flirts. Mrs. Lee and I must dress for dinner."

Cat in tow, the girls hurried off. Cassie came in to put away our tea things and to help me change my dress. I could feel Robert's eyes following me as I readied myself for dinner. I knew he was thinking he had proven his point about my dependence on Cassie and the others who served my family at home. I was still smarting from his having called me an abolitionist. So I was in a most contentious mood when we joined Captain Talcott and the Hales at dinner.

In the presence of the captain's Negro servants, the conversation revolved around the innocuous topics of beach walking, letters from home, and Robert's progress on his engineering projects. But once we had finished our coffee and cake and the girls were taken off to bed, the captain dismissed his servants for the evening and the five adults crowded into the Talcotts' rooms, which were hardly larger than ours.

"Mrs. Lee," the captain said. "I'm sure the lieutenant has told you of the events occurring in Southampton County."

"Yes. But he assures me we are safe here."

"Indeed. The garrison is being reinforced. Extra troops will remain here until the miscreants are apprehended and dealt with. You have nothing to fear."

"I've no doubt of my safety, but I do worry about what this rebellion will mean for the rest of Virginia."

He looked surprised. "I doubt it will mean much at all in the grand scheme of things. From what we know so far, Nat Turner fancies himself some sort of prophet, guided by heavenly visions to lead his people out of bondage. Rumor has it that it was the recent eclipse of the sun that convinced him it was time to act. Clearly he is deranged."

"I quite agree, Andrew," Mrs. Hale said. "The actions of one misguided slave won't undo a system that has flourished for generations." She glanced at me as if seeking my agreement, but I said nothing.

"At tea this afternoon Mary and I were discussing the Colonization Society," Robert said.

"It's a better alternative than an all-out war," Captain Talcott said. "Though I realize many Negroes would have no wish to immigrate to a country where they have no family ties."

"Nor any way to support themselves," his sister remarked. "Freedom would be the worst thing for the Negroes, even if they can't see it that way."

"At least it would be the worst thing for them in America," I said. "Until attitudes toward them soften more than they are at present."

"Of course we can't simply herd them onto boats and set them upon the sea," the captain said. "They first must be taught to do something useful. But under the right conditions, they would benefit. And so would America. A thriving Liberia would demand American trade goods. Not to mention missionary support."

"That would please Mrs. Lee," my husband said. "She is experiencing a great cresting of spiritual feeling these days."

It was true, and it was said without malice or

derision, but in that moment I experienced the cresting of an entirely different feeling. I got to my feet. "Please excuse me. I need some air."

I went outside and walked on the beach until my anger was spent. I sat on a half-rotted log, my chest aching with remorse, watching the waves breaking on the rocky shore and fearing for the future of my marriage. It was much easier to love someone from a distance, when letters were the only source of communication and one could take the time to choose the right word or phrase. Living together day to day in such close proximity magnified the differences between Robert and me. Still, I regretted having been so quick to judge him.

Down the beach a torchlight appeared. Hoping it was Robert coming for me, I got up, ready to apologize for my intemperate behavior. But it was only a fisherman, who passed me without a word. At last there was nothing to do but go home.

The house was dark when I let myself in. Cassie was sound asleep on her pallet outside the bedroom. I undressed in the dark, slipped into my nightdress, and slid into bed. I closed my eyes, though I didn't expect sleep would come anytime soon. I hated quarreling with anyone, most of all my new husband.

"So you've come home at last, Mrs. Lee." Robert drew me close until I lay pressed tightly against him.

"Where else could I go?"

"I am deeply sorry for my remark at dinner. I ought not to be so sensitive to your worries about the state of my soul. My conduct tonight was not that of a gentleman, and I beg your forgiveness."

"I'm sorry I ran out on you. It must have been embarrassing."

"It was. But I had it coming."

"I thought you might come looking for me. I hoped you would."

"You needed to be alone to sort things out. Did you?"

"Not really." I propped myself up on one elbow. "What if we have made a grievous mistake?"

"You regret marrying me already, Molly?"

"No, I regret that I seem always to disappoint you."

"That isn't true."

"It is true. I have seen the way you frown when our rooms are not as tidy as you would like. Or when we are going out somewhere and you think I am not as well dressed as I should be. I cannot be like you. Always perfect, always punctual."

He sighed. "I don't mean to be critical. And I don't know that I can ever overcome my propensity for order and methodology. I will try, sweetheart, but don't expect miracles in my case. Leave something to time." He drew me close and kissed me. "I do love you so, Mary Anna. Am I forgiven?"

Of course I forgave him. How could I not? Especially since half the fault was mine.

He fell asleep, but I lay awake listening to his breathing and the mewing of the kitten next door, sobered by the realization of just how much was at stake. How much of life is by one simple moment decided.

★ 9 ★
SELINA

They hanged that slave Nat Turner. After he was dead they skinned him out, to be sure he wouldn't be causing no more trouble for the white people. We got the news on a Saturday.

Mauma and me, and Ephraim and Billy, plus Lawrence got dressed up and ready to take our apples and vegetables to the Washington market. I had never been before. My daddy usually went with Mauma in the summer when they took a boat across the river with our strawberries and corn to sell. But on this particular day he was feeling poorly and Mauma said I could go.

Washington City was the busiest place. Pigs and goats and dogs running in the muddy streets. Geese honking, people yelling back and forth. Carriages and wagons and carts and people going every which way and more things for sale than I knew was in this world. Bushels of peas and bunches of green onions. Tubs of oysters and strings of fish, umbrellas and bolts of calico. Shovels. Hats. Mauma grabbed me by the hand and we walked around for a while, taking it all in. Then the menfolks got our wagon unloaded and we got down to business.

It was late in the afternoon when a man black as night and big around as a tree stopped in front of us. He looked us over with his mean pig eyes. "Whose people are you?"

Lawrence stood a little bit taller and said, "Who wants to know?"

"Me, that's who." The man picked himself an apple and bit into it, and he hadn't even paid for it yet.

"We belong to Mister Custis up at Arlington," Ephraim said. His voice was quiet as a winter's night after snow has come down.

"Custis? I heard he lets you all come and go any way you please. You all just about free, I reckon."

Billy started to say something, but Ephraim stopped him by shaking his head. To the stranger eating our apple, he said, "You take that apple and go on now. We got to finish up and get on home before dark."

The man took a folded-up paper out of his pocket and gave it to Lawrence. "You might find this interesting. If you can find anybody to read it to you."

I was itching to get my hands on that paper and read every word. I was about to tell that man that I knew how to read and so did Lawrence, but something in the way Mauma looked at me told me not to say anything.

Two women came by and bought our last basket of apples. We packed up our empty crates. Ephraim bought us a loaf of sugar and some vanilla flavoring, and we drove through the crowded streets, across the bridge, and up the road to home.

Missus came out and counted our heads to be sure we all come back, and told us to hurry up because Mister Custis was feeling poorly and wanted some supper before he went to bed. We was all in a hurry too, wanting to know what the newspaper said.

After George took supper up to the dining room, Billy ran through the quarters to round up whoever wanted to come hear. Most everybody showed up, crossed the yard, and crowded into our cabin because it was the biggest. It was still a tight squeeze. People leaned up against the walls and sat on the floor beside Daddy's sickbed. Old Nurse made herself comfortable in my mauma's chair. Nathaniel Parks and his baby sister, Cissy, climbed up into my sleeping loft with me.

Mauma lit a new candle and set it on the table. Lawrence sat in Daddy's chair and unfolded the paper. He cleared his throat a few times and pulled the candle a little closer to the page.

"It says here, after eluding the law for two months, the runaway slave Nat Turner was captured on the thirtieth day of October." Lawrence was running his finger under the words and stopping for a minute to figure them out. "He was taken to trial for the murder of sixty white people and sentenced to die by hanging. On the morning of November eleventh, the sentence was carried out. After the hanging, the body was skinned and left on display as a warning to others who would do harm to their masters."

Outside in the dark, the night peepers and the crickets went quiet. Inside, it felt like some big whirlwind had sucked all the air out. Everybody went still, like in one of Mister Custis's paintings. Even the babies, who had been fussing when they first came in, got quiet. It was the scariest news I had ever heard in my life so far, and I wondered why that man at the market gave us that paper. It didn't seem like Nat Turner had anything to do with us.

Lawrence kept on reading. "In a cornfield Nat Turner had a vision of blood droplets on the corn and knew it was God preparing him to rise up against his oppressors."

"What's oppressors?" Thursday asked.

Ephraim shrugged. "The masters, I reckon. What else does it say?"

Lawrence folded the paper. "Best the women and children not hear any more."

"Huh." Althea folded her arms. "Seem to me like there can't be anything worse than what you already read. Skinning out a man like he was a wild animal. I never heard of such."

"Go on," Billy said. "Tell us the rest."

"It says the whites done killed more than a hundred blacks because of what Nat Turner done. It says some masters made up a new rule, and slaves are not allowed to gather no more."

"We ought to go," Ephraim said, "before Missus finds out we had a meeting. After news like this, she and the mister sure to keep a close watch on us. For a while, anyways." He held out his hand. "Give me that paper."

Lawrence handed it over. Ephraim tore it into little pieces and threw them into the fire, which just about killed me. I had counted on reading it all for myself.

People stirred and started leaving in twos and threes so as not to attract too much attention from the house. Ephraim held up his hand. "Anybody asks you if you heard of Nat Turner, you better say no."

I sure hoped Missus wouldn't ask me, because the Bible says not to tell a lie. But what if you had to, to hang on to whatever kind of a life you had?

Nathaniel handed Cissy to his mauma and climbed down after her. This time he didn't stop to stick out his tongue at me or anything. I guess he was scared too.

After a while it was just Mauma and Daddy and me. Mauma took me on her lap and held me real close. "You all right?"

"Yessum."

"You hear what Ephraim said about not telling nobody about tonight?"

"I heard."

"It's important, Selina. Don't forget and let it slip. If you do, we won't be allowed to go to the market anymore."

Daddy got up and put on his shoes and shuffled outside to the outhouse.

"I don't want you studyin' on this Nat Turner business no more," Mauma said. "It was terrible, but it's over and done." She took my chin in her hands. "If anybody asks, you say you don't know anything."

I remembered a story Althea told me one time about a man who never lied. The king tried to trick him but the man told the truth, and the king figured out that a wise man always tells the truth.

"But, Mauma, what if Missus asks me?"

Mauma didn't answer me. Her face went smooth as stone. After a minute she said, "I got some good news. I was up to the house yesterday when Daniel come in with the mail. Missus got a letter from Miss Mary and tore it open then and there. Miss Mary and her new husband is coming home for Christmas."

★ 10 ★
MARY

Daniel met us at the river landing with the carriage, a red scarf draped jauntily about his neck and a sprig of holly tucked into his hatband. "Miss Mary. Sho is good to have you back to home. Arlington just ain't the same without you."

"I'm glad to be home." I handed him my traveling satchel. "How are you, Daniel? How is your little boy?"

"He had the croup awhile back, but he seem to be right as rain these days." Daniel grinned. "The thought of Christmas coming perked him right up."

"Me too."

Daniel looked around. "Where's Cassie?"

"Staying at Fort Monroe. Captain Talcott's nieces are ailing, and their mother needed an extra pair of hands. Cassie has grown fond of them and asked my permission to stay."

Daniel hoisted the last of our bags into the carriage and held open the door. "Is that ever'thing, Mist' Robert?"

"All but the horse and bridle, Daniel." Robert's cheeks were pink with cold, and his dark eyes shone with the same excitement I felt at being home.

"Sir?"

"A joke. Because Mrs. Lee has seen fit to bring so many trunks on this trip." Robert helped me into the carriage and scooted in next to me. "Drive on."

Daniel spoke to the horses, and we turned for home. Though I had been absent for only six months, the sight of it evoked so many pleasant memories of winters past that my throat tightened. "I wish it would snow so we could go sledding. Do you remember that year when—"

"I do." Robert leaned in to whisper in my ear. "I remember what happened later too. In the storeroom."

I blushed at the memory.

He laughed. "Oh me. Stolen kisses, Miss Molly. Weren't they sweet, though? Perhaps I ought to steal one now."

"Behave yourself, Lieutenant. There will be plenty of time for kisses. If I know Papa, he has seen to it that there is mistletoe hanging from every arch and lantern on the place."

A few minutes later we were home. Leaving Daniel to deal with the trunks, Robert and I went to the door. Old Peter greeted us warmly and waved us inside. Mother rushed over, wearing a new green dress and the gentle, sweet smile that had sustained me all my life, but she seemed much older than when I had left her only six months earlier. Her skin bore deeper wrinkles, and there was a tiredness in her eyes.

She clasped my hands and kissed my cheeks. "Mary Anna. You're home. And dear Robert. How are you, Cousin?"

"Never better." Robert shucked out of his coat and handed it to Peter. "Marriage to your daughter agrees with me."

Daniel came in, staggering beneath the weight of our bags. Mother sent him up to the room where Robert and I had spent our first nights as husband and wife. I pulled off my coat and gloves, and we went into the parlor where a fire blazed. Mother motioned us to sit before the fire and poured from my great-grandmother's teapot. "Your papa has been waiting most impatiently for your arrival."

"Where is he anyway?" I looked around at the banks of ivy, holly, and myrtle decorating the mantel. A ball of mistletoe hung suspended from a red satin ribbon, just where I expected to find it. "I see he had the greens brought in."

"Yes. We had a long spell of wet weather earlier, and he wanted to take advantage of a dry day to get it all cut and arranged." Mother poured herself some tea. "He is in his study at the moment, wrestling with some verse or the other. I should let him know you've arrived."

"Stay by the fire, Mother. I know the way to the study."

Robert stood as I did. "Take your time, Molly. I'm happy to keep Mother company while you and your papa catch up on the news."

I went down the hall to Papa's study and knocked once.

"Come in."

He looked up from his desk. "Ah. Mary Anna."

"I am home, Papa."

"So you are. Come let me look at you." He stood and twirled me around. "None the worse for your six months at Fortress Monroe without your papa."

"And you are none the worse either." I kissed his cheek and noticed a rip in the seam of his shirt. Smudges of ink and cat hair covered the knees of his trousers. Those who criticized my lack of attention to fashion and tidiness might well look to my father for blame. But I found his rumpled appearance endearing. He was a man of many interests and gifts, too busy with his artistic pursuits to give much thought to his wardrobe. The walls of his study were lined with pictures and illustrations done by his own hand. The bookshelves held copies of his original plays and musical compositions.

I loved his lively mind, his lack of pretension, and the absolute self-possession with which he moved through our cloistered little world. "Mother wrote to me that *The Rail Road* was well received."

"It was indeed a successful little play. I hope to mount a production in Philadelphia next year. I am much encouraged to begin work on another very soon."

I noticed a large canvas propped against the far wall. "And what is this?"

"A new painting for the Washington centennial next year."

I studied the outline of the large figure dominating the canvas. "Mother said you are composing a new verse for that occasion as well."

"That is my intent, but I confess I have not progressed very far."

"May I read it?"

"I have spent the morning wrestling with words, and all I have to show for it is the title."

He handed me a sheet of paper written in his curlicued hand. *Lines written for the Centennial Anniversary of the Birth of George Washington Feb 22, 1832. By George Washington Parke Custis of Arlington.*

"I'm certain it will be wonderful, Papa, and a fitting tribute to your stepgrandfather."

He set aside his paper. "After I'm gone you must look to the preservation of all things Washington."

"I will do my best."

"They are very dear to this family, but they belong to our country too, Mary Anna. No one must be allowed to forget him."

Robert materialized in the doorway, and Papa

hurried over to greet him. "Lieutenant. Welcome home."

"Thank you, Father." Robert shook Papa's hand.

"My wife keeps me apprised of the doings at Fort Monroe through Mary's letters," my father said, "but I am very eager to hear from your own lips how your projects are going. None were hampered by that unfortunate Nat Turner business, I hope."

"Colonel Eustis issued an order that restricted us some, but we managed to keep going until the winter weather closed in." Robert crossed the room to warm his hands before the fire. "How did the apple orchard fare this year?"

"The crop was not as ample as it should have been. I suspect quite a few bushels fell into the wrong hands." Papa sighed. "It's unfortunate that this Turner affair has fanned the flames of discontent among some of the Negroes. Though not as bad here as in other places, or so I am told. However, my dear boy, it's Christmas, and I do not wish to mar the occasion with such gloomy talk." He glanced at the mantel clock. "There is time for a walk about the grounds before supper, if you'd like."

I knew Papa wanted time alone with Robert, so I did not invite myself along. They collected their coats and hats and went out. I returned to the parlor, where Mother still sat at her knitting.

"There you are, child. Robert grew restless,

and I sent him off to find you. Did I hear the menfolk leaving?"

"Yes. I think they want to talk politics out of my hearing."

"I'm glad we have some time alone." Her knitting needles caught and reflected the firelight. "You know you can tell me anything that is weighing on your heart."

"I do know that, Mother."

"Somehow I got the feeling you were holding back in your letters."

"That's because Robert likes to add his own postscripts to them."

"Keeping secrets from one's spouse is a bad practice." Something flickered in her eyes. Some unspoken truth lingered in the air, as unmistakable as the scent of honeysuckle. "Suppose you tell me what has you so concerned."

"I want my husband to give more consideration to spiritual matters." I sat down and poured myself more tea. "That was the subject of our first quarrel, in fact."

Mother unwound more yarn. "You must be patient. Let him come to it in his own way."

"I'm trying to. But Robert has a will of iron. The more I push, the more he resists."

"You too have a will of your own. You always have." Mother finished off another row and set aside her knitting. "I have some news that I hope will please you."

"Oh?" I set down my cup.

"I have decided to bring Selina Norris in to train as a housekeeper."

"She's awfully young."

"But she is biddable and eager to learn. She must be trained to do something useful, and I have abandoned any hope of turning her into a fine seamstress."

"Have you told her?"

"Not yet. I thought you might like to do it. She has always been your favorite."

"I don't think she will object, so long as she is allowed to continue her lessons."

"She belongs to us, Mary. She is hardly in a position to object to anything. Especially after that dreadful Nat Turner episode."

"Papa was just saying that some bondsmen have become restless and discontented lately. It seems prudent to allow them as much self-determination as possible."

"Perhaps." Mother rose. "I should speak with George about our dinner. Would you like to rest awhile?"

"I am tired."

"I'll send Rose up to help you."

"I can manage. She can unpack for me later."

"Don't worry so much about Cousin Robert. He is the dearest man I know, and I have every confidence he will do everything in his power to assure your happiness."

I went up to my room. Our room now. Robert's and mine. Rose had seen to the fire, and the room was warm and glowing with soft light. I looked out the window past the winter-drab garden to the far hills where Father and Robert walked side by side, their hands clasped behind their backs. I shucked out of my dress and crawled beneath the covers.

I was home.

Christmas Eve had arrived cold and damp. Father brought in the remnant of last year's Yule log with which to start this year's fire. After supper we gathered in the parlor to prepare presents and hang our stockings, none of us wanting the evening to end.

Now the first gray light of Christmas morning stole into the room. Beside me in the feather bed Robert was still asleep. I leaned over and whispered in his ear, "Christmas gift!"

He came awake and took me into his arms. "Happy Christmas, Mrs. Lee."

"Quit stalling." I planted a kiss on his cheek. "I called Christmas gift first, so now you have to give me something."

"All right." He drew me closer and nuzzled my neck. One hand brushed my bare thigh. "How about—"

I swatted him away. "Shh. My parents are downstairs."

He laughed. "They know we're married."

"The servants will be awake soon. You know how they like to catch us out for their presents."

"All right. If nothing else will do. Look inside my travel satchel."

I tumbled from the bed to retrieve his leather traveling bag. Inside was a small flat package wrapped in red paper. I opened it to find a pair of garnet earbobs set in gold.

"Robert! They are exquisite." I leaned into the mirror to try them on. "They are beautiful, but . . . can we afford them?"

"I saved up to buy them. I thought you ought to have something special for our first Christmas together. Something you can pass on to a daughter someday." He waggled his brows at me. "A child of our own, who will make her appearance sooner rather than later, is my dearest hope."

I chose not to reply, as the idea of motherhood was still too new and strange. I retrieved his present from its hiding place. He sat up in bed, his dark hair falling over his forehead, and untied the green ribbon. "Is this what I think it is? Is this President Washington's silver?"

It pleased me greatly to see how excited he was to own something that had belonged to a man he so revered.

"Yes. I asked Father whether I might give you a single place setting. To take with you wherever you are posted. And if you decide to leave the army, it can always come home again."

He held the fork up to the light, his expression suddenly pensive. "I have thought about leaving the army, but military life is all I know."

"We have plenty of time to decide. For now, let's enjoy Christmas."

We dressed and went downstairs to exchange gifts with Mother and Papa. There was the usual assortment of books and scarves and sweets. By seven o'clock the servants had gathered in the yard, calling out, "Christmas gift!" and we went out to greet them. Papa handed out loaves of sugar and bottles of vanilla, bolts of cloth, and pouches of tobacco.

Selina rushed up and threw herself at my knees. "Christmas gift, Miss Mary!"

I handed her the things I had chosen for her— a book of stories, a bag of candies, a length of pink ribbon.

Her eyes lit up. "I was hoping for a new book. I already read everything Missus give me to read."

"I thought you would be pleased. And the pink ribbon matches your dress."

Selina nodded, her expression solemn. "About to outgrow this old dress, though. Mauma said I growed two inches this year."

"I thought you looked taller."

She laughed. "You don't look taller. You look just the same."

Then Daniel's young son ran to Robert. "Christmas gift!"

Robert pretended to search his pockets. "Let me see, young fellow. I'm sure I put something for you somewhere. Oh, here it is. Do you know a boy who would like a silver whistle?"

"Me!"

Robert handed it over. "Try not to drive your father to distraction with it."

The boy ran to find Daniel. The rest of the servants, old and young, mingled in the yard, exclaiming over their gifts and taking turns thanking us for their treasures.

"Selina?" I put a hand on her shoulder. "I have some news for you."

She looked up, the expression on her round little face instantly wary. "Good news or bad news?"

"Oh, I think it is very good news. Missus wants to teach you to look after the house."

"This house?"

"Yes. She has chosen you because you are smart and helpful."

"Oh."

"What's the matter?"

Selina popped a piece of candy into her mouth and spoke around it. "Nothin', Miss Mary. Whatever Missus want, I got to do."

"Well, you won't have to stop your lessons, if that is your concern."

"I got to go."

Robert saw our exchange and watched her disappear around the corner of the house. "What was that about?"

"Selina is not pleased about becoming a house-keeper."

"And you are unhappy because she is."

"I suppose."

"I love your tender heart, Mary. But she must learn to be useful."

"I don't disagree. But—"

"She is still a child. In time she will come to accept what is required of her. As we all must, black and white."

After Papa's usual Christmas prayer, the servants dispersed. We went inside for our own morning prayers, followed by breakfast. Robert regaled my parents with stories of his exploits at West Point and at Cockspur Island. He was so entertaining that we tarried too long at table and were nearly late for church. And for once, the cause of our tardiness was not laid at my door.

In the late afternoon Christmas dinner was served, the usual feast of turkey, vegetables, and cake. Afterward Papa retired to his writing and Mother to her knitting. Robert and I bundled into our coats and took a long walk in the Arlington wood, pausing to examine a wild holly bush bright with red berries and a shallow pond rimmed with a thin coating of ice. Wild creatures rustled in the undergrowth as we walked along. The faint shouts of children playing in the yard of the Syphax cottage echoed through the trees. Five years had passed since Papa had given Maria Syphax her freedom and seventeen acres of land. It had caused a commotion in the quarters and raised more than a few eyebrows, but I had given it little thought. Papa loved surprising others with his unexpected generosity. The children rounded the cottage and disappeared from view. Robert and I tramped on.

A cardinal perched on a branch above us, a slash of crimson against the copper-colored leaves still clinging to the oak trees. A ribbon of song spilled into the cold air. It was a sweet time, passed without the need for words. It was enough simply to be together on such a blessed day, with our whole lives ahead of us.

The new year arrived. Robert returned to his post at Fortress Monroe, but I stayed on at home to look after Mother, who had taken a chill and was too weak to oversee the house. One morning just after prayers I took her a tray of tea and toast and settled myself in the parlor to answer a letter from the Reverend Gurley.

He was president of the Colonization Society and had taken a keen interest in the activities of our Washington City members. He had asked whether the ladies of our chapter might sponsor a parlor concert to raise money for passage of freedmen to Liberia. *We must not let the loss of those unfortunates who perished from fever deter us from our mission of sponsoring new settlers,* he wrote. *I am most anxious that this early failure not doom our cause.*

I had just begun my reply when there came a tapping sound at the window. I looked up and recognized the face of the boy who had appeared at my schoolroom window back in the spring. I motioned him to come inside and went to the door to meet him.

He shook the caked snow off his shoes and stood shivering on the porch, his teeth chattering.

"My goodness. It's William Burke, isn't it?"

"Yessum. William *Custis* Burke. We been belonging to the Custises for many a generation."

"Well, come inside, William Custis Burke, before you catch your death of cold."

He came into the entry hall, uncertain of where to go next.

"Is something wrong, William?"

"No, Miss Mary." He took a deep breath. "I came to ask you something. I was wondering if you might could teach me to read."

"All children here are welcome to learn. I must leave Arlington soon, but Missus will teach you whatever you wish to know."

He shook his head. "I can't come for lessons with the others. Pap is against it."

"Your sisters attended lessons quite regularly before my marriage."

"Yessum, but he says it's different for a boy. He says they's places where a book is more dangerous to a Negro than a nest of rattlesnakes. He says I'm twelve now and too old to learn."

"That's nonsense. One is never too old to learn."

"That's what I told Pap, but he threatened to take a whip to me if I didn't stop talking about it. So I ain't said any more." William shoved his hands into his pockets. "I already know all my letters, and I can make out a few words. My sisters write words in the dirt for me when Pap ain't around."

My heart ached for the child. "We don't have much time, but we can make a start. And I will speak to Lawrence. He reads very well. Perhaps he can help you after I'm gone."

A grin split his smooth brown face. "I sure would like that, Miss Mary."

"All right. I must finish writing some letters, and then I will send for you. Your pap need not be told the reason why."

We began that afternoon, just the two of us sitting side by side in the small room at the back of the house. While snow collected in the corners of the windows and the wind rattled the glass, William Custis Burke, age twelve, began to unravel the mystery of words and sentences and paragraphs.

★ 11 ★
MARY

1835

Forever after that sweltering July day when my second child was born, I would remember the scent of lime. A small dressing room off my bedroom at Arlington was converted to a birthing room, whitewashed and disinfected with lime. The window was open in the hope of catching a cooling breeze, and every breath of air stirred the faint acrid smell.

Our firstborn, a son we named Custis, had arrived easily and without warning nearly three years earlier during our stay at Fortress Monroe. Robert nicknamed our little boy Boo and declared him the finest child in Virginia.

But this second child, a girl, took her time in arriving. She was beautiful from the beginning, with a shock of fine brown hair and her father's dark, expressive eyes.

Since I had named Custis for my father, it seemed fitting that the first girl should bear my mother's name. Now that there were three Marys residing at Arlington, I chose the nickname Mee for my new daughter.

I wrote to Robert with the news of her arrival

and awaited what I knew would be a joyous reply. But I soon developed a cold that worsened into an attack of fever so severe I could scarcely leave my bed. August and September passed in a blur of pain and misery made all the more unbearable by the steamy Arlington summer, Robert's absence, and the necessity of keeping my children away from my sickroom.

I couldn't have said which was greater—the physical maladies or the pain of knowing I was failing in my responsibilities as a mother. Often in the evenings I could hear Boo crying for me and my mother's soft voice as she tried to soothe and distract him. My daughter was growing and changing every day, and I was too ill to leave my bed. I wrote to Robert imploring him to come home.

One morning, after yet another endless night, Mother announced that she was taking me to Aunt Maria's at Ravensworth in hopes that the cooler, drier air might prove beneficial. I sipped the water she offered and propped myself onto my elbows in the bed. "It won't help."

"It might not. But we must do something, Mary. For the baby's sake, as well as your own."

"Oh, Mother, how is she?"

"Eleanor is looking after her. We're warming cow's milk for her until you are better."

I fell back onto the pillow. "I don't want to leave my children. Where is Boo?"

"Kitty and Eleanor are looking after him. I still cannot imagine why you came up with such a strange nickname for that sweet child."

"It was Robert's doing."

"Speaking of whom, his letter came last evening."

"Last evening? And you are just now telling me about it?"

"You were sleeping when Daniel returned from town. I thought it best to let you rest while you could." She took it from her pocket. "I'll leave you to enjoy it in private."

I broke the seal, my heart beating with the joy of seeing Robert's careful script upon the page. But his message was not at all what I expected. He scolded me for asking him to return home, simply for the pure gratification of his personal feelings, as he so archly put it.

Do you not think those feelings are enough of themselves to contend with, without other aggravations?

I could have wept. I was an aggravation?

I rather require to be strengthened and encouraged to the full performance of what I am called to execute, rather than excited to a dereliction which even our affection could not palliate, or our judgment excuse . . .

I let the letter fall onto my lap and stared out the window. I had not expected such a lecture. Even in my febrile state I recognized that with this letter, something in our marriage had shifted, and my part in it had changed. I was never to need him, never to miss him, but only to encourage him in the work he had chosen, and to welcome him back into my heart and my home whenever he decided to appear. A profound feeling of loneliness swept over me. But I vowed never again to make such a request and risk becoming an aggravation to my husband.

Mother returned with toast and tea and set the tray beside my bed. "Try to eat something."

"I don't want anything."

"I thought Robert's letter might cheer you, but you look quite undone." She peered into my face. "Precious child, has something happened?"

"No. He is well, and as busy as ever."

"We ought to get started soon. I'll send Kitty up later to pack a bag for you."

"I won't leave without my children."

I did not doubt that Eleanor would look after them, but my heart ached at the prospect of parting for who knew how long. I worried that if I did not recover they would not even remember me.

At last Mother relented and sent Kitty to pack their things. Mother helped me dress, but I was so weak with fever and rattled with chills that she didn't bother with my hair. Daniel came upstairs and carried me down to the carriage.

The ten-mile journey to Ravensworth seemed endless. The road rose and dipped, the carriage was cramped and drafty. The children grew tired and restless. Mee woke and began to fuss, and nothing Kitty or Nurse could do would comfort her. We arrived late in the afternoon. I was given a room at the front of the house overlooking Aunt Maria's garden, but I was too weak and too disheartened by Robert's scolding letter to enjoy the view of the summer roses blooming there.

The next day I woke to stiffness and searing pains in my legs. My fever had not yet broken. To my family I confided my fear that I would die. To my husband I said nothing.

A doctor opined that I was in the early stages of rheumatism, which did not explain the recurrent fever nor the painful abscesses that had developed on my thighs. He prescribed warm ointments for the abscesses and continued bed rest—as if I had not spent the past three months resting to no avail.

My birthday came and went without much fanfare. I missed my husband, and in the deepest, loneliest hours of the night I lay awake, fearful that this birthday might well be my last.

Then one afternoon in early October, I watched from the window as a horse and rider thundered onto the road. Even from far away I knew it was

Robert. No one else sat a horse quite the way he did.

He had been away for five months, but I was too weak to get out of bed to greet him. I had been feverish for days. I hadn't had a decent bath in weeks. I smelled of sweat and ointment, and my hair was in knots. Such was my appearance when Robert rushed into my room. He blanched when he saw me.

"Dear Mary." He crossed the room and drew a chair next to my bed. "I got home this morning and your father said you all were here." His voice broke. "I had no idea you were so ill. You never said a word."

"I did not wish to become an *aggravation,* nor to encourage you in the dereliction of your duty merely because I am at death's door."

He had the grace to blush. "I never would have lectured you so had I known how sick you are. And I missed your birthday too. I have not been the husband you deserve, Molly."

"Have you seen the children?"

"Not yet. They are still asleep." He got up and began to pace. "What do the doctors say?"

I gave him the report.

"Can you travel? I want to take you home. Consult with a different doctor. I cannot accept that you will not get well."

Robert was an engineer. His job was solving problems, and he saw my illness as another challenge to be worked out in a methodical and orderly fashion. He consulted with my mother. Our children and servants were readied for travel. In short order he called for a wagon, onto which he loaded my bed, and we traveled home.

The new doctor tried purifying my blood by the application of leeches and by placing heated glass cups on my skin. He prescribed other treatments too unpleasant to recount, yet by mid-November I was still barely well enough to take light nourish-ment while sitting up in bed.

Then my fever broke, and Robert brought in our children. Mee was nearly four months old, and I had scarcely seen her in that time. Robert placed her in my arms and she looked up at me, so solemn and curious, as if to ask where I had been.

Boo climbed onto my bed with the new top his father had brought for him. "Look, Mama. It spins fast."

"My goodness, it certainly does. Did you say thank you to Papa for such a fine present?"

"Yes, Mama." Boo patted my sleeve. "I was scared when you were sick. I didn't cry very much, though. But Mee did. Mee cries all the time."

"You were very brave, dearest. I'm proud of you."

"I know it. You should get up so we can go play in the garden."

"Careful, Boo," Robert said. "We mustn't tire your mother overmuch."

Boo held his toy to his chest. "When will it be Christmas?"

The mere thought of the holiday that required so much effort left me feeling exhausted. For Boo's sake I tried to eat more, in hopes of regaining my strength in time for the festivities. But that year I passed the holiday tucked into Papa's chair, too listless to do more than attempt a few bites of the Christmas feast.

Too, the prospect of yet another separation from Robert when I was still so unwell filled me with dread. Robert's old boss at Fortress Monroe had left the army, and I hoped that Captain Talcott would encourage my husband to follow suit. The children were growing so fast. They needed their father. I needed him too.

But I would never give voice to my feelings. Robert's commitment to duty above all else ran bone-deep in him. I knew what he wanted and what he required of me, and I would not disappoint him.

Our rector at Christ Church prevailed upon Mother to invite one of the seminary students to give the Sunday evening chapel service at Arlington. I was in my bedroom dressing for the occasion when Selina peeked in. At twelve years of age she was on the cusp of womanhood, a sturdy and dependable young girl with a sense of humor she usually kept hidden.

"You going to preaching, Miss Mary?"

I took a second pair of woolen stockings from my bureau. "I can't very well require others to brave the cold while I sit in comfort beside the fire." I bent to pull on my stocking and winced as rheumatic pain seized me.

Selina stepped into the room. "You need help?"

As annoying as it was to admit it, I did need help, and I sat back on the edge of the bed. Selina knelt in front of me and rolled my stocking.

"If you're asking me, you ought to stay inside tonight. You know it's gone be cold as the grave in the chapel. Hold your foot up."

I raised my foot and she tugged my stocking over my knee.

"Give me the other foot."

I did so, and Selina glanced around the room. "You want a jacket to go under your coat?"

"Yes."

Ten minutes later, swathed in so many layers I could barely move, I descended the staircase with Selina and went into the parlor where Mother waited.

"Selina. There you are." Mother looked up from her book. "I can't seem to find the gravy boat. Have you seen it?"

"Yessum. It had to soak awhile after breakfast, but I washed it up and put it back on the side-board."

Mother nodded and glanced at the clock. "I

106

suppose we ought to start for the chapel." She went to the door and rang her bell, and everyone gathered on the path.

It was a short walk, but very cold. The air was sharp and smelled of ice. The purple shadows of evening tinged the patches of snow still lying in the low places.

Mother shivered. "I do hope this young preacher makes short work of the service. I can't remember the last time I felt so cold."

Selina grinned up at me. "Maybe his fiery sermon will warm things up."

Mother frowned, but I couldn't help laughing.

We went inside the chapel and took our seats. The pale-faced preacher, who introduced himself as Mr. Simmons, got right down to business, reading from his Bible in a strong, steady voice. I glanced around to find the Binghams, the Norrises, the Parkses in their usual places. Then I noticed a young man sitting alone in the back seemingly transfixed, his bare hands gripping the back of the bench in front of him.

Just as we rose for the singing of the children's hymn, the door blew open, letting in a blast of frigid air. The preacher delivered a very hasty benediction.

The servants made for the door, eager to return to the warmth of their fires. Selina waved to me and left with her parents. Mr. Simmons sought out Mother to thank her for the chance to hone his skills, and after a quick word with him I tucked my Bible away and started for home.

The young man I had seen earlier followed me outside. "Miss Mary? You may not remember me. William Burke."

"William! My goodness. I didn't recognize you."

"I'm sixteen now. I reckon I've grown some."

"Indeed. But still reading, I hope."

He laughed, his breath clouding the air. "Everything I can get my hands on. Missus lends me her religious books from time to time."

"Dull reading for someone your age. At least I found them so when I was young."

"No, ma'am. They aren't dull to me. I want to be a preacher one day."

"I see."

"I've got a plan to preach outside, like John Wesley did back in the old times. In Missus's book it says he was the best-loved man in all of England."

We reached the back door of the house. Papa had lit the lamps, and yellow light spilled onto the snow. I was ready to go inside but William lingered, his hands in his pockets.

"I sold the gloves and the scarf I got for Christmas last year," he said. "A man at the market gave me a goodly sum for them. Reckon in another year I might can have enough to buy a Bible of my own." His eyes shone in the lambent light. "I never can thank you enough for showing me how to read. It was the best thing anybody has ever done for me. It's a gift, and I sure don't want to waste it."

His earnestness was so touching I felt tears welling up. "I'm sure you won't, William." I handed him my Bible. "Here. It's yours."

He drew back as if he'd been struck. "I thank you kindly, Miss Mary. The Lord sure does move in mysterious ways."

"Just don't let your father find it."

William tucked his new treasure inside his coat. "Don't worry. I got a safe place to keep it."

Despite the double layer of stockings, my feet had gone numb in the cold. "I must go."

William bobbed his head and disappeared into the night, whistling a tune under his breath.

★ 12 ★

SELINA

By the time little Miss Mee came into the world, I had been learning housekeeping for nearly four years. There was more to it than sweeping and dusting. Take the curtains, for instance. Come spring, we took down the heavy winter drapes, washed and pressed them, and stored them in bags with camphor to keep the moths from eating them. Then we had to wash the windows and put up the summer curtains. Soon as summer packed up and moved out, we had to put up the winter curtains again.

I learned to polish the woodwork with a soft cloth and beeswax. Make the wood shine like a new moon. Twice a year I scrubbed everything with a bristle brush to get the dirt out, and then I tackled the chandeliers with rags dipped in ammonia.

Candlesticks and knives and forks and all the other silver things that had belonged to Mister George Washington had to be cleaned and rubbed shiny before putting them back on the sideboard. Missus was forever going on about how the Washington pieces were so important. There was a whale of importance in that room. Besides the silver pieces there were stacks of china dishes and warming plates, and a punch bowl with a sailing ship painted in the bottom of it.

Januarys, Missus would count up all her belongings. She would hand me paper and a pencil, and we'd start with the china closet. She would tell me what to write.

"Missing one wineglass," she would say, and I would write it down. "One glass chimney of a lamp, cracked. One white china teapot, missing. One dinner plate, broken. Two goblets, missing."

I had to write fast to keep up with her.

After that we counted bed linens and the skillets and pans in George's kitchen. Heaven forbid if they was anything missing. Missus wouldn't rest until it was all accounted for.

Besides all the counting up and writing down, I learned where all the different serving pieces supposed to go on the dining table. Charles was the one in charge of the dining room, and he showed me how the bread tray goes between the vegetable platters and how the meat supposed to go at one end with the gravy beside it. Served in a boat. And the soup at the other end of the table, served in a tureen. Boats and tureens looked to me like plain old bowls, but Charles said it was important to know the right names for things, so I learned them.

Keeping a big house, you need a schedule for everything, and we had one. Mondays for doing the wash, Tuesdays for ironing, Wednesdays for beating the dust out of the carpets, and so on all the way to Sunday, which was a day of rest. More or less.

Missus had stopped my reading lessons when I turned ten years old because I could read the Bible as well as anybody, and since that was the main reason for teaching me in the first place, there was no need to keep going. She saw how disappointed I was and told me I could borrow the books she kept on a table in the parlor. But to be honest, they were dry as dirt. Most of them were sermons a preacher wrote down and put into a book. I liked preaching well enough, but not a steady diet of it.

I wanted stories about pirates or the Wild West. Something with a little more excitement to it than a "Treatise upon the Lessons of Saint Paul" or whoever. I still had the book Miss Mary gave me for Christmas, but those stories were for little children and not for a girl about to turn thirteen.

On the day Miss Mary's little daughter, Mee, was born, it was July and hotter than blue blazes. Breathing was like taking in air through a wet blanket. It was a Sunday—supposed to be a day of rest—but Missus kept me busy all morning going up and down the stairs fetching water and linens and liniments and such. The door to the birthing room was shut up tight. I could hear voices in there, Old Nurse and Missus cooing like doves to Miss Mary, who was having a bad time of it, judging from the way she was moaning and crying.

I knew what was happening in that room, and I was partly scared and partly curious. I had got my nature just a few months before, and Mauma, who was waiting for the birthing of her own baby, had sat me down and told me where babies come from and how they get to the outside world. It didn't sound like anything I wanted to try.

Soon as I finished fetching and toting for Missus, I went outside and headed for the summer kitchen. The ground was so hot it scorched the bottoms of my feet. Down in the woods the crows were cawing and the dogs had set up a ruckus. I could smell some of George's tea cakes from clear across the yard. Sure enough there was a pan of them cooling on the sill. I took a couple and got me a gourd and went to get some water from the well. Mauma called it the sweet water of Arlington. There was nothing that could take the heat out of you like a long drink of that pure, cool water.

"Selina Norris."

I spun around so fast that my tea cakes plopped into the dirt.

The stable boy stood there grinning at me. Thornton Gray wasn't much older than me, but he was taller, and thin as a rake. He smelled like hay and leather and horses. His hair was straight and his face was broad until you got down to his chin, which came to a sharp point.

Thornton would tell anybody who would listen that his people was Indians and he was planning to head out West just soon as he was free. We didn't talk too much, me and Thornton, because he usually sneaked away from Sunday night preaching, and during the week he was busy sunup to sundown helping with the horses and the carriages, or else helping the men with the planting. And I was up at the house with my beeswax and candlesticks.

"What do you want, Thornton Gray?"

"I *was* going to ask for one of them tea cakes." He looked down at them, just about as sad as if he was on his way to a burying. "But not now."

I filled my water gourd and took another long drink.

Thornton shook the dust off his bare feet. "Can I at least have some water?"

I handed him the gourd. "How come you're not down at the stables with Daniel?"

"Too hot in there right now."

"You better not let Missus see you standing here doing nothing. She says we must practice great industry at all times."

He filled the gourd and drank it empty again. "Industry. What a word."

"It means we are supposed to stay busy all the time. Because idleness is the devil's workshop."

He laughed, showing perfect teeth. "Missus ain't never seen a workshop in all her born days. And anyway, why don't she just say *busy?*"

"White people like big words, I reckon. I wouldn't mind knowing more of them."

"More white folks?"

"Don't act dumb. You know what I mean."

"Yeah, I do." He filled the gourd again. "Everybody says you the best reader on the place."

It surprised me, how much his words pleased me. My stomach dipped and rose like a rowboat in big waves. "I guess so."

"You a pretty girl too," he said. "Be even prettier if you wasn't frowning all the time."

"I don't frown."

"Yes, you do."

"How would you know what I do? You don't even stay to preaching on Sundays."

"I might, if you would sit with me."

There went that dip in my stomach again.

Just then Kitty come running from the house. "Selina, Missus looking all over for you. Miss Mary's baby has come, and we got to wash up her bedsheets."

"Boy or girl?"

"Girl. Now she and Mister Robert got them one of each. A matched set, Missus says."

Thornton headed back to the stables. "Next Sunday night, Selina."

Kitty glanced at him over her shoulder. "What's he want?"

"Nothing."

"Huh. Boys always want something."

When we got to the back door I stole a look toward the stables, but Thornton was already gone. We went inside and finished everything Missus told us to do. I wanted to see the baby, but Missus said not to disturb Miss Mary, so I went on about my business.

As it turned out, I didn't see much of Miss Mary for a long time because she come down sick in August and Missus packed up and took her and her babies away. They didn't come back until the leaves were gone from the trees and the frost had turned the garden to a brown mess.

Then there was quite the commotion: doctors coming and going and Mister Robert pacing and frowning and the little boy, Boo, crying for his mama and she was too sick to pay attention.

One Tuesday when the ironing was done, I folded Miss Mary's things and carried them upstairs to her room. Missus told me to leave them on the chair in the hallway so I wouldn't wake up Miss Mary if she was resting. But the door to her room was partly open and the curtains was pulled back, and Miss Mary called out, "Who is that in the hallway?"

"Selina. Brought your clean washing."

"Well, come in then."

I went in. The room smelled like medicine and the leavings from a breakfast tray still sitting beside her bed. Miss Mary looked white as a ghost, but she smiled at me. "I haven't seen you lately."

"Missus told me not to bother you. She said you need to get your strength back."

"I do, but I am happy to see you." She motioned for me to set down her laundry on the chest beside the window. "I hear you are doing well, learning to look after the house."

"It's a lot to it."

"Yes, that's true. But it is important to learn something useful."

"I got to go. Missus says it's a sin to waste time."

"She won't mind if you sit with me a minute. I am so tired of being bedfast. I am bored silly, Selina. Tell me, what is going on these days? I am starved for news."

"That's why you so skinny?"

She laughed. "I must look awful."

"I got to be honest. You've seen better days, Miss Mary."

"Undoubtedly." She folded her hands on top of her quilts and waited for me to give her the news.

Downstairs there was seven kinds of noise going on. Mister Robert was laughing with Boo. Mister Custis was practicing on his violin. Charles was in the dining room and the dishes was clattering.

Wasn't much to tell. It was November, and Arlington was settling down for winter. The winter wheat was planted, the gardens laid by until spring. Hog-killing time had come and gone, and the smokehouse was full up with ham and bacon and such waiting to cure. I told her this, and about Mauma still waiting for her own baby.

"How is Sally?"

"She's most nearly too big to get through the door. Her feet hurt her some. But Daddy brings in water every night and heats it up for her. A good soaking seem like it helps. Judah brings slippery elm tea when Mauma's feeling poorly. Mauma says it's going to be hard looking after Wesley and a new baby besides. She says a three-year-old boy nothing but trouble."

Miss Mary just nodded her head.

"Nathaniel cut his foot real bad, and Judah made him a vinegar and ashes plaster. The doctor gave him some bush-elder salve. Althea and Thursday got into a argument yesterday evening. I don't know what about." I picked at a loose thread on my apron. "Thornton Gray said he might sit with me at Sunday night preaching."

Miss Mary frowned. "Which one is he?"

"The one who helps look after your papa's horses. He claims to be mostly Indian. But one day I asked him to speak Indian and he couldn't say even one word."

Miss Mary's cinnamon-brown eyes crinkled up when she laughed. "Do you like this boy?"

My stomach jumped, but I acted like Thornton Gray was nothing special. "He's all right, I guess."

"Ah. I see. Have you been keeping up with your reading, Selina?"

"Since Missus stopped my lessons, there's not much to read around here excepting the Bible."

"I tried reading a few of Mr. Bryant's poems yesterday, but I tired so quickly I gave up. Perhaps you could read to me for a while."

I sat in the chair beside her bed and picked up the book, which fell open to "A Forest Hymn." It was fairly long, and she closed her eyes while I read it to her. Maybe she was picturing the words in her head or maybe she was too wore out to listen. When I got to the end she nodded her head.

"That was excellent. You read very well." She looked out the window, not saying anything for a spell. Then she said, "Isn't it lovely, Selina? I wish things never had to change. I wish Arlington could stay forever just as it is today."

I thought about that. It was slaves that planted the fields and picked the apples and killed the hogs. It was slaves that cleaned the house and cooked the meals and drove Missus everywhere she wanted to go. Miss Mary was all the time doing something for the society that wanted to send my people to Africa—writing letters or selling flowers or reading up on the meetings Missus went to in Washington City.

How could Arlington stay the same if we were all supposed to go?

I heard somebody coming up the stairs, and I handed her the book and got to my feet. "I got to go."

"In a minute." She sat up in the bed and passed her hand over her hair. "Could you bring my hairbrush and my hand mirror?"

I got them off her dressing table and handed them to her. She tried to get the brush through her hair, but it was one big, brown tangle. Knots everywhere. Looked like Judah's old rag mop.

Missus came into the room. "Selina. I've been looking for you."

"My fault, Mother," Miss Mary said. She yanked on her knotted hair. "I'm afraid I have delayed her. Oh, these tangles are quite impossible!"

"No wonder," Missus said. "After four months abed." To me she said, "I'm expecting visitors this afternoon. Be sure the parlor is dusted."

"Yes, Missus."

"And polish that silver tray on the sideboard."

"Yes, Missus."

"And be sure George has started making the sweet biscuits."

"Yes, Missus."

I started for the door, but Miss Mary stopped me. "Selina, before you see to your chores, find my sewing scissors and bring them here."

It didn't look to me like Miss Mary was feeling up to doing any sewing, but I fetched the scissors. And right before my eyes, she started in with those scissors and hacked off all her hair.

★ 13 ★
MARY

1838

"Will we see Indians out West, Mama?" All morning Boo had been clattering up and down the stairs, bringing a succession of favorite toys to the open trunks in my bedroom. Now he plunked his spinning top, which had long since

120

lost its crimson paint, right on top of my best underthings.

I fished it out and set it on the bed. "I should not be surprised if there are Indians."

"Papa says there are. He says they wear beads and blankets and they paddle their canoes up and down the river."

"Well, there is your answer then."

"I want a pony when we get out West." Boo picked up his top and set it into my trunk again.

"Custis Lee. Do not put that toy into my trunk again. If you do, I will leave it behind."

Robert came in. "Here are the books you wanted."

I made space in my trunk next to a chest of my father's old papers, which were very curious and amusing, though many had moldered beyond recognition. For more than twenty years Papa had published recollections of his life as the stepgrandson of George Washington in the *National Intelligencer*. His friends and admirers had encouraged him to collect them into a single volume, and he had asked me to sift through the letters, commissions, deeds, and patents, stretching back to the reigns of James II, William and Mary, and Queen Anne, to find those that might be of interest to the general reader. Some might think such a project a frivolous pursuit, self-indulgent even, but I felt the weight of my family's history and the burden of keeping it alive.

The lives and accomplishments of others, it seems, slip all too quickly behind the veil of time.

Robert set down my books and glanced at our son, who had retreated to the corner in a fit of pique. "What is troubling Mr. Boo?"

"Despite my wishes, he is determined to pack his toys in my trunk instead of his own."

Boo would turn six years old in the fall. Of late he had become willful and obstinate, and I was grateful that for the immediate future our son would fall under his father's watchful gaze. Our daughter, Mee, was three, and Rooney, our second son, was just a year old.

"Custis." Robert's voice brooked no argument. "Would you mind explaining why you have disobeyed your mother?"

"I don't know."

"Then perhaps you ought to go to your room until some plausible explanation suggests itself. And in the meantime think of how you have disappointed both your mother and me with your behavior."

"Yes, sir." Boo retrieved his top.

"I will take charge of that." Robert held out his hand for the toy.

Boo's dark eyes, so like his father's, brimmed with tears. "But it's my favorite."

Robert waited. Boo handed it over and stomped out.

"You see what I must contend with when you

are away?" I folded the last of my shawls into the trunk.

"You must be firm with him, Mary."

"I try. But sometimes I don't know what to do with that boy. I suppose it isn't all his fault. Papa dotes on him because he will inherit Arlington after I'm in the ground."

"All the more reason we ought not to be separated any more than is absolutely necessary." Robert stood behind me and wrapped both arms around my waist. "You cannot know how anxious I have been to get back to all of you, Molly. How I dreamed about you all every night." He kissed the back of my neck. "I have booked the train to Baltimore for early next week. Will you be ready by then?"

Though the mere prospect of the long trip exhausted me, I turned in his arms and kissed him back. "St. Louis, here we come."

He laughed. "Which servants are coming with us?"

"Just Kitty. She is kind to the boys, and they are accustomed to her. Unfortunately, she is given to much daydreaming."

"What about your Selina?"

"Mother can't spare her. Margaret is with child; she can hardly be expected to take Selina's place. Julia is sick too, and there must be someone reliable to help run this house."

Robert left me to my packing, and a few minutes

later I saw him walking in the garden with Papa. Kitty came in, leading Mee by the hand. "Little Miss not feeling so good today, Miss Mary."

"Oh?" I felt my daughter's forehead. It did seem overly warm. I laid Mee on my bed and got a cloth to make a cold compress. Kitty stood there with her hands in her pockets, staring at the ceiling.

"Kitty. Do you not have anything to do? Where's Rooney?"

"Sleeping like a rock the last time I looked."

"When was that?"

"I don't remember."

"Then go check on him, and then ask my mother to come up."

Kitty didn't move. "She can't come up, Miss Mary. She's got comp'ny in the parlor. Missus Palmer and Missus Mason is here."

"Then go look after the baby."

Over the next few days Mee developed a cough and wouldn't eat. As the day of our departure drew near, Robert and I made the unhappy decision to leave her at home in the care of my mother and father.

Papa caught up with me as I was packing a new book of poetry and several novels Mother had given me to help pass the time on the journey west.

"I don't want you to worry about Mee," he said. "It is unfortunate that she must be left behind, but your mother and I will see to her."

"I know she will get the best of care. But I will miss her so." I closed the trunk and locked it.

He patted my hand and smiled. "Having my only granddaughter to look after will be almost like reliving your own childhood."

"Don't spoil her, Papa."

He looked at me, a hint of merriment in his eyes. "You may be certain I will treat her just as I treated you, dearest."

"Oh, then she is completely ruined!"

He laughed. "Tell me, what arrangements has Robert made for furnishing your home in the hinterlands? You are welcome to take some things from here if it makes the move easier."

"Thank you. But we plan to buy what we need in Cincinnati and have it shipped on to St. Louis."

"Well, if you find you need anything from here after you have gone, you have but to ask."

The next day we left for Baltimore and a short visit with Robert's sister, Anne. But Rooney and Boo fell ill, and we were forced to remain for nearly two weeks until they recovered.

At last we left Anne's and continued on toward St. Louis, taking the train to Philadelphia and Harrisburg, and then a canal boat to Pittsburgh, where we waited for the next westbound steamboat. It was my first visit to that city, a bleak and charmless place full of noise and dust from the cotton mills and glass factories that seemed never to shutter their doors. The coal furnaces emitted a constant cloud of black soot and ash that turned everything a dingy gray.

I was already homesick for the lush, green hills of Arlington, and I was relieved when the steamboat came, and at last we arrived in Cincinnati.

After breakfast Robert took Custis on his knee. "What do you think of this journey, Boo?"

"It's a disappointment. I have not seen any Indians yet. Or canoes or anything."

"You will, when we get closer to St. Louis." Robert kissed the top of Custis's head. "I have a great favor to ask of you this morning."

"What is it?"

"I need you to help Kitty look after Rooney while your mother and I go ashore."

"I want to go with you."

"I know you do, but we are on an important errand, getting things for our new house. It wouldn't be any fun for a little boy."

"Kitty doesn't need my help. All Rooney does is sleep all day." Boo rolled his eyes. "He is not much of a companion, Papa."

Robert laughed. "Your brother will catch up with you in no time, and then you will be inseparable. Just as I was with my own brothers."

Sensing that our son was about to launch into full-blown opposition, Robert set Boo on his feet and gave him an affectionate swat on his behind. "Run along now."

I checked on Rooney, spoke with Kitty, and met Robert on deck. We left the waterfront and walked into town.

Robert tucked my hand into the crook of his arm. "Well, dearest wife, what shall we purchase for our new abode?"

Carts and carriages rumbled past. Train whistles screeched. I stepped around a mound of rubbish in the street. "I cannot say, since you have told me so little about it. Am I in for another season of living in rooms the size of a piece of chalk?"

"You will find it a great improvement over Fort Monroe. The house has a proper parlor and two bedrooms. The dining room is not overly large, but it's quite adequate. There is a small accommodation for Kitty and a yard where the boys can play. Best of all, we do not have to share space with Captain Talcott."

My homesickness dissipated in the glow of Robert's happiness at having his wife and children with him. "We need beds and a proper dining table. Chairs. A settee for the parlor."

We found a furnishings store and selected the necessary pieces. While I admired a carved walnut tea table and a pair of handsome upholstered chairs too dear for a soldier's salary, Robert paid for our purchases and arranged for our new things to be shipped by steamer to St. Louis.

We had been invited to attend the wedding of an old friend during our stop in Louisville, and after completing our furniture purchases, we shopped for a wedding gift. Robert bought toys for the children, and I picked up a new handkerchief for Kitty. We stopped for tea at the hotel before returning to the boat, and for a brief time we set aside our responsibilities and worries as parents and simply enjoyed each other's company.

Robert leaned back in his chair and surveyed the activity taking place outside the hotel window. "We have come a long way in the last seven years."

"I should say so." We were both past the age of thirty. No longer young but not yet old, and with so much more of life to anticipate. I picked up the sugar tongs. "Sometimes I find it hard to comprehend that we have three children."

"And each of them entwined so closely to my heart that I feel them with every pulse. I cannot express how glad I am to have you all with me, dearest."

"Even so, something is worrying you."

He stirred his tea. "My orders are to tame a river, and I can't do it without the proper materials and equipment. I don't see how Congress can possibly appropriate the necessary funds when the country is still struggling to overcome the depression."

"Surely they see the absolute necessity of it, regardless of the cost."

"They will weigh the cost against the country's

other needs. Perhaps I will be allowed to finish, perhaps not."

"Well, fretting about it won't change the outcome."

"I suppose not." He sighed. "I only wish I were earning more. The needs of the children will become ever more expensive as they grow."

"Captain Talcott would help you if you wanted to leave the service."

"Perhaps I am better suited to farm some quiet corner of Virginia with you and our children about."

"That would suit me. Papa would gladly hand over the running of White House or Romancoke to you."

"Yes. But I would prefer my own land, and at present we cannot afford it." He finished his tea.

"Well then, I suppose you must be patient with the army. You said yourself that peacetime promotions are scarce as hen's teeth. And you have been a first lieutenant for only two years."

It was time to go. We left the hotel and retraced our steps to the steamer. Boo was thrilled with the new Indian headdress his father had bought for him, but Rooney, the little devil, seemed more intent upon tossing his father's hat into the river.

That evening we left for the thirteen-hour journey to Louisville. The wedding provided a welcome respite from the trials of the long trip. It was a delightful celebration that lasted into the wee hours and was attended by many old friends. After the festivities there was time for a few social calls before the final leg of our journey brought us at last to St. Louis.

The landing was a colorful, noisy swarm of dockworkers, traders, merchants, and copper-skinned natives wearing leather breeches. Carriages and drays lined the docks. A whistle screeched, startling Rooney, who began to wail. Robert took the baby in his arms as we went down the gangplank. Boo, wearing his Indian headdress, clung to my hand, too overcome to misbehave. Kitty, in her rumpled yellow dress, bonnet askew, came last, her arms laden with the children's toys, my shawl, and one of Rooney's shoes.

To the other passengers we must have resembled a small traveling circus. But Robert's joy was so contagious that despite missing our daughter, I found myself looking forward to a new adventure.

★ 14 ★
SELINA

"Brought you a present." Thornton Gray caught up with me on the path up to the house.

I was late reporting to Missus because Mauma was feeling sickly after my little sister was born. For some reason Mauma gave the baby the name of Mary, which made her the fourth Mary at

Arlington behind Missus and Miss Mary and Miss Mee. It seemed like Mauma ought to have picked something less confusing.

My brother, Wesley, was six years old—old enough to help in the garden and tend the chickens, but when it came to looking after Mauma and the baby, he was useless. The night before, Judah brought by some slippery elm tea and told me to warm it up for Mauma when she first waked up. I fixed her tea and cleaned up the squalling baby and made sure Daddy had his dinner bucket filled with biscuits and molasses before he went off to get the fields ready for planting the winter wheat.

The baby had cried and carried on half the night, and now I was sleepy and too tired for any of Thornton Gray's foolishness.

He stuck his hand in his pocket and brought out a strip of lace. It was fine as a spiderweb and so pretty I just about stopped breathing. But Thornton Gray was already too sure of himself to suit me, so I acted like it was nothing special.

"Ain't you going to say anything?"

In the last year he had got his growth on him, and he was nearly a head taller than me. The rest of him had finally caught up with his long arms and legs, and his hair was thick and black as ink. He looked like a man now. He had taken to walking with me to church on Sunday nights, and mostly he stayed for the sermon and the singing. Miss Mary would be pleased about that. But she was out West and too busy to study on what was happening back home.

"It is very pretty." I tucked the lace into my pocket. "Thank you."

"It was the prettiest they had. Come all the way from Europe. That's where they make the best lace in the world."

"You don't say." Missus had let him go to the Georgetown market to help Lawrence sell our fall produce, and now all of a sudden Thornton Gray thought he was a man of the world.

We reached the back door. "I got to go in. Missus don't like it when I'm late."

"Brought you something else." He pulled a folded-up paper out of his pocket. "Keep it to yourself."

I unfolded it. "The *Liberator*?"

"It's a newspaper about freedom," Thornton said. "Some man up in Massachusetts is writin' it."

Dread slithered up my spine and coiled in my insides. It had been seven years since Nat Turner was hanged and skinned for killing white people, but it still scared me every time I thought about it.

"I don't want it. You better burn it before you get us both in trouble."

The back door flew open and there stood Missus. "Selina."

I crumpled the paper and hid it in my pocket. "Yessum."

"You are late."

132

"I'm sorry. Mauma was—"

"Never mind. Please come inside. We have much to accomplish today." Missus glared at Thornton. "Do you not have anything to do?"

"I got plenty of chores." He turned and jogged down the path toward the stables.

I went inside with Missus. She set me to polishing Mister Washington's silver. Again. While I was getting out my polishing cloth, she caught my chin in her hand and said, "Selina Norris. What are you up to?"

The *Liberator* was setting like a lead weight in my pocket. My heart jerked hard against my ribs. "Nothing, Missus."

"Hmm. Are you by any chance courting Thornton Gray?"

"Not especially. He sits with me at church some."

She smiled. "So I noticed."

"He hasn't asked me to marry him or anything."

"At your age I should hope not."

Just then there was a big commotion in the parlor. A yell and then a crash and little Miss Mee started crying. She was always getting into something because Mister Custis carried her on his shoulder nearly everywhere he went. But then he would put her down somewhere and forget to watch her, and she'd get herself into all kinds of hot water. Missus hurried out to see what was the matter this time, and I could breathe again.

Missus kept me so busy the rest of the day, dusting and sweeping and carrying the clean washing up the stairs, that I didn't have time to think about the *Liberator* in my pocket. My plan was to set fire to it as soon as I could. But when I got home that night, Mauma and the baby were sleeping. Wesley was off playing somewhere, Daddy was out in the barn smoking with Daniel, and my curiosity got the best of me.

I sat down at the table, pulled the candle closer, and smoothed out the wrinkled page. A piece by a Mister Garrison caught my eye.

I look upon the Colonization scheme as inadequate in its design, injurious in its operation, and contrary to sound principles. I concede to them benevolence of purpose and expansiveness of heart, but they are laboring under the same delusion which swayed Saul of Tarsus, persecuting the blacks even unto a strange country and believing they are doing God's service. It is agreeable to slaveholders because it is striving to remove a class of persons who they fear may stir up their slaves to rebellion.

Miss Mary and Missus was always talking about the society for sending black people to Africa. They said it was because whites in America would never accept people like me as an equal. They said it was so that black people could have a better life, work for themselves and not for a master. But if Mister Garrison was right, Miss Mary wanted to send me away for her own benefit. Because she was afraid of me. I felt sick all the way to the middle of my heart. Nothing feels worse than to be betrayed by someone you think is your friend.

It was quiet in the cabin, wasn't any sound except Mauma's breathing and the mewling of the baby. With nothing but the candle's feeble glow to light up the darkness, I climbed the ladder to the loft. Folded up the *Liberator* till it was the size of my hand and hid it between the boards in the floor. I pulled my mattress over for good measure. Maybe we would be free one day, and maybe that piece of paper would be my very own kind of jack bag, protecting me from being sent across the ocean to a place I barely heard of.

I knew I was taking a chance keeping it. None of the Custises ever came down to the quarters, but if Mauma found that newspaper, she would raise her very own kind of a revolution.

Daddy and Wesley came in and I heard them taking off their shoes, getting ready for sleep.

The night was clear. The sky was full of stars. I pictured Miss Mary out West looking out at those same bright stars and wishing she was home to Arlington and that it would never ever change. Which meant one thing. If her dream came true, then mine never could.

★ 15 ★
MARY

Dust filtered through the window of the cramped stagecoach, making the baby sneeze. I took him onto my lap and wiped his face.

Boo scowled at Robert as if his father were the cause of all his misery. "How much farther to Arlington, Papa? I miss Grandpa and Grandmama. I'm tired. I'm hungry."

"Almost there, son, and I am proud of you for being such a good traveler." Robert placed an arm around Boo's shoulders. "I bet George has made all our favorites for supper tonight."

After an eleven-day journey from St. Louis, we were almost home. I was soon to give birth to our fourth child, and I was anxious about it and weak with exhaustion.

Our western adventure had been marred by a series of disasters great and small. Upon our arrival in St. Louis we discovered that the house Robert had so glowingly described wasn't available after all. We were forced into temporary accommodations until the home of the explorer William Clark became available. I was overjoyed at the prospect of having space all to ourselves where my boys could give rein to their noisier impulses, but soon I discovered we would be sharing the Clark house with a Dr. Beaumont and his family.

The steamship carrying the new furnishings we had bought in Cincinnati exploded en route, taking our lovely tables, chairs, sofas, and mirrors to the bottom of the river. The boys suffered in the mosquito-laden heat. Kitty came down with a fever. Then winter came and the river froze, trapping us in St. Louis, and we spent a lonely Christmas away from Arlington. St. Louis was a large place, with many agreeable people, but I was more than ready to come home.

Late in the afternoon the stage entered the city. Daniel met us with our coach and saw to the transfer of our bags. Then at last we were home.

I fairly ran from the carriage up the steps to the portico, where my mother waited to greet me with kisses and happy tears.

"Where is Mee?" Leaving Robert and an exhausted Kitty to deal with the boys, I followed Mother inside.

Papa was standing before the large painting of President Washington he had completed a few years earlier. I was shocked to see how bald and stooped he had grown in so short a time. Mee, in a faded pink calico dress, her hair a tumble of curls about her shoulders, was sitting atop his shoulders listening to his story of how a young George Washington had outwitted the British troops.

"There they were, Mee, surrounded by thousands and thousands of British soldiers just waiting to pounce. It was getting dark, and your great-great-grandfather was worried. How could he possibly defeat such a large contingent?"

"I don't know, Grandpapa. What is a contingent?"

The sound of her sweet voice after so long an absence nearly brought me to tears. I wanted to scoop her up and squeeze her but I refrained, for this was a magical moment between my father and his only granddaughter. I waited for him to finish his story, or to turn and see my mother and me waiting in the doorway.

"A contingent is a group of people. In this case, Brits! And they wanted to defeat Washington so they could put down the rebellion."

"What is a rebellion?"

"Never mind. Anyway, our hero ordered his soldiers to set a dozen campfires and keep them burning all night. The British soldiers saw the campfires and decided to wait until morning to attack. And very early the next day, before the sun came up, Washington and his troops stole away. The British readied their weapons and poured into the campsite where they had seen the fires burning the night before. And the whole camp was deserted . . . that is, it was empty. Washington and his men had tricked the British."

"That was a good trick." Mee patted my father's head. "Tell me another story, Grandpapa."

Mother stepped into the room. "Not now, Mee. I have the most wonderful surprise. Your mother and father are home."

Papa set Mee on her feet and opened his arms to me. "Mary Anna!"

I rushed across the room to embrace him, then bent down to my daughter. "My precious child, how I have missed you. Come give your mama a kiss."

Mee hid behind Papa's leg. "I don't want to."

"Oh, of course you do, Mee," Mother said. "We have been talking about this for two weeks. About how your mama and papa and your brothers were coming home."

Just then Robert and the boys came in. Robert kissed Mother's cheek and shook Papa's hand. Custis leapt into his grandfather's arms.

"Papa!" Mee ran to embrace her father. Robert scooped her up and covered her face with kisses until she giggled and squirmed to be set down again. She embraced Custis but ignored Rooney. And me. I could only stand there, exhausted, confused, and numb with disappointment.

Mother whispered to Robert, and he bent down to our daughter. "Have you kissed your dear mother yet?"

She shook her head.

"Then hop to it, child. She has missed you. Maybe more than any of the rest of us."

My daughter marched over to where I stood and

planted a dutiful kiss on my cheek. I reached for her, but she turned away and kissed Rooney, who only blinked in confusion. He had been too young when we left for St. Louis a year ago to remember he had a sister at home.

"I have had a cold supper prepared," Mother said, her voice so full of love and sympathy that I nearly lost my composure. "You must be famished."

We trooped into the dining room. Food was brought to the table, and while we ate, Robert regaled my parents with stories of our year out West. Custis told his grandparents about his friend Israel Beaumont and how they had spotted Indians paddling canoes on the river.

Rooney began to fuss, and Kitty took him up to bed. When Mee's eyes began to droop, Mother said, "Kitty should be back soon to take her up as well."

"I want to take her." I got up and stood behind Mee's chair. "Come along, Miss Lee. Time for bed."

"I don't want to."

My patience deserted me. "It seems there is very little that you want to do this evening, Mary Custis."

Mee turned her dark eyes on Robert. "I want my papa to take me up to bed."

I was tired, heavy with child, plagued with rheumatic pains. I was ready to hand her over, but Robert fixed our daughter with his stern gaze.

"You are being inexcusably rude, Mary Custis. Now go with your mother without any complaint."

She slid from her chair and ran ahead of me up the stairs. I helped her wash her face and hands and change into her nightgown. "Goodness, you have grown so much this barely fits you anymore."

"Grandmama says I am almost a little lady."

"That's true. And ladies are always kind and polite to others. Especially to those who love them more than anything."

She climbed into bed. "Grandmama tells me stories at night."

"All right. What story would you like to hear?"

"The one about the goats and the troll and the bridge."

"That's one of my favorites too." I tucked the coverlet about her shoulders and sat on the edge of the bed. "Once there were three goats that lived in a green grassy meadow not far from—"

"That is not the way Grandmama says it."

"Well, this is my own version."

"The goats lived in a village with a shoemaker and a fisherman."

"Fine. In a village, then. And one day the goats decided to visit the farm that lay on the other side of a shining stream."

"It was not a stream. It was a river, and there was a bridge and it was made of stones and there was moss over the stones."

The long trip finally caught up with me. My

head pounded and my stomach roiled. "Perhaps you ought to tell me the story, then. To refresh my memory."

Mee launched into the tale but soon drifted into sleep. I stood over her bed, studying her sweet face. In the glow of the candlelight, she looked so innocent in repose that I felt a piece of my heart crumble. I had the feeling that she would never forgive me for my absence regardless of the reason. That something precious had been irretrievably lost.

I went across the hall to my bedroom to find Selina unpacking my trunks. Her face lit up when I dragged myself through the door.

"Selina. I thought you'd have gone home by now."

"I saw you had come home and thought you would want your nightdress unpacked right away."

"I am done in. And Mee didn't make life any easier this evening."

Selina fished my nightgown from the trunk. "She just needs to get used to you again is all."

"She is spoiled, I'm afraid."

"I can't lie about that, Miss Mary. Your papa hardly let her out of his sight the whole time you were gone. She's used to being the center of attention." Selina set my traveling case on the dresser. "You need anything else?"

"I don't think so. I'm so tired I could sleep for a

week. But tell me, how is your family? How is Thornton Gray?"

She grinned. "Same as always. Full of himself."

"Have you seen William Burke? I wrote to Mother about him, but she forgot to answer my questions."

"He hasn't been around here in a long while. Mr. Custis sent William to help Mr. Nelson down at Romancoke." Selina folded back the covers on the bed and fluffed the pillows. "Lawrence says William Burke likes a girl down there. Her name is Rosabella. He says she sings like an angel."

"I see."

"William Burke is in love, I reckon."

I couldn't resist teasing her. "And what about you, Selina Norris? Are you in love?"

She laughed and started for the door. "Good night, Miss Mary."

I lay in the darkness listening to the house settling for the night and thinking about William. Papa chose only his most able servants to assist the overseers. The shy, gangly twelve-year-old with a burning desire to read had become a man of some aptitude. A man burning to serve God. Such promise ought not to be wasted. But William was not mine, and as much as I wanted to see him go free, there was nothing I could do.

SELINA

Mister Robert hadn't been gone from Arlington no time before Miss Mary's birthing room was cleaned and limed again and here come another baby into the world. It was the middle of June, the air warm and still. I was putting things away in the upstairs linen press when I heard the baby's first cry. A few minutes later Nurse came out into the hall wiping her hands on a towel and said, "Miss Mary got her another girl. The child is strong, but they's a bad curse on her."

"What kind of a curse?"

"That poor little baby got a red mark on her cheek. Miss Mary's crying about it. But crying won't do a bit of good." Nurse shook her head. "I got to go get some buttermilk for a poultice."

I stood there in the hall wondering what I should do. I wanted to see Miss Mary, but not if she was going to be bawling and carrying on. And I was curious. I had never seen a baby with a curse on its head. Then Missus came out with a armful of dirty linens and I had my work cut out for me.

Next day Missus set me to polishing the furniture in the children's rooms. I got it all spit shiny and started downstairs to see what was next, and that was when Miss Mary called to me from her room.

I went in, a part of me curious and another part scared to see the afflicted child. The red mark was still there, so I guessed the buttermilk hadn't done its job. Miss Mary looked at me with big, sorrowful eyes. When she looked at me like that it was hard to remember that I couldn't trust her quite as much as I once had.

Still, in the *Liberator* Mister Garrison said the colonization people honestly thought they were doing God's work. I decided as long as I was at Arlington, I had to believe that Miss Mary was sincere and doing her best for me.

"Selina, do you know whether Judah has anything that might help my child?"

"Like a spell, you mean?"

"I don't believe in spells and neither should you. Nurse brought up a buttermilk plaster to fade the mark, but it didn't work. Perhaps Judah knows of a different remedy."

"I can ask."

"Oh, this poor child." Miss Mary leaned back on her pillows and shut her eyes tight, but tears came running out anyway.

I didn't know what to do. For some reason she had been weepy ever since she got back from St. Louis. It looked to me like another attack of the mullygrubs was coming on. I didn't want to see her cry, so I headed her off. "Miss Mary, you haven't said what you named this one."

She sniffed and wiped her eyes on the sleeve of her nightgown. "We're going to call her Anne Carter Lee. After Captain Lee's mother."

Good news: there wasn't going to be a fifth Mary at Arlington. "That's a good name. Sounds like a name in a book."

She propped herself up on her elbows. "How would you like to come with me on a trip?"

I was so surprised I couldn't say a word. I couldn't picture Missus letting me go anywhere. Not when President Washington's silver needed polishing every single week.

"Captain Lee thinks I ought to take the children to visit my Turner cousins for the summer. Mother will come with me, of course, and Kitty. But we will need more hands to look after four children."

"But who is going to take care of Arlington if we are all gone?"

"Margaret will be here, and Charles and Peter. And my father will be here to keep an eye on things."

Just like that it was settled. Along about the middle of July we packed up and started out for Kinloch, which was the name of Mister Turner's place. We started out early. Daniel drove Missus and Miss Mary and the children in the carriage, and Thornton Gray got to drive the wagon that Kitty, Cassie, Nurse, and me rode on. Mister

Custis had got a dog for Custis and Little Mary, and the dog rode all the way sitting on top of the trunks. Thornton kept after me to sit beside him, but I didn't want to start any talk about me and him. I sat by Kitty and she told me about her adventures in St. Louis.

It took all day and part of the night to get there. Miss Mary's cousins came out to greet us. We went in and they had supper ready and we ate. White folks in the dining room and slaves on the porch and in the yard. Mister Turner sent one of his slaves to show Thornton and Daniel where to stable the horses, and gave them some quilts for bedding down in the barn.

After I helped Miss Mary get the children ready for bed, I took my quilt and went to the sleeping porch where Kitty and the rest, except for Nurse, were already settling down. Pretty soon Kitty and Cassie started to snore, but I couldn't sleep. After a while I took my quilt out to the front porch and sat on the steps listening to the crickets singing in the grass. Watching the lightning bugs flashing in the dark.

Next thing I knew, Thornton Gray was standing over me dripping water onto my head. "You better get back where you suppose to be 'fore Miss Mary comes looking for you."

I sat up and scratched at a mosquito bite on my arm. "What time is it?"

"Nearly seven. Me and Daniel is fixing to head

147

back to Arlington." He grinned. "You sure you don't want to come with me?"

"Wouldn't matter if I did, now, would it?"

"Reckon not. You still got that paper I give you?"

"Maybe."

"You can trust me, Selina." His voice went real low, in a way that made my stomach jump. "Because I—"

I jumped up and folded my quilt. "I better go in."

"All right then. Reckon I'll be seeing you whenever Miss Mary takes a notion to come on back home."

Daniel drove the carriage into the yard. I waved to him and watched Thornton head to the barn to get the wagon. I went back to the sleeping porch. Kitty and Cassie were awake and waiting on breakfast. We could smell bacon and biscuits and coffee coming from the summer kitchen.

After breakfast came morning prayers, with everybody standing in the yard while Mister Turner read to us from the Bible. Then Miss Mary called me to come up to her room. She had just finished nursing Miss Anne Carter Lee, who was sleeping with her fists curled up like she was ready to fight. I figured with that red mark on her face, she was in for a lifetime of fighting off people making fun of her.

"Selina, I am having a time with my hair." Miss Mary handed me her hairbrush. "Can you do anything with it?"

"I'm a housekeeper. I don't know much about hair, but I might can make you a braid."

"Splendid! I do not want to fuss with it at all."

I braided her hair the way Mauma had taught me and helped her with her dress, an old blue one with wide sleeves that she wore for gardening back home. I could hear Custis and Rooney playing in the room next door and Little Miss Mary shouting and pounding down the stairs. But Miss Mary was staring out the window with the sweetest smile on her face, like she didn't hear nothing but the birds singing.

Finally she turned in her chair and pointed to a stand of trees. "See that oak grove down there? That is where my husband and I first realized we were meant to be married. Oh, he was handsome, even though he was just a boy of twenty. Never shall I forget how dashing he looked in his uniform."

I could see she was missing Mister Robert real bad, and I was afraid she might start crying again. "Sure is a pretty day. What you planning to do with it, Miss Mary? It's too nice to sit inside feeling bad and missing folks."

"You are absolutely right. I think I will take the children for a walk this morning. I want to take my paint box along. Nurse will look after the baby, but I need you and Cassie to help keep an eye on the others."

Sounded good to me. Better than sweeping and

polishing things. I looked through her trunk for her paint box and drawing paper. "You going to need a sunbonnet, Miss Mary."

She sighed. "What a bother. But of course you are right. Mother will never let me out of doors without one."

It took some doing to get the boys and Little Miss Mary ready for the outing. Custis wanted to bring his dog, which he had named Rusty. Rooney had lost one of his shoes and I had to find it. Little Miss Mary pitched a walleyed fit and said she wanted to stay with Missus. But Missus was expecting a visit from her Fitzhugh cousins. She peeled that child off her lap and sent us off with a basket of sandwiches and a quilt for sitting on.

We walked across a meadow until we got to a stream of water. On the other side were a grove of trees and some vines with red flowers hanging down. It made a pretty scene: blue water, red vines, green trees. Miss Mary spread the quilt and opened her paint box. The boys took off, and Cassie followed them to keep them out of trouble. The dog ran ahead, his tail swiping the air like a feather duster.

Miss Mary bent down over her painting and seemed like she forgot the rest of us were there. I picked some vines and started weaving them together.

Little Mary plopped down beside me. "Selina, what are you doing?"

"Making a crown."

"Out of leaves?"

"Uh-huh."

"Who is it for? I know! Me."

"What makes you so sure? Maybe I'm making it for your brother Custis, or that spotted dog of his."

She giggled. "Dogs don't wear crowns. Boys don't either."

"Of course they do. It talks about it in the Bible." I tucked the ends of the vines under.

"I don't care. I want it." She reached for it. "It's pretty."

"Let me tell you something, Mee. In your long life there is bound to be lots of things you will want and can't have. It's going to go hard for you if you can't learn that people don't always get what they want. Even you."

"I'll tell Mama you were mean to me and then you'll be in big trouble."

"Suit yourself."

She jumped up. "Keep your stupid crown. It's ugly anyway."

I shaded my eyes and looked back at Miss Mary. She had finished her sketch and was waving to the boys. Mee ran to meet Custis and Rooney, who had been wading, judging from their wet pant legs.

Miss Mary frowned at Cassie like the whole thing was her fault, and then at her boys. "Custis Lee, what on earth happened?"

"Rusty treed a squirrel, then he got scared and wouldn't cross the creek. I had to go fetch him."

"Mama, I helped," Rooney said. "Rusty was awful scared."

Miss Mary laughed, and it was like sunshine breaking through the darkest clouds. "Then I suppose it is a good thing you brave boys were there to rescue the poor thing."

Custis bent down to study his mother's artwork. "It's pretty, Mama. It looks like a picture in a book. Can I have it for my room?"

"If you wish, precious child."

"I want a picture too, Mama." Rooney collapsed onto her lap and rested his head on her shoulder.

"All right, my sweet. When we come tomorrow, I shall paint a picture just for you."

Rooney beamed at his mother. "And after that it will be Mee's turn."

"I don't want one." Little Mary sat down on the quilt and folded her hands. "I'm hungry."

Miss Mary put away her paint box and opened up the basket. I gave Cassie the crown I made and we ate our sandwiches. The boys took turns slipping bites to the dog.

It was a pleasant time there in the sunny meadow with the birds and insects singing and chirping and the water running over the rocks in the stream. When Rooney and Mee got sleepy, Miss Mary said it was time to go home. I folded the quilt. Miss Mary packed up her paint box.

Cassie carried the sandwich basket, and we started back to the house. The children and Rusty ran on ahead, leaving Miss Mary and me to follow them.

She let go a gusty sigh. I was learning that when she sighed like that, it meant she wanted to talk about something that was bothering her. So I said, "What is it, Miss Mary?"

She stopped walking and reached out for my wrist. "Am I a good mother, Selina?"

Most of the time it seemed like the children were in charge instead of her. Sometimes they minded her and sometimes they didn't. But what did she think I was going to answer? *"No, you an awful parent"?*

The way she was standing there in the sunshine in a plain old dress that was wrinkled and spotted with paint and her hair in a plait, she looked like a ordinary farmwife and not the rich woman who one day would own Arlington and everything and everybody in it. I felt sorry for her.

"Just about the best there is, I reckon."

"My husband scolds me for not being firm with them. He says I must demand their respect. I try, but they don't always listen. Especially Mee."

I thought of times I saw that girl pushing ahead of her brothers to be first for whatever was happening. Snatching for herself whatever she wanted. A toy, for instance. Or the last biscuit on the breakfast table.

"Wesley doesn't listen to Mauma all the time

153

either. But it does seem like Little Mary has a mind of her own, all right."

Miss Mary heaved another sigh. "You were right not to give her the crown you made this morning. She must learn to think of others before herself."

We started walking again. Seemed like our talk had made Miss Mary feel better. I hoped she was right about Miss Mee learning from what I had done. But some people are just born to think only of their own selves, and it seemed to me Little Mary was one of them.

The summer passed slowly. On days when Miss Mary's rheumatism pained her, she sat at a desk in the parlor and wrote long letters to Captain Lee. Then she waited for him to write her back. On good days we went back to the meadow for more painting. When it rained we sat on the porch and listened to Miss Mary reading from the books she had brought from Arlington. Mister Turner played the fiddle, and some nights he stood on the porch and played while Missus and Miss Mary sang. Missus Turner had a fine voice too, and many a night I nearly drifted to sleep listening to the singing.

On days when Miss Mary's many cousins came to visit, Cassie and Kitty were in charge of the three older children. Sometimes I went with them fishing in the stream, and me and Cassie and Kitty taught them to play tag and pickup sticks. Come Saturday night we stayed up late talking to the Turner slaves in the yard and singing our own songs. When Sunday rolled around we had prayers on the porch and Mister Turner read from the Bible.

Then one day it was all over, like waking up from the best dream you ever dreamed. Daniel and Thornton showed up with the wagon and the carriage, and we made the trip back to Arlington.

The minute I got home I knew there was something bothering my mauma. She stomped around the cabin like she was mad at the whole world. Wouldn't hardly talk to me. I helped her with the baby and put the corn pone on the fire, and when Daddy and Wesley came in, we sat down to eat supper.

Many a time Mauma would ask me to read from the Bible before we went to bed. But that night she banged the dishes so loud she woke up the baby, and when Daddy asked her what was the matter she didn't even answer.

Wesley caught my eye and said, "Best leave her be, Sister. She in a fighting mood these days."

So I went up to bed. My bones were tired after the long trip from Mister Turner's place, but my thoughts jumped around like drops of water on a hot skillet. I wondered what was on the other side of the stream at Kinloch. What would have happened if one day I had just kept on walking and never come back? I thought about Miss Mary

155

wanting everything to stay the same. And the feelings the *Liberator* had awakened in me. If there was a wedge between Miss Mary and me, this was it.

I rolled over to the edge of my pallet and reached underneath to touch that folded-up paper that held my dreams in it.

"You won't find it." Mauma's voice in the darkness made me jump. She had come up the ladder to the loft silent as a cat.

I sat up, my heart thumping in my chest. "Who found it?"

"I did, thank the good Lord. Suppose Mister Custis had found it? Or Missus?"

"They never come down here. You know that." I was mad as I had ever been. Over a simple sheet of paper. "It was mine. You had no right to take it."

"You got no business putting this whole family in danger, Selina. Have you forgot what they did to Nat Turner?"

"I haven't killed any white people lately. Don't plan on it in the future either."

"You think because you work in the house and Miss Mary treats you special, the rules don't apply to you. Let me tell you something. If they catch you reading things like that, you liable to find yourself in the slave pen across the river and on your way south. Is that what you want?"

As far as I knew, Mister Custis had never sold

anybody. But wasn't no use arguing with her. I flopped down onto my back. "I'm sorry I worried you. I won't do it again."

"All right then. Get some sleep."

I never would have thought that one piece of paper could mean so much to me. I felt its absence like a missing arm, but I knew Mister Garrison's words by heart anyway. *Men should be as free as the birds in choosing the time when, the mode how, and the place to which they shall migrate. The world is all before them, where to choose their place of rest, and Providence their guide.*

When morning came I went up to the house to polish the silver.

★ 17 ★
MARY

1841

"But I want to go swimming right now."

I looked into the mutinous face of my oldest daughter and wished her father were there to witness just what I had to contend with every moment of that child's life.

"I have told you, Mee, that we will go once we are unpacked and the house is in order."

"Don't call me Mee anymore. It's a baby name and I am not a baby."

I shook out a set of summer curtains and draped them across the back of the settee in the parlor of our rented house in Brooklyn. "Well, you are certainly acting like a baby. Agnes is more grown up than you, and she is barely six months old."

"You love Annie and Agnes and the boys more than you love me. But I don't care."

I reached for her but she pulled away, her arms crossed. I unpacked another set of curtains, heartsick that this child was so hard to love, was so dead set against me.

Kitty came in with Annie in her arms. "Miss Mary, I can't do nothing with this child. Baby Agnes is upstairs sleeping like the dead, but this one here? She has cried for you all morning."

I reached for Annie, who had just passed her second birthday. She was usually a happy child and easy to manage. I loved her all the more for the raspberry birthmark still visible on her face.

Kitty transferred Annie to my arms. "I can unpack that crate for you."

Annie quieted as I jostled her on my shoulder. "Where are the boys?"

"Off somewhere with Jim. Don't worry, Missus. Jim got his eyes on both of 'em."

"Maybe you ought to take Daughter and join them." I eyed Mee. "She seems to have little use for her mother's company this morning."

Mee brightened. "Can Kitty take me swimming?"

"She may not. Go along now, and behave yourself. If you can."

With Annie asleep on my shoulder, I walked to the window and watched Kitty and Mee crossing the yard behind the house. In addition to Kitty and Rose, who helped with the house and with my personal needs, we had brought Jim along to look after Robert's horses and our carriage. He was proving to be an excellent companion for my growing sons. Jim had made a swing for the children, and now the boys were taking turns on it. Custis was nearly ten, Rooney was four, and they were in constant motion from morning until night, when they finally settled with their father and me for reading and evening prayers.

I was pleased to have a spacious house all to ourselves, the yard for the amusement of my children, and a garden for planting the seeds and cuttings Mother sent from home. There was a beach nearby, and on my walks around Fort Hamilton I watched ships coming and going from New York Harbor. Looking out over the pastoral neighborhoods of Brooklyn, it was difficult to believe that the bustle of New York City, with its endless array of fashionable shops, lay just a few miles away. Though Robert's military salary was modest, it was enough to indulge my occasional forays into those shops, where I had already purchased beautiful dresses for my daughters and my mother.

On this blue and gold September day, however, there was no time for walking or shopping. The week before, Mother had requested that I write letters to several of our cousins and acquaintances urging their support of our resettlement efforts.

I eased the sleeping Annie onto the settee, sat at my desk with paper and pen, and unfolded the list Mother had sent. Among the Fitzhughs and Williamses and Turners I spotted the name of Mrs. Pinckney, the woman who at my wedding ten years earlier had offered to buy the carved ivory box my father had just given me. I couldn't imagine that such an acquisitive woman would be sympathetic to the cause, but I penned a note and added it to the stack with the others.

I wrote straight through the day until Rose came in at three to tell me dinner was ready.

"Guess what, Mama?" Custis said as soon as we were seated at the table. "Jim made us a swing."

"I saw it from the window this morning. It looks like the most fun."

"It is fun," Rooney said. "Jim pushed me higher and higher. I went higher than Mee."

"Oh, Rooney, you did not," Daughter said, picking up her glass of milk.

"What about you, Custis?" I worried constantly about my elder son. I wanted him to have the same carefree childhood I had enjoyed, but he seemed always to be serious and preoccupied.

"I swung once or twice, but then I let Mee have my turns. She's younger than me."

"That was kind of you, son. But there is nothing wrong with enjoying yourself." I took a bite of Rose's excellent apple pie. "You ought to have fun while you can. Your formal schooling will begin soon, and then you won't have as much time for leisure."

"I don't know why you can't keep teaching me, Mama."

"Well, my precious child, for one thing I am not very good at mathematics."

"Maybe you take after Grandpapa. He says he was not any good at it either. He says President Washington worried about it all the time." Custis buttered his biscuit. "Did Grandpapa worry about you?"

"No. But I was not expected to excel in the same subjects as boys. I was more interested in art and books and riding my horses anyway." Rose appeared to refill my water glass. "I suppose that's why to this day I'm not very fast at numbers."

"But Papa is. He can teach me. And then I could stay right here."

"Are you worried about leaving home and going away to school?"

He shrugged. "Maybe. I guess so."

"Fairfax is not so far from Arlington. You will be home often."

"If I were going away I would not be the least

bit worried," Daughter said, finishing her second slice of pie. "I think it would be wonderful. When I grow up I am going to travel all over the world and never come back to Virginia."

She cast a defiant look my way, undoubtedly seeking a reaction.

I waited for Rose to clear the table before replying.

"We will miss you, Daughter. But no doubt you will see many exciting things. You must write to us and tell us all about your travels."

She pushed back from the table. "Since you won't take us swimming, I am going up to my room."

"Mama, may Rooney and I go back outside?" Custis asked. "Jim said he would show us the hayloft."

"Rooney needs his nap, but you may play until your father gets home."

Custis grabbed his cap and ran outside. Kitty came in and took charge of Rooney and the still-sleeping Annie.

I poured a cup of tea and retreated to my desk, where I finished my correspondence and then opened a packet of notes and clippings from my father's collection. Work on his book had progressed only in fits and starts over many years, and I had no idea when it would finally be finished. But I enjoyed the peek into the lives of my ancestors. Among them was a woman called

Sorrowful Margaret. I was curious about her and pored over Papa's old papers, searching for more of her story.

An hour later a carriage rolled into the yard. A tall, red-haired woman in a straw hat and a yellow calico dress emerged, made her way to the door, and rang the bell. I hurried to answer before another buzz should awaken my sleeping children.

"Mrs. Lee?" Bright blue eyes appraised my ink-stained fingers and hastily pinned hair.

"Yes?"

"I'm Ellen Wilcox. I live in the yellow house at the end of the road. I ought to have come earlier to welcome you, but I understand you have a large family and I thought perhaps I should give you time to settle in."

I was surprised at how much her call pleased me. I'd had little time for socializing, especially since Agnes's birth and our move to Fort Hamilton.

"Please come in." Grateful that Rose had dusted the tables and swept the floors just that morning, I led my guest into the parlor. "Would you care for tea?"

"Oh, my dear, please don't trouble yourself. I'm certain you are busy enough looking after your family. Four young children, I hear?" Mrs. Wilcox settled onto the settee.

"Five. I have an infant daughter."

"My heavens. How do you have time to breathe?"

"My servants are indispensable to me."

Rose bustled in and stopped short when she saw my guest. "Oh, Missus. I didn't know you had comp'ny."

"What is it, Rose?"

"I was wanting to know what you want me to fix for Mr. Robert's supper this evening. I meant to ask you this morning after prayers, but it slipped my mind." She backed toward the door. "It can wait, though."

Mrs. Wilcox watched her go, and it seemed to me the air suddenly chilled. "I wasn't aware that you kept slaves, Mrs. Lee. I think you'll find that few New Yorkers approve of the practice."

"It is an unfortunate necessity, but both my mother and I have devoted much energy toward their eventual emancipation."

"Eventual? Why not now? Why perpetuate a cruel and inhumane system that cannot possibly stand?"

I was momentarily stunned at her lack of good breeding. No one I knew would dare pay a social call and then proceed to criticize the hostess. In her own parlor! It was true that on the plantations in the Deep South, unspeakable cruelties were inflicted upon those in bondage. The thought of it shamed and sickened me. But Arlington was more akin to a country estate than to a plantation, and my father demanded far too little of his servants, to his own detriment. He asked nothing more of

164

them than to support themselves by growing their own gardens, and to assist in the upkeep of the house and grounds. Their lack of productivity was the chief reason he was always in debt.

And as it happened, Cassie, who had accompanied Robert and me to Fortress Monroe when we were first wed, had been emancipated along with her husband, Louis. My father rarely explained himself to me or to anyone, and I had no idea what had prompted him to let Cassie go. Cassie and Louis had come to New York to seek their fortunes. But I was disinclined to explain any of this to my ungracious caller, or to make of them an example to defend myself against her disapproval.

"I cannot expect you to understand a situation with which you seem to have no experience, Mrs. Wilcox. Perhaps we shall have to agree to disagree on this point."

She got to her feet and fussed with her straw hat. "Perhaps you are right. I must go."

I walked her to the porch and stood there while she climbed into her carriage and rode away.

Then Robert arrived, looking preoccupied, and went straight to the parlor with his paper and pen. I couldn't know whether he was working out some engineering problem or stewing over some political issue. He would tell me in his own time.

Rose came in to announce supper. Custis, Daughter, and Rooney took their places at the table and bowed their heads as Robert blessed our meal. Then came the best part of my day, when my children got to see their father, who always was full of playful affection and kindly advice. Between bites of Rose's beef pie, Robert quizzed Custis about his reading, teased Daughter about sewing for him, and listened to Rooney's detailed description of a lizard he had found in the grasses near the swing.

Dessert was served. Robert finished the last of his pie and leaned over to ruffle Rooney's hair. "Want to play cowboys and Indians?"

"Yes!" Rooney jumped up, nearly overturning his water glass. "I'll race you to the parlor, Papa!"

Robert laughed and let his son win the race. Soon my husband was on all fours with Rooney on his back. Custis hid behind the curtains, drawing an imaginary bow against the cowboy and his horse.

Mee and I were alone at the table. "Daughter, don't you want to join the game?"

"No, it's silly. And besides, it's a boys' game."

"Want to walk with me down to the stable to see Kate?"

"She is your horse, not mine. I want a pony of my own."

"I know you do. Perhaps we will get one while we are posted here." I retied the blue satin ribbon that had come loose from her braid.

From the parlor came a loud yell and a thump.

Custis ran into the dining room. "Mama, Rooney fell off Papa's back and hit his head."

"Is there any blood?" Daughter's voice held an unmistakable note of hope.

"Nope, Rooney's fine. Papa says he needs a cold compress."

I got a basin and a towel and went into the parlor. Robert was holding Rooney on his lap and rubbing our son's back. "He's all right, Mary. Just a bump on his forehead."

Together we soothed Rooney. Custis went in search of Kitty, who soon returned to get all of the children ready for bed.

Robert kissed each of his children in turn. His tenderness with them brought a lump to my throat. I counted myself lucky, for no father anywhere on earth was more attentive to his children or more earnestly concerned with their welfare.

The children went upstairs with Kitty. Robert and I settled in the parlor, I with my knitting, he with his book. He took a letter from his pocket. "I almost forgot to give you this."

I opened Mother's letter and read it, first with eagerness and then with dismay. I handed it to Robert. "She says they can't afford a visit this autumn after all."

He scanned the letter for himself and handed it back. "I'm sorry Father is in such dire circumstances. He ought to find a way to make Arlington pay for itself. White House and Romancoke are self-sufficient. I fail to see why Arlington must remain in such poor financial shape."

"White House and Romancoke are working farms. Papa never intended Arlington to be anything other than a place to entertain and to show off the Mount Vernon treasures."

"But something must be done to satisfy the creditors and keep the house going."

"I agree. What do you suggest?"

"The servants must become more disciplined and productive. More acreage ought to be placed under cultivation. Winter wheat and corn have done well. Father ought to try livestock production."

"He tried sheep farming once. It was a disaster. But we must think of something."

"I can do little besides offer my opinion. If it is asked." Robert closed his book and placed it on the side table. "If only I had twenty thousand a year, I could put everything in tip-top shape."

"If we had that kind of money, this entire conversation would be moot."

"I suppose."

"Is everything all right? You seemed preoccupied when you arrived home this evening."

"Just the usual aggravations that come with the job of post engineer. I had hoped the mapping of the coastal fortifications would be completed by now. And there has been another delay in the funding for dredging the sand bars." He sighed. "I shouldn't be surprised. President Tyler cannot seem to get along with anyone, even with the members of his own party. I would rather not see the government fractured at a time when we have so much potential for progress."

"Perhaps his cabinet can talk some sense into him."

"One can only hope. Will you forgive me, Mary? I find that I am too tired for reading after all."

"I will be up soon."

He kissed my cheek and made his way upstairs.

I turned up the lamp and resumed my knitting, thankful that I had not mentioned the intense pain that had been building in my legs all day. Though Robert hadn't said so, I knew he worried about the future of his military career if the government could not agree upon its priorities. He rarely spoke of his unfinished work on the Mississippi River, but it pained him to leave any task undone. To remind him of my infirmities would only increase his unhappiness, and I would not add the weight of a single feather to his burdens.

Upstairs my family settled for the night. I heard Rooney giggling and the sound of the windows being closed for the evening. It was getting late, but I was too unsettled by worries about Papa's finances and Robert's career to think of sleep. And Mrs. Wilcox's reminder of the thousands of the enslaved in the Deep South—for whom whips and chains were as much a part of every day as air and sunlight—sorely troubled me.

What could my meager efforts for the Colonization Society really accomplish? I could raise money from daylight to dark and it would never be enough to save all of the poor wretched souls who languished in bondage. For all our good intentions, sending a few hundred freedmen to Liberia each year was like spitting into the ocean. Still, if I could give even one family a chance for a better life, wasn't it worth trying?

The stairs creaked and Robert, his hair tousled and his eyes heavy with sleep, peered into the parlor. "You're still up."

"Too many problems on my mind."

"Mine too. But we can't solve them tonight. Come to bed, Molly."

He held out his hand. I took it and together we ascended the stairs.

★ 18 ★
SELINA

1844

I stayed so busy helping Missus with the dusting and polishing that I forgot all about my birthday until Thornton Gray grabbed me by the hand. He led me to a remote part of the garden and pressed me up against the brick wall of the carriage house, which was still warm from the sun. Darkness was gaining on the late-autumn sky, but a thread of sunlight came in through the trees.

Thornton kissed me—not for the first time—and put a book into my hands. "This is for you."

It was pretty. On its red cover was an illustration of a flower and the word *Poems* in gold letters. I will say this: that boy knew the way to my heart. Reading was a kind of enchantment that came over me whenever I had time for a book. Sometimes a story was the only thing that made it possible to keep going.

"Where did you get this?" was all I could think of to say.

He still was holding on to my hand. "Mister Custis let me keep a little from the extra hauling I did for him. You twenty-one now. I thought you ought to have something special."

Twenty-one. In some ways it didn't seem like I had been on earth for that many years. I thought about getting older only when I saw how gray my mauma and daddy were getting to be and how big Wesley was growing. He was twelve now and tall as Daddy. Our little sister, Mary, was right behind him.

"Got something to ask you," Thornton said.

I knew what it was he was fixing to ask, but I said, "What is it?"

He leaned against the wall beside me, and we

looked out at the sky. Pale stars came out, shivering in the purple sky. "I reckon we ought to go on and get married."

"That is not a question."

He laughed. "You know what I mean, Selina. Will you?"

I looked at the clumsy boy who loved me and felt my heart beating too hard. His words were not much of a surprise. I knew from the day he brought me that scrap of lace from the market in town that one day he would want to marry me. But what kind of life could we have, still the property of other people?

I had kept my promise to Mauma not to bring any more copies of the *Liberator* into our house, but I kept my ears tuned to the conversations in the parlor when Missus's friends and cousins came to call. There was plenty of talk about the Quakers, who were writing in the newspapers calling for slavery to end. In his newspaper, Mister Garrison was still railing at the colonization people who wanted to send us to Africa. Missus said freedom would come one day, and she was worried that we would find out it was nothing like we expected. Where would we live and how would we eat?

I thought about those questions all the time as I was polishing the silver and beating rugs and dusting tables in the parlor. I remembered the summer I was ten years old and Peter, who was in charge of letting people in and out the door of the house, told us after preaching one night that Mister Custis had set Maria Syphax free. And gave her some Arlington land and a house besides.

When she got wind of it, Judah set down her sewing and cocked her eyebrows and said it wasn't no big surprise to her and anybody with one eye and half sense could see why he'd done it. I didn't see it back then. I asked Mauma and she told me to shush.

And now Mister Custis had finally listened to Nurse's constant begging to free her daughter. Cassie married a boy name of Louis and they had gone up North. I didn't think for a single minute freedom was going to be a cakewalk, but I was at least as smart as Cassie, and I figured if she could make her way in the world, so could I. There was no telling how long it might take, but my dream still was shimmering out there in front of me, shiny as a new dime.

Thornton grabbed my hand, and we started up the path to the cabin. "You know you love me, Selina Norris. You know you gone say yes."

"When we get free, then I'll think about it."

Thornton spat into the dirt. "You just dreamin', girl. You and me? We liable to be dead and buried long 'fore that day comes. Might as well take whatever happiness we can get while the gettin's good."

"Thornton Gray, stop pestering me." I held my

new poem book to my chest and changed the subject. "I got a letter from Rose last week. From all the way in New York. She went shopping with Miss Mary and the new baby, and Miss Mary bought Rose a new bonnet."

"Missus Lee got herself another young'un?"

"Yes. Another boy, named after his daddy. He was born right here while Miss Mary was home last year. You don't remember?"

"Too many children to keep up with, I reckon. Seem like she runs home to Arlington ever' year to bring a new baby into the world. How many she got now?"

"Six. Three boys and three girls."

"Lordy. How many children we gone have, Miss Selina Norris?"

We reached the quarters. It was dark. Yellow light spilled from the windows of the cabins. A bitter wind blew in off the river, and I was getting cold. "Thank you for the poem book. I got to get inside. Mauma will wonder where I am."

Thornton shoved his hands into his pockets. "You gone tell her I proposed?"

"Maybe."

"Well, when you make up your mind let me know, and I'll come and get you. We can stay with my pa for a while. Till we can get a cabin of our own."

"If I decide to marry you, I want a proper wedding. With a preacher and everything."

"Ah, Selina. Don't be that way. That kind of a wedding is for white folks. And it don't make no difference in how we feel. We gone be just as married as Miss Mary and Mister Robert is."

Through the door of the cabin I could hear Mauma and Wesley talking, their voices low. Smoke drifted up the chimney and into the black night. "I got to go."

"Marry me. You know you want to." Thornton leaned over and stole another kiss. I went inside.

Mauma was putting the clean dishes away. Wesley was reading the Bible Miss Mary gave him last Christmas. Daddy was already sleeping in front of the fire. There wasn't an iota of joy in any of them. And if they remembered it was my birthday, nobody said a word about it.

I sat down at the table across from Wesley so we could share the lamplight and opened up my poem book. But the words danced on the page and refused to settle into my head. Wesley began reading aloud from the book of Isaiah. Mauma recited the verses right along with him, but something changed in me that night. All I could pray was that I might be spared from such a life as this. A life heavy with longing and burdened by sorrows too mournful to recall.

★ 19 ★
MARY

We were going home for Christmas, and I wanted to visit some of my Brooklyn neighbors before we left. On a brisk morning in late November, after breakfast and morning prayers, Robert left for his office on the post. I dressed and pinned my hair as best I could. I was expecting our seventh child, clumsy at everything, and too far along to ride my little mare, Kate. I bundled into my cloak and gloves and summoned Kitty and Rose. "Where are the children?"

"The girls upstairs, playing with they doll babies," Kitty said. "Robbie is still sleeping."

"Be sure to give him his breakfast as soon as he wakes. You know how grumpy a hungry two-year-old can be."

"Don't worry, Miss Mary," Rose said. "We're keeping an eye on them. I just now saw Rooney outside with Jim, helping pitch hay for the horses."

"My son is wearing his gloves and coat, I hope."

"I put them on him myself," Kitty said. "But I ain't guaranteeing he's gone keep 'em on. That boy is way too full of mischief, if you're askin' me."

Rooney had grown into a fearless eight-year-old, the most rambunctious of all my brood. I worried constantly about his safety.

I left the house and in the sunless November morning walked the short distance to Mrs. Lane's. A plump, gray-haired woman with bright blue eyes and a ready laugh, she greeted me warmly, and we settled before the fire in her cozy parlor talking of mutual friends and family news and plans for Christmas. She was reciting the ingredients for a plum pie when I heard a noise outside and looked up to see Kitty rushing through the gate and up the walk.

"Mrs. Lane! Mrs. Lane!"

Kitty rushed inside, her eyes wide with fear. "Jim sent me to fetch Mrs. Lee home. Rooney has gone and cut his fingers off."

I got to my feet and grabbed my cloak. "What happened?"

"Do you want me to come with you?" Mrs. Lane asked.

"I'm all right. I must go."

"Of course, my dear. I hope it isn't as serious as it seems. And do let me know if there is anything you need."

We started for home, Kitty holding tight to my arm.

"Kitty, what happened? You know how Rooney is. Was there no one watching him?"

"Jim said he turned his back for just a minute, and the next thing he knowed, Rooney was up in the hayloft playing with the straw cutter. Jim told him to leave the cutter alone and come on down, but I reckon the cutter must of slipped or something. He says they was blood ever'where and he hollered at me to come and fetch you home."

We ran into the yard, where Jim was cradling a screaming Rooney in his arms.

"Oh, Jim, how bad is it?" I unwound the bloody bandage.

"Sliced off the ends of two fingers, Missus. I got 'em wrapped up in my handkerchief so's the doctor can sew 'em back on. But we got to get Mr. Rooney to the infirmary right quick." Jim was already moving along the street. "I done sent for Captain Lee too."

For the sake of my injured son, I tried to remain calm as I struggled to keep up with Jim. Inside, I was falling apart. Three years before, Annie had accidentally poked out her eye with the scissors and now had sight only in one eye. As if the birthmark was not enough of a cross to bear. And now this.

At the infirmary I held Rooney on my lap while the doctor applied salve and bandaged his hand.

"There." The doctor stood and patted Rooney's shoulder. "You are a brave and good lad, little Mister Lee. The captain will be proud of you."

Rooney shook his head. "No, sir. I am a bad lad, and my papa will be disappointed because I should have minded Jim."

That night Robert and I took turns sitting by Rooney's bedside. In the wee hours of the morning I left to make tea. When I returned to the shadowed room, Robert looked up, and I knew he was thinking of the awful day when our little Annie had lost her sight.

"Oh, Mary. If only children could know how their careless acts overwhelm us with sorrow," he said quietly, "they could not so cruelly afflict us."

Rooney whimpered and tore at his bandages. I reached out to still his hand.

Robert sipped his tea. "I saw the girls when I arrived home. Annie asked me whether Rooney's accident means we are still going to Arlington for Christmas."

"We can't travel with Rooney and risk those stitches coming undone." I busied myself straightening Rooney's blankets so Robert wouldn't see my disappointment.

Christmas Day began before daylight. Custis and Mary had gone ahead to Arlington. Annie, Agnes, and Rooney woke and began clamoring for their gifts. Robert had filled their stockings, and the parlor soon rang with laughter and bright chatter. Kitty brought in Robbie, who was just barely old enough to know that this was a special day. Robert took him from her arms and carried him around the house to admire the greenery and the brace of glowing candles on the dining room table.

"Today is Christmas," Robert told his two-year-old namesake. "What would you like for a present?"

"A carriage and some horses!"

Robert laughed and handed him to me. "What do you say, Mama? It seems a modest enough request."

"Mama, I don't feel like church today," Rooney said.

"I will stay with him," Robert said. "Kitty can look after the baby if you want to take the girls."

I went upstairs to help Annie with the little veil she wore when we ventured into public. She was only six years old, but old enough to feel self-conscious about her birthmark and her sightless eye. Rose came up to help dress Agnes, and the three of us set off for church, our boots crunching on the snow.

The church was beautifully decorated with candles and greenery. I sat between my girls in our usual pew near the front and helped them through the readings and the hymns. That evening Robert and I dined with the Stauntons and arrived home in time to kiss our children good night and hear their prayers. I added my own intercession, that I might be equal to the charge God had given Robert and me.

All too quickly Christmas passed, the new year arrived, and I prepared to go home to await the arrival of our seventh child. Robert's duties made it impractical for him to accompany me, but the journey was a short one, and he consoled himself with thoughts of my return to Fort Hamilton in early summer.

One afternoon in early January, he came into our bedroom as Rose was folding my things into my trunk. I dismissed her and walked into my husband's waiting arms. I had grown accustomed to having him home every night, and I dreaded our separation.

Robert spoke against my hair. "I am already lonesome for you all."

"I will miss you too."

"I want you to spend some time in the mountains next spring. You need to regain your strength. And a visit to the hot springs would do you a world of good."

I glanced up at him.

"You do your best to hide your pain from me, but I can see it in your eyes, Molly. Promise me you'll go."

"All right."

"Just don't stay away too long." He pulled away to look into my eyes. "I shall be waiting for you, and most eager to kiss my newest child. And you know the rest of these *chillen* cannot do for very long without their papa."

A week later we were home. I brought the Christmas gifts we had bought in New York for

Custis and Daughter. Our son had returned to boarding school, but Mary was still there and greeted me with her usual haughtiness.

"Happy Christmas, dear child." I handed her the package I had brought. "I missed you so much on Christmas morning, Mary, and so did your papa. He sends you all his love and kisses."

"Thank you, Mama."

"Aren't you going to open your present?" I had gone to three bookshops in New York in search of *The Christmas Annual* for her. It was an expensive book, lavishly illustrated and very popular with the younger set. I hoped it would soften her heart.

She tore away the paper and glanced at it, the disappointment plain on her face. "A book?"

"Yes. It's *The Christmas*—"

"I am almost eleven. I can read the title for myself."

"Mary Custis?" My mother pinned Daughter with her steady gaze. "Do you not recall the conversation I had with you just this morning?"

My daughter rolled her eyes and planted a cool kiss on my cheek. "It's quite a lovely book, Mother, and I am certain I shall enjoy it. Thank you ever so much."

She spun on her heel. Holding her back straight and her head high, she started down the hall, her satin slippers peeking from beneath the ruffled hem of her dress. Watching her go, I was struck with a wave of maternal melancholy. My eldest daughter was on the verge of young womanhood and about to enter a private world of dreams and secrets I could never share. It was a natural progression, this burgeoning of possibilities, of private hopes and fears, but as she reached her bedchamber and the door closed behind her, I could not help feeling that something vital had been torn from me.

"Well then," Papa said, setting Agnes onto her feet. "Come along, my pets. You must be hungry after your trip. Shall we eat?"

As always, George had sent some lovely things from the kitchen, but fatigue and Daughter's cool reception had stolen my appetite. I picked at my food until the others finished and Rose came in to clear the table.

Ever attuned to my feelings, Mother left her place at the foot of the table and laid a hand on my shoulder. "Mary dear, let's sit in the parlor for a while."

Leaving Papa and the servants in charge of the children, we went into the parlor, where a fire burned merrily in the grate. A leftover ball of mistletoe, decorated with red ribbon, still hung in the archway. The remnants of the Yule log smoldered in the grate.

Mother retrieved her knitting needles from the basket at her feet and settled into her favorite chair. She peered at me over the top of her round spectacles. "You mustn't mind Daughter's behavior. She is headstrong and too eager for her independence."

"Sometimes I feel she hates me. I wish I had never left her here to accompany Robert to St. Louis. I don't know how to make it up to her. How to win her love."

"A wife's place is always with her husband. One day your children will be grown and away, making their own lives, and there will be only you and Robert to love and comfort one another."

"Oh, I hope our children won't forget about us." I searched her face, but it was as placid as the river. "And I hope you haven't felt that I have abandoned you, Mother."

"Abandoned? Certainly not. But lonely all the same." She reached for another ball of yarn. "You are the only chick in my nest. It isn't our place to question the ways of Providence, but sometimes I do wonder why none of my other children lived past infancy."

"When I see Annie and Agnes laughing and whispering together, I often wonder what it would have been like to have had a sister of my own."

Mother's hands stilled, and she looked at me with a quizzical expression before her normal serene smile slid back into place. But in that unguarded moment I glimpsed something secretive and troubling in her eyes.

Rose came in with a tray and said, "Miss Mary,

your papa told me to bring you something to eat, in case you was feeling peaked. Since you hardly touched your dinner."

"Thank you, Rose."

When she had gone Mother said, "Is there any more word from Cassie? I have been so worried since you wrote that you had found her and Louis in New York."

"Thanks to Lily and Eddison." In the comfort of my mother's cozy parlor I felt my appetite returning. I poured tea, slathered a biscuit with butter and jam, and took a bite. "Lily took me to see Cassie just before Rooney's accident."

Mother's needles clicked as she finished off another row. "Your aunt Maria was here during Christmas and mentioned she had heard Eddison is working as a steward on a steamer."

"Yes. Papa was right to free them. They seem to be doing well. I wish the same for Cassie and Louis. But Lily told me after Louis got sick they had to sell everything except their clothes just to pay the rent." I took a warming sip of tea. "I offered to pay their passage back here so they could stay with Nurse until they got on their feet, but Cassie wouldn't hear of it. It seems there is a great deal of pride in the matter."

"Eleanor would be all too happy to welcome her daughter back. She misses Cassie. But perhaps their pride will serve them well in the end," Mother said. "And perhaps we ought not to let your papa know they are struggling. If he knows they are having trouble, he might be more reluctant to let any more of our servants go."

She finished off the last row of stitches, slipped the needles free, and held up her handiwork for my inspection. The blanket was knit of the softest wool in shades of yellow and cream. "For your new little one. I was so busy during the holiday I feared I wouldn't finish it in time."

I felt such a rush of love for my mother that I found it hard not to cry. "It's beautiful. And very practical for a baby arriving in the dead of winter."

"I'm glad you like it." Mother brushed at my hair. "You look tired, child. Perhaps you ought to get some rest."

I went to my room and wrote to Robert, advising him of our safe arrival. Downstairs, the door to Daughter's room remained firmly closed.

A bit later Selina came up. "Miss Mary? You busy?"

I set aside my pen and paper. "Not really. How are you? I know I have not written in some time, but after Rooney's accident things got so busy I scarcely had time to breathe."

She nodded and leaned against the door frame. "Missus told us about his accident. He always was the curious one. Reckon it got the best of him this time." She fidgeted with the hem of her apron and fixed her gaze on some point outside the window.

"What's the matter, Selina? Is something wrong?"

She sighed. "Not wrong, exactly. Reckon I'm curious. Like Rooney."

"About?"

She sighed. "Menfolks, Miss Mary. I don't understand them at all."

"Men in general, or one in particular?"

"Particular, I guess."

"Thornton Gray?"

She shrugged. "He's all the time teasing me and carrying on, and I can't tell when he's serious and when he is fooling, and I never know what to say back to him."

"Why, you just tease him right back. Make him wonder what you're thinking."

"Yesterday he asked me did I think he was handsome."

"Oh, I hope you didn't tell him yes."

"See, that's the problem. I wasn't sure what to say, so I changed the subject."

"Well, the next time he asks something like that, just smile mysteriously and say something like 'I haven't made up my mind yet.' Men are like foxhounds, Selina. They love the thrill of the chase. Don't make it too easy for him to catch you. And one day you will look into his eyes, and you will know whether he is the one. Just as I knew Captain Lee was the one for me."

"Huh. How long you reckon that's gone take?"

"If I knew that, I could write a book and make a fortune."

Kitty pounded up the stairs. "Selina, Missus asking for you."

"Coming." Selina bobbed her head in my direction and left with Kitty.

Four weeks later, on a frosty February morning, my nose filled once again with the scent of lime.

★ 20 ★
SELINA

The seventh Lee child came into the world on a blustery day in February, perfect as the china doll baby her big sister Agnes carried around everywhere she went. Miss Mary had already used up every possible combination of names in her close family, so this time she cast a wider net and settled on Mildred Childe, after one of Mister Robert's sisters. He himself was still in New York when Mildred Childe got here, and it was some time before he came home to see her. When he did he decided to call her Precious Life instead of Mildred, and so far the name has stuck.

I was worried about Miss Mary because back in May, Lawrence had come home from the Georgetown market with news that the country was in a war with Mexico. I looked it up on the globe in Mister Custis's study while I was in there dusting his bookshelves. It was so far away I couldn't figure out what we had against those people that we would start a war with them. Lawrence said the disagreement was over the exact spot where Texas ended and Mexico started, and the Congress meeting across the river from Arlington decided to do something about it.

I was in the dining room drying the glassware and putting it back in the cupboard when I heard Mister Custis telling Missus that Mister Robert was sure to go to Mexico with the army and it wasn't any use for Miss Mary to go traipsing back to Brooklyn, New York, with seven little children hanging on her skirts.

Sure enough, a little bit later Mister Robert came home and started going to meetings in Washington, getting ready to leave his family again. I could see the sadness building up in Miss Mary's eyes when she looked at him, and I tried to keep her mind off of it by talking about her flower garden and helping her sew clothes for the children.

Custis was away at school, but every morning after prayers she gathered Little Mary, Rooney, Annie, and Agnes in the little room at the back of the house for their lessons. She sewed clothes for Miss Agnes's doll baby, and when the younger children were asleep, she worked on her papers at the desk Mister Custis had set up for her in the ballroom. On Mondays and Thursdays she taught the slave children their lessons, writing out words for them on the same slate I used when I was a child. When the windows were open and I happened to be crossing the yard, I could hear her teaching the story for the day, and the children singing "Old Ralph in the Wood." Sometimes it made me wish I was eight years old again.

One morning I went outside to empty the water I used for scrubbing the floors when Rose caught up with me. It was laundry day and the bed linens were on the boil, sparks flying up from the fire. Rose stood over the kettle stirring the sheets and pillowcases with her wooden paddle, sweat running down the side of her face and her feet floured with dust.

"Guess what?" She set down the paddle and stood there with her hands on her wide hips watching me struggle with the heavy wooden water bucket.

I tipped the bucket over and watched the water make itself a trench in the dirt. "I'm too busy to guess, Rose. You got something to tell me, just say it."

Rose and me were not friends. We got along and got the work done, but she didn't like me much because she thought Missus favored my whole family more than any of the others. She didn't like that I was the only one Miss Mary wrote letters to when she was away. I didn't like that Rose had got to travel all the way to New York and had come back with her nose in the air, talking about the city this and the city that and acting like she knew everything.

"Randall asked me to marry him, and Miss Mary and Missus is throwing us a wedding."

I felt like somebody had stabbed me with the kitchen knife. "You're fibbing, Rose."

She cocked one hip. "I ain't neither. You don't believe me, you can ask Miss Mary herself."

I wasn't about to do such a thing. If it was true, and Rose was getting the thing I wanted for myself, it would hurt me, and regular life was already painful enough.

"It's gone be in September." Rose took up her paddle and stirred the linens. "Everybody at Arlington, black and white, is coming. Gone be a fine time. Missus and Miss Mary bought me a new dress and new bonnet, special."

I wrung out the mop and set it in the empty bucket. "I got to finish dusting Mister's bookshelves."

Rose said, "You gone marry Thornton Gray?"

"That's for me to know and you to find out."

Rose glanced around to be sure Missus wasn't watching and then stuck out her tongue.

Sometimes I hated her.

Missus's cousins from Ravensworth were coming to Arlington for a visit. I worked past dark that night, making sure the house was ready for company. When I finally let myself out the back door, the moon had come up and was painting the trees with silver. Lightning bugs flew around my head as I took the long way home. I was still bothered by the notion that Miss Mary was giving Rose a big wedding, and I wasn't ready to go home to the noise and busyness of Mauma's cabin.

I knew Thornton Gray was close by. I could feel his eyes watching me, even before he said my name.

"Walk with me down to the river." His hand found mine in the dark. His thumb pressed against the calluses I'd got from so much mopping and sweeping. "You working too hard, Selina Norris."

"No choice."

"We all got choices. Just not very good ones. Come on."

"I'm too tired. Been up since before dawn."

"I got news." I could feel his smile. He knew good and well news was the one thing I couldn't say no to.

We walked down the hill toward the river. Lights from a few passing boats lit up the water. We sat down on the grass. My shoulder bumped his. "I'm listening."

"We had us a secret visitor last night."

"What do you mean?"

"Man name of Humphries. He works with those people writing papers like the *Liberator*."

"He came here? To Arlington?"

"Yessum. In the middle of the night. He talked to Austin Bingham and Nathaniel, and to some of the Parkses too."

"What did he want?"

"To tell us they's people in Maryland ready to help any slaves wanting to escape."

"That's crazy. Nobody in his right mind would risk getting caught and whipped." Nat Turner crossed my mind right then. "Or worse."

"Mister Custis don't whip nobody. Remember when George Parks got caught taking apples from the cellar? All Mister Custis did was take away George's tobacco for a week and give him some extra work to do. Never raised a hand to him."

"He might, though, if people was to run off. Besides, Mister Custis already let Cassie go. Before that he let Lily go. And he freed Maria Syphax when I was a baby. Miss Mary says one day he will let the rest of us go. Anybody who thinks they can get free by running is crazy."

"Huh." Thornton was quiet a minute. Then he said, "Reckon that makes your brother, Wesley, crazy then. Nathaniel told him what Humphries said, and Wesley said he might up and try it one of these days."

My stomach went tight. "Wesley acts wild sometimes, but he's barely fourteen. He is not old enough to—"

"He's old enough to know his own mind, Selina. Old enough to know there is no future for him here."

"Not now, but one day—"

"One day! One day! I am tired of hearing that.

You think the world is gone stop turning and wait for us to get free so life can begin? You think we are not gone get old and gray just setting here waiting for old man Custis to take a notion to let us go? You been working in that house since you was nine years old and what has it got you, besides misery and calluses?"

"I got to go." I stood up and shook out my skirt.

"Selina. Wait. Don't be mad at me."

"I'm not mad." I started walking up the hill.

He caught my hand. "Then give me a kiss."

His lips were warm and soft as a velvet ribbon. Maybe he was right and it was a mistake to wait any longer before I said yes to him. I would soon turn twenty-two years old. Just about the age Miss Mary was when she married Mister Robert. Now she was close to forty with seven children, and it had all happened quick as lightning.

Freedom might come next week or next year or in ten years. Or never. But even if dreams born in bondage might never come true, I couldn't help thinking about what might happen if I ever was free. I was a good reader. Maybe I could teach little children, or find myself a boarding-house to run. Maybe I could be a lady's maid. On the other hand, maybe Thornton was right not to count on something that might not ever come to pass. Maybe I ought to marry him and take what-ever little scrap of happiness might come my way.

We reached the path that led to the quarters. It

was a warm spring night, and everybody was still outside enjoying the mild weather. Children chased lightning bugs while their mothers stood in open doorways talking. Down in the woods the menfolk stood in a tight circle, smoking their tobacco and sharing a bottle. Somewhere, ham and cabbage still simmered over a fire. The air was full of the smell of it.

I looked up at Thornton. "You still want to marry me, Thornton Gray?"

"Naw. I'm out of the mood now."

You could have knocked me over with a single breath. I stared at him, humiliated, tears spurting out of my eyes, my mouth opening and closing like a fish. Finally I blurted, "Oh. I . . . I was just teasing you anyway."

He laughed. "Joke's on you, Miss Norris. Of course I want to marry you. Say the day. Tomorrow? Sunday?"

"I want to tell Missus and Miss Mary first."

"Get their permission? You think they care what goes on down here? No, they don't. Long as we say 'yessum' and 'no sir' and clean up their messes so their lives run smooth."

"I want their blessing anyway."

"Suit yourself. It's all right with me." Thornton nuzzled my neck. "When you gone marry me, Selina Norris?"

I smiled mysteriously. "I haven't made up my mind yet."

★ 21 ★
MARY

"And how is the rheumatic pain these days, Mrs. Lee?"

Mother had summoned the doctor because of my ragged cough that had persisted for nearly a month. I sat on the edge of the bed while he tapped on my chest. The smell of frying ham wafted up the stairs. Through my open window came the shouts of my children at play on the lawn and the murmur of bees in the pink roses still blooming in the garden.

I was weary of keeping up the pretense that I was not slowly becoming an invalid. There were days when the least movement brought intense pain. Nights when the blue pills the doctor had prescribed offered no relief. But my mother was standing next to the doctor, an anxious expression on her sweet face, and I couldn't bring myself to tell him that with each month that passed, walking up and down the stairs became more difficult. Simple things such as lifting my babies and buttoning my own shoes caused such sharp pains that I had to bite my lip to keep from crying out. And there was Robert to consider. He was in Washington, awaiting new orders, and there was no point in his worrying about something he could not control.

"It's no worse than usual, Doctor."

"The warm baths will help with the stiffness." He took a bottle of black syrup from his bag. "This ought to help with the cough." He pinned me with his pale eyes. "You need rest, Mrs. Lee. You've only just delivered a child."

"It has been six months."

"Nevertheless. A woman with your history of complications must guard against getting overly tired. Though I am certain it's easier said than done, when one is the mother of so large a brood." He helped me lie back on the bed and then leaned down to speak so that Mother wouldn't overhear. "Perhaps you and Captain Lee ought to consider your family complete. Take appropriate measures to prevent any more children."

Never had anyone spoken so frankly to me about such a personal subject. I was hardly the blushing bride, but I could feel heat rising to my face. I could muster no reply except to thank him for coming to see me.

He picked up his bag. "If that cough isn't better in a week's time, send for me."

Mother walked him out, and a few moments later I heard his buggy clattering down the road.

Kitty came in and placed the baby in my arms. "Miss Mildred Childe hungry, I reckon. Pitched a fit the whole blessed morning."

I raised my chemise to let Precious Life nurse. Kitty stood gazing out the window.

"Have the children had their breakfast?"

"Yes, Mrs. Lee. And Missus already had morning prayers too. She plans on teaching the girls they lessons this morning so you can get some rest. Rose got Mr. Rooney and Mr. Rob helping Ephraim in the garden."

"I am not sure how much help a three-year-old will be to Ephraim, but Rob will enjoy it."

"Yessum, little Mr. Rob sure likes digging in the dirt."

I shifted the baby onto my shoulder and patted her back until she released a satisfying burp.

Selina came upstairs carrying a set of fresh linens and opened the door with the toe of her shoe. "Missus said you need clean sheets. I'll put them on the bed if you feel up to sitting in the chair while I do it."

Precious Life was already asleep. I handed her back to Kitty and got out of bed. With a quick bob of her head, Kitty left the room.

Selina stripped the linens from the bed and piled them on Robert's chair. I watched her hands expertly smooth the clean linens over the mattress, thinking how quickly the years had passed. She was no longer a child, terrified over a drop of blood, but a young woman who had turned into an exceptionally fine housekeeper.

She tucked the sheets under the mattress and

drew them taut. "Saw the doctor calling here this morning. You all right, Miss Mary?"

"Just a cough. He says I ought to rest more."

"Huh." She regarded me, one brow cocked. "The same as what I have been telling you."

"It is. I should have listened, O wise one."

"Yes, you should. But you never do. Wasn't I the one who told you not to go riding in the rain? Didn't I say you was liable to catch a cold?"

"You did." I couldn't help smiling at her intensity. "But in my defense, it wasn't raining when I started out."

"No, it was not. But your bones was aching something awful, and that's a sure sign of rain." Selina scowled and fluffed the pillows with more force than was necessary.

"What is the matter with you this morning, Selina?"

"Nothing, Miss Mary."

Something was afoot, but I was too tired to coax it out of her. "I ought to get up and get dressed, but that bed certainly looks inviting. Just like a fine hotel room in New York."

Selina removed a feather duster from her apron and began dusting the chest of drawers. "What was it like in New York?"

"It was so many things all at once. Scary and exhilarating, madding and enchanting. More kinds of people on the streets of Manhattan than you can even imagine exist in the world. Bartenders

199

sweeping glass off the sidewalk, street vendors warming their hands over braziers on the corners, ragmen with carts and horses, stylish women and their maids carrying boxes from the finest stores. Street after street of stores and tearooms and theaters. You would have found it quite an interesting place."

"Huh."

"I didn't venture into the city too often. Mostly I stayed at home in Brooklyn with the children. I made a few sketches of the city, but I'm afraid they aren't very good. I'm out of practice."

"Huh."

I watched her flick the feather duster over the headboard and the windowsill. "I haven't seen much of you lately."

"Been busy downstairs and helping with the summer garden. The squash and corn did real well this year. Mister Custis told Lawrence this is the finest crop he ever saw at Arlington."

"That must have made Ephraim and the other men happy."

"I reckon so."

"And what of Thornton Gray? I hear he has become indispensable to Daniel."

"Daniel says Thornton knows horses as well as he does. But I don't think Daniel is about to give up his job as carriage driver. Reckon Thornton will be driving the wagons and tending the stables awhile longer."

Selina's hands stilled.

"And?"

She whirled around, her checked skirts swirling around her ankles. "Miss Mary, he asked me to marry him."

"I see." Selina was a woman now, with a woman's feelings and dreams. It pleased me that she had found someone to love her. I smoothed my wrinkled gown. "I suspected as much. I have seen the way he looks at you in chapel when he thinks no one is watching. Have you given him an answer?"

"I told him I hadn't made up my mind yet."

"Ah. Good for you."

"I'm going to say yes, but I want a proper wedding with a preacher."

"You know Virginia will not recognize your marriage."

She frowned. "Why not?"

"Because only those unions between free persons have legal standing."

The look on her face made me queasy with shame that she should be denied even this small dignity. "However, if you wish a service of Christian marriage, I will try to arrange it."

Selina crossed the room and seized my hands. Her eyes were wet with tears. "This is the nicest thing anybody ever has done for me."

"Well, we had better not count on it until we hear from the minister, but I will do all I can to convince him to perform the ceremony."

Selina scooped up the dirty linens. "I got to go."

I dressed and went down to the dining room, where my breakfast had been kept warm on a tray. I had just taken a bite of my biscuit when I heard Robert's footfalls in the entry hall. I got up and went through the parlor to the front door. "Back from the city already?"

He leaned down, smelling of soap and the garden, and pressed a rosebud into my hands. "Good morning, Mary. Mother just told me the doctor has been here. And that you are to rest. What are you doing out of bed?"

"I can't stay in bed all the time. And Papa went to some trouble to set up a desk for me. I intend to make use of it while the children are at their lessons."

He brushed at the corner of my mouth. "You've a bit of biscuit there. Go ahead and finish your breakfast before it gets cold."

"Will you sit with me and keep me company?"

We returned to the dining room to find Papa happily munching from my plate. He looked up and stopped chewing. "Mary Anna, was this yours?"

"It was, Papa. I was late to breakfast owing to a visit from the doctor."

My father blushed, even to his bald pate. "I do apologize, my dear. I shall send for another plate right away."

"No need. I'm not very hungry, and it won't be long until dinner anyway."

He eyed the last bit of ham on the plate. "Well, if you are quite sure."

"Mary," Robert said, "do you feel up to a short turn in the garden?"

Leaving my rosebud on the table, I retrieved my straw hat and we went out into the peerless beauty of the late-summer day. Robert held tightly to my arm as we strolled across the gently rolling hills, listening to the noisy gossip of jays in the trees.

"I didn't expect you home from Washington so soon," I said. "Mother said you were to be tied up with meetings all day."

"Well, one meeting, anyway. With General Totten."

I pressed a hand to my midsection. A meeting with his commanding officer could mean only one thing.

"I received my orders this morning," he said. "I'm to report to General Wool at San Antonio de Bexar. In case I am needed in the field in Mexico."

"I see. Though just why a married man with seven children would seek to put his life in peril is utterly beyond my powers of reasoning. Especially when you said yourself you are not even certain Congress ought to have declared war on Mexico."

He sighed. "I wish I felt more justified in our

203

cause, but it is not my place to make such judgments. General Totten feels that I can be of use to General Wool, and I am prepared to render whatever services might be required to bring this matter to a swift end."

My chest was already aching, filling up with drops of loneliness that would become a torrent in the bleak months that lay ahead. "When do you leave?"

"In a week or so. I have been assigned an orderly, an Irish fellow by the name of Connally. He is in charge of procuring mules for the garrison. As soon as he's ready, we'll be on the way."

The day had grown hot. The slant of sunlight flooding through the trees burned my eyes. We took a brief turn in the gardens and started back to the house.

"How long will you be gone?"

"Hard to say. But I hope that I—"

"Papa!" Our three sons raced to greet us. Rob launched himself into Robert's arms. Rooney wrapped his arms around Robert's legs. Custis, nearly fourteen, stood apart, his eyes searching mine.

"Papa, guess what?" Rob said. "Me and Rooney helped Ephraim in the garden."

"Did you?" Robert kissed our smallest son. "I am pleased that you find ways to be useful. And how about you, Rooney?"

"Worked like a Trojan until it got too hot."

Rooney squinted up at me. "Mama, may we ask George to make us some lemonade?"

Robert set Rob on his feet. "Ask him to make enough for everybody. I could use something cool to drink myself."

Rooney and Rob headed for the kitchen.

Custis fell into step with his father and me. "The papers say the army is preparing for an assault on Mexico," he said. "Papa, do you think there will be a war?"

"That depends upon whether the Mexicans will stand down from their border dispute."

"But we can't let the killing of our soldiers last spring go unanswered, can we, even if they were fighting in disputed territory? Wouldn't that make us look weak? What is President Polk going to do about it?"

We reached the house. Robert stopped on the wooden steps and placed a hand on our son's shoulder. "For one thing, he is amassing more troops on the Texas-Mexico border. Perhaps a show of strength will be all that is needed. I hope so, since I have just this morning been ordered to proceed there."

"You're going to fight?"

"If it comes to that."

Ten days later, out on the porch, Robert kissed each of our children good-bye. Custis struggled to appear manly, but his eyes were wet.

205

Rooney stood bravely between Agnes and Annie. "Don't worry, Papa. When Custis goes back to school, me and Rob will take care of Mama."

"Thank you, son. I know you all will do your best while I am away." Robert bent to Daughter. "Be kind to your mother, Mary Custis. And write to your poor old lonesome papa."

Mary, stoic as ever, merely nodded. Rob wept as if his little heart had shattered, and his tears nearly made me lose my composure too. Precious Life slept peacefully in my arms, too young to know her papa was leaving her. I couldn't help wondering how old she would be when he came back to us.

Daniel brought the carriage around and loaded Robert's trunks. Mother and Papa came out. Papa shook Robert's hand and clapped him on the shoulder and said gruffly, "Good luck, son."

"Thank you, Father." Robert turned to my mother, who was having a hard time holding back her own tears. "Look after my Mary for me," he said. "She takes on too much."

As if I had any choice, with seven noisy, needy children under my care.

"You must make her get enough rest," Robert said.

"Try not to worry about us, Robert," Mother said. "Only come home safely."

He bent to kiss our sleeping daughter. "We must pray for a swift conclusion to this Mexico business, Mary, for I am terribly homesick for you already." His lips, soft and warm, brushed mine. "Take care of yourself, my dearest wife."

My throat ached with unshed tears. "And you do the same, my love."

"Mr. Robert?" Daniel stood beside the open carriage door. "We ought to get going if you plan on catching that train to Wheeling."

"All right." Robert climbed inside and closed the door.

Daniel clicked his tongue to the horses, and the carriage rolled down the drive. Rooney wrenched himself free from my father's grasp and chased after it.

I turned and carried Precious Life inside, my emotions a raw tangle of resentment at Robert's going, pride in his bravery, and fear for his safety. The baby stirred and began to fuss. I kissed the top of her head, the weight of my impending vigil already pressing hard against my heart.

★ 22 ★
SELINA

Rose wasn't fibbing after all. Miss Mary and Missus gave her a wedding bigger than any we had ever seen down in the quarters. The new pink dress they bought her was trimmed with satin bows on the sleeves and a ruffle on the skirt. Her bonnet was of the same color and tied with wide ribbons.

Missus and Miss Mary and her girls dressed up for the occasion in silk dresses and fancy hats. Mister Custis wore his old straw hat, a pair of threadbare fawn-colored breeches I had folded up a thousand times, and a sour expression that said he thought the whole thing was nothing but foolishness. He marched down to the quarters with his Bible and read some verses, and there under the big trees, Rose and Randall promised to stay together for the rest of their days, and that was that.

George fixed us a ham with biscuits and the strawberry jam we had put up back in the spring, and a cake with boiled icing. Nathaniel and Wesley set up tables to hold everything. Randall and Rose sat side by side in Mauma's best chairs, stiff and straight as Chinese royalty. Presents piled up at their feet like it was Christmas—new quilt tops, a candlestick, oilcloths for the table, jars of preserves. Judah gave them red flannel sacks filled with a special wedding potion to wear around their necks. Charles—who ran the dining room for Missus and who had showed me how to set a table and what a gravy boat was for—gave them a baby cradle, which set off a lot of laughing and teasing. But Rose and her new husband would never have a need for it. Rose had already told Mauma she wasn't about to bring more babies into slavery. Mauma told Rose: easy to say, hard to do.

My cousin George brought out the harmonica he had got from a store in Washington during a trip to market and played while we danced. After a while Miss Mary's children got restless, and she let them go back up to the house with their grandparents. Pretty soon Daddy and Mister Bingham and some other of the menfolks drifted into the woods.

I looked around for Wesley. I hadn't seen him since he and Nathaniel finished setting up the wedding tables. Lately it seemed like my brother was always mad about something. Once or twice I asked him what was the matter, but he wouldn't say anything. Mauma said it was because he was turning from a boy into a man. Maybe that was true, but I couldn't stop worrying about him and his wild notions.

"Selina." Thornton appeared from out of the crowd and tried to kiss my cheek, but I slapped at his hand. He drew back. "Looks like somebody swallowed a hive of bees this morning."

"I don't think we ought to kiss in front of everybody. That's all."

"Why not? We gone to be married soon."

Just then, one of the Bingham children turned over a table. Plates and forks clattered to the ground. People scrambled to pick them up, and that seemed to be the end of the wedding celebration. Folks started back to their own cabins or scattered to the chores that never did take a holiday, no matter what.

"I got to help Mauma carry her chairs home."

"I'll do that. You a lady. And ladies don't go around toting furniture." Thornton crossed the yard, and I heard him telling Mauma he was there to help. He had dressed up in his best gray pants and blue shirt, and his hair was shiny as a raven's wing. Mauma said he was too skinny and his cheekbones too sharp to be handsome, but Thornton Gray suited me just fine.

Miss Mary crossed the yard, holding her skirts up from the dust. "Selina. You mustn't feel envious of the wedding we gave Rose. I have written to the Reverend Keith about performing your ceremony."

"What did he say?"

"I haven't had a reply yet." She placed a hand on my arm. "I saw the way you were watching Rose today. Sometimes it's very difficult to stand by and witness the happiness of others. I wanted to remind you that your day is coming."

There are times when feelings go deeper than words, and the things that are most important fall between the cracks and stay there. The wedding was over and done. There wasn't any use in letting Miss Mary know what I thought about it.

"Reckon when the reverend will write you back?"

"I have no idea. But I shall speak to him myself the next time I see him."

Rose and Randall came over. He was holding on to her tight, like he thought the wind might blow her away.

"Miss Mary, we can't thank you enough," Rose said. "We sure had us a fine wedding."

"I'm very glad, Rose. This will be something to tell your children and grandchildren about one day."

Rose didn't bat an eyelash. She looked up at Randall and then at Miss Mary and said, "Yessum, we surely will. Me and Randall, we want lots of children."

And I thought, *Rose, when did you learn to lie like that?*

★ 23 ★
MARY

Dear Mrs. Lee,

I regret that my extended travels and a subsequent illness have prevented my replying to your letter of last September. I beg your forgiveness for my tardiness. While I can appreciate your wanting a marriage service for so valuable a companion as Selina Norris, I am afraid I must refuse. The church—

"Miss Mary?" Daniel came into the room where Papa had set up a work desk for me and set down the bulging mail pouch. "Looks to me like you got some mail from Mr. Robert."

Setting aside the disappointing note from the minister, I opened the pouch to find letters from Robert for me and the children. "Yes. At last. Thank you, Daniel."

He went back into the hallway and I heard him greeting Old Peter, who still manned the door for Papa every day. I sorted the letters for Rob and Rooney and the girls. Desperate for the scent of my husband, I lifted his letter to my nose. But there was only the faintly musty smell of paper and sealing wax. I ran my fingers over his neat handwriting, every letter perfectly formed, and imagined his hands—strong and browned from months in the hot Mexican sun—gripping his pen. I pictured him hunched over his small camp table, tired and dusty after a day in the saddle, penning his letters by lantern light, pouring out his homesickness and his most ardent wishes onto the page.

Now he wrote from Cerro Gordo describing the valley town and its inhabitants—dark-haired women selling fruits from carts in the street, old priests smelling of incense and wine, olive-skinned children who peered at him shyly from the windows of brown adobe huts as he rode past on his new mount.

I have named her Grace Darling and you will see why when you meet her, for she is exceedingly well formed, of calm and sweet temperament, and fleet of foot.

He mentioned little of the dangers he faced, knowing that such news would only make our separation harder to bear. Instead, he wrote of our children.

I have written to Custis at school where I trust he is diligently applying himself. I hope the girls are well. How I wish I had them with me here, for they would be such a comfort to me. Tell Rooney and Rob to stay out of trouble.

> Kiss them all for me, dearest
> Mary, and believe me always
> your affectionate husband,
> RE Lee

"Mama?" Rooney stood in the doorway in muddy boots, his shirt and trousers sopping wet. "Rob and I were playing pirates and, well, I sort of fell in the river."

I got to my feet, sucking in a sharp breath as a pain traveled along my leg. "Where is your brother?"

"Oh, he's all right. Jim and Kitty were with us, and Grandpapa too. Jim fished Rob out. They're coming now, but I got here first." He crossed the room to my desk, trailing water onto the wooden floor. "What's the matter? Why are you crying?"

I tucked away Robert's letter to read again later. Letters took more than a month to reach me. This one would have to assuage my loneliness for many weeks to come.

"I'm fine, child. But look at you. Go find Selina and ask her to fetch you some clean clothes."

Just then Kitty and Jim arrived with Papa and Rob. A sorrier lot I had never seen, but my father was having a fine time.

"Now, do not be cross with us, Mary Anna. Boys need to be boys. And there was no harm done."

He grinned sheepishly and wrung water from his shirt.

"You are the worst boy of all, Papa."

But it was impossible to be angry with a portly, balding, disheveled old man in a battered hat and tattered breeches so clearly besotted with his grandsons. They needed a man other than the servants to emulate, and Papa was happy to oblige.

An hour later the boys were bathed and changed, the girls had finished their lessons, and we gathered in the parlor, where I handed out Robert's letters. The children took turns reading aloud his charming descriptions of the birds and turtles and snakes of Mexico. He had included little hand-drawn sketches for each of his children, along with reminders to study hard and to write to him.

Rooney's lip trembled. He folded his letter and set it aside. "I miss Papa. I don't know why he had to go so far away."

I wanted to scoop him into my arms, but he thought himself too old now for such comforts. He slid off the chair and went in search of my father.

"Mama, may we make a picture to send to Papa?" Annie perched on the arm of my chair and turned her good eye in my direction. "This morning I saw some bluebells blooming. If I make a picture, maybe he won't be so homesick."

"That's a lovely idea. He can pin it to his tent and think of you every time he sees it." I drew her onto my lap and kissed her.

"I want to send him a picture of my cat," Agnes said.

"He will like that, I'm sure. And we must remember to—"

"Mary Anna?" Mother appeared in the doorway, a letter in her hands.

"What is it, Mother?" I kissed my children and sent them off to their various pursuits.

She crossed the room and took the chair closest to the window. "Your aunt Eleanor writes that your cousin Lorenzo is ill. She needs help in caring for him. I would go to Audley myself, but I am simply not strong enough these days to make the trip."

"Of course you must stay here. I'll go. I'll take Rooney and the girls with me. Kitty and Eliza can help you with Rob."

"What about Daughter?"

"She will escape Arlington as soon as she can wangle an invitation. Mary seems to prefer almost any place to being at home with us."

Rooney had left his papa's letter behind. I slipped it into my pocket.

"Thank you for taking this on," Mother said. "It won't be easy looking after Lorenzo and keeping up with the children too."

"Annie and Agnes can help me with the baby.

And I'd like to take Selina with me, if you can spare her."

"Surely your aunt Eleanor has a housekeeper of her own."

"Yes, but I will need someone to help me keep myself and the children organized. Selina was a great help the summer we spent at Kinloch. Besides, I feel I owe her a trip to distract her from disappointing news."

"The Reverend Keith has refused to perform her wedding?"

"It's spineless of him, really. Of course the marriage won't have any legal standing, but it means so much to Selina. It seems petty to deny her merely for the sake of appearances."

"I shall write to him myself," Mother said, smiling at last. "Even he won't be able to resist the power of *two* Custis women."

She looked out the window, and I followed her gaze. A carriage was winding along the road from the long bridge, the top of it just rising into view.

"Callers," Mother said with a weary sigh.

"I can tell them you are not up to visitors today."

"No, I'll manage. You should write to your aunt Eleanor and start packing. From the tone of her letter, the sooner you can get there, the better."

Arrangements were made quickly, and I set off on the sixty-mile journey to Aunt Eleanor's with

217

the children and Selina. That evening we stayed at the home of friends in Clarke County, reaching our destination the following afternoon just as a spring thunderstorm broke.

Aunt Eleanor—who preferred to be called Nelly—welcomed us with a buffet supper and comfortable beds and many expressions of gratitude. Looking into her troubled eyes, I was glad I had come.

While Selina settled the children, I went down the dark hallway to check on Cousin Lorenzo.

The sickroom was dimly lit, the air close and still. A merciless rain pelted the windowpane and ran in sheets down the glass. Lorenzo's lips were cracked and dry, his eyes too bright and full of pain. I crossed the room, poured water from the washstand into a basin, and wrung out a linen towel to place on his forehead.

"Cousin Mary."

I took the chair beside the bed and clasped his hand. "Lorenzo. We are so sorry you are not well. Mother was too ill to come, but she sends her love."

He nodded.

"Is there anything you need? Some water, perhaps?"

"No, nothing."

A loud thump sounded overhead, followed by a blood-curdling scream. Lorenzo smiled. "Ah. The Lee children are here."

"Half of them, anyway."

"What news is there of Cousin Robert?"

I shared the latest from my husband's letters. "He's bringing home a pony for the children, but I haven't told them yet because we have no idea how much longer he will be away. If I tell them now, I won't ever have a moment's peace."

"I suppose not." His eyes fluttered and closed.

"I ought to let you sleep. But call for me if you need anything." I removed the wet compress from his forehead and got to my feet.

"Mary?"

"Yes?"

"If I don't get well, promise you will look after Mother. She has no one else since Father died. And since we moved from Woodlawn she has so few friends to call upon."

"I promise. But you mustn't think like that. You will get well, now that the weather is warming."

I left him and went to the room Aunt Nelly had prepared for me. Selina was there and had already shaken out my dresses and placed them in the pine clothes press in the corner. On the washstand sat a pitcher and basin, a fresh towel and soap. The blue coverlet on the tester bed had been folded down, the curtains drawn for the night. I took off my shoes and collapsed into the only chair in the room. "Are the children settled?"

Selina looked done in too, after the rigors of the trip, but she smiled. "They were too tired to give me much trouble tonight. Once they are rested up, it will be a different story, I expect."

"Well, you don't have to manage them by yourself. Aunt Nelly's girl Flora will help."

Selina took out the leather traveling case containing my combs, hairbrushes, and perfume. She unpinned my hair and dragged the brush through a thick brown tangle. "You got yourself a rat's nest right there, Miss Mary."

"Oh, I know it. Precious Life likes to amuse herself by pulling on my hair every chance she gets."

Selina chuckled and kept working the brush through the tangles. The feel of her strong hands on my head was hypnotic. I closed my eyes.

"I remember the time right after Little Mary was born when you up and cut off all your hair with the sewing shears," she said after a time. "I couldn't believe you would do such a thing. Since Mister Robert said your curls was your best feature."

"He said that?"

"Right after he got home that time and saw what an awful shape you were in. You shocked him, the way you looked so peaked. I heard him telling Missus he was afraid you would die."

"I nearly did."

"The good Lord wasn't ready for you up there, I guess." She gave my hair a few more brush strokes before fashioning it into the loose braid I favored for sleeping. "There you are, Missus Lee. Anything else you need before I go?"

"I can't think of a single thing."

She stood in the doorway with the familiar look of questioning in her eyes. I knew what she wanted to ask and I hated to disappoint her.

"The Reverend Keith has finally replied to my request to conduct your wedding. He is being unreasonable about it."

"You mean he won't do it."

"So he says. But he has not yet heard from Mother." A picture of her rose in my mind, her sweet expression and gentle manner that masked a spine of granite. "Few mortals there be who can resist the determined will of Mary Fitzhugh Custis."

Selina brushed at her skirt. "I'm not surprised the preacher refused. Thornton said he wouldn't bother with it."

"He's afraid some in the congregation might not like it. They may feel it sets a bad precedent."

"How can marrying folks in the sight of God be a bad thing?"

"Precisely the point. I believe he will agree to it, once he hears from Mother. But if he doesn't we can find another preacher. Perhaps some young seminary student would be eager for the practice."

Selina jammed her fists into her pockets.

"I know you are disappointed, but—"

She looked at me in that intense way she had,

that made me feel she could see my words forming on my tongue before I uttered them. She laughed softly. "I wondered why you wanted me on this trip. But nothing can make up for being made to wait and wait. Good night, Missus Lee."

"Selina, you mustn't give up on this. I certainly haven't. We cannot give up on anything we feel is worth fighting for."

"If you say so."

She left the room, closing the door behind her.

"Mama? Rooney broke Angelina's neck." Agnes stood before me holding her favorite doll. It had indeed sustained a grave injury. Large cracks ran along the doll's forehead and across her neck. I drew Agnes into my arms. She was the most delicate featured of my daughters, "the pretty one," some said, and the one with the tenderest heart.

"Poor dear Angelina has a cracked cranium," I said. "Go ask Flora for the cement and I will make her good as new."

"Can you make a new dress for her too?" Agnes smoothed the wrinkled satin of the doll's dress. Once a vibrant pink, it had faded now to almost white.

"Not right away, child. I'm here to take care of Cousin Lorenzo, remember?"

She nodded. "I heard Flora and Selina talking last night when they thought I was asleep. They say poor Lorenzo is going to die. They say it might happen today. I never saw anyone die before. Is he going to die, Mama?"

"I hope not. Aunt Nelly and I are doing all we can to make him well. And you mustn't listen to the servants' gossip." I kissed her forehead and sent her off to find the cement.

I finished the letter I had begun to Robert earlier in the day, but I was worried about Lorenzo. In the two weeks since our arrival he had grown steadily weaker. The doctor visited with some regularity, prescribing cold compresses, warm salves, syrups, drinks, and pills, none of which made any difference.

I enlisted Selina and Flora in keeping the children occupied out of doors where they could expend their energy in endless games of hide-and-seek or cowboys and Indians among the trees, or fish in the stream that ran through the back of the property. They held picnics on the front lawn and made daisy chains for Aunt Nelly's old dog, Blue, who wore them without complaint.

Occasionally I heard Selina reading aloud from one of the children's books I had brought along, and I couldn't deny the sense of pride I felt that she had learned her lessons so well. Of all my young scholars, she had proven the most capable.

"Mary dear?" Aunt Nelly, unkempt and bleary-eyed, appeared in the open doorway, a basin of water in her hands. "I've just helped Lorenzo to tidy up, and now he is asking for you." She looked exhausted and so frail and filled with worry that I feared for her health too.

I took the basin from her hands. "Why don't you get some rest? I'll sit with him for as long as he wants me."

She didn't argue. "It was a long night. He kept going in and out of delirium. I wonder whether I should send for the doctor again."

"I can't see what good it will do. We have done everything he told us to do and it hasn't helped."

Aunt Nelly's eyes filled. "I suppose you're right." She cupped my chin in her hands. "You have been a most tender and efficient nurse, Mary Anna. A source of great comfort to him. And to me."

She started up the stairs, and I went into the sickroom. The gentle spring breeze stirred the curtains at the open window. Outside, Rooney and the girls were engaged in a lively game. Their voices carried on the cool morning air.

I looked down at my cousin. "What can I do for you, Lorenzo?"

"Just sit with me for a moment."

I pulled the chair close to his bed and sat facing the window.

He smiled. "I hear your children at play."

"I'm sorry. I try to keep them quiet. But they are young. Full of high spirits and exuberance."

"I was not complaining. I enjoy the sound of

them. It reminds me of when I was young and the future seemed bright with hope." He licked his lips. His hand moved along the coverlet, seeking mine. "I must ask you to do something for me."

"Anything."

"Send for my son. I want to see him once more before I die."

I didn't bother to deny the hopeless nature of his condition. "All right. I'll send a letter this afternoon."

"And I want you to write out my will. There is paper and pen in the desk."

I retrieved the writing materials and returned to his bedside. His voice suddenly weakened, and I leaned close as he dictated his wishes regarding provisions for his mother's care and the disposition of his property, livestock, and servants.

When it was done he scrawled his signature on the page and then lay back on his pillows and closed his eyes. I sat beside his bed as the day wore on and his breathing grew faint and irregular. Late in the evening, I stepped into the hallway and called for Aunt Nelly.

She came downstairs, her Bible clutched to her chest. "Mary, would you read to him? Prepare my boy for life beyond the grave?"

Her tears fell upon the coverlet as I read. We sat with him perhaps for another hour as his breathing grew even shallower and more ragged before his soul at last departed for heaven.

Aunt Nelly summoned her servants and began funeral preparations. Alone in my room I penned a letter to Lorenzo's son.

Washington Lewis
Virginia Military Academy

Dear Washington,

I am grieved to tell you that your dear father expired at eleven o'clock this evening. He went peacefully after an illness of some weeks, despite the best efforts of everyone here. His last wish was that he might see you again before his time on earth was ended. Your grandmother is bearing up as well as one can expect. Undoubtedly the funeral will have taken place before you can get here, but I do urge you to come home as soon as travel can be arranged.

Your father requested that I write down his will mere hours before he left us. I am certain you will not be surprised to learn that you are to inherit the bulk of his estate, slaves included. I urge you to treat them with compassion and let no motive of worldly interest induce you to act in an unkind or ungenerous part toward them. We must make allowances for them and endeavor to hasten the day when they are allowed to go free.

Your cousin,
MC Lee

★ 24 ★
SELINA

1847

Fall rolled around again, and Miss Mary hadn't said a word about me and Thornton getting married. Of course it was a busy time. Mister Custis packed up and went to visit his other plantations, White House and Romancoke. Missus and Miss Mary all the time was having company. Friends from Washington City came to call, along with cousins and aunts and such.

Miss Mary's favorite cousin was Miss Martha Williams, nicknamed Markie. Miss Markie usually shared the bedroom of Daughter when she came to visit Arlington. She was very fond of cats and they seemed to like her too, always following her around.

Missus and Miss Mary still had hopes of freeing slaves and sending them off to Liberia, and they went to Washington every little whipstitch to meet with other people who thought the same.

One morning at the end of November, while Missus was waiting for Daniel to bring the carriage around, she told me to find Rose and have her help me beat the dust out of the rugs. I said I would tend to it, even though it was cold and I wasn't in a hurry to work outside.

"Rose has been sick lately," I told Missus, who frowned as she tied the ribbons on her bonnet.

"She hasn't said anything to me. What's the matter with her?"

"I don't know, Missus. Maybe some kind of a cough. Yesterday I went looking for her and she was in her cabin sitting over a bucket of hot water. Reckon the steam made her breathe better."

Just then Miss Mary came into the hallway. She had been at her desk since breakfast, reading the passel of newspapers Daniel brought from town every day or two. She put on her coat and hat. From upstairs came the voices of the children and the thump of footsteps on the floor.

"Selina has just told me Rose is not well," Missus told her. "Apparently a congestion in her chest."

"How odd. I saw her and Randall last evening and she seemed fine. The two of them spoke with great animation, in fact." Miss Mary smiled at me. "The happiness of newlyweds, I expect. It doesn't seem possible they have been married more than a year already."

But time had crawled by for me, waiting for some preacher to marry Thornton and me.

Just then Miss Mary said, "I've received a note from the Reverend Keith. He has had a change of heart, thanks to my mother."

I thought I might just rise up and start floating above the floor like a spirit. "He will marry us?"

"Yes." Miss Mary's smile took up most of her face. "Mother and I want to host your wedding, just as we did for Rose. The minister can't come until December, and in cold weather we think the parlor might be more suitable than out of doors."

I was nearly at a loss for words, thinking that I would be married in the same place where Miss Mary had married Mister Robert.

Miss Mary said, "Will that suit you, Selina?"

My heart flopped around in my chest like a fish on a line. "Oh, yes, ma'am. That suits me just fine."

They left for the city. I was dying to find Thornton and tell him the news, but I had to scrub the floors and clean the lamps and find Rose for help with the rugs.

I let myself out the back door and went down to Rose's cabin. It was some ways from the main house, down the path and close to the farm at the bottom of the hill. She didn't answer when I knocked, so I went on in.

Rose was lying on the pallet beside the fire, and I could tell even before I touched her that she was burning up with fever. I got down on my knees and said, "Rose? You ought to have sent Randall to ask Missus for the doctor."

"No doctor." She pushed me away.

"What's wrong with you?"

"Judah made me a potion and I drank too much of it, I reckon."

"What kind of a potion?"

Rose stared at me like I had mud on my face. "If you been paying attention you would know."

Then it hit me. Rose had a baby on the way and she was trying to stop it from coming. "Judah made you up some squaw mint tea."

"She calls it pennyroyal, but it's the same by any name." A tear rolled down her cheek and onto her pillow. "It didn't work. Steam bath didn't work either."

I had seen the pennyroyal growing in Judah's garden. It was a pretty plant with a spiny stem and blue flowers shaped like a fan. But it was dangerous. "Mauma says pennyroyal is liable to kill you if you take too much."

"I just as soon be dead as have a slave baby for old Mister Custis to claim."

Her eyes went hard with defiance, and as much as I loved Miss Mary, I couldn't help feeling a kind of admiration for Rose. There was something daring in her determination to defy the Custises, even if they had given her the wedding of the century.

"Missus will help you when the time comes."

"You always take their side." Rose wiped her eyes on her sleeve. "Sometimes I think you like bein' a slave."

"One day we will go free."

Rose laughed, but it was not the joyous kind of laugh. "Wishful thinking is what that is, Selina Norris."

"Miss Mary says it will happen."

"And you believe her?"

"She keeps her promises. She told me just this morning, her own preacher is coming to marry Thornton and me. In the parlor up at the house."

"In the house? What a surprise. You always been her favorite. You and the rest of the Norrises." Rose sat up. "You got to help me, Selina."

A long time ago I heard Missus Bingham telling Mauma about a girl who tried to burn her baby out with a candle and burned herself up instead. I wasn't about to light Rose on fire. "I don't see there is anything I can do. That baby is going to come and that's that."

She took a crumpled paper from her pocket and handed it to me. "You read a lot better than I do."

"You tore this out of Miss Mary's New York newspapers?"

"Don't worry. It's a old one I found in the bin behind the stables. Miss Mary won't be looking for it no more."

I took the paper to the window and held it up to the gray winter light.

Mrs. Bird—female physician where can be obtained Dr. Vandenburg's Female Renovating Pills from Germany. An effectual remedy of suppression and all cases where nature has stopped from any cause whatsoever. Sold only at Mrs. Birds, 83 Duane St near Broadway.

Rose said, "I don't know that long word starts with a *R*. Or the one starts with a *S*. But it supposed to help if your nature has stopped. I know that much."

I didn't know what they meant either. I hadn't ever seen them in the Bible or my poetry book. "Does not matter what they mean," I said, "since the only place to get the pills is all the way up in New York."

"You got to get me some before Missus sees my belly getting bigger."

"You are the one who has been up to New York. All the time bragging about it."

"I was mostly in the country. Miss Mary took Kitty with her when she went to town. I don't know nothing about New York."

"Well, I surely don't either. And how do you think I can get there, Rose? Just jump on a train and ride it clear to Broadway Street?"

"You Miss Mary's pet. I bet she would let you go."

"And what reason would I give?"

"Ain't Cassie living up there now? You could say you want to go visit her."

"It's not that easy. Miss Mary says New York is a dangerous place. People going every which way. Besides, I don't want to lie to her."

Despite her fever, Rose jumped up and snatched the paper from my hands. "Never mind. I'll think of something else."

If looks could kill, the one she gave me just then would have struck me dead.

"One day you gone wake up, Selina Norris, and figure out what a fool you been all your life."

I left her there and went back to the house. The children were asleep or working on their lessons. I told Kitty that Rose was sick and I needed help beating the rugs. We hauled them outside and took the carpet beaters to them, dust flying up around us in a thick gray cloud.

The next day Rose came back to work in the house like nothing had happened. I studied her to see if I could tell she still had a baby coming, but she looked like always to me. She tried to stay out of the sight of Miss Mary and Missus, and she wouldn't speak to me except when she had to.

Rose never had been my best friend, but I felt sorry for her. I knew what it felt like to feel strong about something and not be able to do much about it. But then it was December. There was the usual Christmas preparations at the house, and I couldn't think of anything except that I was about to marry Thornton Gray.

Mister Custis came home from his trip just before my big day. He was in a terrible mood when I took Missus her tea tray that afternoon. I overheard him complaining that the price of wheat and corn was less than it had been, and he might have to think of some way to make up the money he borrowed to cover his debts. He was in such a dark mood I was afraid Miss Mary might just send the word to the reverend not to come, but the preacher showed up on the day he was supposed to.

Missus had given me a bolt of light blue material for a new dress, and Mauma helped me sew it up. I still had the piece of lace Thornton had given me that long time ago. We put it on the cuffs, and Mauma sewed a ruffle on the bottom of the skirt.

Thornton wore a blue shirt and gray trousers, and he looked better than I had ever seen him. He smiled at me and held out his hand, and a joy that broke like morning came over me then.

The house was decorated for Christmas with greens and candles and a big ball of mistletoe in the archway. The parlor was too small to hold everyone from the quarters, so there was only me and Thornton and the Custis family, Mauma and Daddy, and my brother and sister.

The preacher stood with his back to the fireplace and talked about how Jesus had showed up at a wedding in Cana to bless the couple and pour the wine. He said God looked favorably on couples who married in His sight. Then he said to Thornton, "Do you wish to wed this woman in the sight of God and these witnesses?"

Thornton grinned at me. "I sure do, sir."

"And, Selina Norris, is it your wish to marry this man and to live with him under God's holy covenants as long as you both shall live?"

I wasn't sure what a holy covenant was, but it sounded like a good thing so I said, "Yes, sir."

"Very well. Then you are wed and may God bless you."

That was it. Thornton kissed me in front of everybody for the first time.

In the dining room we had cake, and punch served in the bowl with the painting of the ship in the bottom. Missus invited the preacher to have some refreshments, but he took off like he couldn't get away from us fast enough. I wondered what she had told him in her letter that made him change his mind. When I told Thornton the preacher was coming to marry us after all, he said Missus must have sent some money for the church along with her note. I never did ask about that.

After the cake was gone, we thanked Missus and Miss Mary for the fine wedding. Missus just nodded her head, but Miss Mary squeezed my hands and said, "You are welcome, Mrs. Gray."

It was the first time I ever heard my new name and it sounded strange and wonderful in my ears. Thornton helped me on with my coat and held my hand as we walked down to our cabin. People had brought presents the same as for Rose and Randall. There were candles and jams and a new quilt. But no baby cradle. Old Judah made jack bags for us, filled with basil to bring us money, cinnamon for love, and rosemary for protection.

Two days after Christmas, I wrapped up a slice of mince pie to take to Rose. It was her favorite, and I felt bad that I wasn't able to help her get the pills from New York. Every time we crossed paths I could see the fear and desperation boiling up inside her.

It was freezing cold and slap-up dark by the time I finished my work at the house. I hurried along the path to Rose's cabin, the bare trees above me creaking in the wind. Yellow light from her window spilled into the darkness.

I was about to knock on the door when I heard a strange hum coming from the inside. I cupped my hands and peered through the crack in the door. Rose and Randall had tied blue ribbons around their heads and were walking in a circle around a water bucket and a candle set in the middle of the floor. Casting some kind of a spell, it looked like.

"Be it day or be it night / Keep us safely from their sight. / Fire and water, moon and sun / Shield us till the journey's done."

I turned around and ran home to Thornton.

"What's got into you, Selina?" He got up from his chair as I ran inside, my heart jumping out of my chest.

I set the mince pie on the table and told him what I'd seen.

He pulled me close. "Sweetheart, whatever Rose does is on her head, not yours."

"I suppose so. But it was scary all the same."

Maybe it was the endless talk about abolition and Liberia and running away that in the deepest part of the night made me feel like something dark and deadly was about to swoop down and swallow us. But wrapped in Thornton's arms I felt safe, a wren in its nest.

Thornton said, "Missus Gray, you know what I'm thinking?"

"I never know what's going on in that head of yours, Mister Gray."

He laughed. "I'm thinking we ought to eat that piece of pie."

He got a fork and we shared the pie, sitting side by side listening to the night wind and an owl hooting from somewhere far away.

The next morning Rose and Randall were gone.

★ 25 ★
MARY

Shortly after Rose and Randall disappeared, a new year began. Robert was still in Mexico, having assisted General Scott in the taking of the capital. Robert's letters were entertaining and terrifying, one missive describing the delights of Mexican chocolate and the strangeness of black-eyed senoritas who wore no stockings, the next recounting a close call with a band of enemy soldiers that had obliged him to hide for hours beneath a rotted log while mosquitoes feasted on his flesh. He described reconnaissance missions accomplished in the dead of night and the horror of bodies littering the battlefield after the Battle of Vera Cruz.

No longer only an engineer, he had become a skilled warrior who had tasted the smoke and blood, the noise and fear of the battlefield. Now he knew the thrill of danger, the challenge of outthinking and outmaneuvering the enemy. I worried that in his pursuit of excellence on the battlefield he had pushed himself far beyond the bounds of prudence, and that his return to the more mundane duties of diverting rivers and constructing fortifications would only increase his discontent with military life.

On a warm afternoon near the end of May, at the conclusion of lessons with the servants' children, I taught them a new hymn called "Little Drops of Water." After we had sung it twice, I released them to their chores in the vegetable garden and joined Mother in the parlor with my sewing. Annie and Agnes needed new dresses, and the baby was outgrowing her things too. Daughter came in and was plunking away on the piano she'd persuaded me to buy for her when Papa returned from Washington City.

"The Mexican senate has finally ratified the Treaty of Guadalupe." Papa waved his newspaper in the air. "It's the talk of the city today."

"I suppose President Polk is crowing about his victory in this matter." I took another spool of thread from my sewing basket.

"He is indeed, and well he should. Between this treaty and our acquisition of the Oregon Territory, the United States of America is now doubled in size."

"I'm happy the war is ended, but I fail to understand why we could not have simply purchased the land in the first place and avoided war altogether. My children have suffered terribly without their papa."

Mother adjusted her spectacles. "And we have all been deprived of the comfort of Robert's company."

"Indeed. But I expect this treaty means your vigil is at an end, Mary Anna, and Robert will be on his way home soon." He chuckled. "No more black-eyed senoritas for him. The way he carries on with the ladies, you are lucky one of them didn't steal him away."

"Carries on? You mean those harmless letters he sends to Markie and our friends? It is nothing he doesn't freely share with me. He gives me no cause to doubt his affections or his fidelity."

"A truthful husband is a blessing beyond measure, is it not, Mr. Custis?" Mother looked up at Papa, her brows arched, and it seemed to me that the air suddenly thickened.

"Indeed, indeed." Papa patted his pockets and

glanced around the room. "I seem to have misplaced my pipe."

"You left it in the dining room this morning," Mother said, not missing a single stitch.

"Ah. Thank you, my dear. I cannot think how I would get on in this life without you."

Mother continued her sewing.

"Well, I want to get to my study," Papa said. "On the way home this afternoon I thought of a wonderful line for the poem I'm working on. I ought to write it down before it slips my mind." He left the room, his footsteps echoing in the hallway.

"Mother?" I reached across to still her hands. "Is something wrong? Between you and Papa?"

"Everything is as it has ever been, my child. Don't let your father's teasing spoil the happiness of this day. Your Robert is safe and coming home."

A week later Robert's letter arrived announcing his departure from Mexico City. He was expected on the twenty-ninth of June, just a day before the seventeenth anniversary of our marriage. The entire household dressed up to await his arrival.

Custis, nearly sixteen, was home from school. Daughter, my budding musician, was about to turn thirteen. Eleven-year-old Rooney and four-year-old Rob stood on one foot and then the other, and raced each other to the window each time we heard a sound in the yard. Annie and Agnes, nine and seven, sat primly on the settee in the parlor, holding hands. And Precious Life, who had been a newborn when Robert left, was now a beautiful dark-haired and mischievous two-year-old who had no memory of her father at all.

Late in the afternoon, Rob ran to the window and shouted, "Mama! Somebody's coming."

With Life in my arms I went to the window, expecting to see the carriage coming into view. But a horse and rider appeared on the road.

"It's Papa!" Rooney wrenched open the door and ran into the yard.

Robert reined in and lifted Rooney into his arms. "Kiss your old papa, Roon!"

He dismounted and the children swarmed their father, basking in his laughter and his generous embrace.

"You are late, Papa," Rooney said when the commotion subsided.

"The train was late and I missed the carriage, so I borrowed this noble steed and rode home as fast as he could trot."

Robert handed off the reins and stepped onto the porch. I couldn't take my eyes off him. Twenty months in the Mexican sun had browned his skin and deepened the fine lines around his eyes. He had shaved off his side whiskers and his mustache, and there were tiny flecks of gray in his dark hair. Tall and impeccably dressed in his uniform, he had never looked more handsome. I had never loved him more.

His eyes sought mine and held. He smiled, crossed the porch, and gathered me and the baby into his strong arms. "Dearest Mary" was all he said.

Three years passed, and Robert was assigned to oversee the construction of Fort Carroll, near Baltimore. Anti-slavery sentiment in that city was running high, so I brought none of my servants with me when I took our younger children to join him there. Custis was at West Point. Daughter, as usual, was visiting relatives. Annie and Agnes were at home at Arlington with their grandparents, studying with their tutor, Miss Susan Poor. Only Rooney, Rob, and Life made the trip with us.

Our home on Madison Avenue was a new redbrick row house built in the traditional style, with long windowless rooms arrayed along a central hall and doors leading to both front and back. There was a lovely garden and plenty of room for Grace Darling and for the pony, Santa Anna, that Robert had shipped directly to Maryland, much to our boys' delight.

On Sundays we took our children to church, after which there were afternoon games on the lawn with Robert happily entangled among his children, horses, cats, and dogs. I was content to sit in the sunshine with my books or with my little writing desk, penning letters to the various members of the Virginia legislature.

The Colonization Society had long been in debt, and in order to continue its work we needed cash. Since Virginia had benefited handsomely from the labor of the enslaved for generations, we felt it was time to offer them a choice about their own futures. Though our legislature had joined several other states in appropriating funds for Liberia, the amount allocated was woefully inadequate. Now the task was to convince them of the need for more, despite the constant opposition from Mr. Garrison and the other abolitionists.

One day in late spring Robert and I settled with our books beneath the shade of an old oak near my garden. The first of my tulips nodded in the slight breeze off the river, the new grass shining in the slanted light.

Rooney rounded the house. "A letter for you, Mama."

"Thank you, child." I broke the seal. "Where is your little brother?"

"In the paddock with Santa Anna. But don't worry, I'll keep an eye on him."

He ran off, and I scanned the letter. "Oh dear."

"Bad news, Molly?" Robert looked up from his book, his finger marking his place.

"Mother writes that Aunt Nelly has fallen ill."

"Can Mother tend to her? The girls will be perfectly fine at Arlington with Miss Poor and your father to look after them."

"I don't think so. She has been ill all spring.

And Aunt Nelly is past seventy and apt to need more care than Mother can manage even if she could withstand the trip to Audley."

He sighed. "I suppose you ought to go, then."

I set aside Mother's letter. "The school term is nearly done. I may as well take the children home for the summer."

"If you must. But it will be too quiet here without you." He rose and crossed to my chair, then bent to kiss the back of my neck. "Come back to me soon, Miss Molly."

I pressed his hand to my cheek. "Don't I always?"

I packed up the children and we made the short trip to Arlington. The girls smothered us with kisses and draped a necklace of jasmine blossoms around their baby sister's neck.

"We missed you something awful, Millet," Agnes told her. "We've a wonderful surprise for you in the stables."

Life's face lit up. "I love surprises. What is it?"

"Come and see," Annie said, taking her sister's hand.

"Kittens," Mother whispered in my ear as the girls headed out the door. She looped her arm through mine. "Come inside. I've some exciting news of my own."

I followed her into the parlor, shedding my shawl and hat along the way.

"Our plans for sending a new group of freedmen

244

to Liberia are nearly complete." Mother sank into her chair, and I saw how pale and worn she looked.

"You are taking on too much, Mother."

"No more than usual. It is only that I am getting older. And I do want to see more families making a new start in freedom before I die."

I couldn't imagine Arlington without Mother in it. "You won't leave us for a long time yet."

"God will choose the time and place, as He always does." She handed me a sheaf of papers. "I have written some letters that you must attend to if I am unable."

"It seems to me I ought to be here taking care of *you* instead of running off to Audley. Though of course someone must look after Aunt Nelly."

"I have plenty of people to look after my needs. But poor Eleanor is alone since Lorenzo died."

"What about Washington? He inherited everything. The least he can do is provide for his grandmother."

"People don't always do as they should. And I am certain your aunt would much rather have you to nurse her than some stranger Washington might engage."

"I was hoping to take Selina with me to Aunt Nelly's, but she can stay here to oversee the house."

"Selina is not able to do much work herself these days."

"I haven't had a letter from her in some time. Is she ill?"

"No. But another baby is on the way. I was certain she had written to you about it."

I digested this bit of news. Selina and Thornton were already the parents of two girls, Emma and Annice. *We are both mothers now, Miss Mary,* she had written after the birth of the first one.

"Take Eliza," Mother said. "I can spare her now that Life is older and her sisters are here to fuss over her."

The next morning I set out for Audley. As the carriage wound slowly along the narrow roads and up into the cool foothills, Eliza kept up a steady stream of chatter, filling me in on all the gossip from the quarters. Ham was worried that all of his hair was falling out, and Judah had made a concoction of sage, whiskey, and quinine to pour over his head.

"It ain't helped none, though, that I can see, Miss. His head still shiny as a baby's bottom." Eliza grinned, revealing a missing tooth. "Judah cured my canker sore, though. With blue violet tea."

"Eliza, you know that my father pays the doctor to visit when anyone in the quarters gets sick. You are not required to rely upon Judah's home remedies."

"George in the kitchen? He swears Judah's potions work better'n anything that doctor got. He had hisself a bad toothache awhile back, and her chickweed poultice fixed it right up." Eliza looked up at me from beneath her red-checked bonnet. "You ever had any blue violet tea?"

"Never."

"Well, let me tell you, Miss. It's awful slimy goin' down. But it do the trick."

We stopped for the night and set out again at dawn. At last we reached the road to Audley, and I willed Daniel to hurry. I was famished, and my hip ached after two days in the carriage.

Eliza peered out the window. "This your aunt's place?"

"Yes. The house is up ahead. We will be there soon."

"What's the matter with her, anyway?" Eliza asked, frowning. "Whatever it be, you should of brought Judah. She cures everybody at Arlington." She sighed. "Mostly, anyway. She couldn't cure Rose, though. But I don't reckon nobody got a cure for—uh-oh." She clapped a hand over her mouth.

"What was the matter with Rose?"

Two dogs ran into the road, barking and nipping at the horses. Daniel halted the carriage in Aunt Nelly's yard and jumped down to open the door. "We're here, Miss Mary. You go on in. I'll tote your trunks in for you."

I went in to find Flora waiting in the parlor. She crossed the room and clasped my arm. "Oh, Miss Mary. I am so glad you got here. Miss

247

Eleanor been so poorly all day. I been tryin' to do for her as best as I can, but she don't want to eat a bite or stir from her bed."

"I'll go up to her now. Could you get my girl Eliza settled? And perhaps make some tea?"

"Yessum. I'll see to it."

I climbed the stairs to Aunt Nelly's room. It was the largest bedroom at Audley, light and spacious with tall windows that framed a view of the distant mountains. But today the curtains were closed, the lamps unlit, and the air thick with the smells of illness and food left too long on the tray.

I went to the bed and bent over Aunt Nelly. "Auntie? It's Mary."

She stirred and opened her eyes. "Mary dear. I was afraid you wouldn't come."

"Of course I wanted to look after you." I smoothed her damp gray tendrils off her forehead. "How long have you been like this?"

"I don't rightly remember. A few weeks, I suppose."

"What does the doctor say?"

"Stomach ailments and old age. There is little to be done for the former, and nothing of course for the latter."

"Flora tells me you are refusing to eat. This must not go on if you expect to recover."

She sighed. "Sometimes I would rather go on to my heavenly reward. I am so alone here now without Lorenzo."

248

"Wash doesn't visit?"

"Now and then, but he spends most of his time with the farm manager going over the books."

"When was the last time you ate anything?"

"Last evening, perhaps. Everything I eat makes me deathly sick."

"Well, I must find something you can tolerate. And you must get some fresh air."

But she had fallen asleep, her mouth slack, her thin, veined hands folded on the counterpane.

I went downstairs.

"I put your things in the room where Flora showed me," Daniel said. "Anything else you need, Miss Mary, before I head on back home?"

"No, nothing. Tell Mother I will write to her in a few days."

"Yessum. I surely will." He turned to Eliza. "You take care of Miss Mary."

I went out to the kitchen to see what I could find for Aunt Nelly. A basket of root vegetables and half a roast chicken sat on the table. I made soup, ladled it up, and took it upstairs on a tray along with a slice of toasted bread and some apple butter.

I parted the curtains and opened the window to let in the spring breeze. While the soup cooled, I helped Aunt Nelly to bathe and change into a clean nightshift. I brushed out her thin tufts of white hair and then drew my chair next to the bed.

"Eat this soup now, and no arguments."

She ate a couple of spoonfuls. "Not bad for a woman who rarely cooks."

"I have been doing all of the cooking these last few years. The people of Baltimore look most unfavorably on those who keep servants. Regardless of how well they are treated. The city is rife with abolitionists these days."

"Yes, so said your dear mother in her letter. I imagine you feel the absence of your Selina most keenly."

"She has become indispensable in so many ways. But she is expecting her third child later this year."

"Is she? It seems only yesterday your mother wrote to me about her wedding."

I noticed with some satisfaction that Aunt Nelly had almost finished her soup. Perhaps loneliness was the greatest of her ailments. "It will be four years this December since Selina's wedding."

"Time goes by too fast, Mary Anna." Aunt Nelly picked up her knife, but her hand shook.

"Here. Let me." I spread some apple butter onto the bread. "Bon appétit."

She smiled. "It has been a long while since anyone has spoken French to me."

"I am no longer fluent, I'm afraid. Too many years teaching little children their alphabet and how to do sums."

"Your own children must be all about grown by now."

"Precious Life is five. Custis is eighteen."

"Your mother wrote that Custis is at West Point."

"Yes."

"Following in Robert's footsteps."

"But I pray not to war. I couldn't bear to have my son or my husband in harm's way."

Aunt Nelly finished her toast and set down her knife. "I was hungrier than I thought. Your company is like a tonic to me, Mary. I see far too little of my family these days."

"A week or so of good nourishment and fresh air and you will be good as new." I leaned down to kiss her withered cheek. "Would you mind if I retire early? The trip has made my rheumatism act up again."

"Of course not, my dear."

"Call if you need me. I am in Lorenzo's old room."

I slept until the crowing of the rooster in the yard and the bright spring sunlight awakened me the next morning. I called for Eliza to bring water and towels for my morning ablutions. I had been too tired to unpack my trunks the previous evening, so I set her to shaking out my dresses and shawls and putting away my traveling case and umbrella.

The smell of baking biscuits and coffee filled the air. Leaving Eliza to finish my unpacking, I went upstairs and peeked into Aunt Nelly's room. She was still sleeping peacefully.

251

Down in the kitchen, Flora was busy frying up ham and eggs. She bobbed her head when I came in and indicated the coffeepot on the stove. "Help yourself, Miss Mary. I ain't had time to set the table yet."

"Don't bother, Flora, if it's only us. I would just as soon have my breakfast here."

She picked up her spatula and expertly flipped the eggs. "Suit yourself. They's hot biscuits in the oven. What do you reckon Miss Eleanor gone eat this morning?"

"A boiled egg and a biscuit. No butter, though. She liked the apple butter I gave her last night, so perhaps some more of that. Some weak tea if you have it."

"Yessum. I'll see to it. You want to take it up there when it's ready?"

"Yes. She seems to be more interested in food when there is family news to distract her."

Half an hour later I knocked on Aunt Nelly's door and went in to find her dressed and sitting in the wing chair by the window. "It's a fine morning, Mary."

"Indeed. It's good to see you out of bed and looking so chipper."

"I slept very well. Or as well as anyone my age can expect to. What did you bring me this morning?" She lifted the clean kitchen towel Flora had placed over the breakfast tray and wrinkled her nose. "I don't like boiled eggs. I never eat them."

"Well, I hope you can make an exception today, since Flora went to some trouble to fix them."

She sighed.

"There is more apple butter. You like that. And there's some lovely tea."

"Don't cajole me. I am not a child."

"Of course you aren't. I only meant to—"

She pushed away the tray with such force that it toppled onto the floor. Apple butter splattered my shoes and the hem of the counterpane. The tea made a brown puddle on the carpet.

Flora pounded up the stairs and rushed into the room. "Land's sakes. What in the world's going on in here?"

"An accident," I said quickly. "Will you bring a mop and—"

Flora was not fooled. She glared at my aunt. "I'll see to this mess. Won't be the first time."

Aunt Nelly gazed out the window as if none of this had anything to do with her. Allowances must always be made for the old and the infirm, but my patience was at an end. I went outside to the neglected, overgrown garden. In the shed at the end of the gravel path I found tools and an old pair of gloves several sizes too big. Returning to the unruly flower beds, I weeded and hoed and snipped and pruned until the sun passed its zenith and blue shadows fell across the yard.

"Forgive me, Mary."

I turned around to find Aunt Nelly standing

beside my newly pruned bed of Bon Silene roses. Despite neglect, a few of the bushes were full of tiny buds that would flower when the weather warmed. I pulled off the oversized gloves and pushed my hair from my damp forehead. "What are you doing out of bed?"

"I took a nap earlier. The day's nearly gone, and I felt I should find you and apologize. You were only trying to help me this morning, and I was inexcusably rude."

I blotted perspiration from my face with the sleeve of my dress and leaned against my rake, the hours of exercise and solitude having restored my patience with her. "It must be hard when one is older to—"

"Old age is no excuse for lack of manners. Will you sit with me awhile? It's very pleasant on the porch just now, and I have asked Flora to bring us some tea and biscuits." Her faded eyes held a measure of the old mischief I remembered from my childhood. "I missed my breakfast this morning, and now I'm starving."

Leaving the pile of weeds for the yard man to clear away, I put away the garden tools and joined her on the porch. The cool breeze wafted down from the mountains, bringing with it the smells of new grass and wild plums.

Flora arrived with the tea tray. Without uttering a word, she set it down and marched back inside.

"Flora is still angry with me." Aunt Nelly

poured tea and nibbled on a biscuit. "She and Henry have both become such a trial of late that I would free them if I could. But of course they belong to Wash, and my grandson won't listen to a single thing I say. On any topic."

I knew how she felt. To be a woman was to be under the absolute control of fathers, husbands, sons, brothers, or uncles, powerless to manage one's own money or to make decisions about anything. Of course it wasn't the same as slavery, but womanhood was its own kind of bondage.

"Everyone is having trouble with servants these days," I said. "The Northern agitators are putting notions into their heads. I'm for freeing every last one of them, as soon as they are equipped to make a decent life for themselves."

"Your mother wrote to me that her maid ran off."

"Yes. After we went to the trouble of holding a wedding celebration for her." I took a sip of my tea. "I had no idea Rose was not content. But it seems the better they are treated, the less loyal they become."

Aunt Nelly munched on a biscuit.

"We've not heard a word from them since. Neither of them had any idea how to survive without Papa's protection. I do wonder if they are even still alive."

Aunt Nelly stirred sugar into her tea. "Such a troublesome business. Tell me, how is your cousin

Markie? And those brothers of hers? I never hear much from that sweet girl anymore."

"I had a letter from her just before I left Baltimore. She is home from a trip to New York with Orton. She didn't mention Laurence, but I assume he is well. It seems she and Orton had quite an exciting time. Orton wrote to Agnes about it. Her first letter from a boy pleased her a great deal."

"Perhaps romance will bloom one day."

"I hope so. Orton is a fine boy. Of course they are much too young right now to think of romance."

"Time will pass quickly enough." Aunt Nelly sighed. "I feel terrible for Markie. I'm not sure I could have taken over as head of my family when I was her age. I do hope she was able to have fun in New York."

"I expect she will turn up at Arlington sometime this summer, and then I shall hear more of her adventures firsthand."

"How I would love to hear all the news from Arlington in person. Letters are lovely, but they are no substitute for a real visit."

"You know you are welcome at any time. Mother would love having you visit."

"Yes, but the trip would be too tiring for me now. And there would be no one here to mind the servants. But as the years go by I do miss my dear old Tub more than I can say."

I laughed at the mention of Papa's childhood

nickname. "You had better not let him hear you call him that. He is quite sensitive about it. Not even Mother calls him Tub."

"She could get away with it. I remember when they were first married. She was just sixteen years old and suddenly the mistress of a large house. Oh, she was a shy little thing, but she has managed her home admirably. He still adores her, you know."

I thought then of the tense and strange conversation that had taken place in the parlor the day Papa announced the end of the Mexican War. "Sometimes I feel there is something not quite right between them. Something they are keeping from me. In her unguarded moments Mother seems terribly sad. But she won't tell me anything."

"Every married couple has their private hurts and disappointments." Aunt Nelly patted my hand. "Your mother lost all of her children in infancy. Except you. That is a terrible sadness no woman ever overcomes."

"I suppose not. But I don't think that's it. I think it has something to do with Papa."

"You are imagining things."

"I don't think so."

"Leave it alone, Mary Anna." Aunt Nelly's tone was suddenly as chilly as the breeze coming off the mountain. She got to her feet, rattling the empty cups on the tray. "It's getting cold. I'm going in."

★ 26 ★
SELINA

Miss Mary said I was not welcome in Baltimore and she would have to do without me, but it was just as well since my nature stopped shortly after Thornton and I got married and then my Emma was born. Judah rubbed my belly with a balm of oils, Gilead buds, leeks, and horseradish, and Mauma put a knife under my bed to cut the pain, but nothing helped. Birthing a baby is the hardest work I have ever done, and in my opinion it never gets easier just because you know what to expect.

I wrote to Miss Mary after Emma's birth and again when Annice came along, but by the time number three got here it didn't seem like another one was any news, and I was too busy for letters anyway.

Now it was almost Christmas again. The air had turned cold and the trees were bare. Mauma was looking after my children and I was back at the house doing what I always do, keeping things clean and orderly and helping Missus with her holiday plans. The Lees and their brood were coming home from Baltimore, so there was the usual decorating of the parlor with greens and candles and the laying of the Yule log in the parlor fireplace. Thornton had gone out early with Ephraim to find mistletoe, and they came back with enough for the house and the cabins in the quarters.

Thornton held a sprig of it over my head and winked. "Give me a kiss, little mama."

I swatted away his hand. "It was too many kisses made me a mama in the first place. I don't need another child, thank you anyway. This cabin is already full to bursting."

He laughed. "Ain't we got us a fine family?"

"Selina?" Ephraim stood in our open doorway, his arms full of fresh greens that gave off the sweetest clean smell. It had started to snow. White flakes covered his hat and shoulders. "Missus asking for you."

I bundled myself up and stepped out into the bitter cold, and Ephraim crossed the yard with me. We went in the back door and along the corridor to the parlor. We passed the schoolroom, where the tutor, Miss Poor, was lecturing Miss Annie and Miss Agnes about something or other. Annie was paying attention, writing in her notebook, but Miss Agnes was watching the snow come down. She gave me a little wave as I went by.

Missus looked up from the pile of candles she was arranging on the mantel. "Oh, good, Ephraim. Those look lovely. Fetch the ladder and put those in the archway."

"Yessum. Where you want this mistletoe?"

"Where it is most likely to be useful, I suppose."

He laughed and so did she.

It did my heart good to see Missus so happy. Lately she had been sick as a kitten and moping around, even though the fact that Miss Mary and her family were coming home was usually news that perked her up considerably.

"What can I do for you, Missus?" I handed her another candle, which she set on the mantel.

"Mister Custis has tracked in mud into the front hallway."

"I'll see to it."

"The silver chocolate service needs polishing." She looked out the window where the snow was blowing sideways across the frozen ground. "If this snow keeps up for a day or two we shall have a fine day for skating and sledding. After being out of doors the children will want their warm cocoa."

"When they supposed to get here?"

"Tomorrow. Though I won't be surprised if they are delayed by the weather. Mr. Custis says the river is already beginning to freeze."

George came in carrying a big pot of soup. "Gettin' so cold out there, Missus, I figured you and the mister might want something hot to warm your bones."

"Yes, George, thank you. Please leave it on the sideboard."

"Yessum."

"Were you able to get the mincemeat for the Christmas pies?"

"Yessum. I already got the crusts made and ready for the oven onct Miss Mary and her fam'bly gets here."

Missus finished placing the candles and stood back to admire her efforts. "There. I always think Arlington looks its best at Christmastime."

We all scattered to do what she told us. I cleaned up the mess Mister Custis left in the entry hall and set to work on the silver chocolate service. It took me forty forevers to polish the pitcher, which had curlicues and etchings all over that had to be scrubbed with a brush dipped in the polish, and then there was a dozen cups with tiny handles that made them hard to clean. When that was done I started on my regular chores of mopping and polishing and making the bedrooms ready for six more people.

Would have been even more folks to prepare for excepting that young Mister Custis Lee was stuck at West Point learning soldiering like his papa before him and wasn't allowed to come home. It made me sad to think of him up there with none of his kin to say Merry Christmas to on Christmas morning. And Daughter, who knew whether she would turn up? That girl acted like she was not even a member of her family. She was always off to visit other folks, and once in a blue moon she would swoop into Arlington with her trunks and hatboxes and birdcages and scrapbooks and start demanding this and that. I hated to say it because she was Miss Mary's firstborn daughter, but I hoped she wouldn't turn up and spoil the happy time the rest of the children had anytime they were all together.

I finished up and put on my coat. It was almost dark by the time I headed back to the cabin. My skirts dragged through snow that was nearly knee-deep and soft as powder. The wind tore at my cloak and whistled in the spaces between the cabins scattered along the path.

"Selina!"

I stopped in my tracks. "Who is that?"

"Louisa Bingham."

"What is it? Your man sick again? I'm all out of poultices, if that's what you're after. You got to see Judah if you need—"

"We all fine." Louisa pulled me into the space between two cabins where the snow had piled into a drift. My feet were completely wet and stinging with the cold. "Austin come back from town this afternoon with a package for you."

"A package? Who from?"

"Now, how would I know that? He said some man at the market give it to him and said it was from a friend." She pushed a small flat box into my hand. "I got to go. My babies is hungry."

I slipped the package into my pocket and went home. Mauma was at my cabin and had already fed the two oldest girls. Mercifully they were asleep and the fire was burning in the grate. I got out of my wet clothes, and Mauma got a towel and rubbed my feet until the feeling came back into my toes.

The baby began to fuss, and I opened my dress to let her nurse. "Where's Thornton?"

"Gone off with Wesley to find us a Christmas tree." She made a clicking sound with her tongue. "Thornton Gray worse than a child when it comes to Christmas." Mauma got to her feet and put on her coat and the pair of old men's boots Missus had given her last year. "I ought to go and see about your daddy's supper."

She went out into the cold. The baby fell asleep, and I put her down beside her sisters. I stirred the pot of beans Mauma had left simmering on the stove and set the table. Then I remembered the package still in my coat pocket.

I got it and took it close to the fire. It was wrapped in brown paper and tied with a piece of twine that had gone black from so much handling. I tore it open, and a square of folded tissue fell out. I opened it, and there was nothing but a single stem of dried flowers.

Pennyroyal.

It had to be a message from Rose. I figured the pennyroyal was her way of saying she had made it to freedom. Maybe it was meant to make me sorry I hadn't helped her in her hour of need, or maybe it was meant to make me feel stupid for not trying to get away myself. I turned the box toward the firelight to see if there was writing inside it somewhere, but there was nothing. I wondered where it had started out from. New York maybe—if she had found Lily and Cassie. Or maybe she was in Baltimore where folks seemed willing to help slaves wanting to run.

I heard Thornton and Wesley coming back. I threw the box and all into the fire and watched the edges blacken and curl. Thornton brought the tree inside. Next day we put on some bits of ribbon and sprigs of holly and the bird's nest I had found years before, walking out from church one night. It was falling apart, but you could still tell it was a nest and that babies had been born in it. I couldn't say why I had kept it all those years. I only knew I wasn't ready to let it go.

The next morning we went up to the house to call Christmas gift. It seemed strange not to have Rose and Randall there among the other families—the Binghams and Dotsons and Derricks. Daddy wasn't feeling well and Mauma stayed home to tend to him, but Wesley and my sister Mary were there. Wesley was a grown man now, nineteen years old and our daddy made over, with the same long, narrow Norris face and wiry build. Too old for toys. Missus gave him new knitted socks and a flannel shirt, and he barely said boo to her about it. Just nodded his head and took off down the path to the quarters.

After Missus and the Lees finished giving us our presents, Thornton took the children home and I stayed to help Missus with tidying the house. She and the Lees dressed up in their Christmas finery, the colonel in his uniform, and off they went to church. In the afternoon they came back, laughing and teasing one another and tracking snow into the entry again. George had made them their usual feast. More cleaning up after that. By the time I finished putting everything away, the house had grown quiet and the winter light was almost gone.

I was in the back hall putting on my boots and coat when Miss Mary came in munching on a cookie that smelled like citrus and nutmeg. She had changed out of her church clothes and into an old lavender dress with a rip in one sleeve and the hem falling down.

"Selina." She stepped over a pile of boots and mittens the children had left and brushed her fingers together to get the crumbs off. "You startled me. I thought you would be gone by now."

"I'm just going." I glanced at her dress. "You ought to let me put up that hem, Miss Mary, before you trip over it."

"You look too tired for sewing. But I don't wonder at it. My children are enough trouble to make a preacher swear."

We both laughed.

She said, "Is Thornton at home?"

"Yes. Watching my children."

She grabbed my arm, her brown eyes snapping with mischief. "Let's play hooky."

"What?"

"Hooky. It's a new word I learned from Rooney. Apparently the boys at school use the term to describe skipping their classes. I think you and I deserve to shed our responsibilities for a while."

She grabbed Mister Custis's old hunting coat from the bench against the wall. "Let's go sledding."

"Now?"

"Why not? We've a little time before it's truly dark."

I couldn't think of what to say.

"Have you ever gone sledding?"

"Not since Mauma took me when I was little."

"Come on, then."

We went out the back door and across the yard to where the children had left a sled. Miss Mary grabbed the rope and we trudged up the snowy hill in the cold, our breath making puffs of fog in the air.

At the top of the hill, we stopped and looked up at the sky. A single star winked down at us, golden and bright. Purple shadows colored the drifts of snow. I could see our footprints leading back to the house. It was a pretty scene, like an illustration in a book.

"Ready?" Miss Mary eased herself onto the sled. She scooted to the back to make room for me. I climbed on and tucked my skirts around me. She pushed off and then we were flying, bucking and bumping over the snow, the two of us helpless with laughter as the sled gathered speed and the snow flew into our faces. It was as perfect a moment as I ever had since my wedding day. We weren't mistress and slave then. We were just friends. Mary and Selina.

When we got to the bottom and slid to a stop, Miss Mary said, "Shall we go again?"

I could have stayed out there all night, but Thornton was waiting for me at home, the baby needed to be fed, and I had started to shiver in my damp clothes. And Miss Mary had no business being out in the night air, which was sure to make her bones ache even worse.

I got off the sled and brushed the snow out of my hair. "I got to go. And I expect Colonel Lee is looking for you by now."

"I suppose you're right. If not my husband, then at least one of the children needs something." Miss Mary leaned the sled against the side of the shed, her quick breaths clouding the air. "I do love them all—desperately—but they are a noisy set and sometimes their demands are too much. Do you know what I mean?"

"I do. But I reckon all mothers feel that way from time to time."

She pulled something from her pocket. "I've been saving this for you."

It was ten dollars. More money than I had ever seen in my life.

"For your children," she said. "For their future."

I thought about Rose then, about how she had run off and risked punishment rather than bring a baby into slavery. It was on the tip of my tongue to tell Miss Mary about the pennyroyal, but for some reason I held back. It would be some time before I understood why, on that night of purple shadows and bright stars, I had kept silent.

★ 27 ★
MARY

April 12, 1853
Mrs. MC Lee

Dear Madam,
It has been so many years since I had the chance to greet you that you may not remember me, as I have spent most of my time at White House, a very pleasant place to live that has many advantages to other places about there. I have also spent much time at

Romancoke, attending to business for Mr. Nelson when he was too sick to go out. I was but a boy of twelve when you commenced my lessons in the schoolroom at Arlington, and it comes as a surprise to myself when I remember that I am thirty-four years old now and married, with four children of my own.

I had hoped to see you at Arlington at Christmas, but Selina told me Colonel Lee is the superintendent at West Point now, and you were there for much of the season.

I am writing because Rosabella and I wish to take our children to Liberia to start over in freedom. I hear there is a ship leaving late in the fall, and if your father will give us our freedom we mean to be aboard when it sets sail. I asked him about this at Christmas but he seemed to be thinking about other things and never did say whether he would even think about it. Mrs. Lee, I hope you will intervene as I am very anxious to study for the ministry at the seminary in Monrovia. I still have the Bible you gave me when I was sixteen, but it is quite worn out from daily reading.

Your humble servant,
Wm. Custis Burke

William's letter arrived on Friday, but I was too busy boxing up books and clothes to send to the girls, who were at Arlington with Papa and

Mother, to read it. Both Rob and Life were suffering from coughs made worse by the raw April weather, and on this gray, rainy Sunday I stayed home with them while Robert went off to church. It was one of many times I felt torn between allegiance to my husband and the responsibilities of motherhood.

Robert was not happy with his duties at West Point. The endless meetings, the petty politics, and the disagreeable climate added up to a daily misery for him, which I tried my best to assuage. He wanted me by his side whenever possible, but this morning he had encouraged me to look after the children, promising a long afternoon just for the two of us.

I was eager to share William's letter with him in hopes he could advise me on the best argument to use with my father. William had earned his chance at a better life, but convincing Papa to relinquish ownership of six of his servants would not be easy, even with Mother on my side.

"Mrs. Lee, I brought you some tea." Eliza glided into the room and set the tea tray on the table beneath the window. From there I had a view of the barracks and the Hudson River, now shrouded in gray mist. "You need anything else, Missus?"

Her voice sounded strained. "Eliza, are you all right?"

"Yessum. Just tired is all. Miss Mildred had herself a bad coughing fit before daylight this morning, and it took me some time to get her quiet."

"Oh, I know it. Rob had a restless night too. Thankfully, they are sleeping now." I poured the tea. "I suppose that new cough syrup the doctor sent over is finally working."

"What those babies need is some of Judah's slippery elm tea, that's what."

"Mother is coming for a visit next month. If the children are not completely cured by then, I'll ask her to bring some."

Through the window I watched Robert cross the yard and unlatch the gate.

"Colonel Lee is home, Eliza. Would you bring another cup? I'm sure he's chilled to the bone after walking in this weather."

"Yessum. I'll be right back."

She left, and Robert came into the hallway. I heard him removing his wet things.

"Mary?"

"In the parlor."

He paused in the doorway, and I could sense that something was wrong. He took from his pocket a telegram and handed it to me. "Brace yourself, my dear."

Papa's message was as terse as it was urgent. Mother was gravely ill and I was wanted at home.

"Don't worry about Rob and Life," Robert said. "Eliza and I can manage."

I couldn't seem to move my feet.

Eliza returned with the teacup but there was no time to waste.

I climbed the stairs and tossed some clothes into my trunk. I looked in on my sleeping children and kissed them good-bye. Robert sent for a coach and driver and accompanied me to the train station.

"Try not to worry, Molly." He kissed my cheek and handed me into the train car. "Send word on her condition as soon as you can."

I waved to him from the window as the train chugged toward Washington.

On Tuesday, rumpled, gritty-eyed, and sick with worry, I arrived home and dropped my bags in the entry hall. The house seemed strangely quiet. I called for my father, but it was Agnes who rushed to greet me.

"Mama, I don't have a grandmama anymore!"

Papa emerged from the parlor, looking as unkempt and bleary-eyed as I. He shuffled toward me, arms outstretched. "Mary Anna, your mother has gone. I do not know what to do."

"This is so sudden, I can't believe it. What happened?"

"On Thursday last she complained of a head-ache, and the doctor came and said it was nothing serious." Papa rubbed at his eyes. "But the next day she was worse, and he gave us little hope for her recovery."

"We were with her, Mama." Agnes leaned her head on my shoulder. "Annie and I both. We were on the bed with her and she told us not to cry. We said the Lord's Prayer with her and then she left us."

"I'm sorry you had to endure that without me or your papa."

Agnes sniffed. "I know she's in heaven now, but she is the first person who has been taken from me, and it seems so hard."

Selina came in, her face so full of sorrow that I nearly lost my composure.

"Miss Mary? I heard you had arrived. George is making you all some breakfast. It's just about done."

"All right."

Selina fumbled for her handkerchief. "I sure am sorry. The missus was always good to me."

"Thank you, Selina."

Presently, Charles came in, and I could see that he had been crying too. "Miss Mary, they's some breakfast on the table if you feel like eating."

I didn't want a bite, but Papa was in no condition to do anything. I would need my strength to make the necessary decisions and to weather the heartache ahead. I sent Agnes to fetch her sister, and we ate in sorrowful silence.

"If Grandmama were here we'd have morning prayers now," Annie said when our meal was finished.

"And so we shall." I took Mother's bell from its place on the sideboard and walked out into the warm April sunshine to summon the servants, just as my mother had done every morning of her life. I read a few verses while the servants wept quietly and birds trilled in the garden outside the window.

Afterward I found Papa sitting alone in his studio. "We must choose a spot for her grave."

He slumped in his chair. "I cannot do it. You must find the proper place for her, Mary."

I walked down the slope toward the river to a spot in sight of the gardens Mother had so loved. I sensed Selina's presence before she spoke.

"Miss Mary, I don't know if it will comfort you to know I was with your mother when she breathed her last."

I turned around. "I only wish I could have been here for the moment when that precious soul took flight."

Selina wiped her eyes. "It was peaceful. It was after midnight and we were all there gathered round her bed. Your papa was on his knees beside her when the girls came in. They were scared, and Missus asked them to come up and lie down beside her and say the Lord's Prayer with her. I said, 'Missus, is there any word you want to tell me for Miss Mary?' And she said, 'Oh, Selina, I hate that she will be shocked when she hears this.' And that was the last words she said to me."

I turned back to the patch of green I had chosen for her resting place.

"You got to be strong now, for your girls. 'Specially Miss Agnes. She is taking this loss very hard." Selina moved to stand beside me and shaded her eyes. "This where you going to put her?"

"Yes. I think it would please her to be in sight of the garden and the river."

I telegraphed Robert, summoned Ephraim to dig the grave, and sent word to the Reverend Dana to come and conduct the service. The next morning I went into the garden alone to pick flowers for the mourners, who had begun arriving the previous evening.

At noon a handful of our friends joined my cousins and aunts and my daughters for the service. I found my father alone in Mother's bedroom, staring out the window.

"Papa. It's time."

"Who—" His voice faltered. "Who is to bear the coffin to the grave?"

"Austin, Lawrence, Daniel, and Ephraim. They were among her favorites."

"Are the servants assembled?"

"Yes. Annie and Agnes are in the parlor with Uncle William. We are all waiting for you."

He shook his head. "I will remain right here."

"But—"

"Leave me now, Mary Anna."

I went out to organize the mourners. After the minister's address and the usual prayers, Annie, Agnes, and I joined hands. Uncle William followed us in the procession to the gravesite. I handed out the flowers from Mother's garden to those assembled, and when the coffin was lowered into the ground we tossed the flowers upon it.

Agnes threw her arms around me and sobbed.

For her sake I staunched the flow of my own tears and swallowed the ache in my throat. "It's only her body that's in the grave, precious child."

"I know. Maybe her angel spirit is looking down on us right this minute."

"I am certain of it."

"It is beautiful, isn't it, Mama, to look through the green trees and at the blue sky above and think she may be there."

The servants moved away from the grave. I looked up in time to see Maria Syphax, Charles's wife, standing apart from the others, a single rose in her hands. Because Charles was in charge of our dining room, I saw him daily when I was home, but I saw Maria only occasionally, as she rarely ventured from the property Papa had given her. Now she crossed the lawn and stood before the open grave for a moment before dropping the rose onto Mother's coffin. Her eyes met mine, and for a moment I experienced a most peculiar and unsettled feeling. But it quickly passed, and Maria hurried away.

I found the minister standing among the small knot of family and friends still assembled and thanked him for coming.

"It was my honor, Mrs. Lee." His face had grown pink beneath the spring sunshine, and he tugged at his collar. He produced his handkerchief and blotted his face. "Your mother was a fine woman. Everybody who knew her will remember her grace and her efforts on the behalf of others."

"I have often thought that she alone of all our household was ripe for heaven. My father always said she was everything that was lovely and excellent."

"Indeed. She truly was one in a thousand." He bowed to me and the girls. "My carriage is here and I must go. But do call upon me if there is anything else I can do for you or your father."

Annie and Agnes and Uncle William accompanied me back to the house. George had prepared a meal, but none of us was really hungry. The girls picked at their food until I sent them up to their room to rest. Papa remained behind the closed door of his bedroom.

Selina came in. "Is there anything I can do for you?"

"I can't think of anything."

"I'm going on home now, but I set some cake and fresh coffee in the parlor for you all." She crossed the room and clasped my hands. "I know this is the worst thing that has ever happened to you, but you got to do the best you can. And look after your papa. He is grieving so."

The following days passed in a blur. Mother's obituary appeared in the local newspapers. Letters arrived from members of the American Colonization Society, urging me to continue her work. Robert's letter spoke of his own inconsolable grief. I read it alone, sitting in the garden Mother had so loved.

Dearest Mary,

This is the most affecting calamity that has ever befallen us. The blow was so sudden and crushing that I yet shudder at the shock and feel as if I had been arrested in the course of life. I suppose the best way to honor her memory is to seek to emulate her in word and in deed. I pray that when I die my last end may be like her.

"Mary Anna?" Papa came into the garden wearing his favorite straw hat. "I thought I'd find you here."

I folded Robert's letter to read again later and got to my feet, brushing the dirt from the hem of my skirt. "You seem much improved this morning."

"We must learn to bear that which cannot be

changed." He gazed up at the house and garden, the sloping lawn. "Everything is just the same. Our home, the park, the lawn, and this beautiful garden she loved so well. Her imprint is all over this place, and yet I feel so utterly alone."

"I know it, Papa. You won't be alone, though." I linked my arm through his. "I must return to West Point soon, but Annie and Agnes will remain here with Miss Poor. And Markie has offered to stay as long as you want her."

"Whatever would we do without Markie?" Papa plucked a blossom from the lilac bush and held it to his nose. "I have always been partial to lilacs. I know of no other flower with such a lavish fragrance."

He tucked the flower into his shirt pocket. "Please do write to your sweet cousin and ask her to come. At least until you and the children are home for the summer."

"All right." We started up the path. "Perhaps this is not the best time, but I must ask you for a great favor."

"A favor?"

"I had a letter from William Burke last week. He says that he has asked you for his freedom. He wants to go to Liberia."

"So he said."

"But you didn't give him an answer."

"I thought the absence of my permission served well enough."

"That's hardly fair, after the years of excellent service he has given you. The least you could do is give him a definitive answer."

Papa's steps slowed. "Manumitting six servants costs a considerable sum of money. And I have made provisions in my will for their emancipation." He waved a hand. "Five years at the outside, after I am in my grave, they can all go."

"God willing, you will be here for many years yet. By then William and Rosabella might be too old for such an undertaking. William is already well past thirty. And his children ought to have their chance now, while they are young."

He grunted.

"If you won't do it for them, or for me, do it for Mother. You know it's what she would want."

"It's hardly fair, Mary Anna, to bring your mother into this discussion when she is not even cold in her grave."

"I am sorry to bring this up now, but William says there is a ship leaving in the fall, and in order to book passage, he must first prove he is free. Then there are the applications to complete and letters of recommendation to procure, not to mention outfitting them for travel."

He halted and peered down at me. "Refusing you now will not mean the end of this discussion, will it?"

"I'm afraid I shall have to keep bringing it up until I get the result I want."

He sighed. "I am too tired to fight you. Have the papers drawn up and I will sign them."

"Thank you, Papa."

"But hear me, child. I will not contribute one cent to their expenses."

We returned to a house still in mourning. Papa hung up his hat and plodded off to his studio. Annie and Agnes were at their lessons with Miss Poor; the hum of their voices penetrated the thick silence. I could hear Selina moving around upstairs, dusting the furniture and changing the bed linens. Mother's little bell rested on the sideboard where I'd left it.

Everything was the same, everything was different. I felt my mother's presence surrounding me. I remembered the last morning we'd spent together in the garden, surrounded by lilacs and arbutus and the scent of roses. She wore a red sunbonnet faded to pink by many wearings and her old black garden boots. In the summer sunlight her skin was pale, the bones of her hands thin as wire. She bent to pull a handful of weeds, an expression of serene contentment on her face.

This is how I would remember her—happy and at peace. I smiled to myself. *We did it, Mother. William Burke is going free.*

I went to Mother's writing desk to get paper and ink for writing to Markie. At the back of the drawer lay a single letter, creased from many readings. The ink had faded, but there was no mistaking my father's sprawling hand. Wondering why she had chosen to save only this letter, I pulled it out. Addressed to my mother while she was visiting at Kinloch, it was full of news about the servants at Arlington House, prospects for the corn crop, and sorrow at the loss of so many of our family.

Death indeed, my Dear Wife, has used his scythe with an unsparing hand of late in my unfortunate family. He has cut off the young, the gay, the innocent, and the good and the happy. I need not expect to be exempt.

"Mama?" Annie poked her head into the room. "What are you doing?"

"Writing to Cousin Markie. Your grandpa wants her here while your papa and I are away."

"Oh." She perched on the arm of my chair. "What's that?"

"A letter from your grandpa to your grandmama." I glanced at the date and was surprised to see that more than thirty years had passed since he had written it.

"May I see it?"

"It's nothing to interest a girl of your age. Besides, if I know Miss Poor, she will set you to your mathematics lessons soon."

"Mathematics. Ugh." Annie wrinkled her nose. "Boring as dirt."

I sent her off to join her sister and returned to Papa's letter.

One duty I have yet to [*here the page was smudged and I could not make out his handwriting*] the duty of affection and gratitude to you, Dear Wife, to leave you all my possessions and hope they may make you some amends for the unhappy moments I have caused you . . .

An image of my mother's face, her expression full of some private grief, rose in my mind. The letter confirmed that which I had always suspected, but which no one would admit: that my father had hurt her in some profound way. So profound that she had kept this letter for three decades.

I returned the letter to the drawer. I hoped that whatever had passed between them had been acknowledged, forgiven, forgotten. I wrote to Markie, urging her to come to Arlington for a long visit. Shortly thereafter I returned to West Point. But the questions regarding my parents lingered long after time had softened the sharp edges of my grief and the scent of my mother's garden had faded into memory.

★ 28 ★
SELINA

On that sorrowful day when we put Missus under the ground, I saw Maria Syphax coming across the yard dressed in black and holding a pink rose in her hand, and my heart like to have stopped beating.

I was barely out of my baby time when Mister Custis gave Maria Carter seventeen acres of land and her freedom, but from time to time I overheard Mauma and Judah whispering about "that high yellow woman." Maria Carter was a few years older than Miss Mary, and she had married Charles from the dining room the year Miss Mary turned eighteen, but I was too young to recollect it.

Her cabin in the woods was packed to the ceiling with children, or so Judah said. Maria didn't spend too much time in the quarters, but I had seen her enough to recognize her the minute she walked right past us to drop her flower onto Missus's coffin. She did not speak a word. She just turned and looked at Miss Mary for the longest time and then went back the way she had come.

I could of told Miss Mary why Maria had come.

What she was looking for. What she knew. But my lips were sealed.

Some words are best left unspoken. Some secrets are best left buried with the dead.

★ 29 ★

MARY

Mrs. Pinckney lived in a plain-looking house in Georgetown, its unremarkable façade offering no clue to the opulence within. I handed my calling card to the servant who opened the door and stood in the entry hall in my mourning clothes, admiring the tall gilt-framed mirrors and French tapestries lining the walls and trying to calm my nerves. I had not seen Mrs. Pinckney since my wedding celebration. From time to time I had written to her on behalf of the Colonization Society, and she had responded with modest donations. But I wasn't certain she would receive me. Or that she would be amenable to my plan.

"Mrs. Lee?" The girl who had admitted me to the house returned. "Please come with me."

She led me into the parlor, where Mrs. Pinckney waited behind a gleaming silver tea service. Mrs. Pinckney dismissed her girl with a wave of her hand and rose to greet me.

"Mrs. Lee. This is a pleasure I never anticipated,

after more than twenty years. I must say you have hardly changed at all since your wedding day." She peered into my face. "Though of course you look tired now, my dear, but who can blame you after such a crushing loss? I was so sad to learn of your dear mother's death. She was certainly a bright example to everyone who knew her."

"Thank you. Of course I thought so."

Mrs. Pinckney motioned me to a chair and took her time pouring the tea into paper-thin china cups, setting out the sugar tongs and the crystal milk pitcher. I looked around at the room, which seemed to have been arranged for a Beaux Arts exhibition. Every shelf and surface was crowded with Chinese porcelains, bronze sculptures, and a collection of French ormolu clocks. A set of miniature paintings of hollow-cheeked saints and fat, smiling cherubs adorned the fireplace mantel.

"What brings you here?" Mrs. Pinckney asked. "It must be important, since you are in mourning."

I took the cup she offered, using the moment to compose myself. I hated asking a favor of any-one, especially someone I barely knew, and I felt guilty for what I was about to do. The plan, which had seemed so easy in theory, now filled me with sadness, but I had no other option, and now I steeled myself to follow through.

I sipped the tea, set down the cup, and opened the small cloth bag I had brought with me from

Arlington. I took out the carved ivory box my father had given me on my wedding day.

"Do you remember this?"

Her eyes lit up. "Of course I remember. May I see it?"

I handed it over, quashing my distaste at having her touch something so precious and so personal. She opened and closed the gold-hinged lid.

"It is still one of the loveliest things I have ever seen," she said.

"You once said that if I ever wanted to sell it—"

"Oh, my dear. Is it that bad? I have heard rumors that Arlington is in dire straits. One does hear these things, you know. But I never dreamed the situation would come to this." She made a *tsk-tsk* sound. "Your father is the most generous host in Virginia, but one does wish he had exercised more financial prudence rather than forcing his only child to give up her own personal treasures."

"You misunderstand my purpose, Mrs. Pinckney. This has nothing to do with my father or with his management of the estate. I'm selling the box to help a friend with some expenses."

"I see. Anyone I know?"

"I don't think so."

She ran her fingers over the box lid. "I would like to think about it."

I couldn't bear the thought of having to subject myself to further conversations on the subject.

And time was of the essence. "I'm afraid I need a decision today."

"Oh, I see. You have other buyers interested, I expect."

I didn't correct her. I waited while the many clocks ticked loudly in the silence. Finally she said, "I can offer you eight hundred for it."

I had hoped for a thousand, but I decided not to push my luck. Nor to prolong the agony of parting with something I so dearly loved, even if in doing so I was contributing to something far more important than my own sentimental feelings. "All right."

Mrs. Pinckney rose. "Please enjoy your tea while I write a check. I'll be back in a moment."

The deed was done. The ivory box sat on the side table, the jewels catching the light. I was overwhelmed with guilt when I thought of Papa and of how happy he had been to give me such a beautiful keepsake on the most momentous night of my life. I hoped he would never know I hadn't kept it.

Mrs. Pinckney returned and handed me the check. "I hope your friend appreciates your sacrifice."

I tucked it away and got to my feet. "I must go. Thank you for receiving me."

She smiled. "I cannot think of a single person in this town who would not receive the daughter of Mary Fitzhugh Custis. She was one of a kind."

I left the house, and Daniel drove me home. Papa was in the garden talking with Ephraim, his ratty straw hat pulled low over his eyes. It was high summer, and the vegetable crop was coming in faster than we could harvest it. He looked up and waved as I went up the steps and into the house. I put away Mrs. Pinckney's check, removed my hat, and started down the stairs.

"Miss Mary, is that you?" Selina, carrying a basket of squash and beans, peeked in from the rear hallway.

"Yes. I just got back. I want to walk down to visit Mother's grave."

"Huh. It won't do anything except make you sad all over again." She shifted the basket onto her hip. "You want me to go down there with you?"

"Not today. I think I want to be alone with her."

"At least try not to come back with your eyes all red and puffed up. Miss Agnes and Miss Annie are still taking this death awfully hard."

"I know it."

"I noticed there's some roses just opening up this morning. If you want to take some to her."

"I will." I collected the shears from the basket Mother kept beside the back door and let myself out into the garden. I snipped half a dozen stems of ruby-red buds and walked down the path to Mother's grave. In the three months since I had put her there, the grass had begun to cover the red wound in the earth. The cuttings my daughters and I had planted were taking hold. One day her grave would be surrounded by the flowers she had so loved.

I placed the flowers on the handsome headstone Robert had purchased for her. "Guess what, Mother. You were right all those years ago when you told me to be patient with my husband. Last week Daughter and Annie were confirmed. And Robert too."

I still couldn't quite believe that something I had so long hoped for had finally happened. The previous Sunday night I had sat in our pew at Christ Church in my mourning clothes, the suffocating heat pressing down, watching Daughter and Annie kneeling at the Communion rail. It was a moment of inexpressible happiness amid so much pain, and I reached over to clasp Robert's hand. He kissed the back of my hand, stood, and walked to the front of the church to join his children. Whether he had chosen to be confirmed at that moment in order to ease the pain of my sudden bereavement or to honor the woman he had for so long called Mother, I couldn't say.

I wished that she had lived to witness that glorious event. I could only hope that the full knowledge of it may have swelled the tide of joy wherever her spirit had gone.

From the top of Federal Hill in Baltimore I could see the *Banshee* riding at anchor among sailing vessels and steamships crowding the harbor. A flock of geese winged above the breakwater where the river roiled with wind-whipped whitecaps. Beyond the teeming wharves, the city's monument to President Washington pierced the pewter-colored sky.

Beside me in the carriage, Robert's sister, Anne, fussed with her skirts and retied the ribbons on her bonnet. "Are you sure this is a good idea? It isn't exactly the best day to be out and about. You're able to visit so seldom anymore, I would hate for you to get sick and spoil our time together."

"I've looked forward to this visit too. But I've waited for years for such a day as this. I can't let disagreeable weather keep me away."

The carriage drew up at the wharf, and the driver jumped down to open the door. Anne peered out at the dozens of black families standing near the *Banshee*. A cold rain began to fall.

"If it's all the same with you, Mary, I think I will wait for you here." She sent me a sharp glance. "No sense in both of us getting sick."

I left the carriage and made my way to the center of the group. Since July I had corresponded regularly with William Burke and his family during their preparations for beginning anew in Liberia. Our letters flew back and forth as William and Rosabella filed the necessary applications with the Colonization Society, collected letters of reference, booked passage, and outfitted themselves and their children for the voyage. Now at last they were on their way, along with some 257 other freedmen.

"Mrs. Lee, what a surprise to see you."

The Reverend Gurley pushed through the throng to clasp my hand. He was no longer president of the society, but he still took a keen interest in the activities of all the chapters, including mine in Washington City.

He raised his umbrella to shelter me. "Not the best weather for commencing a journey, but I expect our freedmen are happy to be under way at last." He glanced around and checked his pocket watch. "I would have thought our sponsors would have arrived by now."

"How many are going this time?"

"Just three. But they are competent men and well prepared to assist our families in getting settled. This group will make nearly ten thousand people we have resettled so far."

"It's a start, I suppose."

"Yes, but we must revive our finances in the new year. Now that Mr. Webster and Mr. Clay have passed on to their rewards, I worry about who will champion our cause."

I was deeply troubled about that myself. Mr. Clay had expired the previous July. Mr. Webster had followed him just three months later. I feared that Mr. Garrison's continuing attacks upon us in his *Liberator* and other writings might turn the tide permanently against us. "Won't the money the state legislatures have appropriated keep us going for a while?"

Two little boys ran past, jostling us, and the minister took my elbow to steady me.

"Perhaps. But when we are obliged to purchase slaves in order to free them, even the thirty thousand a year set aside in Virginia does not go very far."

"Mrs. Lee?" I recognized William Burke's voice even before he reached me.

He nodded to the Reverend Gurley, then clasped my hand. "Mrs. Lee, I can never thank you for all you have done for Rosabella and me, and our children."

"Pardon me, Mrs. Lee," the minister said. "There are our sponsors, arrived at last. I must speak to them. You are welcome to my umbrella."

He soon was lost in the burgeoning crowd milling about the pier.

William held the umbrella above our heads as the mist grew heavier. "I'm glad you came to see us off."

"I couldn't stay away on such a momentous day."

"I have some news I hope will please you," William said. "I have been accepted to the seminary in Monrovia."

"Oh, William, that is wonderful news. I'm deeply pleased."

"It never could have happened if you hadn't given me those secret reading lessons."

"Lawrence and my mother deserve most of the credit. I was away so much of the time when you were growing up."

"But it was you who got me started, and you gave me that Bible when I was just sixteen. You convinced Mr. Custis to give us our freedom and gave us the money to pay for this trip." He reached into his pocket and handed me a roll of bills. "This is what we had left after we paid for everything."

"You ought to keep it. There are sure to be more expenses once you reach Liberia."

"Yes, I imagine there will be. But I'd rather you use this to help some other family who wants to emigrate."

We heard a commotion and peered from beneath the umbrella. The sponsors were organizing the passengers, checking their papers, directing them to the gangplank.

"I reckon I ought to go find my wife." William handed me the umbrella. "God bless you, Mrs. Lee. I will write to you when we get there."

"I would like that."

He turned and was swallowed in the crowd moving toward the gangplank. Soon the last passengers were aboard. The pier was nearly deserted. I looked around for the Reverend Gurley, but he had gone. Only a few dockworkers remained to load the last of the cargo. Behind me, the carriage waited.

Despite the mist and the chill, passengers crowded the deck to wave good-bye. Huddled beneath the large umbrella I couldn't see William, but I took out my handkerchief and waved, my throat swelling with tears as the *Banshee* cleared the harbor and faded into the mist.

★ 30 ★
MARY

1857

I was headed for my schoolroom, my arms full of books for reading lessons with the servants' children, when I saw Papa trudging up the path from the stables. Four years had passed since my mother's death, but he had never completely recovered from the loss. He had given up his pen and easel, preferring his solitary walks among the clear streams and cool shades of Arlington. He was often gone for hours, lost in the quiet beauty of the revolving seasons and in his own private reveries.

On that bright October morning I set down my books and met him at the door. He was red faced, perspiring heavily though the air was still cool from the morning's frost.

"Are you all right?"

He shook his head. "I'm feeling very strange this morning."

I sent for the doctor, but his condition worsened rapidly. Before I knew quite what was happening, he called me to his side, and I could see that he was failing.

"You are a good daughter, Mary Anna." He clasped my hand. "My dearest love, besides your mother."

"And Arlington."

He smiled then. "And Arlington."

He summoned his grandchildren, took his leave of them in the gentlest way, and asked for our pastor. But before the elements for administering the sacraments could be prepared, my very kind and indulgent father fell insensible and slipped away.

Unlike Mother's funeral, which was small and personal, his was a very public affair. The Welsh Light Infantry and the Veterans of the War of 1812 joined a thousand mourners who crossed the long bridge over the river and made their way to Arlington. Six of our servants bore his mahogany coffin to the grave next to my mother's.

When the service ended I stood for hours receiving the endless parade of politicians, soldiers, lawyers, artists, newspapermen, and plantation owners swarming the lawn.

The pastor sought me out and took my hands in his. "Mrs. Lee. When your dear mother passed, I had hoped it would be many more years before your father joined her. Four years seems hardly enough time to recover from one loss. And now you have lost them both."

Overcome with grief and exhausted from days of preparations, I could only nod.

He surveyed the milling crowd. "I haven't seen Colonel Lee."

"He's on his way home from Texas."

"I didn't realize he had left West Point."

"Oh, yes, quite some time ago, and very happy to leave it behind."

"Well, I'm sorry the burden of this death has fallen upon your shoulders, but I suppose that's the difficulty of military life."

"One of many, I'm afraid."

He nodded. "Will you excuse me?"

He crossed the yard, and the mourners began to disperse. I gathered my children and we returned to the house.

Selina was there, taking care of everything with her usual quiet efficiency.

"There's food on the sideboard whenever you all get hungry, Miss Mary. And I put all the calling cards on your desk. There's a bunch of telegrams, too, from people who knew Mr. Custis."

"Thank you. I will get to them as soon as I can."

"No need to be in a hurry about it. Colonel

Lee can help you sort it out when he gets here."

Unfortunately for my husband, there were much thornier things to sort out when he finally arrived home. As the only one qualified to be executor of my father's will, he shouldered the difficulties of sorting out Papa's wishes regarding his properties and the disposition of the slaves. Papa left behind a very injudicious will, in which there was no distinction between the good and the bad, and this rendered our task very difficult.

And there were other worries. Some of the servants claimed that on his deathbed, Papa had promised to free them all. Several of them simply left, slipping away into the night. Others dawdled at their chores, broke things, or feigned illness. Anything to disrupt the serenity that had so long reigned at Arlington.

Wild rumors ran rampant.

"Listen to this," Robert said at breakfast one morning, rattling his copy of the *New York Daily Times*, which Daniel had delivered the previous evening. "'It is already whispered about town that foul play is in process in regard to the Custis Negroes on the Virginia plantations; that they are now being sold South and that all of them will be consigned to hopeless slavery unless something is done.'"

"But it isn't true." I stared out at the bleak December landscape.

"Of course not." He tossed the paper aside. "The

servants know full well that I intend to free them as soon as your father's debts are discharged. But I will not sit here and let such vile accusations pass unchallenged."

He excused himself to paper and pen, and a few days later the *Times* printed Robert's tersely worded correction of the facts:

Mr. Custis left his property to his daughter and only child, and her children. His will was submitted to the Alexandria County Court for probate on the first day of its session after the arrival of the executor at Arlington and is there on record in his own handwriting, open to inspection. There is no desire on the part of the heirs to prevent the execution of its provisions in reference to the slaves, nor is there any truth or the least foundation for the assertion that they are being sold South. What Mr. Custis is said to have stated to his assembled slaves is not known to any member of his family. But it is well known that during the brief days of his last illness he was constantly attended by his daughter and granddaughter and faithfully visited by his physician and pastor. So rapid was the progress of his disease after his symptoms became alarming that there was no assembly of his servants and he took leave of but one, who was present when he bade farewell to his family.

No sooner had Robert quashed those rumors than an outrageous article appeared regarding plantation owners who sought any means to increase the number of slaves as a way of increasing profits. It included a mock obituary of my father:

Among such was the late George Washington Parke Custis, owner of several properties across Virginia, a man of notorious licentiousness which was strictly Virginian in its impartiality for color.

Markie, who had returned to Arlington as the new year arrived, was incensed.

"Oh, Mary, what an ugly lie. You ought to hire a lawyer and sue the lot of them for libel."

"Robert says we must ignore everything until the public gets its fill of gossip. I don't care if they want to say things about me. I'm alive and can fight back. But attacking someone as fine and generous as Papa now that he's gone is inexcusable. He doesn't deserve it."

But the following week I made a discovery that changed my mind.

I was still working on his *Recollections*, and his desk was piled high with bills, receipts, half-finished poems and plays, untidy stacks of correspondence from his political friends in Washington, and carefully preserved newspaper clippings about his ancestral home.

Making my way through the mountain of paperwork, I found copies of land deeds and bills of sale for equipment for his mills and other holdings. Tucked into the back of a ragged green cloth letterbook was a note signed in Papa's own hand.

Maria Carter, acknowledged as my daughter on this first day of January in the year of our Lord 1826, is hereby granted complete and permanent emancipation and the parcel of land comprising seventeen acres of land in the . . .

The words blurred before my eyes. Maria Carter, born a slave five years before me, educated at my own mother's knee, wed to Charles Syphax for these many years, was my father's child. My half sister.

I didn't want to know this. I wanted to believe he had been a different kind of man. I put away the ledger, furious at myself for having been so naive, furious at him for having taken his secret with him into the ground. Maria was not the only mulatto at Arlington, but I had never made any connection between them and my father. Now I wondered whether the others were also his children.

The last vestiges of guilt over having sold the ivory wedding box he had given me evaporated. I was glad to be rid of it, for now his entire life seemed to me nothing less than one enormous lie.

★ 31 ★
SELINA

1859

Spring took its own sweet time returning to Arlington, and my children, who slept stacked head to toe like sticks of firewood in the sleeping loft, suffered from the constant chill. Thornton kept the fire going day and night. Judah brought by poultices and tonics every day or so, and Mauma doctored my babies while I kept house for Miss Mary. Her rheumatism had finally got the best of her despite pills and potions and trips to the hot mineral springs, and now she mostly depended on me to do for her, and on crutches or her rolling chair to get around.

So I was surprised one morning in March to see her making her way across the yard to my cabin. I set down the potatoes I was peeling and went to the door. "Miss Mary, what are you doing out here?"

"I'm worried about your children. Especially Annice."

I glanced at my daughter, who was sleeping on her side, trying to breathe easier. "She is having the worst time of it."

Miss Mary handed me a bowl. "I had George make some chicken broth for her, but if she is not improved by tomorrow I will send for the doctor."

She bent stiffly over my sleeping children, laying her hand against their cheeks. "Oh, I wish I could find more comfortable quarters for you."

I was wishing the same thing, but there wasn't anything to be done about it as long as we belonged to Arlington. And it didn't seem we would be away from there anytime soon.

Colonel Lee spent most of his time going over books of numbers and trying to keep the abolitionists away. But they came anyway, to the fields and the stables, and talked to the menfolks about nothing but how to run away and how we were now free because old Mister Custis was dead and buried. How all we had to do was rise up and demand our freedom. But every time Thornton told me what they had said, all I could think of was Nat Turner skinned like an animal when I was a girl. The terror of it was never far from my mind.

Miss Mary left me to see to Annice, then went back to the house.

The next morning right after prayers, Colonel Lee called us into the parlor.

"You all know that Mr. Custis demanded little of you when he was alive. And now you are all waiting for manumission. In order to speed that day, I must first put the finances of this house in order. This was the wish of Mr. Custis as stated in his will."

I stole a look at Lawrence, the market man. He was the one we all looked up to when it came to matters of liberation, but I couldn't make heads or tails of the look on his face.

It was true that Mister Custis let us do as we pleased. As long as the work got done he never raised his voice or his lash. But still, we were his property the same as the sheep and oxen and President Washington's silver. The president had bought and sold slaves too, and Mister Custis didn't see anything wrong with keeping us in bondage. It was the way he had been raised from his boyhood at Mount Vernon. Keeping slaves was the only thing he knew.

Lawrence looked like he was finally about to speak up, but then he changed his mind, and we waited to see what Colonel Lee was going to say next.

"As much as I disliked breaking up families, I had no choice but to hire out all those who were able to work," the colonel told us. "This has caused unhappiness among you. I will do all I can to make those of you who remain here as comfortable as possible. In return I ask you to be patient and to remember that Mrs. Lee from her earliest days has done all she could on your behalf."

I didn't doubt that he believed every word he said. But he had thrown Ruben, Parks, and Edward in jail last fall for sassing him. He wouldn't think twice about doing it again if people didn't mind their tongues.

Miss Mary sat by the window with her hands folded in her lap. She still thought Africa was the answer to the problem of what to do with us, but that idea didn't sit too well with my brother, Wesley, who had been one of the first to be hired out. At twenty-six he was taller than our daddy and strong from working the orchards and the wheat fields. From time to time we got word of him from the place he was working down in lower Virginia.

Colonel Lee dismissed us, and we headed to our chores. I took care of my usual cleaning, dusting, polishing, and mopping chores, changed the linens on the bed, and brought Miss Mary's ten o'clock tea into the room off the parlor where she went to do her reading and work on her book. She had been writing that one thing off and on for many years. It must have been some whale of a story.

"Thank you, Selina." She poured herself some tea and took a sip. "How is Annice today? And the rest of the children?"

"Annice seems some better this morning. The rest of them are about the same."

"The doctor will be here this afternoon to see about that burn on Austin's leg. I'll have him look in at your place."

"Thank you, Missus."

She smiled. "I think that's the first time you have ever called me Missus. I have always thought of my mother as Missus. I suppose I still do."

"This is your house now. Reckon you're the mistress over everything."

"Yes, and it is nothing but a pure trial these days." She waved her hand over a stack of newspapers on the desk. "I refuse to continue reading these stories about how terribly we are treating you all. Most servants would be grateful to be in such gentle hands."

I picked up her shawl that had fallen to the floor and folded it. There were times when my children were small and I would come to her with some concern about them, or when I needed an extra loaf of sugar or vinegar for a poultice, that I thought she understood my life. But she had never known how it felt to want more than you could have. How the longing for it made the days seem longer and the endless round of chores harder to bear.

She reached for her shawl. "Tell me, Selina, are we truly being unreasonable in our expectations of our own servants?"

A feeling of dark humiliation rose up in me then. Until the colonel's speech that morning, I had never allowed myself to think that I was a piece of property. Something that could be bought or sold whenever the owner took a notion. I told myself that I was different from Rose and Kitty and Judah because of my friendship with Miss Mary. Now I saw that despite her kindliness toward me, in her eyes I was just like the others. At the mercy of rules that were made up just for profit. The thought of it burned like fire in my veins.

"Now, Miss Mary, how do you expect me to answer a question like that?"

She acted like she hadn't heard me. "Do we starve you? Beat you? Sell you South? We do not. And think of all those we have already freed. Eleanor, Cassie, Lily, Eliza. And soon, the rest of you. Yet these reporters persist in their villainous attacks upon my husband and upon my father's memory in language I would not pollute my lips by repeating."

It was the longest speech she had made in some time, and surely the angriest. I had known her all my life, and sometimes I still couldn't figure out her moods. One day her words would be soft and sweet, curling right around your heart like a flowering vine. The next day, sharp as a fishhook. Lately there had been mostly fishhooks. When she got that way it was best not to cross her. "You want me to throw the papers out for you then?"

She sighed. "No, I suppose I ought to keep them until my husband has finished with them."

I made my escape and spent the rest of the day staying out of her sight. I felt like my heart had been split in two. Despite it all, one half still belonged to Miss Mary. The other half belonged to myself.

Late that night, when the children were asleep, Thornton pulled me close. He had worked in the stable later than usual, and the smell of fresh hay still stuck to his skin.

"Got some news today," he said quietly. "Wesley has run off and took your sister, Mary, and George Parks and some others with him."

A cold chill crept over me then, like I had walked on somebody's grave. "Does Colonel Lee know?"

"Lawrence said the colonel found out last night. From the overseer."

"Huh. How did McQuinn find out?"

Up in the loft one of the boys cried out, and I heard my older girls quieting him. In the corner, an injured rabbit Annice had rescued and was nursing back to health scrabbled in his cage.

"Somebody come up from Romancoke with the news," Thornton said. "I hope Wesley and all of them get away clean. Colonel Lee don't look kindly on anybody who don't do what they supposed to do."

"He thinks everybody ought to be like him. Do your duty no matter what."

"Mama?" Emma called down from the loft. "You and Daddy gone be talkin' all night?"

"Nope," Thornton said. "We are all done talking for now, baby girl. You go on back to sleep." He wrapped his arm around my waist. "You too, wife."

But I stayed awake until the stars faded,

308

thinking about my brother and sister. Not knowing exactly what to wish for. If they got away, I might never hear of them or see them ever again. If they got caught, they would pay a hard price for running, and I understood now that even my friendship with Miss Mary would not be enough to spare them.

★ 32 ★
MARY

Two years had passed, and I was still struggling to come to terms with the fact that I had at least one mulatto half sister living on the property, when Robert strode into the parlor one morning, his face taut. I was not certain I could absorb any more distressing news, or go on pretending everything was well. I hadn't told anyone what I had discovered about Maria and my father.

I set down my pen. "Has something happened?"

"I have received word that the Norrises and George Parks have been apprehended in Maryland. Apparently they have been jailed there for several days."

"Given their ingratitude and bad conduct, perhaps you ought to let them remain there."

"I would leave them there if I could, but we can't afford to pay the jailer to keep them."

I set aside the stack of Papa's letters to General Washington that I had been reading. "Give them their freedom, then. Let them find out for themselves how difficult it will be for them to make their own way in the world."

"And what would that do, except to encourage others to run away?" Robert stood looking out the window, his hands clasped behind his back. I could feel the tension building in him. "No. There must be consequences. They must be brought back and held accountable."

He was a military officer and unaccustomed to insurrection. I feared for those unfortunates, even if by choosing to run they had sealed their own fate. "You intend to make an example of them."

He sighed. "It grieves me to think of it. Why is it that they cannot see that hard work and cooperation will bring about their freedom much sooner than fomenting this constant trouble?"

"We have the legal right to keep them, but thanks to the abolitionists we have lost our moral authority over them." A sharp pain ripped through my hands, and I dropped my pen onto the desk. "In their minds they are already free. We may control their bodies, but not their spirits."

"Moral authority or no, they still must be taught a lesson. I cannot see any other way to restore order."

"Give them some extra work, then. Hire them

out to someone farther away. But spare them from the lash. For my sake."

"I seem to remember that you have complained often of their conduct of late."

"Yes, but I see no point in whipping them other than to make the others resentful and less likely to follow your orders. Mercy ought to temper justice, even in this case. Especially in this case."

"I am not unaware that we are speaking of Selina's family, and that you two have formed an uncommon bond. But—"

"I must depend upon her, Robert. Especially when you are away. And think of Leonard and Sally Norris. How it will hurt them to see their children punished."

He went to the door. "I find the necessity of disciplining the Norrises highly distasteful. I would spare you this unhappiness if I could. But I must do what is necessary to maintain order. This is the only way to preserve Arlington for you and the children."

His mind was made up.

I kept busy with my writing. I had chosen Benson Lossing, a family friend, to serve as coeditor of my father's *Recollections*. As Robert awaited the return of the runaways from Maryland, I buried myself in letters to Mr. Lossing regarding publication of the book. But even the tasks of choosing a publisher, comparing royalty rates, and assembling the photographs Mr. Lossing requested did little to keep the shame and dread at bay.

The day the Norrises came home, I heard the commotion in the quarters and the sound of horses' hooves in the yard. Selina had arrived early as usual to help me get dressed and to tidy my room. She went about her tasks with her usual efficiency, but in complete silence. I had no words, either, for the sorrow that weighed heavily on our hearts. Though we never discussed it, we both knew that some part of our friendship would be irretrievably lost, left out on the whipping post that had gone unused in my father's lifetime, but which I saw now had stood for years as a silent warning, a call to obedience that I mistook for loyalty.

I couldn't bear the look of anguish and accusation on Selina's face. The smell of the food George sent from the kitchen made my stomach churn. I had Selina prepare my headache bag, and then I sent her home for the day. I closed the windows to mute the anguished cries coming from the yard and drew the curtains against the light.

I must have slept, for it was nearly dark when Robert came into the room and dropped into the chair beside my bed.

"Is it over?" I sat up, propping a pillow behind my shoulders.

"It is. The overseer refused to follow my orders. I had to send for the constable to carry them out."

"Oh, Robert. Are Wesley and his sister—" Imagining their terrible punishment, I could not finish my thought.

"They have been punished, but not beyond the bounds of human endurance. They will recover with no lasting effects. And Parks as well."

"You know what the newspapers will say if they get wind of this. They will accuse you of mistreating Papa's slaves."

"Undoubtedly." He sighed. "The law provides for the disciplining of servants. I did not enjoy it, but it had to be done."

"What happens now?"

"I have arranged to have them transported to the Hanover County courthouse until they can be hired out to work again. The railroads are looking for good men. I expect Parks and Wesley will find work there. An agent in Richmond will see that Mary Norris is suitably employed."

He dropped his head into his hands. "That we might soon be rid of this entire situation is my most fervent prayer."

As worried as I was for Selina's family, and for her own grief, I could see what this day had cost my husband. Robert was unabashedly sentimental when it came to his own family and unable to look with indifference upon the suffering of others. The ideals that had guided him all his life—fairness, discipline, and a responsibility to his family and to his servants—were crumbling before our eyes as our servants, aided and abetted by the roving abolitionists, reached toward freedom.

"Have you had any supper?"

Robert shook his head. "I am sick to my soul. How about you? Have you been abed all day?"

"Just about. I sent Selina home this morning. I can't eat either."

"God help us, Mary. Perhaps we ought to pray."

Days later, just as I had feared, the New York *Tribune* published a sensationalized account of Robert's punishment of the runaways, accusing him of the worst sort of mistreatment of "the Custis slaves." I thought Robert surely would refute such vile reportage, as he had refuted the erroneous *Daily Times* story regarding my father's will, but this time, weary and heartsick, he said nothing.

The events of that tumultuous spring faded as summer waxed and waned. October arrived with its glorious days of golden sunlight and bright autumnal color, and I spent more time out of doors. On mild days when my rheumatism permitted a short walk, Selina and I strolled in the garden talking of our children, my forthcoming book, the new kittens that had been born in the stables. I had long since given her free access to my library, and occasionally we discussed the poems of Mr. Bryant, who had become a favorite of hers.

By unspoken agreement we never mentioned Wesley and Mary.

Thornton's birthday was coming up, and one morning in mid-October Selina asked if she might have the ingredients for the special eggnog we served at Christmastime.

"I got the eggs and the cream," she said, offering her arm to steady me as we walked among the mock orange trees. "But I need some of the brandy and rum Mr. Custis favored."

"Remind me when you need it, and I will see to it. We haven't much use for spirits these days." I stopped to remove a few dead blossoms from Mother's Bon Silene roses. In the six years since her death it seemed they had grown ever more luxuriant. "I am surprised that Thornton Gray allows brandy and rum into his good Baptist household."

"He says we are half Methodist with some Episcopalian sprinkled in, and there is no harm in a glass of eggnog for special occasions. Even for the children." She plucked a bright purple aster and handed it to me. "Reckon you must miss your own children, especially the older ones grown and gone. By my account, even Miss Mildred is thirteen now."

"Yes. The baby of my family isn't a baby any longer. As she is very quick to remind me."

Selina chuckled. "Annice and Emma are just the same. They don't have any idea of the tribulations waiting for them on the other side of childhood."

"If they did they would not be in such a hurry."

315

"That's the truth. Reckon all we mothers can do is pray for them."

"Oh, I do. All the time. It brings me a measure of happiness to remember them to God. Although I sometimes think—"

"Somebody's coming." Selina shaded her eyes as a horse and rider appeared. We started back to the house.

A uniformed rider thundered past, headed for the fields where Robert was overseeing the harvesting of the late-season rye.

Selina frowned. "Who was that?"

"I think it's Lieutenant Stuart. I wonder where he's going in such a hurry."

My question was answered almost immediately. Robert returned from the field and, without stopping to change into his uniform, summoned Daniel and the carriage. Selina and I reached the door just as Daniel drew up in the yard. Lieutenant Stuart saluted me as he rode past in a cloud of dust.

"Summons from the War Department," Robert said, brushing the bits of rye from his trousers. "President Buchanan has sent for me."

"The situation must be dire if you are not taking time to change your clothes."

"Yes. A report of an insurrection."

"Where?"

Robert opened the carriage door and climbed inside. "Harper's Ferry."

316

SELINA

One of the cats found his way into the office where Colonel Lee kept his papers and ledgers and such, and tipped over a whole bottle of ink onto the floor. It took a great deal of scrubbing with acid and hot water to remove it, and by the time that was done, Miss Mary was calling for me. I found her sitting by the window in her rolling chair, staring at the winter-brown garden.

"What can I do for you, Miss Mary?"

She shrugged.

"Must be some reason you rang that bell." I bent down to look into her tired brown eyes. "Unless it was the cat that rang it."

A ghost of a smile crossed her face then.

"Seems like the mullygrubs got ahold of you today." I took her hands. They were stiff and cold and thin as bird's bones.

"I shouldn't be so gloomy. But I feel very much alone with my children away. Even Markie has made herself scarce of late. But I suppose there is nothing to do but keep busy."

I dragged a chair over beside hers and sat down. "Seems to me like there is plenty for you to do. They may not know it yet, but your girls need those letters you write most every day."

"Mary Custis is almost thirty years old and a law unto herself. I have no influence with her now. Not that I ever did."

"She always was a headstrong girl, that's true. But you did your best for her."

"I suppose. My other girls don't behave as I would wish them to either." She smiled. "Now I know how my mother felt, despairing of my ever finding a husband. I want to see my own daughters settled and happy with families of their own, but it will take very special men to tame their ways."

"Huh. From what Miss Agnes says, Mister Orton Williams has taken a liking to her. I won't be surprised if they get married one day."

"Perhaps. They have corresponded since childhood. Agnes thinks very highly of him. Orton is a good boy. Colonel Lee likes him."

"Well, there you are then. One daughter down and three to go. The other girls will find themselves suitable husbands by and by."

"I hope so. But Mildred is only thirteen, and already such a tempestuous girl. I pray God will change her heart before Satan takes possession of it."

It was all I could do not to bust out laughing. "You were a wild one yourself when you were Miss Mildred's age. Leastways that's what Eleanor always said. She said you used to do just as you pleased and say whatever came into your head, no matter what anybody thought."

"Yes, and it was that very behavior that scared my mother into thinking no one would have me. I suppose I still do as I choose."

"Yes, you do. And yet here you are. Satan hasn't got ahold of you yet."

Miss Mary went on like she had not heard a word I said to her. She had a great deal on her mind that day.

"Rooney will not apply himself to his studies. And Robbie is so undecided about his future that I despair of him too." She let out a gusty sigh. "I have been too indulgent to the faults of my children, Selina, and for that I have been punished."

I wasn't about to get into a conversation about who got punished and for what. "What about that man who's helping you with your book? Didn't you tell me he asked you for some pictures?"

"Mr. Lossing. Yes, he wants more pictures of the Washingtons and of Arlington. He has recommended Derby and Jackson to publish it, instead of Mr. Lippincott, but I have yet to make an answer."

"Well then?" I could feel impatience building up inside me. White people always thought their problems were so much worse than anybody else's. It was true she was often in pain and worried about her children. And Mister Custis had left a

319

mountain of debts behind. But Miss Mary was still one of the richest women in Virginia. She had a fine house filled with books and carpets and paintings and enough linens and silver to run a hotel.

Try living in a one-room cabin with a man and six whiny, sick children, and then talk to me about who deserved to get the mullygrubs.

"I ought to finish going through the papers my father left," she said finally. "And make up my mind about a publisher. And I should reply to the *African Repository*. They want permission to print the letter I received from Rosabella Burke last year."

"Daniel told me you got a letter from William."

"Rosabella wrote as well. She and William have added several more children to their family, but Rosabella reports she is in excellent health. William is busy with his preaching and traveling to other churches."

"He always wanted to be a preacher."

Miss Mary stifled a yawn. "I don't know what's the matter with me. I have so little energy these days. The years are catching up to me, I suppose."

"George boiled up some beef last night. I'll make you some beef tea. Unless you want one of Judah's remedies."

"What does Judah recommend for an affliction such as mine?"

"Pokeberries soaked in brandy. A wineglass full, three times a day." I got to my feet. "If you try that remedy you might want to keep a chamber pot close by."

She laughed and motioned for me to roll her chair from the window over to the table where her papers and pens and boxes of Mister Custis's things were set out.

I fixed some beef tea and brought her some bread and fastened the curtain back from the window to let the light in. "Daniel just got back from town with the colonel. I expect Mister Robert will be in to see you in a little while. That ought to cheer you up."

But she was already busy with her work, her nose buried in a dusty book.

I went out the back door and crossed the yard. Since Colonel Lee had hired away most everybody, Arlington was strangely quiet. Until I got to my cabin. Mauma was there like always. Judah and Kitty were there too, and several of the Binghams, and my daddy and the few men the colonel had kept on the place to put the crops by. Thornton had been sent down to White House to do the same there.

A stranger was standing in my cabin with a bright fire in his eyes. In the quarters there'd been talk of a white man going among the Virginia slaves stirring up a furor. I figured this must be him.

"Selina," Mauma said. "This man got news from that abolitionist Mister Robert captured at Harper's Ferry last month."

"That's right." The man took off his hat. Above the tanned part of his face, his forehead was pale as the moon. He turned ice-blue eyes on me. "You might ought to send your children out to play while we discuss this."

Two of my babies were sleeping on a pallet next to the stove. I shooed the older ones into the yard.

"You people might have heard of John Brown," the man said. "He's been stirring up trouble in Kansas for quite a while."

"We don't need any trouble here," I said. "We've got as much as we can handle already."

"John Brown come to Harper's Ferry to call attention to the plight of you slaves here in Virginia. And the master of this very house is the one who took his artillery and a company of marines to storm the engine room where John Brown and his followers were holed up. Mister Brown was seriously wounded."

"We already heard about that." Judah puffed on her corncob pipe, and the smell of tobacco filled the room. "Tell us somethin' we don't know."

"Mister Brown was taken to court, where he was convicted of murder, treason, and insurrection. They hanged him yesterday."

"That don't surprise us none." My daddy knocked his own pipe against the bottom of his shoe. "But why tell us about it now? Nothing we can do."

"There is plenty you can do. Among John Brown's

effects the authorities found maps, papers, and plans for even bigger insurrections. But those plans depend on the bravery of people like you who will stand up and throw off the yoke of oppression. Demand your freedom." He pointed to Judah. "Look at you. Thin as a rake and dressed in rags. Wouldn't you like to be free?"

She frowned. "And do what? Go where? I'm nearly eighty years old."

That stopped him in his tracks for a minute. But then he said, "You can't expect folks like John Brown to fight for you if you are not willing to fight for yourselves. To die if necessary. To mingle your blood with that of John Brown and the millions of slaves who have died at the hands of their masters. Anarchy and revolution! That's what it will take to dispel the poisonous miasma of bondage and assure you of the right to live as free men and women. My friends and I stand ready to help anyone who chooses to leave Arlington. We can go tonight."

Perry Parks stood up. "I'm gone with you."

"Me too." Daniel's son stood up. "I ain't afraid. Not one bit."

"Then you be a crazy fool," Judah told him.

The man said, "Be ready as soon as it's dark. Wait in the woods behind the chapel. Someone will come for you."

Then a shadow filled the doorway, and there stood Mister Williams, the county constable who

323

had whipped Wesley and Mary for running away.

"What's going on here?" He stared at the stranger. "Who are you?"

"A champion of the oppressed."

"You are trespassing on Custis property. Go on now. Don't let me catch you here again."

The man jammed his hat onto his head and squeezed past Mister Williams. "You can't stop the tide once it's started to rise, Constable."

The abolitionist faded back into the woods quiet as a ghost. Mister Williams looked around the cabin. "You people best forget everything that man told you. You mind the colonel and do your best, and you will get your freedom by and by."

"By and by," Perry muttered. "Huh. Words don't cook rice."

Mister Williams whipped his head in our direction. "What did you say, boy?"

"I said you're right and I'm going to act nice."

"That's the spirit. Now, all of you get on back to work."

★ 34 ★
MARY

1860

Waking just after dawn, I eased from my bed to light the fire Selina had laid for me the previous evening. The kindling caught and flared, chasing the November chill from the room. I opened the curtains to the wide expanses of the sky and the river.

Loneliness cast a special luster on the dying leaves of autumn, and I felt suspended—small and alone—between those two great infinities. In this world we have only each other to guard against the cold universe. Except for Markie and the few servants still rattling about Arlington, I had no one. Robert was in Texas with the army, and my children were scattered like dandelion seeds just at the time when we might have given comfort to one another.

Lately the talk around Washington City was of nothing but the coming election and the probability that Lincoln would be elected president. The newspapers were full of reports from South Carolina, where the leaders seemed intent upon secession. It was a foolish notion, and I said so in my letters to Texas. My husband agreed. He wrote hurriedly from San Antonio.

Disunion will mean anarchy. Secession is nothing but revolution. The aggression of the North and the selfish and dictatorial bearing of the South are equally egregious. I cannot anticipate so great a calamity to the nation as the dissolution of the Union.

"Mary?"

Markie had come up the stairs and was standing in the doorway, her dark eyes bright with anticipation. She waved a brown-paper-wrapped package in my direction. "Guess what I have here?"

"I can't guess. I haven't had any breakfast yet."

She laughed. "It isn't hard."

"Is that my book?"

"Yes!" She crossed the room and bent to kiss my cheek. "It's the *Recollections*. Published at last, and I, for one, am so proud of you."

I tore off the paper and ran my fingers over the cover. Seeing my father's name alongside my own brought a wave of emotion—pride, regret, and a deep longing for days that could be no more. "Where did you get it?"

"The bookstore in Washington City. I wanted to give it to you when I arrived last night, but there wasn't time. I do hope Derby and Jackson haven't already sent you one."

"They should have. But correspondence from Mr. Derby has been sparse of late."

Markie flopped onto the chair beside my bed. "He probably forgot. All this talk of Lincoln and secession has everyone preoccupied. I can't imagine the union will be dissolved, though."

"Neither can Robert." I crossed the room and handed her his letter, which had come in yesterday's mail.

She read the letter. "Oh, he seems so distressed. Perhaps I should write to him."

"If you like. He enjoys your letters."

"I shall write to him tonight to enclose with yours. For now I want to speak with George."

"I am sure he can find something for us to eat."

"I want to ask him to make something special for dinner tonight. To celebrate the fact that we have another author in the family." Markie grinned. "Uncle Wash would be so proud of you."

That evening we dined by candlelight on boiled ham made from my great-grandmother Washington's recipe, gravy and potatoes, and a dried apple tart with sweet cream. Every bite was delicious, but the many empty chairs around the table brought a lump to my throat. I couldn't help feeling guilty, knowing that Robert was making do with much plainer fare.

Markie was still at Arlington a few days later when a letter arrived from White House.

Dearest Mama, Rooney wrote in his looping hand.

We have a son, healthy and strong, and Charlotte is well. We have much to be thankful for, but I do regret that Papa is so far away and it will no doubt be some time before he can greet his first grandchild and namesake. Yes, we have named our baby Robert Edward Lee in hopes he will grow into as fine a man as his grandpa. Charlotte asks that you visit as soon as the weather warms, as she is most eager to show off her handiwork. The Arlington servants engaged here are well and ask to be remembered to Papa when next you write to him.

In his last letter to me, Papa addressed me as "Fitzhugh." He thinks that I ought to give up my nickname now that I am a married man and a father. To please him I shall make the effort, but I suppose I shall always think of myself as plain old Rooney.

With love and kisses
to all at Arlington,
Your devoted son,
Fitzhugh Lee

I passed the letter to Markie. "Oh my. So our Rooney is Fitzhugh now? It sounds much too serious for him. But I suppose it seems more dignified."

She picked up the *Daily Times* and we fell silent, absorbed in our reading. I had hoped for a letter from Robert, but the secession movement was gaining support in Texas and he was preoccupied with concerns for his men. Their constant worries about their futures as soldiers, and as husbands and fathers, had led to several resignations and to a deep despair that even a man of my husband's talents found hard to overcome. Everyone was taking sides. The country my great-grandfather had fought to establish was being torn asunder by conflicting passions. I could see nothing ahead but disaster.

Markie sipped her coffee. "You seem preoccupied this morning, Mary. And not just about the next election. Something else is bothering you, I can tell."

Publication of Papa's book had stirred unpleasant thoughts of him and his other daughter. The secret lay like a stone in my heart. Before I could decide whether to tell Markie about my mulatto half sister, Selina came in to scrub the floors, Ephraim arrived to ask about pruning the roses, and George informed me that we were out of lard and flour. The next day Markie left on an extended visit to our kin in Kent County, and the moment in which I might have unburdened myself to my cousin was lost.

Lincoln won the election, and by the time Robert came home from Texas the following spring, I had much more serious things to occupy my mind. South Carolina had made good on the threat of secession, and other states quickly followed. In early April the newspapers reported accounts of the firing upon Union troops attempting to supply Fort Sumter, just off Charleston. Their actions seemed to embolden the men of Virginia, who voted to join the Confederates.

Each day brought us closer to disaster. Robert refused President Lincoln's offer to lead the Union forces and huddled with his brother Smith and his old friend General Scott, debating whether to resign his commission in the United States Army.

"What shall I do?" he asked one evening a few days later. The girls had gone off to bed and we were alone in the parlor, where a small fire blazed against the April chill. "General Scott advises that if I am to resign I should do so at once. And he's right. I cannot retain the respect of my fellow officers when my loyalties are so divided."

Plainly, this was the greatest struggle of his life, and there was so little I could offer him. "Both parties are in the wrong, but somehow the Union must be preserved. I can't pray that God will prosper the right, because I see no right in this matter. But I know you, my dearest husband. Whichever way you go will be the path of duty. You will think it right, and so I shall be satisfied."

"Thank you, Mary." He got to his feet. "I should like some time alone."

He went into his office and closed the door.

The stairs creaked, and our daughters came into the parlor.

"We are too upset to sleep," Agnes said. "Is Papa all right?"

Charles came in to clear the dining room and light the lamps.

"Colonel Lee sure looked worried tonight," he said, shaking his head. "Hardly touched his dinner. You need anything else, Mrs. Lee?"

"Nothing. Thank you, Charles."

"Yessum. Reckon I ought to go on home then."

The door closed behind him. The girls and I sat in gloomy silence. Agnes pressed a handkerchief to her eyes. "Oh, Mother, Arlington feels just as bereft as it did when Grandmama died. So cold and sad. How can Papa possibly decide to leave the army? It has been to him home and country for my entire life."

"I think it's stupid to even think that the country can be split in two," Mildred said. "Papa ought to stand with the Union."

"And let Lincoln's troops overrun Virginia and tell us how to manage our own affairs?" Mary Custis slammed her book closed and glared at her sister. "You are naive to think he wishes anything less than the total destruction of the South. Secession is the only way to prevent it."

The clock chimed midnight, and Robert's door remained closed.

"I'm tired of this death watch," Agnes said. "I'm going to bed, Mama."

When morning came I found Robert sitting in the parlor, staring out the window, weary but utterly calm. Two letters lay on the table beside the chair.

"Mary. Where are the girls?" His voice was in tatters, his cheeks so hollow and shadowed I was afraid he had fallen ill.

"Getting dressed. George should be up with breakfast soon."

Moments later the girls joined us in the parlor. Charles bustled in to set the table. Selina arrived to begin her chores but quickly withdrew when she saw us there, rumpled, bleary-eyed, and anxious.

Robert stood. "I suppose you will all think I have done very wrong."

He handed me the letters. The first was but a single sentence addressed to the Secretary of War.

Sir: I have the honor to tender the resignation of my commission as Colonel of the 1st Regt of Cavalry.

The other, to General Scott, explained his struggle to separate himself from his profession of thirty years and thanked his old mentor for his kindness.

Your name and fame will always be dear to me. Save in defense of my native State, I never desire again to draw my sword.

My hands shook as I handed them back to him. I was terrified for him. For all of us. "Are you certain, Robert?"

He nodded.

"Then so am I."

He summoned Billy to deliver the letters to the War Department, and thus our fate was sealed.

April 26, 1861
Richmond

My dear Mary,

I am very anxious about you. You have to move and make arrangements to go to some point of safety, which you must select. The Mt. Vernon plate and pictures ought to be secured. Keep quiet while you remain and in your preparations. War is inevitable, and there is no telling when it may burst around you.

"Mother?" Agnes joined me in the parlor. "You are pale as milk. What is it?"

I handed her the letter. "Your papa thinks we may be invaded."

Only three weeks earlier, Robert, newly appointed to lead the Confederates in Virginia, kissed us in farewell and rode away from Arlington. Now he was preparing for the worst while I still prayed for some miracle to save us all from the coming carnage.

Agnes frowned. "What should we do?"

"Pack up the Washington treasures, as he directs. But I'm not certain we need to leave just yet."

"I read in the paper last week that some in the South are burying their treasures in their back-yards," Agnes said.

I had stopped reading the papers, especially those from the North, for they were full of hatred for my husband.

If Mr. Custis could have lived until now, he would have good cause to be bowed down in grief and sorrow to behold his son-in-law following in the steps of Benedict Arnold.

I promptly penned a succinct reply to the Washington paper.

I cannot conceive why Lincoln has assembled such an army if it is not his intention to attempt to crush the South. I have but one great consolation now, that my dear parents are both laid low in their graves, where but for my children I would most gladly lie beside them.

"So will we bury the silver, Mother? The paintings and the plates? And where shall we go?"

"Hush, child. Let me think."

"We could go to Ravensworth. Aunt Maria will

take us in." Agnes indicated the letter. "Papa says we must decide on our own where to go."

I called for Selina. Together we filled two crates with our silver, our papers, and those of President Washington. Those I sent by rail to Robert for safekeeping. My books and engravings were locked into storage. Draperies and carpets, the Washington china, and the punch bowl that had been used at my wedding were hidden in the cellar. My girls and I worked feverishly by day and lay down at night in rooms stripped bare save for our beds. I slept fitfully, knowing that sooner or later I must flee. Dreading the moment when I must take my daughters and make for safety on my own.

A few days later I was outside, enjoying a rare moment of quiet among my flowers. The May morning had dawned warm and fair. The first roses of the season had come into bloom, and the air around me was thick with their sweet fragrance.

Markie's brother, Orton Williams, rode into the yard and began speaking even before he dismounted.

"Mary, the Union army is camped just across the river." His face was tight with worry. "General McDowell intends to use Arlington as a base for protecting the capital. You are going to have to get out. Today, if you can manage it."

"But that's impossible."

"The servants and Mister McQuinn can help

you. Just take the most valuable things. I'd stay to help you if I could, but I'm needed elsewhere." He looked toward the house. "Is Agnes here?"

"In the study, packing up her grandfather's globe."

Just then Agnes appeared on the porch. Orton strode across the yard and spoke with her most earnestly, though I couldn't hear what he said. He retraced his steps and planted a swift kiss on my cheek. "Markie sends her love and says to tell you she will catch up with you as soon as she can. Take care of yourself, Cousin. And pray this war is over swiftly."

Orton swung up and rode away. I summoned the overseer and gave him instructions for looking after the grounds. I set Daniel and his son to packing up our trunks, some paintings, and our housekeeping items. Daughter and Agnes went back and forth from the house to the wagons, loading their belongings. I was too busy and too frightened for emotion until Selina appeared with a bundle of clean linens.

"Here you are, Miss Mary. These are the ones scented with the lavender you are partial to."

My heart was so heavy and my nerves so frayed that my reserve crumbled.

Selina frowned. "Now, you listen to me. You are just as well to dry those tears. We all got to be strong until this is over. Nothing we can do to change it, so we have to get through it best we can."

"I know it. I wish you could come with me. But Robert says the army will start taking servants as contraband."

"I can't risk it. Besides, who would look after my children?"

Mr. McQuinn, the overseer, arrived to help Daniel and Ephraim load the piano. When that was done he brushed his hands together and looked around. "That's just about got it, I reckon, Mrs. Lee. Except for that walnut cupboard in the north hallway. If you want to take it, I can make room for it somehow."

"Missus?" Daniel looked worried. "If we don't get going soon we gone be half the night getting to Ravensworth, and you told me yourself what your cousin said about the soldiers camping all around these parts."

"He's right, Mama," Agnes said. "We ought to get started." Her eyes filled. "I miss Papa so much. And I sincerely hate leaving my home."

"It can't be helped, child. Go get your cat, unless you intend to leave him behind."

She ran into the house. I turned to Selina. "I want you to have the cupboard."

"I can't take your cupboard, Miss Mary. I used to leave Mr. Robert's buttermilk in there most every night."

"Well, he won't have time for buttermilk until this war is over, and heaven alone knows when that will be. You may as well take it. And the blue-

and-white pitcher we keep there too. I know you have always admired it."

Selina stood there with her hands on her hips, her eyes welling up.

My own eyes burned. For thirty years Selina had been my comfort; at times she had been my conscience. I wanted to do something to help her. Something to keep her safe. But there was little I could do.

On impulse I took the last of the money I had with me from my travel bag and pressed the bills into her hand. "This isn't much, but it might save the day if you can't get the produce to market this fall."

"I can't take your last dollar. You've got to eat too. You and the girls."

"I'm related to half the population of Virginia. They won't let me starve."

Agnes returned with her tom snuggled securely in the crook of her arm. "I'm ready, Mama."

Selina shoved the bills into her pocket. "All right then. You planning to stand there till sundown, or you going to give me the keys?"

"What?"

"Well, somebody's got to look after Arlington till you get back."

Without another word I handed Selina the keys. Daniel helped me into the carriage. The reins snapped and the wheels turned, taking me into exile.

SELINA

Before Miss Mary's flowers had even finished blooming, the Yankee soldiers arrived. Dozens of blue-coated men on horseback and in wagons loaded with guns and tools and I don't know what all poured over the bridge and up the road to the house. White tents sprang up all over the grounds. The men chopped down trees for their cooking fires. They dug trenches and practiced marching, their orders shouted through a thick, gray cloud of woodsmoke hanging in the air.

Mister McQuinn kept his cold eye on the few of us still living in the quarters. In the long shadow of evening he would come up to the yard to drink with the officers on duty. Some nights I could hear them laughing, and I wondered if they weren't on the same side, even though the overseer was collecting his money from Colonel Lee.

Lawrence came back from southern Virginia with reports that the Yankees were building as many forts as fast as they could. Every day they dug trenches somewhere around Washington City, and Lawrence said those trenches were full of guns and ammunition. Day and night I worried about my children. The war was supposed to be about freedom, but moving around in Arlington's empty rooms, I sometimes felt like my dreams were further away than when I was a child learning my letters at Miss Mary's knee.

Miss Markie showed up to get the things she kept there when she was in residence, and it was a pitiful sight, seeing her so full of grief for the old house. She locked herself inside the room and cried until she was out of tears. Then she asked me to come in and help her pack her trunks. While I was in there folding petticoats and shawls and whatnot, one of Miss Mildred's tomcats slipped into the room. Miss Markie scooped him up and cried some more.

I handed her my own handkerchief to wipe her eyes.

Finally she said, "Oh, Selina, this poor old house looks so desolate. Isn't it strange, how quickly everything has changed?" She set the cat on his feet and picked up her hatbox. "Last year we were all so happy here, so peaceful. Who in their wildest dreams could have conjured this present state of affairs?"

Miss Mary had sent Daniel with the carriage to take Miss Markie home, and he came in to tote her trunks outside. "You 'bout ready, Miss Markie?"

She blew her nose and looked around the room like she was trying to memorize it. "As ready as I can be, I suppose."

I went into the yard with her. My mother and old Judah, plus Young Daniel and Ephraim, crowded around Miss Markie, grabbing her hands, telling her good-bye and good luck and remember us kindly to Miss Mary and the girls. I handed her a letter for Miss Mary and watched the carriage roll down the hill and out of sight.

The next week when Daniel came back to fetch more of Miss Mary's things, he brought me a letter. I walked past the soldiers' tents and stacks of firewood they had made from Miss Mary's trees and sat on the lawn where I could see the river.

July 7, 1861
Kinloch

Dear Selina,

Your letter brought a ray of sunlight into this present darkness. I am greatly cheered to know that my gardens still survive despite the occupation of the Yankees. Please remind Ephraim that the lilac bushes nearest the rose garden must be pruned, and tell him not to forget to tend to my mock orange trees.

Precious Life has returned here from school and her lively presence is a balm to my empty days. The Genl writes as often as his schedule allows, but of course no letter can substitute for his kind and loving presence. My Turner cousins remember you well from our visit here when my children were small and have asked about you most sincerely. I have told them of your taking over as keeper of the keys and how that fact brings some measure of peace to my fevered mind.

I expect things to get worse before they get better. Just last week Aunt Maria wrote that a neighbor was accosted on the road and threatened by a band of perfectly lawless troops from New Jersey. Every day there are rumors of marches and countermarches, and in this atmosphere I cannot help feeling that some crisis is approaching.

> That God may protect us and
> bring a swift end to this late
> unpleasantness is the constant
> prayer of your devoted friend,
> MC Lee

Three weeks later we got word that Confederates beat the Yankees in a fight in Manassas. Lawrence said surely the war was over, but no. It went on.

When Christmas came I went into the woods and cut some mistletoe and greenery for my cabin. My daddy made some corncob toys for my children. But it was nothing like in the olden times when everyone dressed up in their best clothes and went up to the house to call for Christmas gifts. I wasn't sure whether Thornton was still at White House or if he'd been hired out to the railroad. I didn't know where Miss Mary was either. There had been one letter after the news from Manassas that said she was moving some-place farther from the fighting. I hadn't heard a word since.

The next spring more soldiers showed up at Arlington. They cut more of the old trees that had sheltered my children; they helped themselves to the contents of the smokehouse and cleaned out the wine cellar. I could understand that. Even Northerners had to eat. But then one day I was up at the house polishing the staircase banisters and sweeping cobwebs from the windows when a bunch of rowdies crashed through the door and started helping themselves to the things Miss Mary had left in the parlor.

I went in there with the broom in my hand. "What do you think you're doing in here?"

One of the soldiers, a redheaded man with a face that looked like he lost a fight with an ice pick, grinned and said, "Spoils of war."

"That's right," said another one. "Nothing you can do about it, neither." He picked up a little wooden side table. "This is real nice. My wife will enjoy it."

I pointed my broom at him. "Don't you touch Miss Mary's things!"

"Aw, don't worry about it. She's so rich she won't hardly miss them."

Another soldier came in carrying one of Missus Washington's engravings that Miss Mary had locked in a closet in the rear hallway. "Hey, fellas, lookee what I found. I bet this is worth something."

I left them and went into the yard, where more Yankees were swarming like ants. I stopped the first one I saw, a tall, pale-faced man who stank of sweat and whiskey. "Where is General McDowell?"

He frowned at me. "Who wants to know?"

"I do."

"Is that so? What's your name, girl?"

He looked at me like I was another piece of furniture, one more possession belonging to Arlington, and I thought about Missus counting our heads after a trip to the market, to make sure we all came back. I thought about standing with her in the china closet writing down what all was broken or missing, and how even Miss Mary thought of me as one more thing that belonged to her. Something broke inside me. I was done with being owned.

I stared at his hard, pale eyes. "I am Missus Gray."

"Mrs. Gray, eh? Well, the general was headed to his tent the last time I saw him."

I crossed the yard, stepping around the puddles left from the night's rain, and found the general sitting behind a little desk in his tent, the flaps tied back to let in the river breeze. He was barrel-chested and in a blue uniform with a double row of brass buttons that shone in the morning light. His dark hair was trimmed and parted. His mustache and goatee were tidy. General McDowell would have been an appealing man if it hadn't been for the bad manners he allowed his soldiers.

When I stepped to the door, still holding my broom, he set down his pen and leaned back in his chair. "Yes, what is it?"

"General McDowell, your men are stealing from this house."

He frowned. "And you are?"

"Mrs. Gray. I didn't say a word when they helped themselves to our food, but now they are breaking into locked closets, taking things that once belonged to President Washington."

He shrugged. "If that's true, it's—"

"It is true. I just watched them with my own eyes."

"All right. I'll speak to the captain and—"

"You think they will listen to him? You ought to take care of this your own self. Because the war will end someday. If I was you I would not want to be the one responsible for the loss of President Washington's belongings."

He pushed back from his desk and reached for his hat.

I leaned on my broom and watched him walk up the front porch steps and into the house.

A little while later a wagon pulled up and a couple of soldiers started loading things onto it. General McDowell came over and said, "You may not believe me, but I have the most sincere sympathy for your mistress's distress."

I didn't say anything. Just gave him a hard look. Because I didn't see any trace of sympathy in him.

"As far as it is compatible with my duty, I shall always be ready to do whatever may alleviate it." He waved his hand toward the wagon. "To that end I have decided to remove Mrs. Lee's things to the Patent Office. They will be safe there until the war is over."

"All right then. Reckon I ought to go feed my children. If there is any food left."

"We won't starve you out. You have my word on that." He tipped his hat. "And now you must excuse me, Mrs. Gray."

I started back to my cabin. My knees had gone weak with the sudden realization of what I had done. A slave telling off a general of the United States Army. But I had to do it. Even though I wanted to leave Arlington for a home of my own, I still felt tied to that old place, with its years and years of memories.

My heart was heavy for the loss of things the soldiers had taken that would never be returned. But my feet were so light it seemed like I was floating. The shame and despair of being human chattel had gone from me, rising up like incense to the sky because the Yankee general had seen me as a person. My own words ran round in my head like a song heard over and over. *I am Missus Gray. I am Missus Gray.*

More of the Binghams left Arlington that summer, some of them riding the soldiers' supply wagons that went back and forth across the river. Lawrence paid no attention to Mister McQuinn's orders and spent more and more time in the city, coming and going whenever he took the notion. When he came back he brought news of fighting in places like Shiloh, New Orleans, and Chattanooga.

Without the routine of keeping the house and tending the gardens and fields, time seemed to slow down, until it was hard to keep up with the days and months passing by. Before the war everyone at Arlington looked forward to Christmas, but that year it was just a regular day. I didn't care for myself, but it was hard to look into the expectant faces of my poor little children knowing there was nothing I could do to make a celebration for them.

Late on Christmas afternoon, the overseer came by with a rabbit he had shot, and we fixed it for dinner. I was glad for my children to have something besides corn pone and sweet potatoes, but one rabbit couldn't turn the day into any kind of a happy occasion. Word had come that Thornton had gone to Romancoke, and I wasn't sure when I would see him again. I didn't know where Miss Mary was either.

Two weeks later I was outside getting some wood for the fire. Snow was coming down hard enough to cover the bare patches in the yard and soften the edges of the stables and abandoned slave cabins. Darkness was gaining on a winter sky the color of a wet stone. I picked up the sticks of firewood and started back to the cabin.

Mister McQuinn appeared out of the white mist and shoved a paper into my hands. "Christmas present from General Lee."

I set down my burden and unfolded the paper.

Know all men by these presents that I, Robert Edward Lee, executor of the last will and testament of George Washington Parke Custis, deceased, acting by and under authority and direction of the said will, do hereby manumit and forever set free from slavery the following named slaves belonging to the Arlington estate.

My hands shook so hard the words wouldn't stay still on the paper. I leaned against the wood-pile to steady myself.

George Clark, Charles Syphax, Selina Gray and Thornton Gray and their six children . . .

My knees would hardly hold me up. My eyes traveled with great speed down the page.

Margaret Taylor and her four children, Lawrence Parks and his nine children . . . Julie Ann Clark and her three children. Sally Norris and Len Norris and their three children Mary, Sallie, and Wesley . . .

My parents, and my brother and sister who had run away and been flogged for it . . . they were free, thanks be to God and all the angels and General Lee.

The Binghams—their names were written down too, on this glorious piece of paper more precious than gold. I wondered where they were and if they knew they were free.

I brushed the snowflakes off the paper and kept on reading. The second page had a list of Mister Custis's slaves from his other places— White House and Romancoke—and at the bottom the general had signed his name with his seal and the date: December 29, 1862.

"It means you are no longer in bondage." The overseer flapped his hands. "You're free as a bird."

"I know it. I can read."

"You can leave here whenever you take a notion to. You and your children." He bent his head against the cold and left me alone in the snowy yard.

Forever free. I folded the letter into my pocket and stood there in the pure silver light of that winter's night while the news sank in. Maybe it was the wind and the snow that burned my eyes until everything was a wet blur. But I don't know. Maybe it was tears.

★ 36 ★
MARY

1862

"Mama." Mildred glared at me as we climbed into the carriage, her sweet young face the very picture of mutiny. "Must we move yet again?"

Mary Custis settled herself opposite me and rolled her eyes at her youngest sister. "Why, no, Mildred Childe, it isn't at all necessary. It's just that it's such great fun playing hide-and-seek with the Union army."

My head pounded and my stomach roiled. "Mary Custis, please. The situation is distressing enough without your sarcasm. Show a little compassion."

In July, the Battle of Manassas and constant rumors of troop movements near Aunt Maria's house had forced us farther north and east, to Kinloch. Union troops lined the roads, battlements sprang up amid the greening meadows, sentries guarded bridges. Danger waited around every corner. I worried constantly for my husband and children, and for Selina and her family, at the mercy of the Yankee soldiers who had overrun my home. A thousand times I wished I could have sent her to a place of safety, but no place was safe.

Cousin Elizabeth and Thomas came out to see us off.

"Be careful, Mary," Thomas said. "And keep an eye out for our Charles. Kinloch seems empty when my children are running hither and yon."

My own family was scattered to the four winds. Annie had gone to the Wickhams' at Hickory Hill with Rooney's wife, Charlotte, and my little grandson. Agnes was in Richmond staying with Mrs. Warwick, a friend of the general's. And Custis was ordered to North Carolina.

Elizabeth passed a basket through the open carriage window. "Take this, Mary. It will tide you over until you reach your aunt Eleanor's."

The carriage lurched, and we turned our eyes toward Audley, with its sad memories of Cousin Lorenzo. Once we were settled there, friends of Aunt Nelly's who lived nearby came to call, bringing news and greetings from other of my acquaintances who could not travel. I worried constantly about what was happening at Arlington. Was Selina all right? I hadn't heard from her in months. Were the Washington treasures still safe?

And most of all, what was happening with Robert? I lived for his letters. In early August a letter came, written from the town of Huntersville.

I returned here yesterday, dearest Mary, to visit this portion of the army . . . The soldiers everywhere are sick. The measles are prevalent throughout the whole army and you kno that disease leaves unpleasant results, attacks on the lungs, typhoid, etc. etc. especially in camp where the accommodation for the sick is poor. I traveled from Staunton on horse-back. A part of the road I passed over in the summer of 1840 on my return to St. Louis after bringing you home. If anyone had told me then that the next time I traveled on that road would have been on my present errand I should have supposed him insane. Give love to Daughter and Mildred. I did not see Rob as I passed through Charlottesville. He was at the University and I could not stop.

Mildred joined me on the porch and peered over my shoulder. "A letter from Papa? Is he well?"

"Yes. Worried about the measles among his men."

"I received a letter too, but it was written days ago. He says to give love to everyone here, and to tell Sue Washington that her father was sitting on a blanket sewing a strap on his haversack.

Papa said Sue ought to be there to do it." Mildred frowned. "I don't see why men can't do their own sewing. After all, we women have to do plenty of their chores while they are gone."

"And no doubt we shall be called upon to do many more before this war is finished."

She sat down beside me. "Well, I hope it's over soon. I am thoroughly tired of being a refugee."

"We ought to be grateful so many friends and relatives are willing to receive us. These are perilous times, Life."

"I know it, Mama. But last evening I overheard Mrs. Harrison saying there are terrible rumors about you and Papa. People are speculating about your separation in the papers." Mildred's young face clouded. "Mrs. Harrison says the stories are full of the most vile slander. I just want this war to end so we can go home."

I had seen those papers for myself, but I had hoped to shield an impressionable girl from such ridiculous lies. I poured out my heart to Robert, who replied with his usual calm reasoning.

As to reports you say are afloat about our separation I know nothing. Anyone that can reason must see its necessity under present circumstance. As to the slander with which you say the papers abound, why concern ourselves? They are inserted for no good intention you may be sure.

"Listen to me, Precious Life. There are those who think your father is a traitor to his country, and they cannot refrain from telling all sorts of untruths. We must not let them dampen our spirits. We know the truth, and the truth must suffice."

"Yes, Mama." Mildred threw her arms around me. "I knew it wasn't true. I am sorry they hurt you, though."

"Well, thank you for that, child." I gazed out over the yard to the road winding into hills already tinged with autumnal color. "Your papa says we ought to establish ourselves somewhere for the winter. I'm thinking of going to his mother's house."

"To Shirley? I haven't been back since Rooney and Charlotte's wedding. It might be fun to see it again. It's so lovely and peaceful there."

"You have your schooling."

"If the war is still on this fall, I shall not return to school."

"Oh, yes, you will. Your papa will be deeply disappointed if you don't finish your studies."

"But what I am studying *for?*"

"Knowledge is its own reward."

"That's what Charlotte says too." Mildred released an exaggerated sigh and fluffed her skirts. "I do miss her, and her sweet little baby. And I miss Arlington and my cats. And I miss Papa most of all. It's awful to have one's family going every which way."

"There is no prospect of returning to Arlington just now. Besides, if it's safe to travel next month I must visit the baths. Rob and Daughter have agreed to take me."

"Oh. Is your rheumatism bad again?"

It was worse than ever, but I didn't want to burden Mildred when there was nothing she could do. "Yes, but the hot springs will help. Now go fetch my knitting. I promised some socks to your father."

As winter closed in I took Agnes and Annie and moved to White House. Charlotte had returned from Hickory Hill with a few servants and my grandson, a bright sunbeam in the midst of so much misery. Mildred returned to school. Daughter left to visit friends in Kent County.

We occupied ourselves with our knitting, with reading and writing letters to my sons and the general. From Savannah the following spring Robert wrote of the blooming of that city's lush gardens, so perfectly describing the yellow jasmine, redbuds, orange trees, and azaleas that my heart broke for the unseen beauty of my own gardens. I longed for news from Arlington and for word from Selina. But I was a wanderer—a gypsy endlessly on the move. It was unreasonable to expect that her letters could find me.

If not for my grandson I should have fallen even further into despair, but little Robert was so much like my own Rooney at that age that I couldn't help laughing at his antics. Charlotte, however, was often tearful and driven to distraction. She was a pretty little mouse of a girl with chestnut hair and fair skin, and accustomed to getting her own way. War had brought out her inner strength, but her constant worries for Rooney's safety stole her energies.

One evening when she seemed particularly done in, I sent for tea and settled her amid the cushions on the parlor sofa. "I am worried about you, Chass. Perhaps you ought to return to Hickory Hill where there are more people to look after you. I can keep the baby with me if it will help."

"I couldn't ask you to do that, Mother. Not when your rheumatism is so severe."

"It is a hindrance, but Lu and Peggy and my girls are here to do the things I can't do. Surely the five of us can contain one small child."

"Perhaps. But I could never part from my little boy, even for a day. He is all I have of Rooney for the moment. Besides, there is a good reason for my malaise." She rested her hand on her middle. "I'm with child again."

"Are you? Does Rooney know?"

"I haven't told him yet. He would only fret, and the baby isn't due till fall." She drank her tea. "Don't tell the general yet either. He sees Rooney all the time and he might let the cat out of the bag. I want to be the one to tell Rooney, when the time is right."

"I shall be quiet as the tomb."

"Don't talk about tombs. Not now. It's bad luck." Charlotte refilled her cup.

From upstairs came the sound of the baby's laughter and the pounding of feet along the hallway.

"I'm so glad to have Annie and Agnes with us," Charlotte said. "Especially Annie. She is so cheerful and full of fun despite her blind eye. I only wish Mary Custis were here. I haven't seen her in such a long time."

"She is always off visiting somewhere. Her father worries she may be wearing out her welcome among our friends and family. Her tendency to rely so heavily upon the generosity of others distresses me."

A knowing smile lit Charlotte's face. "As does Rooney's impulsiveness. He has told me so, many times. It's no secret that you and the general thought we were too young to marry."

"I'm sure Mr. Wickham had his reservations, too, about a daughter marrying at so early an age."

"I have always been grateful that you both gave your blessing anyway. Rooney has proved a most satisfactory husband. He is industrious and thoughtful and kind. We have our son. And soon another child. When this war is over we shall be sublimely content."

Lu, one of the servants, came into the parlor. "Letter for you, Mrs. Lee."

"Which Mrs. Lee?" Charlotte asked.

"Mrs. General Lee." Lu handed me the letter. "It just now come for you, Missus. They's a package come for Miss Agnes too. Reckon I'll take it on up to her." She turned toward the door. "Supper's gone be ready in a little while."

She left, and Charlotte rearranged her pillows. "Is it from the general? What does it say?"

I scanned the letter. "Northern troops may come up the Pamunkey River to try to take Richmond. He says we should all get out of the way." I let the letter fall into my lap. "I am thoroughly tired of running."

"But we must think of the children. We can't sit here and risk being trapped behind their lines."

"Of course not."

I returned to the letter. "He thinks I ought to come to Richmond. He says, 'I can soon make arrangements for your comfort and shall be very glad of your company.'"

"He sounds awfully lonesome," Charlotte said. "I think it would do him good to have you with him. What do you think, Mother?"

"I must think about it." I read the last of the letter. "He says to sell the corn and the wheat as soon as it can be harvested."

"Yes, he wrote me the same last week. I have asked the overseer to take care of it, but who

358

knows whether he will take me seriously. He doesn't like taking his orders from a mere woman."

"Nevertheless, you are mistress of White House. If he won't listen, then we shall be forced to dismiss him."

"And replace him with whom? Able-bodied men are scarce as hen's teeth these days."

Agnes pounded down the stairs and rushed into the parlor. "Guess what? Orton Williams has sent the most charming letter. And he's sent his Bible for safekeeping."

Charlotte smiled. "Is it my imagination, or is love in the air?"

Agnes blushed. "He is awfully handsome and just as kind as can be. Don't you think so, Mama?"

Oh, the high hopes I had for my sweet Agnes. At twenty-one she was at the height of her beauty, an openhearted young woman full of life and promise. Clearly she was smitten, and nothing would have made me happier than a match with Orton.

"I'm going to put his Bible in my trunk." Agnes fairly floated toward the stairs.

"Supper soon," I said.

"I'm not hungry," she sang.

I was still at White House in April when Robert wrote that General McClellan's forces were on the move and urged me again to leave. *There is no telling from what quarters the enemy will proceed,* he wrote.

I hated the necessity of abandoning the simple home where George Washington had married my great-grandmother, but I once again packed my things and prepared to depart for Marlbourne. Its owner, Mr. Ruffin, an admirer of my husband's, had kindly offered to shelter me and the girls.

The carriage came for us on a bright May morning sadly reminiscent of the lovely spring day just one year earlier when I had left Arlington.

The girls climbed into the coach. "Are you ready, Mama?" Annie asked.

"Not quite. I'll be right back."

"Where are you going?"

"To leave a note for the Northerners."

Agnes laughed. "I doubt the cretins can read."

I scribbled the note.

Northern soldiers who profess reverence to Washington: Forbear to desecrate the home of his first married life, the property of his wife, now owned by her descendants.

I signed it *A granddaughter of Mrs. Washington* and pinned it to the door.

The driver helped me into the coach.

We drove out of the yard and onto the road. I couldn't look back, but Annie did, and her eyes filled with tears. "Oh, I really wish from the

360

bottom of my heart that the Yankees were all in the infernal regions!"

I didn't bother to chide her, for I could not have agreed more.

★ 37 ★
MARY

Just months after my departure from White House, General McClellan's forces stormed the property. They seized the few remaining servants as contraband, pillaged the house, and burned it and the barns to the ground. Some time later I received a note from one of the Northern soldiers professing his protection of the house, but the pile of rubble spoke for itself. I could only pray to live long enough to see a day of retribution.

Even before I learned of its destruction, I wrote to Robert requesting that he make arrangements for me to join him in Richmond. But now I was behind enemy lines and needed an escort to pass through them to the city. Major Roy Mason was dispatched to meet me at General McClellan's headquarters.

The general was nearly twenty years younger than my fifty-four years, and such a handsome man—thick dark hair, a luxuriant mustache, pleasantly even features—that had I been young and a Yankee woman, I might well have enjoyed his attention.

"I trust you had a comfortable journey, Mrs. Lee." He bowed slightly and motioned to his aide, who left the room and returned momentarily with a tea tray.

"As comfortable as can be expected under the circumstances."

He poured a cup of tea for me, but I left it untouched. "My husband has assured me of safe conduct to the Confederate capital."

"Of course. I thought you might like to rest awhile before you go on."

"Thank you, but I haven't seen my husband in more than a year. I should like to continue on as soon as you can manage it."

He nodded. "I have arranged for a carriage to transport you across the Meadow Bridges. Major Mason will remain with you until you are safely on the other side."

The major came into the room. "I'm ready when the lady is, sir."

The journey took me across the bridges and along a narrow winding road to a cluster of farm buildings set beneath a stand of old trees. As eager as I was to see Robert, when the carriage finally rolled to a stop I felt a moment of misgiving.

I had missed my husband terribly. I longed for the comfort of his daily companionship. But a solid year of constant uprooting and travel along with my worsening rheumatism had taken their toll. I was plump now, and gray haired. Daily I grew more firmly convinced that the South had been right to resist Northern tyranny. I worried that Robert would find me too much changed.

"Here we are, Mrs. Lee," the major said. "Gooch's farm. General Lee will meet you here and take you on into town."

He helped me out of the carriage. And then there was my dear Robert, coming lightly down the farmhouse steps, a smile on his face, his arms spread wide in welcome. I was shocked at the change in him. His hair and beard were snow white. His entire countenance, which had always been youthful, now reflected the enormous weight of his responsibilities. But his bearing as he descended the steps was regal, his gray uniform impeccable, his black boots polished to a high shine.

Beneath the shade of an old hickory tree, we embraced.

"Dear Mary." Robert drew apart to peer down at me. "I have been very anxious for your arrival. I couldn't sleep last night for thinking of it. Did the enemy treat you all right?"

"General McClellan was most solicitous."

"Very good. Our hosts have prepared dinner."

"I'm not hungry. I would rather go on to Richmond and get settled."

"So would I, but I don't see how we can refuse their hospitality."

Taking my arm, he led me up the steps and into the house, where we were met with warm greetings and a surprisingly elegant repast. As soon afterward as was polite, we thanked our hosts and continued into the city.

I expected to share Robert's quarters at the Spottswood Hotel, where he had established his headquarters, but I soon learned there was no room for me there. Richmond was overrun with refugees from across Virginia and elsewhere. Every house was filled to overflowing. Some had been converted to makeshift hospitals, forcing people to bed down in churches, abandoned schoolhouses, and outbuildings.

Robert had arranged rooms for me at a plain wooden two-story house on Leigh Street. He saw to my trunks, kissed my cheek, and returned to his work. I sank into my chair, feeling deflated. After so long a separation I had hoped for a few hours alone with him, but the first great lesson of my marriage had been that duty would always and forever come before personal pleasures. I could do nothing but wait for him.

As the summer unfolded I met my neighbors, Mr. and Mrs. Caskie, who had a house at Eleventh and Clay Street. Their daughter Norvell was a lovely young woman, fond of fashion and of bantering with Robert when we dined with them. Mildred was back at school in Raleigh, and the other girls were visiting in North Carolina. I missed their endless chatter and took pleasure in Norvell's talk of clothes and books and the handsome young Confederate officers who came and went from the city in an ever-changing parade.

One morning I was occupied with my knitting and only half listening as she described a wedding she had recently attended. Word of the burning of White House had just reached my ears, and I was too angry to think of such trivial matters as weddings and the latest styles in hats.

Custis came up the walk and knocked at the door. He had been ill and was taking care of his papa's many requests while he recovered.

"Mother?"

"Come in, son."

Custis bowed to Norvell. "Miss Caskie, I trust you are well."

"I am. And how are you? I was just telling your mother about a lovely wedding that took place here last Saturday."

I put down my knitting. "Custis, I found your father's other pair of spectacles. He left them here one evening and forgot them. I suppose you ought to send them as soon—"

"Mother, I have come with terrible news."

I steeled myself for the worst. "Your father—"

"He is fine, so far as I know. I've had a letter from Rooney." Custis knelt beside my chair. "It's the baby. He caught a cold, a severe one, Rooney says, and he did not recover."

Norvell rushed to my side. "Oh, Mrs. Lee, I cannot imagine how difficult this is for you. Your poor little grandson. Is there anything we can do?"

Custis rose. "I'm certain your gentle ways and bright company will be a balm to my mother's spirits, Miss Caskie. Especially as my father cannot come home just now to comfort her." He patted my hand. "I'm sorry I can't stay, Mother. You ought to write to Rooney. He is convinced his daily sins are the cause of this calamity."

I went at once to Hickory Hill to offer Charlotte whatever solace I could.

In late August I returned to Richmond. The house on Leigh Street seemed strangely quiet. Daughter had come and gone, and so had my husband, who was now encamped near Orange Court House.

Mrs. Caskie invited me to tea, and I was glad for the distraction. We had just concluded our light repast when a visitor arrived. Mrs. Caskie went out to the porch to greet him and then brought him inside.

"Mrs. General Lee, this is Dr. McCaw. He is chief physician at the hospital up on the hill."

The young doctor pressed my hands most warmly. "I have heard many lovely things about you, Mrs. Lee, since your arrival here. Mrs.

Caskie tells me you have turned your house into a veritable sock-making factory."

"One must have some useful occupation to pass the time, and my husband is constantly asking for more socks for the men in the field. It's only a small thing, but the men seem to appreciate it."

"Dr. McCaw, please do sit down," Mrs. Caskie said. "We've just finished our tea, but I can make more if you like. It won't take a moment."

He perched on the edge of a horsehair settee. "Thank you, but I haven't much time. I've come to ask a favor."

Mrs. Caskie joined me on the sofa, her hands folded in her lap.

"I'm sure you have read in the papers that the number of patients at Chimborazo continues to grow as this war goes on," he said. "Most of my patients are sick rather than wounded, but that doesn't mean their needs are any less important."

Mrs. Caskie said, "My husband says we might find ourselves caring for more wounded if the fighting increases. He says the presence of so many railroads serving Richmond virtually assures we will receive some battlefield casualties."

"It's possible. But my present situation requires many more hands to look after the soldiers we already have. My staff of physicians is adequate, but they can't spend as much time as is needed in simply visiting with the men. Listening to their stories. Helping them write letters home."

I thought of my husband and my own sons—all of them now in the service of the Confederacy—who might at any moment find themselves sick or wounded, alone and far from the comforts of family and home. "How may I help you, Dr. McCaw?"

The young physician beamed. "I hoped both you ladies might use your influence to encourage others of your acquaintance to visit my patients on occasion. It would certainly free up the doctors' time, and the presence of a lady always elevates the atmosphere of any place."

"I will help in any way I can," I said. "I would like to visit the men myself."

"So would I," Mrs. Caskie said.

"Splendid." The doctor got to his feet. "I ought to get back to the hospital. I cannot thank you ladies enough. Come anytime. Whenever it suits you. The men will be delighted, and my staff will be deeply grateful."

"My goodness," Mrs. Caskie said when he had gone. "I do hope we can help those poor men. When do you suppose we might visit? I will see about getting a carriage for us."

"I promised Robert twenty-five pairs of socks weeks ago, and I have hardly begun to knit them. Perhaps when they are finished."

"Let's plan to go then. I'll ask Norvell. I'm certain she will want to do her part."

I returned home just as Perry Parks, the

Arlington servant who had accompanied Robert to Richmond, arrived.

"Miss Mary!"

"Perry. I didn't expect to see you here."

"The general sent me back from Gordonsville with Custis. We got to catch up to Mr. Robert this evening."

"How is he?"

"Tired out some, after overseeing General Longstreet and General Hood. From what I know, they been busy cuttin' the Yankees' railroad lines and such. I look after him best as I can."

"It's good to see a familiar face from home. How are you?"

"I was feelin' poorly shortly after Malvern Hill, but the general nursed me back to health. I tol' him if he ever gets tired of soldierin' he might find work up at that hospital up yonder. I tol' Mr. Robert couldn't any doctor have done no better." He fished a letter from his pocket. "Custis said to bring by this letter that come for you this morning. He said he woulda brought it himself, but he's busier than a long-tailed cat in a room full of rockers."

I glanced at the envelope. "It's from my daughters."

"How is young Miss Mary, and Miss Agnes, and Miss Annie? And Miss Mildred? I surely do miss them. I miss ever'body from Arlington."

"Oh, Perry, so do I. All were fine, the last time I

heard from them. Mildred is at school. Daughter just left to visit friends at Cedar Grove. Annie and Agnes are in North Carolina. It has been awhile since I had a letter from them."

" 'Spect you're wanting to read it, then."

Perry set off down the street. I went inside, removed my bonnet and gloves, and opened the letter.

August 25, 1862
Jones Springs, North Carolina

Dearest Mama,

Two weeks ago our precious Annie was stricken with typhoid. We are presently at Jones Springs which we hoped might offer a more efficacious climate for her recovery The doctor at first prescribed the usual treatment—cold baths and the blue fever pills. She rallied for a time and begged me not to tell you and Papa, knowing how this news would worry you. She is failing. Last evening the doctor returned and prescribed brandy and cream mixed with morphine. I sit with Annie day and night and I pray hourly for her recovery, but I think you had better come.

Give love to Papa and my dear brothers when you see them and to Mary and Mildred when you write. I heard Mary was in Richmond but Mrs. Hardin, a friend of Mrs.

Caskie's, was here last evening and said she heard Mary planned a visit to Cedar Grove. Please hurry.

Your daughter,
Agnes

A train was quickly outfitted for my use, and I arrived in North Carolina to find Annie still alive but wracked with palpitations and violent fevers that lasted for hours. Agnes had grown so thin and pale from looking after her sister that I feared for her well-being too.

"Oh, Mother, thank God you have come in time."

Agnes led me into a dimly lit room where Annie lay shivering despite the summer heat.

"She has been like this for days. Last night I slept beside her to keep her warm, but nothing seems to help." Agnes fell into my arms and began to sob. "I know we are supposed to pray 'Thy will be done,' but she is only twenty-three. Too young to die."

I bent over Annie's bed and called her name.

"She can't hear you, Mama. The fever has made her deaf."

Agnes touched Annie's hand, and Annie opened her eyes.

"Mama." It was a mere whisper in the silent room.

"Yes. I'm right here."

Agnes glanced at the clock on the fireplace mantel. "It's time for her morphine. The doctor says to give it to her every hour." She mixed the drug in a small glass with a bit of brandy and cream.

We lifted Annie so that she could swallow, and soon she closed her eyes.

"She will rest for a few minutes now." Agnes collapsed into the chair beside the bed.

"When was the last time you ate anything, child?"

Agnes shrugged. "I don't know. The days and nights all run together. She has been so sick these last days I have barely had any sleep."

"Is there food in the house?"

"Some eggs, I think. Maybe some milk."

"I'm going to make you something to eat and then I want you to sleep. I will watch over your sister while you rest."

"But you are exhausted too. I know the trip was hard on you, Mama, but I didn't know what else to do."

"You are too young to shoulder such a burden alone. You ought to have sent for me sooner."

"Annie begged me to wait. She thought she would get better." Agnes closed her eyes. "But I admit I am tired."

I made my way to the kitchen and prepared a supper for the two of us, then I sent Agnes to bed and took up my vigil beside Annie. Between prayers for her recovery, I wiped her face and administered the morphine and wished for my husband's steady arm. But we were alone in the long dark night, Agnes and I, with no one to help us save God.

As the bright days of autumn crawled by, Agnes and I settled into a routine. She looked after Annie in the daytime, and I took over at night, alone with my thoughts and fears. I didn't know where Robert was or how to reach him. But sending for him would have been futile, for he was engaged in a cause more important than any one family, even his own.

Annie lingered, semiconscious, until very early in the morning of the twentieth of October, when she opened her eyes. Agnes came to my room to wake me. "She wants her hymnbook."

In that moment I dared to hope the fever had broken and she would be well again. But by the time I dressed and got to her room, I could see the end was near.

Annie turned her head on her sweat-drenched pillow. Her small hand lay atop the hymnbook resting on the yellow counterpane. She clasped mine. "You are still here, Mama."

"Where else would I be when my little girl needs me?" I spoke aloud, though I knew she couldn't hear me. In that moment I recalled such precious memories from her years on this earth. Her bright laughter, her inquisitive mind, the way she and Agnes complained loudly and often about attending school at the "Staunton jail." Her sweet and innocent attentions to the cadets at West Point when she was still too young to court them. Now she would never know the joys of marriage and the comforts of husband and home.

Her face twisted as the pain hit her, and she shivered violently.

Agnes brought the morphine, then climbed beneath the covers to try to keep Annie warm. "Oh, Mother, she is going. I can feel it. What can we do?"

I took Annie's cold hands in mine and pressed them to my chest. "She is in the hands of God. He will do all things well for her."

Annie opened her eyes. "Mama, I am ready to rise."

The mantel clock emitted seven soft chimes. And then my darling Annie was gone.

We braided her hair and laid her out with flowers gathered from the garden. A friend offered his own cemetery plot, and there we laid her to rest.

Agnes packed our trunks. With hearts made even heavier by the necessity of leaving Annie behind, we returned to Richmond.

I never learned precisely how the news reached Arlington. I supposed Perry must have gotten word to his father. Somehow the news was delivered, and in early December I received a letter from Selina.

November 25, 1862
Arlington, VA

Dear Miss Mary,

There is no one this side of heaven who can know how much your heart hurts at the loss of your Annie. And there is nothing I can say that will ease the pain. Tell the general and the rest of your children that everyone here grieves with them. Miss Annie's smile always reminded me of a light in the window of a dark house, how it could make you seem less alone when you looked at it. I have no doubt she is making some corner of heaven brighter now. But I don't suppose that will bring you much consolation. Any mother expects to pass on ahead of her own children, and I imagine this is a shock that will only grow less so with time.

You were the one who told me how a book can brighten the darkest of times, and when I heard Miss Annie had passed I got out the poem book you gave me when I was just a girl. Do you remember? In it was a poem which is too long to copy the entire thing, but I send you a few lines in hopes they will somehow comfort you.

Everything at Arlington is the same. Soldiers everywhere. The house dark and still of an evening. We had a snow the other night, the first one this winter, and I thought about the night you and I went sledding on the hill. I remember we hit a hard bump that lifted us both off the sled and I thought we would go flying off into the snowbank and break our necks, but you held on tight and we got over the bump and the rest of the ride was pretty smooth. I suppose that is what you must do now. Just hold on tight and get over this bump till life brings you better days.

Your humble servant,
Selina Gray

PS: Here is the poem from Mr. WC Bryant, the same you used to read to me when I was small.

And then I think of one who in her
Youthful beauty died
The fair meek blossom that grew up
And faded by my side
In the cold moist earth we laid her
When the forests cast the leaf
And we wept that one so lovely
Should have a life so brief
Yet not unmet it was that one
Like that young friend of ours
So gentle and so beautiful should
Perish with the flowers.

After the loss of my home—which even savages would have spared for the sake of the former association with my father—after the loss of White House with its ties to my Washington kin, after the deaths of my little grandson and my dear Annie—all in the space of a single year, and despite my constant prayers for mercy, the cruel hand of death once more gripped my family. A few weeks before Christmas, Charlotte gave birth to a little girl who developed a lung infection and died before her parents could name her.

Once again I wrote to Robert with sad news.

His letter, written from his camp at Fredericksburg, arrived just as I prepared to leave Richmond for Hickory Hill.

I have grieved over the death of that little child of so many hopes and so much affection and in whose life so much of the future was centered.

I felt the loss too. But my family circle was irretrievably broken, shattered beyond repair. Even the news that Robert intended to free all of the Custis servants at the end of the month failed to cheer me. Their freedom had been the chief object of my life's work, but two years of war and death had rendered me indifferent to joy, numb with grief, and burdened by losses that went too deep for tears.

February 16, 1863
Richmond

My dear husband,
I am worried to learn you are bogged down in such heavy snow and hate the thought of your suffering, and the toll this winter is taking upon your men and horses. I am pleased to know that George has arrived to cook for you and Perry is still there to look after you. The $8.20 per month that you are paying them ought to enable them to lay up something for themselves.

No doubt you have heard our government has passed an impressment act allowing for the taking of supplies and the purchase of crops at a negotiated price. Of course there is no way to enforce it, and the rising price of everything here, from corn and flour to meat and salt, has set everyone on edge. In certain quarters there is talk of rebellion, but I cannot imagine it will make any difference, as Governor Letcher and President Davis seem to be blind to the suffering of this poor old city.

I enclose two pairs of socks. Please use them yourself, my own love, and refrain from giving them away. Every soldier is precious but none more than you, to your countrymen and to your family who cherishes you so.

Your devoted,
MC Lee

I set aside my letter for posting and took up my needles. I was still running my knitting factory, turning out as many pairs of socks as I could between visits to our sick and wounded soldiers. One day at the end of March, as I sat by the window with my knitting, a woman in a tattered blue dress came rushing up the walk to ring my bell. Agnes let her in.

"Mrs. General Lee." Her voice shook when she addressed me. "You don't know me. My name is Minerva Meredith. My husband works at the ironworks. I'm sorry to barge in here like this, but we need your help. That new law they just passed is starving us to death. Our children are barefoot and in tatters. Something must be done."

I could see the desperation in her eyes. But people thought I had more influence than I actually possessed. "I understand, Mrs. Meredith. Everyone is suffering. It isn't fair. But I don't know what I can do."

"Come to our organizational meeting. It's tomorrow at the Baptist church in Oregon Hill."

Agnes, who had been busy making coffee for our visitor, came into the room. "My mother is hampered by rheumatism, Mrs. Meredith. It won't do to have her out in this chilly weather. But I will stand in her place."

"Agnes, I don't think it's wise to—"

"I know I must be mindful of Papa's position, but you would go if you were able, and Mrs.

Meredith is right. Something must be done."

"I will write a note to the governor. But I don't think—"

"Oh, bless you, Mrs. Lee," our visitor said. "He surely will listen to the wife of General Lee. Bless you both."

Agnes gave the weeping woman some coffee and sent her home with a few slices of bacon and a cup of flour from our own dwindling stores.

The next morning dawned warm and fair. Agnes went off to join Mrs. Meredith's meeting, and as I was not expected at the hospital that day, I found my walking cane and took advantage of the fine weather to post my letter to the governor. I was just returning from the very short walk when I heard a commotion in the streets and Agnes calling for me.

"Mama! There's rioting in the streets. Mrs. Meredith organized a march on the governor's office, but when we got there he wouldn't come out to see us."

She ran up the walk, took my arm, and we went inside.

"What happened, child?" I sat down and put my cane aside. "I thought Mrs. Meredith would wait for my note to reach Governor Letcher."

"The men from the ordnance factory came to the meeting, and they didn't want to wait another day. So we met at the statue of General Washington and marched over to the governor's mansion. But he wouldn't come out, so we left.

Mrs. Meredith and Mrs. Jackson and the men started calling out for others to join us. Now they're raiding the warehouses and the stores, taking food and clothes, shoes, even jewelry. The police are arresting people and taking them off to jail." Agnes paused for breath. "I knew it would be bad for Papa if I were thrown in jail, so I came home."

"That was wise." I was exhausted just from listening to her account.

"But I'm not sorry I stood up for them," Agnes said. "And I'm proud of you, Mama, for writing that letter."

"It won't do any good now, I'm afraid."

Agnes collapsed into her chair. "Anyway, it was very frightening, but thrilling in a way. Just wait until I tell Orton."

The riots lasted only a few hours, but for weeks following the arrests, everyone in the city was jittery. Letters from Robert had grown even more sporadic, and my sweet Agnes became increasingly despondent, waiting day after day for a letter from Orton.

By the middle of June the weather had turned fair and warm. Agnes and I took our books and our coffee out to the small garden at the back of the house where a few spindly roses were in bloom. We had just settled down to our reading when a skinny gray kitten wandered in, mewing pitifully.

Agnes picked her up. "Oh, you poor thing. Mama, this little baby is half starved. I'm going to give her some cream."

"If you do, there won't be any for tomorrow, but go ahead, child, if you want to."

Agnes got to her feet. "I'll be right back."

She went inside and I returned to *Les Misérables*. I had forgotten the pleasures of reading in French that I had so enjoyed as a girl, and soon I was so absorbed in the story that it was some time before I realized Agnes had not returned.

Leaning on my walking cane, I got to my feet and went inside. Agnes lay sobbing on the settee, a letter on her lap.

"Darling, what is it? What's happened?"

"Oh, Mama, Orton is dead. He was caught behind enemy lines in Tennessee last week and convicted of spying. The Yankees hanged him."

Sorrow for her and hatred for the lawless Yankees boiled in my veins. Agnes clung to me, keening so brokenly that my own tears fell. I thought of Annie. One daughter was dead in body, the other in spirit. I wasn't certain which was worse.

SELINA

1864

Freedmen's huts sprang up all over the beautiful grounds of Arlington, and besides that the soldiers had a large military school established there. Nothing looked the way it had in the days when Miss Mary was young, with her children playing at her feet.

War news came to us almost every day. We heard when General Lee won his big victory at Chancellorsville in the spring of '63, and we heard the Yankee soldiers cheering in the summer of '64 when General Sherman burned everything in his path on the way to destroying Atlanta. I had heard little from Miss Mary since she weaved a funeral wreath for her own daughter, but one day in October I received a short letter from Richmond. It was two years since Miss Annie had passed from this earth. Mister Robert was desperately trying to hold back the Yankees, but even Miss Mary could see that the war couldn't go on much longer.

I fetched my paper and pencil and sat down to write her back.

November 8, 1864
Arlington, VA

Mrs. Lee,

I received your letter and was happy to hear from you, and I was hoping to see you once more at Arlington but I suppose that is not possible now. I was sorry to hear of Mr. Rooney's terrible troubles. To be wounded in battle and then kidnapped from his own home and taken prisoner was trouble enough. But the news that his wife has gone the way of her two sweet babies surely must be too much for one man to bear, and I know that you grieve for him as well.

Thornton keeps up with all the war news and we cannot help hoping the fighting will soon be over. We have heard of a piece of property in the valley, not far from Alexandria, that he wants to buy and make a farm of it. The house is not much to look at it and he says the land is very poor, but I am anxious to get it. I have done the best I could at Arlington having so many inferior persons to contend with, and I will be happy to have a comfortable home of my own.

My children are well. Emma is a fine-looking girl. She has big dreams of finding a good job in Washington and Annice, too. It will be good when they are old enough to be on their own, as the cabin is crowded as usual and I am once again with a baby on the way.

Remember me kindly to Miss Agnes and Miss Mildred, remember me kindly to Mr. Custis and also to Mr. Robert. I trust I may see the day yet when you will have Arlington, and I hope that I may yet be able to see you as I am very anxious to.

> No more from your
> humble servant,
> Selina Gray

The cabin door swung open and Thornton came in with Annice, both of them carrying an armload of firewood.

"Mama, guess what?" Annice dumped the wood in front of the fireplace and made herself comfortable on my chair underneath the window. "Mister Lincoln has been elected president again. Everybody says this is sure to be the end of the war."

Thornton threw another log on the fire and muttered something I couldn't understand. Ada woke up and began to fuss. I set down my pencil and took her onto my lap, though she was getting too heavy for me to hold, with another child waiting to enter the world. Her braids had come undone and I fixed them back, one eye on my husband. Something was bothering Thornton, but he wouldn't tell me unless I asked. "What is it that's got you worried, Mister Gray?"

"Saw Austin Bingham this morning. He's got his eye on that farm down in the valley. I'm worried he'll buy it out from under us 'fore we can save up what we need."

"Where would he get that kind of money?" Ada was getting heavy, and I shooed her off my lap.

Thornton shrugged. "They say some of the Northerners is willing to make loans to freedmen. I'm thinking about looking into it."

"Huh. What do you reckon those Yankees will want in return? I don't suppose they're making loans simply out the goodness of their hearts."

Thornton eyed me sharply. "I know you're still loyal to Miss Mary and you don't like what the Northerners have done to Arlington. But we got to think of ourselves now. If the Yankees want to help us get our own land, we got to consider it."

"He's right, Mama," Annice said. "Arlington is our past. Green Valley is our future. It's gone happen, soon as the Yankees beat the Confederates once and for all." She got up to pour her papa some coffee. "I don't know why General Lee keeps on fighting now that Mister Lincoln has already freed the slaves. But I surely hope he gets beat, and soon."

I could see the end of the war would be best for everybody. I wanted that place in Green Valley as bad as I'd ever wanted anything. Even if the general's men won and the North lost, wasn't nobody going back to slavery times. I was sure

Miss Mary knew it as well as anybody. But I also knew her heart, and her general's fierce pride. If he lost his war it would crush them both.

Annice brought me a cup of coffee. I held on to the warm cup and watched the fire crackling in the grate. This was another of those times in the long friendship of Miss Mary and me, when getting my own wish would mean Miss Mary couldn't get hers.

★ 39 ★
MARY

Shortly after Dr. McCaw's visit to Mrs. Caskie's, I made my first visit to Chimborazo Hospital. Perched high on a hill on Richmond's east side, the hospital was a city unto itself, with its own soap house and icehouses, a guardhouse, gardens, and stables. An apothecary, a carpentry shop, and a blacksmith shop ensured that Dr. McCaw and his large staff had whatever was necessary to see that their patients, who often numbered into the thousands, received the best of care.

The wooden barracks of the soldiers, first built for military training—some one hundred buildings in all—had been converted into ninety wards, each holding forty beds. I was pleasantly surprised on my first visit by the whitewashed walls and the curtains at the windows, each room adorned with vines or flowering plants.

I soon learned that the true boss of the operation was Mrs. Pember, a no-nonsense widow from Charleston who had taken over as matron and instituted her own set of rules and her own way of doing things. She seemed to resent my presence among her patients, as any visit from the wife of General Lee caused a commotion that took more time to contain than she was willing to invest.

Not wishing to go where I was not welcome, I began visiting the smaller hospitals scattered about Richmond. The ladies of St. James Church had taken up the cause of Miss Sally Tompkins, who had opened a hospital at the home of John Robertson, a local judge. Miss Tompkins welcomed my visits to her patients.

Though hollow-eyed with sickness and sorrow, the men never failed to greet me in the most respectful and gracious way. Their pitiful entreaties tore at my heart, as there was so little I could do for them. But I sat for as long as my rheumatism would allow, reading to them, helping to write letters home, or simply listening to their recollections of happier times. They took such pride in having served under my husband's command. Often they told stories of his care for them—the gift of a warm blanket or new socks from the general's own trunk, a leave granted in the midst of a conflict, a word of encouragement when a comrade fell—kindnesses that endeared him to his men. He felt each one's agony and shared their hardships in his letters home. *Every day is marked with sorrow and every field has its grief, the death of some brave man.*

"Mrs. Lee."

I paused beside the bed of a young man whose limbs were wrapped in bandages. Blood had seeped through the linen and dried to the color of rust. His eyes were sunken and fever bright. He reached for my hand, and I clasped his as tightly as my crippled fingers would permit.

"Mrs. Lee. Will you do a favor for a soldier of General Lee's?"

"Of course, child. Whatever I can."

"It's my mother, ma'am. My sister writes that Mother is deathly sick and wants to see her only son—that's me—before she expires. I put in my request to General Longstreet a month ago, but I haven't heard a word." He grasped my hands so hard I winced. "Can you ask General Lee if I can go home?" Tears coursed down his cheeks. "I just want to go home."

Every refugee and every soldier in Richmond wanted the same thing. The soldier had a duty to his country, yet I could not remain unaffected by his fervent plea. He was no older than my Rob, and his grievous wounds would plague him for the rest of his days. If he survived.

"If I had it in my power I would put you onto

the cars myself this very afternoon. I cannot promise anything, but I will write to my husband."

"Thank you. You are God's own angel, Mrs. Lee."

"What is your name, young man? Where is your home?"

"Henry Lawson, ma'am. From Mooresville, Alabama. It's on the Decatur Road."

I rose from Mr. Lawson's cot and stayed for the rest of the afternoon, reading the Bible to a moonfaced young man from Tennessee, wiping the fevered brow of another from Georgia, spooning soup into the mouth of yet another. The effort tired me to the depth of my bones and robbed me of my last ounce of optimism. But never had I felt more committed to our cause, never had I felt more deeply satisfied.

Miss Tompkins came into the room, her arms full of fresh bandages. According to Mary Chesnut, who knew everyone and everything that happened in Richmond, Miss Sally Tompkins was barely thirty years old. But her tired expression and pale complexion made her seem much older.

"Mrs. Lee," she said quietly. "You're still here."

"There were many who needed a kind word today, and I could see you were too busy with the most critical cases. You are very good with them, Miss Tompkins. Everyone in Richmond sings your praises."

"And yours." She set the bandages on a chair in

the parlor and pressed a hand to the small of her back. "Mrs. Chesnut says you are tireless in your efforts to supply socks and blankets to our soldiers. Three hundred pairs of socks last month!"

"Some of the ladies from St. James have taken up the cause. I could not accomplish half as much on my own."

"Nor could I. They are the lifeblood of this hospital." Miss Tompkins motioned me to a chair. "I don't have any tea, I'm afraid. But there is coffee, if you like."

"Thank you, but I must go. My daughters will wonder what has become of me."

"Shall I have my orderly drive you?"

"If you can spare him."

I left Miss Tompkins to her patients and entered the carriage for the trip home. I had moved to a house on Franklin Street that afforded more room for my daughters and me. I was glad for the additional space, though it meant I now saw less of the Caskies.

Darkness was falling when the orderly drew up at the gate. He helped me out and I crossed the street, leaning on my cane, passing houses still brilliantly lit despite the privations of war. The sound of distant cannon fire from Fort Harrison punctuated the conversation of soldiers milling about on the corner. They stood in twos and threes, smoking and offering up their opinions on the conduct of President Davis, General Hampton, and General Beauregard. Even Robert's decisions were loudly questioned and dissected. It was quite a shame that such brilliant military minds were not employed on the fields of battle, I thought, where their superior judgment would surely have brought a swift and victorious end to the fighting.

Agnes had arrived home ahead of me and set the lamp in the window.

"Mama, there you are!" She took my coat and hat and helped me into my rolling chair. "You are late. I was worried."

I felt a stab of guilt at having caused her any distress. Since Annie's death and the horrific loss of Orton Williams, Agnes had grown quieter and spent more time with me. Mary Custis spent her days going from house to house visiting anyone and everyone she knew.

"Mary has gone to an engagement party for a friend of Mrs. Chesnut," Agnes said. "We are not to wait up for her. And you and I both have letters from Papa."

I rolled my chair to the parlor, every bone in my body protesting even the slightest movement. A trip to the hot springs would have brought much relief, but there was no prospect of such a visit anytime soon.

"Papa is amazed that people in Richmond are still having parties," Agnes said, handing me her letter. "He is quite incensed at such frivolities when half the city is starving."

Richmond was indeed a paradox. Food had grown ever more scarce and expensive. President Davis called upon Virginians in the countryside to send anything they could spare for the refugees. Sausages, pieces of beef, sacks of flour, and tins of lard came to our assistance. Tea was a luxury at twenty dollars a pound. Butter was two dollars a pound when it was available at all. Muslin for dresses cost eight dollars a yard.

Those who had managed to retain their fortunes and those who had profited from the war continued to hold lavish parties—their forced gaiety a defense against the fog of melancholy that hung perpetually over the capital. They seemed unaware of the difficulties surrounding the refugees—the scarcity of food and of decent accommodation, the lack of kitchen facilities. People with plenty of rooms to spare refused to rent them out. Our soldiers in the field were ragged and without proper shoes, a situation that could have been improved had the rent money gone to their aid.

Until the war, unrelenting hardship had been merely an abstraction to me, like something from Mr. Hugo's novel. Life as a refugee in Richmond brought it all too vividly to life. Like many others, my daughters and I ate fatback and field peas and the occasional ham gifted to us as the family of General Lee. We dressed in homespun and calico, our boots worn paper thin, and we turned a deaf ear to those who criticized the conduct of the war. I had no use for such people. They did not belong to our Southern patriots. They were unworthy of a single drop of blood that was shed in their defense.

Agnes brought me a cup of coffee—bitter and black—and the letter from Robert. She removed my shoes and gently massaged my feet. "What does Papa have to say?"

"He is sending one of his shirts for that old soldier at Miss Tompkins'."

"The old Irish gentleman Mrs. McGuire told us about?"

"Yes." I scanned Robert's letter. "He says he can send another shirt if we need it. But he requires a new pillowcase."

"Poor Papa. But where on earth does he think we can find the material for a new one? Mary used the last scrap of muslin to patch her skirt."

"We'll manage somehow. He sends a pair of drawers that need mending too. Listen to this: 'If no sick or wounded soldier requires them, ask Daughter to put them in my trunk.'"

Agnes laughed. "Isn't that just like Papa, to give away his drawers? Do you think any soldier would want them in such a condition?"

"They clamor to own anything belonging to General Lee."

Agnes sat back on her heels. "Yesterday I saw Mrs. Chesnut in the street. She says now that

Lincoln has been reelected, President Davis is worried Grant's forces will overwhelm Papa's. And Papa says himself that Grant is getting ready to prepare some great blow that will finish off the Confederacy."

"We must pray for victory."

Her face clouded. "Forgive me, Mama, but lately God has not paid much attention to the prayers of us Lees." She got to her feet. "You spent too much time at the hospital today and now you are done in. Promise me you will stay home and rest tomorrow."

"I'm all right. And how can I even think of rest when your papa's men are desperate for socks and drawers?"

Agnes sighed. "Even if we had ten times as many ladies helping us, we could not supply all of their needs."

"That is no excuse to do nothing. The Confederacy must somehow prevail."

She regarded me with a most quizzical expression. "Who would have thought the great-granddaughter of Martha Washington would one day become the Confederacy's most loyal supporter? The war has changed you."

Of course it had changed me. No living soul with half a heart could fail to feel anything but outrage toward the Northerners, especially toward that bloodthirsty subhuman savage, William T. Sherman. Not satisfied with destroying military targets such as rail lines and supply depots, he drove women and children from their burning homes and shot their chickens, turkeys, and piglets in the yards where they stood, as if those poor dumb animals were his mortal enemies. He torched churches and desecrated cemeteries, for no purpose other than to demoralize a broken and defenseless people. He laid waste to Atlanta and continued his march to the sea, destroying everything in his path. He cared nothing for the rules of warfare or for the suffering left in his murderous wake.

Is it any wonder I had begun to dwell more upon the crushing hardships of the Southern people and less upon the ancestors my father had taught me to revere? Such shameful conduct hardened my heart against the Union in a way I had once thought impossible. In the face of so much senseless savagery, the Southern cause became fully mine.

"The war has changed us all, Agnes, though not necessarily for the better." Suddenly I was famished. "What have we for supper, child?"

"Beef soup and bread. I'll bring you a tray. You stay put."

"Kindly bring my pen and paper too. I met a young soldier today who needs my help in getting home."

"Papa can't spare anyone who might soon be well enough to return to the front."

"This young man is not likely to see further

action, and General Longstreet seems to have lost his request for leave. I promised to ask your papa for his help."

Agnes smiled in a way that reminded me of my lost Annie. "You never give up, do you, Mama?"

"It's something I can do for good."

The war entered its fourth year with no end in sight. Following our crushing defeat at Gettysburg, Robert had warned President Davis that a long siege would strain his remaining troops to the breaking point. Men were dying, and there were none to replace them. Since February the legislature had debated whether Virginia ought to emancipate all the slaves in order to press them into military service. The debate spilled over into my sock-knitting circle one morning in March when Mrs. Winkler—no stranger to strong opinions —stormed into my parlor, her cheeks blazing.

"You cannot imagine what I've just heard, Mary." She nodded briskly to Norvell Caskie and Agnes, sat down, and took out her knitting. "General Forrest himself has decided we ought to let the Negroes fight right alongside our boys. As equals! Whatever is that man thinking?"

"My father said we cannot afford to care for the color of the arm that strikes the invaders of our homes," Norvell said, "even if using the Negroes to help us win the war would rob us of our victory. But honestly, I am so tired of war I don't care who turns up to fight with us. So long as it is over soon."

"What does General Lee say about this?" Mrs. Winkler turned her penetrating gaze upon me. "I know he tells you everything."

"Not everything. He must be mindful of his letters falling into the wrong hands. But he has made known his support of arming the Negroes, regardless of the effects such a move might have upon our social institutions. He has long believed that slavery must end."

"And Papa has paid the price for his views," Agnes said. "The Charleston newspaper called him a 'federalist and a disbeliever in slavery.' It's true Papa thinks slavery must end, but even the *Examiner* has questioned his loyalty to the South. And after everything he has sacrificed for the cause. I know we aren't supposed to hate anyone, but I can't help it. I despise anyone who questions my father's decisions."

Setting aside her work, Agnes went to the kitchen to get our coffee. Presently she returned with the tray, and Norvell helped her pour.

"People can talk all they want to about our precious social institutions," Norvell said, taking up the conversation again. "But, Mrs. Lee, if we can't win at Petersburg, and soon, then nothing will matter at all."

"My husband has proposed a plan to President Davis."

Agnes set down her cup and unwound a new

ball of yarn. "The problem is that the president is having too much fun giving parties to listen to my father."

Robert had suggested to President Davis that we abandon Richmond to the Yankees, concentrate our dwindling forces farther north, and make a stand there. But the president hesitated, and by April 2, Communion Sunday at St. Paul's, it was too late.

I woke to a hazy morning that obscured the bursting of shells in the distance, a sound that had become so familiar I scarcely took note of it anymore. Church bells rang out across Richmond as the haze gave way to a brilliant sun and thousands of people headed for services.

Every pew at St. Paul's was filled. There were women in widow's weeds, a smattering of government officials, and Confederate officers in their dress uniforms.

"Look, Mama, there's Miss Tompkins from the hospital," Agnes murmured. "The poor thing looks worn to the bone. And there is Mrs. Winkler, just behind the president's pew."

I followed her gaze to the opposite aisle, where President Davis had just taken his seat. He wore a fine dark wool suit, a white shirt, and a black tie. Apparently he had taken plenty of time to consider his wardrobe and complete his toilette. Too bad he hadn't given equal attention to my husband's advice.

Our rector, Dr. Minnigerode, gave the call to worship. From the corner of my eye I spotted a Confederate messenger sliding into the side door. He handed a note to the sexton, who hurried over to President Davis and handed him a telegram. The president read it, and even from my pew I could see the color drain from his face. He got to his feet and hurried from the church, his aides at his heels.

At his departure, a kind of quiet desperation descended upon us. Dr. Minnigerode struggled to complete the Communion service. We remained in our seats until the final prayer was uttered, but our thoughts were for our country. And by our country, I mean the South.

The service ended. We rushed from the church. Out on the streets, chaos reigned. The sidewalks outside the government buildings were piled high with burning documents. White ash and curling pages blew across the streets. Men were packing railroad cars with crates of records and the contents of the Confederate treasury. Families carrying their belongings mobbed ticket offices, seeking a way by boat or by train out of the city. Banks were overrun with people taking out their cash. As the city emptied, the streets became choked with panicked people, horses, wagons, and carriages.

"Mama, where shall we go? Is there any word from Papa?" Agnes helped me into the house and into my rolling chair. "I'm so scared I cannot think."

I was too angry at President Davis to be afraid. And I was not going anywhere. The end of the Confederacy was at hand, and Robert would expect to find me here. And after four years as a refugee, I was too exhausted to move again. Even if the worst happened, I no longer cared. "Where would we go, child?"

"I don't know. But we can't stay here."

"We can and we will."

I directed Agnes to lower the window blinds and seal the shutters. We sewed our few remaining valuables into the linings of our homespun skirts. Agnes made toast and coffee, but we were too frightened to eat. We sat in silence, listening to the ever-increasing commotion in the streets.

About seven o'clock that night, Mr. Winkler knocked on the door. He and his wife had secured passage on the same train that would take President and Mrs. Davis to Danville.

"You are sure you won't come with us, Mrs. Lee? It would be my honor to look after you in the general's absence." Mr. Winkler shook his head. "I am afraid this city will descend into chaos in another few hours. There's bound to be looting and fighting, and there won't be anyone to stop it."

"You're very kind, but we will be all right here. You must go and look after your own family."

"I don't like to bring this up, but there's talk the Yankees may arrest Southern sympathizers. I wouldn't put it past them to arrest the wife of the Confederate leader."

"Nor would I. Nevertheless, I have made up my mind to stay."

He sighed, whether from relief or genuine regret I could not say. "We may never meet again, Mrs. Lee. But my family will pray for God's mercies for you and the general."

He went out into the street and left us to the terrors of that awful night. Orders had been given to burn our tobacco warehouses, and in the dark of night this was done. When the wind shifted, the flames quickly spread across the city. The old timbers upon which many of Richmond's buildings rested split and burned, sending bricks and glass flying. Agnes and I huddled together in the shuttered house, listening as doors of houses were ripped away and chimneys collapsed.

Before dawn, the house next door caught fire, the orange flames licking the wooden door and the porch railings. I had been half asleep in my chair, too frightened to lie down, and the smell of smoke roused me. "Agnes, fetch the water bucket. Hurry, child."

She ran for the bucket, and I wrenched open the door. A wave of heat blasted our faces.

"Get back, Mama." Agnes dashed outside and

tossed the water onto the fire. The old wood popped and hissed.

Twice more she filled the bucket and doused the timbers. The fire went out, but we were too unnerved to sleep. We passed the rest of the night watching from the window as the glow of larger, more distant fires devoured the city.

In the morning we ventured outside where a steady breeze, still thick with smoke, blew cinders that stung my eyes. Soldiers moved about the deserted streets, retrieving bodies from the rubble of collapsed buildings. Refugees were picking their way through the piles of ash and debris, searching for whatever might be salvaged. Everywhere there were charred buildings, smoldering fires, piles of brick and glass, soot and ash. Our soldiers were leaving, marching toward the river and over the Mayo Bridge, the only one remaining in all of Richmond. When they were safely across, that bridge too was destroyed.

Later that morning the Yankees arrived. They lowered the Confederate flag and raised the Stars and Stripes. In the shadows of our ruined city their band played "Yankee Doodle" and "The Star-Spangled Banner," just to make certain we knew we were now an occupied city. As the day wore on, women arrived at my house on Franklin Street, their eyes red with weeping, seeking reassurance that Robert would somehow repulse the Union and win the day. But I harbored no such hopes and had no words to comfort them.

A Yankee captain came up the walk and rapped at the door. "United States Army!"

Agnes got to the door first. "We well know who you are, sir. What do you want? We haven't anything worth stealing."

"I am told this is the home of Mrs. General Lee."

I came up behind Agnes, my clothing rumpled, my eyes still burning. "I am Mrs. Lee."

He removed his hat. "I am ordered to post a guard here, ma'am, for your protection." He summoned a young Negro man who left his mount at the gate and started up the walk.

"I appreciate your concern for my safety, Captain, but under the circumstances, I wonder whether posting a black man to guard the family of the Confederate general is the right thing to do. Some might misinterpret it, I fear."

He blinked and raked a hand across his chin. "You may be right about that. I hadn't thought of how it might look."

He sent the black man back to retrieve his horse, and soon another young man made his way up the walk to take up his post. He stood there all day and all night, and in the morning when I woke he was still there.

"Agnes, take that poor boy something to eat."

"Let him starve. I hate Yankees. I shall hate them till I die."

I hated them too, in the abstract. But this soldier,

so pale and thin in his too-large uniform, was hardly more than a child.

Agnes took him some corn pone and bacon and some coffee, for which he thanked us most kindly.

"Where are you from, young man?" I asked.

"Ohio, ma'am." He wiped his mouth on his sleeve. "But I haven't been home in over a year." He handed me his dishes. "I sure do thank you, Mrs. Lee. For what it's worth to you, I don't think there's a Union soldier anywhere who doesn't admire your husband. He is a mighty warrior. Even General Grant says so."

A week later a report reached us that Robert—aided by our son Rooney—was still in pursuit of the enemy, still refusing to be vanquished. Robert was reported to be in good spirits.

But General Grant wrote to him, seeking peace, and Robert, knowing he had run out of time, soldiers, and options, agreed to surrender his army.

The two met on April 9, Palm Sunday. All of Richmond wept for hours at the news.

Later many newspapers would praise Robert as a peacemaker, calling the surrender his finest hour. But I knew him as others could not. A long military career had prepared him for any eventuality except defeat. Regardless of praise, surrender would be the harshest ordeal of his life.

On the day Robert arrived home, after a grueling

ride of more than a hundred miles, the streets were lined with admirers who had stood for hours in a strong April shower waiting to see him. Women ran into the street to hand him baskets of food, garlands of flowers, scented handkerchiefs. Men wept openly, their hats in their hands. Little boys stood in awe, their hands raised in salute as Robert, accompanied by Rooney and a procession of twenty riders, guided his beloved Traveler through the ruined city.

Custis had arrived home the day before, and now he stood at the window with Agnes and me, watching for Robert to make his way through the throng to Franklin Street.

At last we spotted him, sitting erect in the saddle and looking every inch the professional soldier, though his trousers and boots were caked with mud. He reined in and dismounted with such difficulty that I feared he would fall.

"Custis, go help your father into the house."

"He would hate that, Mother. He must come in under his own steam."

The crowd followed Robert to our door, where he handed Traveler's reins to a weeping bystander. He mounted the steps, turned, and raised his hat in acknowledgment.

For a moment he stood silhouetted in the open doorway. Then he squared his shoulders, came inside, and shut the door. Agnes burst into tears, flew into his arms, and covered him with kisses.

He held her close, patting her shoulder and murmuring to her until she quieted, then he stepped back and opened his arms to me. Sorrow was carved deep in the lines of his face, but never had he seemed more beautiful. Virtue exists independently of victory, and never had he been more exemplary.

I fell into his arms, my tears falling fast. The entire fabric of our marriage was woven of partings and homecomings. There had been no sadder parting than the day he rode away from Arlington to join the Confederacy, no sadder homecoming than this.

Rooney rushed in, disheveled after his long ride in the rain, his face ashen.

Robert turned and placed a hand on our son's shoulder. "Fitzhugh, I—"

"Papa. I just ran into a Yankee colonel in the street. He says somebody has shot Lincoln."

★ 40 ★
MARY

1865

As Lincoln's funeral train wound its slow way toward Springfield, Robert wrote to our friends, seeking a quiet little house in the woods where we could live in peace. He was exhausted, his spirits low, his prospects uncertain. He was fifty-eight years old, no longer a military officer, and stripped of his citizenship. The question of what to do with the rest of his life loomed just as large as the need to find a permanent place to live.

In early June an offer came from Mrs. Cocke, the mistress of Oakland, who invited us to be her guests at Derwent, a small cottage on the estate. We packed at once and took the canal boat from Richmond to Cartersville. From there a rough, jostling drive of about six miles brought us to the house. Lying just a few miles south of the James River, it was a retired little place with a straight-up house. The only beauty it possessed was a fine growth of oaks surrounding it. It had been rendered habitable, but all the outbuildings were dilapidated, and the garden was a mass of weeds.

The lower level comprised two rooms and a kitchen. Upstairs were two more rooms too small to accommodate five adults in anything approaching comfort. The cottage was stuffy and, according to Robert, hotter than a field tent in August. But he needed someplace quiet, and the quiet at Derwent was so profound I could number the acorns falling from those splendid oaks that overshadowed it.

Agnes spent her time looking after me, keeping me company when Robert went out for his solitary rides on Traveler. She was still so heartbroken over Orton, so quiet and sad that she scarcely noticed the heat and the isolation. But for poor Mildred, Derwent was a trial. At twenty, she was a lively and pretty girl with no friends about, reduced to a lonely existence reading novels and tending the chickens.

One afternoon when Robert returned from a long ride, I brought up the subject of our future.

"Mrs. Cocke is very kind, but we cannot prevail upon her hospitality forever." I brought his tea, and we sat by the open window, hoping for a breeze. "Our daughters need a permanent home."

Robert tossed his riding gloves onto a vacant chair and heaved a sigh. "What would you have me do, Mary? I agree this is not the ideal situation, but our future must be guided by circumstance."

In that moment he seemed so discouraged and all seemed so dark that I was tempted to think Agnes was right, and God had indeed forsaken us. I was sorry that I had troubled my husband by raising the question. "You're right. Something will turn up. It must."

He shook his head. "I expect to die a pauper. I see no way of preventing it. If only I can get enough for you and the girls, I am content."

Summer came, and Robert was offered several positions at large salaries.

"Perhaps you ought to consider the offer from the insurance company," I ventured one night. It was too hot to sleep, and we lay in the dark listening to the sawing of cicadas in the grass, our borrowed bed linens going damp in the heat.

"What do I know about such an enterprise?" Robert turned his pillow over to the cooler side. "I couldn't contribute anything useful. They only want my name, Mary, and the Lee name is not for sale."

Then one day Judge Brockenbrough, the rector of Washington College in Lexington, rode in with a letter inviting Robert to become president of the college. As desperate as we were for an income and a home of our own, I was not in favor of it. For one thing, the salary was only fifteen hundred dollars a year, and for another, I had not forgotten Robert's unhappiness during his years as superintendent at West Point. Washington College, which was, according to the judge, practically insolvent, with an outmoded curriculum and a dwindling enrollment, did not seem any more promising.

"I know it seems we have little to offer you, General Lee," the judge said. "But the trustees intend to provide a president's home that will be erected according to your specifications, and we intend that Mrs. Lee shall have the lifetime use of it."

I knew then the deal was sealed, for nothing had worried Robert more than the question of how to provide a suitable home for me and his three daughters. His entire life was a response to the call of duty, and now his foremost duty was to his family. And though I prayed daily for my girls, it seemed unlikely that any of them would find good and honest men to love them as I was loved. The war had taken all but the very old, the very young, and the infirm.

The judge went on. "Further, the trustees pledge their support in your reorganizing the course of study as you see fit, and in the disciplining of the students. You won't encounter any interference from us, sir."

Robert turned the letter over and over in his hands. "It's a kind offer, and I shall give it my most serious consideration."

"We hope to have a new president installed for the fall term, General." The judge got to his feet. "I do hope we may have your answer soon."

With a courtly bow to me and the girls, he descended the steps and rode away.

"Well, Molly, what do you think?" Robert sat down next to me and clasped my hand. "Would you mind very much being the wife of a college president?"

I reminded him of his years of discontent at West Point. "If you are happy, I will be satisfied. But you ought to be certain such work will not be too disagreeable."

At the end of the month he wrote to the college, accepting their offer, and in mid-September he swung up on Traveler for the four-day ride to Lexington. I remained at Derwent with my daughters until November, when Rob arrived to escort us to our new home.

"Good news, Mama," Rob said, kissing my cheek. "Custis has joined the faculty at VMI, so he will be right there in Lexington to help you and Papa."

The prospect of having my firstborn so near cheered me, for I wanted nothing more than to gather up the tattered remnants of my family and mend them, to make them as whole as it was possible to be.

We boarded the boat and arrived in Lexington on December second with Daughter and Mildred.

"Mary." Robert held Traveler's reins in one hand and handed me a box of chocolates with the other. "There are no roses blooming this time of year, but I wanted to welcome you home."

I squeezed Robert's hand and reached up to stroke Traveler's face. The horse rewarded me with a hot, grassy snuffle that made us laugh.

Robert looked around. "Where is dear Aggie?"

"Helping Mrs. Cocke close up Derwent. She will be along presently."

Mary Custis and Mildred came ashore and kissed their father. Rob settled me into the carriage for the short ride to the college.

By the time the last of the trunks was unpacked, Christmas Day was upon us.

A letter from Selina arrived.

412

We had a better harvest this fall, Mrs. Lee, and were able to save quite a bit toward buying our land. We bought small gifts for all our children this year which were greeted with much excitement as I am sure you can imagine. Do you remember the fun we had at Arlington trying to catch each other out for Christmas gifts? How often do I remember those days and long to see you again.

I wished then for one quiet afternoon with my old friend, talking over times gone by. I regretted the great burden I had placed on her shoulders. I still had the few dollars I had sewn into my hem during the last desperate days in Richmond. It was the only money under my personal control and the only currency that was worth anything. The defunct Confederacy was bankrupt; the bonds the government had issued were worthless. I took my threadbare dress from the clothes press and ripped open the hem.

December 25, 1865
Lexington, VA

Dear Selina,
We are settled at the college. All of my children except for Rooney are here for the holiday. You can imagine how their presence cheers me, yet the empty places at our table bring sadness, too, to this holy season.

Yesterday Custis and Rob went out to cut greens for the house and I was reminded of our many Christmases at Arlington. Of the days that are no more.

I am much encouraged that you are planning to purchase the farm. Nothing can ever repay your courage and loyalty to me and to Arlington, but perhaps these few Yankee dollars might hasten the day when you will have a home of your own.

With kind remembrances
to your family, I remain
yr devoted friend,
MC Lee

"Mama?" Precious Life wedged herself into the corner of my chair. "What's the matter? Why are you crying?"

I tucked away the letter. "Oh, don't mind me, child. I'm just an old woman in mourning for the past."

"You aren't old! But, oh, I miss Arlington too. I know Papa is excited to have a job at last, but Lexington is so dreary. And I simply detest those Federals at the garrison. I think they make a fuss about the freedman's bureau sometimes just to embarrass Papa."

Mary Custis and Agnes came in, their faces smudged with flour, aprons streaked with gravy.

"We did it, Mother," Daughter announced. "We made Christmas dinner by ourselves."

Agnes grinned and dropped a curtsy. "Dinner is served."

Mildred summoned Robert from his reading, and soon we were gathered around the table. Robert said our blessing, and for a moment it was possible to pretend that the war had never happened. That sweet Annie had never died. That Arlington was still mine.

If the trustees had thought that in hiring Robert Edward Lee they were getting a mere figurehead, they were soon disabused of that notion, for he threw himself into the improving of his college with everything that was in him.

His duties gave purpose to his days, and though I sometimes glimpsed a fleeting look of sadness in his eyes, he seemed content. Daily there came numerous requests for photographs of General Lee, for a snippet of his hair, for one of his buttons. And as he was very busy from morning till night, I attended to those requests. William Burke had written from Liberia with such a request, and one morning in autumn I received his thanks for my response.

August 16, 1867
Mrs. MC Lee

Dear Madam,
    I received your letter by the ship Goleanda, which afforded us all much comfort to hear from you and your family and many friends

415

and relation. We regret exceedingly to learn from your letter that you are still a cripple from rheumatism. We are glad to hear however that your health is good. Mr. Fitzhugh Lee I have no doubt will find the White House a pleasant place to live as it is a pretty place. I am glad to learn that your youngest son Mr. Robert Edward is such a prosperous farmer. Remember me kindly to these young gentlemen of yours and tell them I shall never forget them and that they have our best wishes. Remember us also kindly to the young ladies. Accept our thanks for the likeness of yourself and the general. Robert Edward is quite proud of it and calls it his Gen Lee. He is a remarkable fine child. He will be four years old the 9 of September.

The Gen looks about the same except that his beard seems to be frosted as though he had passed through many severe winters. Since my last attack of sickness old age begins to show itself very plainly in my beard and head. I shall be forty-eight the 8 of Sep'ber. I am able to preach once on Sabbath and to attend to a Bible class in the afternoon and look after my apprentices during the week who are learning the business of tanning and shoemaking. I have quite a number of coffee trees growing and I hope to send the Gen some coffee from my farm before long. Rose is quite busy all the time, having cows to milk and 18 in the family to look after. She is quite complaining at this time as she is expecting in a week or two. Mr. Gurley writes me that Ephraim is dead and that my mother is still living. I wrote to Selina but have not heard a word from her. Rose joins me in the kindest remembrance to yourself and the Gen and all the family. Please write as often as you can and tell us all the news.

Yr humble servant,
Wm. C Burke

I pictured my mother then, and thought of how happy she would have been to read William's letter, to know that despite those who criticized us and the work of the Colonization Society, we had made a difference in the lives of the Burke family. I could never repine of our actions that led to this result.

The years rolled on. Much was happening at the college. Enrollment was up, and the school was again solvent. Construction was completed on the new house. At Robert's request, large porches wrapped around the sides of the house, so that I might take advantage of the pleasant weather from the confines of my rolling chair. The house had running water for every purpose and a furnace with air ducts that brought welcome warmth to every room during the winter. Dear old Traveler and his equine companion Lucy Long were ensconced in a fine brick stable attached to the house. The milk cow had her own outbuilding, as did Mildred's many cats. At the rear of the property sat a woodshed and a greenhouse.

My daughters adjusted to life in a small mountain town. Occasionally young men from the college would find the courage to call at the house, at which time Robert and I ceded the parlor to the young people and occupied ourselves with our books in the dining room.

One evening in late September two students came to call on Precious Life and Agnes. Fitzhugh and Rob had recently returned to their farms after a visit to us. Mary Custis was on another of her extended visits to our Turner cousins.

The weather was lovely, cool and clear, and Robert opened the bay windows in the dining room, from which we watched the lengthening shadows fall across the lawn. The campus was quiet. In the distance the old bell in Washington Hall tolled the hour. I sighed at the beauty of it.

Robert looked up from his book and smiled. "Are you happy, Mary?"

"I am content."

"There is a difference."

"Yes. I still dream of Arlington."

From the parlor came the sounds of our daughters and their young men harmonizing as Mildred played the piano.

Robert closed his book and stared out the window for a long time. Since the war he had come to believe that taking a military education had been the greatest mistake of his life, and often he lapsed into pensive reveries upon which I rarely intruded.

But that evening I said, "A penny for your thoughts, my love."

"I am thinking of my responsibility to almighty God for these hundreds of young men. Five years have gone since we arrived here, and there is still much to be done."

"The trustees are pleased. The students revere you. You have saved this college from financial ruin. I would say you have acquitted yourself very well."

"Perhaps, but sometimes I wonder whether I can be certain of my acceptance into heaven."

"Oh, Robert. You need not fear. A more upright and conscientious Christian never lived."

"Thank you, Mary. But I'm afraid I won't live much longer, and I will leave too much still undone."

On that golden September evening I did not feel as if he could die before me, and I was selfish enough to wish that I might be spared such a loss. My life was of so little consequence compared to his, and nothing could add to his estimation in the hearts of his countrymen.

"You are tired and working too hard, that's all."

He watched two students hurrying toward the chapel and chuckled to himself.

Relieved at his sudden change of mood, I said, "What are you thinking?"

"I was recalling last Friday's chapel service. You know the rector's words are never among the briefest of human utterances."

"He does tend to go on and on."

"Friday he prayed over us for so long, classes were delayed. My faculty were quite annoyed." He turned to me, his dark eyes twinkling with mischief. "Would it be wrong of me to suggest that he confine his morning prayers to us poor sinners at the college, and pray for the Turks and the Chinese and the other heathen some other time?"

We laughed and returned to our books until the clock chimed ten. Then he rose and went into the parlor. The music fell silent, and I heard the sound of the window blinds being lowered.

"Good night, young gentlemen," Robert said firmly, sending our callers on their way.

A week later on our regular church evening, a terrible storm commenced, and continued during a very protracted vestry meeting. The general had been so unusually occupied all day that he'd had no time for any recreation except a little snooze after dinner in his armchair.

When I went into tea at seven he had not returned from the vestry meeting, and I sat down with my sewing to wait for him, one eye on the raging storm outside, my ears attuned for the sound of his return.

Half an hour later he came in, and I heard him put his hat and coat in his room. He came into the dining room where our tea awaited.

"You have kept us waiting a long time, Robert. What have you been doing?"

He stood at the foot of the table to say grace but did not utter a sound as he sank back onto his chair.

"You look very tired. Let me pour you a cup of tea."

He made no reply, but simply looked at me with an expression that alarmed me.

"Custis!"

Our son came in, took one look at his father, and knelt beside his chair. "Are you all right, Papa? What do you want?"

When Robert made no reply, Custis sent for Dr. Madison, who had been at the vestry meeting. A few minutes later the doctor arrived, along with Dr. Barton, and they both bent anxiously over my husband.

Dr. Madison asked for cold compresses and hot applications for Robert's feet. The doctors began undressing him, and he was perfectly able to help pull off his things, but he couldn't speak.

"What's the matter with him?" Custis spoke with the doctors while my daughters and I hovered near Robert's bed.

"More than likely an attack precipitated by over-strained nerves," Dr. Madison said. "After a good rest he ought to be good as new."

But after sleeping continuously for two days and nights, Robert was no better. My daughters and I took turns sitting beside his bed, speaking to him in softest tones and holding his hand. Mildred had always been his greatest comfort, and with increasing urgency she tried to revive her beloved papa, regaling him with stories of her school days in Raleigh and reminding him of the many teasing letters he had written to her.

"Remember my pet squirrel Custis Morgan?" she asked one afternoon, silent tears slipping down her cheek. "Remember when he got out of his cage and you told me to hold his head under water or else make squirrel soup?" She rested her head on his chest. "Remember when you wrote to me that your pet rattlesnake had died? Say you remember it, Papa."

She looked up at me with such desolation in her eyes that my own tears began to fall. I sent her to her room to rest and took her place beside the sickbed.

Days passed. The doctors gave him medicine, which roused him somewhat. In those lucid moments I sat beside his bed, talking to him of our children and of the good wishes for his recovery that had come in from around the country.

The following Saturday he greeted me with an outstretched hand and kindly pressure. "Mary."

I took his hand. My hopes revived. "You look much stronger today. Before you know it you will be good as new and riding out on Traveler. He has missed you."

A terribly sad look crept across his face then. He shook his head slowly and turned his face to the wall.

On Sunday night he suddenly became insensible and lay in that condition until Tuesday, when all hope was relinquished. I called for my children and we sat up all night, every moment almost expecting it to be his last. He lay breathing most heavily and, the doctor said, entirely unconscious of pain. It was a terrible night, everyone frightened and in tears.

Custis handed me a cup of tea. "I think we ought to send for the Reverend Pendleton."

The minister arrived and knelt with us around Robert's bed. We recited the prayer for the sick. Afterward I sat with Robert's hand in mine, all moist with heavy perspiration, until about nine o'clock in the morning. Mildred went for Dr. Madison. He simply looked at Robert, shook his head, and walked away.

"Mama," Custis said quietly. "Why don't you lie down for just a little while? You will make yourself sick just sitting here."

Agnes agreed. "Let me help you get into bed.

We will come and get you if there is any change."

"At least have some tea and change your dress," Precious Life said. "It will make you feel better."

I allowed her to help me to my room, where I had tea and changed my dress. I was gone but for an hour, and when I went back Robert had begun to struggle for breath. After two very severe struggles, his breath seemed to pass away gently, and he then lay cold and insensible.

Custis kissed his father's cheek. He went into the hall and retrieved his coat and umbrella. "The girls will stay here with you while I telegraph Fitzhugh and Rob."

"All right."

"Where is Mary these days?"

"Kinloch."

"I'll wire her too, but I doubt she can get here in time for the funeral."

"Typical." Agnes wiped her eyes. "Mary never loved Papa as much as we do. She won't even care that the most wonderful, kindest, and most handsome father in the entire world is gone."

"Agnes, don't criticize your sister, please. Not now."

"Sorry, Mama, but it's so hard to refrain."

Robert's hand was growing cold in mine.

"Please leave me now. I want to be alone with your papa."

"Of course," Precious Life said. "But we will be right outside if you want us."

I sat in the silence as the morning wore on. My mind moved in reverse across the many years with Robert, back to our shared childhood at Arlington, back to the joy of our wedding day, to the thousand small kindnesses Robert had shown me during all the years of our marriage. Rosebuds at my breakfast plate. Strong arms lifting me when I was too weak to walk. Sweet words comforting me in the deepest night. His unfettered delight in his children. The extraordinary sacrifice he had made for the Confederacy.

I couldn't think of a future without him in it. With the extinguishing of his breath, my life had shed the last vestiges of meaning, for everything in our house was always done with a reference to his comfort, his wishes. Now there was no object in having anything done.

Outside, the bells at Washington Hall tolled.

Custis returned. "I've sent for Mary and the boys." He placed a hand on my shoulder. "The news is out, and the whole city has gone into mourning for Papa. You had better prepare for another stream of visitors."

A torrent of tears fell onto that most noble face as I bent to kiss Robert for the last time. I had never so truly felt the purity of his character as in that moment, when I had nothing left to me but its memory.

"Good-bye, my dearest love. My own heart. Good-bye, beloved warrior."

★ 41 ★
MARY

1873

The newspapers took note of my return to Arlington and were effusive in their praise.

> Mrs. Lee is a lady whose noble character and Christian graces render her an object of reverence to all who meet her. Mrs. Lee conversed upon the matter of her lost home without one single expression or shade of bitterness.

No shade of bitterness. Did they suppose I had forgotten for a single moment that my home was taken from me without any conscience or common decency, despite the countless kindnesses my father showed to the Northern people?

Let them think what they will. I will never be resigned to the loss of Arlington. If justice and law are not utterly extinct in the United States, I will have it back.

This is the story I tell myself. Hope, after all, is the comforter of the wretched. But death's swift scythe—so keen and unsparing—had taken so many who were so dearly loved.

It was my husband I missed most. He was a

bright star that moved in its singular orbit, bringing light and warmth to my darkest days. Without his strong arm and loving heart I lost much of the will to fight. It was lassitude and not capitulation that accounted for my seeming acquiescence to common thievery.

During my long absence, whenever I thought of Arlington in its present condition, it seemed like a terrible dream. Daily I had been almost maddened by accounts of fallen Union soldiers being interred on my own property. The dear old house was rarely out of my thoughts either waking or sleeping, until the longing to revisit it became almost more than I could endure.

Perhaps I ought to have been content with my memories. But memory is a treacherous thing, and in the end I felt I could not die in peace until I had seen Arlington once more. With Rob and a carriage full of Fitzhugh cousins, I went home.

Beneath a brilliant summer sky we drove through familiar hills stained with lemon-colored light, the rattle of the carriage wheels startling flocks of sparrows that lifted and winged above the river, black against the sun.

Rob buried his nose in the latest edition of the Washington City newspaper. My cousins nattered on about subjects of no consequence, attempting to draw me out of my melancholy reverie. But I could think of nothing but Arlington.

The scent of lilacs coming through the carriage

windows transported me across the years to mornings in the dew-drenched rose garden with my mother, to the humming of insects in the whispering grass and the press of the sun on our heads as it spread its light across the gray surface of the river.

I thought of crisp October mornings on horseback with my father, the woodsmoke curling from the chimneys of the servants' quarters, the surrounding trees resplendent in the mellowed luster of autumn.

Rob folded his newspaper and set it aside. "The papers say the Syphaxes are pressing their claim to the acreage Grandpa left to Maria."

To this bit of intelligence I made no reply. I had managed to keep thoughts of my father's former slave to myself, and to shield my children from the unpleasant truth that had come to light only after his death.

We crossed the long bridge and turned up the steep lane to the house. Filled with a mix of anticipation and disquietude, I leaned closer to the window. The hills where children both black and white had played were stripped of trees and occupied by the Freedman's Village where two thousand former slaves crowded together in idleness. I couldn't help feeling a jolt of anger that all of my efforts to improve their circumstances had borne such meager fruit.

The carriage halted at the door, and I looked

beyond the village to endless rows of graves, the white marble tombstones stretching into infinity. Placed there out of nothing less than pure malice by a man my husband had once called a friend. I felt dizzy and sick with grief.

Rob laid a hand on my arm. "Are you all right? We can turn around and go back to Ravensworth if this is too difficult for you."

His gentle attention calmed my racing thoughts. "No need for that, child. We're here now. I will be all right."

"Cousin Mary?" The youngest of our party, only sixteen, caught my hand. "May we go down to Arlington Spring? Mother says there is a boat landing and a dance pavilion."

"That was a long time ago. I have no idea what is left of it now."

"I remember it, Mama," Rob said. "I'll take them down there."

The cousins spilled from the carriage and headed off toward the river.

Rob said, "Shall I carry you inside the house first?"

But I had no wish to go inside. I sent him off with the others and sat in the carriage, the door open to the breeze coming from the river. Birdsong wafted over the ruined gardens where I had spent so many happy hours with my sketchbook and paint box. Across the river, the half-finished monument to President Washington shimmered in the morning light.

A group of former slaves crossed the yard on their way back to the Freedman's Village, and I thought of Selina. Through many years, the necessary daily contact between mistress and servant had ripened into a mutual attachment. But I feared that despite our continuous exchange of letters, time and circumstance had frayed the bonds of friendship.

"Mrs. Lee."

My eyes flew open, and I realized I had drifted into sleep. And that Selina—as if summoned by a dream—had come to see me.

I was shocked at the change in her. Though I was fifteen years her senior, she looked nearly as old as I. Her hair was threaded with gray, her hands careworn, and her eyes—which had so often glowed with curiosity or amusement or compassion—were devoid of light.

For a moment we regarded each other in silence. Not because there was nothing to say, but because there was too much.

Selina spoke first, and then it was as if all the years that separated us had not happened at all. "I'm glad you came back. I have been very anxious to see you. How are you, Mrs. Lee?"

"Truthfully? I am terribly weary these days."

She handed me a glass of water. "I heard you were coming today, and I came to see you. I thought you might be thirsty after such a long trip. Nothing is sweeter than the water of Arlington."

I made room for her in the carriage and drank deeply of that sweet, cold water.

"I never thought I would live long enough to see you again," she said, blotting her face with her handkerchief. "Then I read in the paper that you were visiting your kinfolks at Ravensworth."

"I should have written to you that I was coming, but I made up my mind at the last minute. I'm grateful for your letters. They have been a comfort to me, especially since the general's passing."

Selina looked out across the river. "It has been a long time you've been gone from here, but I still have hope you will get Arlington back one day."

"Me too. Though so much has changed that it would never be the same. I shudder to think how much more would have been lost if you hadn't stayed on."

"I won't lie, Miss Mary. I underwent a great deal to stay here as long as I did. Your things were taken away by everybody, to the Northern officers in their tents and all over the grounds." Selina shook her head as if she still could not quite fathom their lawlessness. "When they moved away they gave them to the persons that waited on them. The quartermasters and officers took what they wanted."

"Yes, so you said. It pained me terribly to read that letter."

"It pained me terribly to write it."

"I still wonder what happened to my father's bookcase. I promised it to Custis."

"I cannot tell you anything about it. I don't remember seeing it since you left, but I suppose it was carried off like everything else." Selina looked away. "Then the Yankees buried those men in Missus's flower garden just for spite. It was a blessing your mother didn't live to see it. It would have broken her heart."

The day was growing warmer. I held the cool water glass to my cheek. "I don't want to think about it anymore. Tell me about your children. Are they well?"

"For the most part. The youngest had a bad fever last spring, but she's all right now." She paused. "Thornton and I paid off the loan on our land. It's free and clear."

"I'm very pleased for your family."

"It's poor right now, but we made a decent enough crop last year, and we have plans to build it up. Our oldest boy is twenty-one now. He's tall as Thornton, and a big help to his father. Emma is getting ten dollars a month working as a chambermaid in Washington. Sarah too. Annice has been doing nursing the past three years."

"I'm not surprised. Annice always was a tender-hearted child. I remember the way she doctored injured animals when she was small."

Selina chuckled. "Rabbits, coons, birds with broken wings. It seems strange to me that she is

432

on her own now. Time passes so fast it nearly takes my breath away. But I still have four of my children at home with me. Florence is the baby. Seven years old." She shifted on the seat and gazed out the window again. "You probably heard my brother spent some time in the army. On the Northern side. I don't suppose that comes as a surprise to you, though."

Wesley Norris had paid a heavy price for his actions. And so had Robert. But there was nothing to be gained by reopening old wounds. Instead, I said, "Your last born is growing up. I wish I could see her."

"I wish you could too. Florence is a handsome child. Takes after her father."

"You always were crazy about Thornton Gray."

"Ever since the first day I laid eyes on him." A smile stole across her face, making her seem almost young again. "Of course I didn't let on to him how I was feeling. Not at first, anyway."

"You knew exactly how to flirt with him."

"Huh. Everything I know about flirting I learned from you."

We laughed, and it was like old times.

It was growing warm inside the carriage, and Selina blotted her face again. "I saw your youngest boy once, a few years back, and he reminded me so much of the general it gave me a turn." She regarded me solemnly. "I imagine you miss Mr. Robert terribly."

433

"Some days his absence is more than I can take. Agnes and Mildred look after me. And so does Custis. But you cannot imagine how dreary my days are without him."

"But you still have his children to remember him by. And there's hardly a soul in the whole South who doesn't love General Lee. That's got to make you proud."

"Yes, but it was only after his passing that I realized I was not as appreciative of his fine character as I should have been. I wish I could see him once more, to tell him so."

"I remember the day he asked you to marry him." The old light came back into Selina's eyes.

"You cannot possibly remember that. You were barely out of the cradle."

"I was almost nine, and I remember everything. Mauma had been up to the house to get lye| soap for the washing and heard you telling Missus all about it. The news was all over the slave quarters before Mr. Robert rode away that day."

A burst of laughter erupted outside the carriage. Rob and my young cousins were returning.

"Reckon I ought to be going," Selina said. "Thornton will be wondering where I got to."

I handed her the empty water glass, and she got out of the carriage.

"I almost forgot. I stopped by your folks' graves this morning." She reached into her pocket. "Found this piece of green and this rosebud blooming there. It's the same that you planted at your mother's grave."

In my mind's eye I saw the garden as it was then, the masses of rosebuds, the grass steeped in dew, and the bees murmuring in the hedges. And my mother kneeling in the dirt in her faded poke bonnet, forever so gentle and patient with me despite my untamed ways.

Selina reached through the open window and clasped my hand. The years fell away and she was once again my pupil, my housekeeper, and my confidante. My old affection for her came rushing back. "Oh, Selina, I only wish that—"

"I got to go now, Miss Mary. You take care of yourself and don't you be staying out in the cold and damp like you used to. It's bad for your bones."

She briefly squeezed my hand and stood back while Rob and my cousins piled in beside me. The last rose I would ever take from Arlington lay in my lap, a slash of bright pink against the dark silk of my dress. As the carriage rolled down the drive, I looked back to see Selina hurrying down the path, and I thought of one of General Washington's observations, the first I had memorized as a girl. *True friendship is a plant of slow growth and must undergo and withstand the shocks of adversity before it is entitled to the appellation.*

We had known joy, but we had weathered much

adversity. We knew too well the sting of betrayal, the bitter taste of grief.

Many times when overcome by illness and death, crushing defeat and unremitting physical pain, I wondered whether there is any purpose in human suffering. Whether there is any reward for having borne the unbearable. The poet says the wound is the place where the light enters you. Perhaps it's true, and it's only in the broken places that we find healing and grace. I don't expect to learn the answer this side of heaven. Perhaps the hope of perfect knowledge is enough.

The carriage slowed, and I looked back. Selina was growing small and indistinct as we neared the bridge. We topped the hill. She lifted her hand in farewell.

I raised my hand to the window. Good-bye, old friend. Good-bye.

★ 42 ★

SELINA

For weeks after the general died you could read of nothing else in the papers. Emma came to Green Valley to visit one Sunday afternoon a few days after he passed, bringing the *Daily Times*, which contained accounts of mourning all over the South. Sitting in my parlor that looked out over our vegetable patches, I read the dispatches from Richmond and Selma and New Orleans. Everywhere businesses and shipping concerns closed. People draped their doors in crepe and evergreen. Flags flew at half-mast.

People couldn't seem to say enough good things about the general. The governor of Virginia said he filled up the full measure of our conception of a man. Some important judge in New Orleans said he was heroic and honorable and had won the admiration and affection of every heart in the land. Even the New York newspapers that Thornton brought home that autumn called General Lee a noble American. Already there were plans for statues to be put up in his honor.

It was impossible for me to think of him as somebody about to be remembered in cold hard stone, for in life he was full of warmth and light. It is true he caused a great deal of grief and hardship in my family, and that is something I never could forget. Every time I thought of what had happened to Wesley and Mary, I got that same bees-in-the-stomach feeling I'd had as a child. I couldn't blame Miss Mary for what the general had done, but Wesley did. Wesley always said the general had freed him twice, that his rage against all the Lees had liberated him long before that snowy December evening when the emancipation letter arrived.

Still, General Lee had promised my freedom and

kept his word. He was a man who made a hard choice in joining the Confederate side, and he saw it through and lost everything. Even if he was going to be remembered forever with statues everywhere, those statues couldn't make up for what that hard choice had cost him. He and Miss Mary had endured more hardship than comes to most mortals in a lifetime, and their story was still tragic, the same as the Greek heroes you read about in books.

I wrote to her when I first heard the news. It was some time before she replied. I still have the letter saved in the bottom drawer of my bureau.

The kindness of everyone is unceasing but life seems so aimless now, so blank. His memory will be cherished in many hearts besides my own. I may soon follow him, but his children—what a loss to them.

What news is there of Arlington? I long for it still and there is so little hope of my ever seeing it again.

When she finally did come home to Arlington, we sat in her carriage talking over the old times. That sunny June morning when I saw her carriage coming along the road, I remembered all the years when I had stepped from the door of my cabin to cross the yard and enter the back door at Arlington. Taking those fifteen steps separating slavery and freedom—and back again as the shadows of the evening fell across the yard. And all the time the hope of liberation glittering like a brook when the sun shines on it. On that homecoming day we spoke as equals—Mrs. Lee and Mrs. Gray—and not as mistress and slave.

Her appearance that morning shocked me. She looked so old and frail I feared she might not survive the trip back to her kinfolks' house. I thought of a story Althea had told me once when I was a child. There were slaves who lived on an island, and these slaves could predict when someone was about to die because in the dark, sparks of fire would gather around their heads, spirits from the other side coming to guide them. I hadn't seen any sparks surrounding Miss Mary, but it felt like something was gathering around her that day. When I watched her carriage head back across the river, I knew I would never see her again.

"Mother?" Annice stood in the doorway of my home, a bag in her hands. "Brought you some apples from the Green Valley market. Daddy says to tell you he will be home in a little while."

"Thank you, child."

"Are you all right?"

"Fine. I was woolgathering. For some reason Miss Mary has been on my mind lately."

"Oh?" Annice started for the kitchen. "I barely remember her. The papers sure made a big to-do about her visiting here back in June."

"She remembered you, though. She recollected the way you looked after animals when you were little."

China rattled as Annice made coffee. She came back to the parlor with two cups and Miss Mary's blue-and-white pitcher on a tray. I had kept it all those years as my own personal treasure.

Annice lit the fireplace and sat down beside me. "Did I tell you I got a new patient last week? A Mister Morrison. He is a relative of General Jackson's wife, or so they say."

An hour passed while she chattered on. The gray sky outside my window deepened to a silver twilight that settled over the valley. The fireplace popped and hissed. My younger children ran in and out, letting in the raw November air.

Thornton arrived from the market. He set down his empty boxes and came over to kiss me and his daughter. He had grown stooped in the years since we were young and courting by the light of fireflies, and his hair was threaded with gray. But inside, he was the same determined boy with the teasing eyes who had captured my heart with gifts of lace and newspapers when I was just a girl.

"How was the market today, Daddy?" Annice rose to fetch a cup for him.

"Fair to middling. Weather's turning, and that always sends folks home early." Thornton warmed his hands before the fire. He reached inside his jacket and took out a letter. "This came for you, Selina. From Lexington."

I tore it open, anxious for news of my oldest friend. A silver locket spilled out, the same as she wore on her summer visit to Arlington.

November 10, 1873
Lexington, VA

Dear Selina,

I know you will be sorry to learn that Death has visited my family twice in the last three weeks, and we who are left behind are in such disbelieving sorrow that cannot be described. Sweet Agnes left this earth on October fifteenth after an illness of some weeks, succumbing to complications of the digestive system the doctor said. You know Mother loved us all, but Agnes was her favorite and the blow of her death was one from which Mother could not recover. Five days ago she expired quietly and has been laid to rest next to my sainted father in the chapel here, along with Agnes.

You may know that the trustees at Washington College appointed Custis as the new president after my father died. My sister Mary is off somewhere, leaving Custis and me to rattle around in the house alone. Rooney and Rob are settled elsewhere and I do not yet know what my future plans will be.

Before her mind began to wander in her final hours, Mother extracted my solemn promise that I would write you with this news. She spoke often of your long friendship, and she remained until her last breath in your debt for your care of Arlington and the treasures that meant so much to our family and our country.

After my father's death she was often cheerless, but her visit with you last summer seemed to elevate her spirits, and I had hoped that I might have the comfort of her presence a good while longer. But God has seen fit to take her unto Himself and I know she is happy now in Heaven with her beloved warrior who was the chief object of her lifelong affection.

In going through her papers this morning I found a note expressing her wishes that her few pieces of jewelry be divided among her children and her servants. You are not a servant any longer, of course, but I enclose this locket knowing she would want you to have it.

Yours sincerely,
Mildred Childe Lee

It takes a lot to make me cry, but this news wrung every last tear from my eyes. Pain rose up in my chest and wrapped itself so tightly around my heart that I could barely speak. It seemed too much for Miss Mildred and her brothers to bear, that Miss Mary and her sweet girl were gone in one fell swoop. But it is a fact that even the worst pain has a way of eventually knitting itself up, the same as a broken bone. Miss Mary's children would have to go on because life gives us no other choice.

I held the locket in my palm and thought about the past. Which is a different place, a faraway speck on the map of life, and the only way to get back there is in memories. Staring into the crackling fire, I could almost see Miss Mary once again singing to us in the schoolroom, bending down to tend her flower garden, sitting beside the fire with her sewing, waiting anxiously for a letter from Texas or St. Louis or Mexico.

I remembered the way her brown eyes lit up with pleasure on my wedding day and the smell of her dresses when I took them to the laundry—dirt and the oil of roses mixed with paint and lavender. I remembered the hushed busyness outside the birthing room when she brought her babies into the world, and one thrilling ride on a snow sled when purple shadows painted her beloved hills and the nest of stars above us glittered in the winter sky.

She was born into privilege, but it hadn't shielded her from the many great sorrows of her life. I prayed her soul was at peace, and I thanked God for the world of books she had opened up for me on those long-ago days in the sunny schoolroom at Arlington. Knowledge is one kind of freedom, and the only kind she could give me back then. My mother once said anytime a slave learned to read and write it was a miracle. It was Miss Mary who sat me down with chalk and slate and primers brought from Washington City so that the miracle could proceed.

The logs in the fireplace burned down to orange coals. Annice lit the lamps and Thornton went to the door to call our children in for supper. But I sat where I was, Miss Mildred's letter on my lap, and thought about the day when I first stood with my husband on this worn-out patch of ground and we cried like children because the money Miss Mary had sent meant that finally it would be ours.

"Mama?" Annice said. "Come on and eat. Your supper's getting cold."

"In a minute."

I tucked away the letter and the locket and went to the table and bowed my head while Thornton asked God to bless our meal. Life had not been any kind of easy, but I had a lot to be thankful for. The Bible says that even the sparrow finds a home and the swallow finds a nest where she may lay her young. I thought of the slave cabin at Arlington where I had come into the world, where I had learned to be a wife, where I had birthed my own children. There were some good memories mixed in with the bad. But it was not my home. It never was.

A bird doesn't live in the nest where it was born, but in the sky in which it flies.

AUTHOR'S NOTE

This novel owes its existence to two fairly recent discoveries of historical materials. In 2007, a trunk belonging to Mary Custis Lee, the eldest daughter of General and Mrs. Robert E. Lee, was discovered in a bank vault in Virginia. Inside the trunk were several hundred items Miss Lee had collected, including papers, letters, postcards, and clippings. Among the papers was an 1872 letter from Selina Norris Gray, a former slave at Arlington, to Mrs. Robert E. Lee.

In September of 2014, a volunteer for the National Park Service, which maintains Arlington House (now the Robert E. Lee Memorial), spotted a photo for sale on eBay. The seller in England had found it in a box of "unwanted" photos at a British garage sale. The park service volunteer recognized the woman in the photo as Selina Norris Gray. Mrs. Gray had been Mrs. Lee's housekeeper and personal assistant and had taken charge of Arlington and its Washington treasures when Mrs. Lee was forced to abandon her home at the start of the Civil War.

As a student of history and especially of the life of General Lee, and as the author of a number of historical novels, I was thrilled with these new finds and intrigued by Selina's story. At a time when slaves were deserting Arlington, why did Mrs. Lee leave Selina, rather than the white male overseer, in charge? How had such a deep trust developed between mistress and slave? Why did Selina choose to stay when other slaves simply walked away? And how did she come to be recognized as the "Savior of the Washington Treasures"?

At the same time I had recently read yet another biography of General Lee in which his wife was marginalized, criticized, and denigrated. I set out to write this novel with several goals in mind: to bring Mary Anna Randolph Custis Lee out of the shadow of her iconic husband and give her the credit she deserves, and to explore the friendship between Mary and Selina, which lasted until Mary's death in 1873. Just as important, I felt that Selina's story, which is largely unknown outside a small circle of historians, deserved to be told.

From the very beginning of her life, Mary inspires controversy. Almost all historians give her birth year as 1808, but Elizabeth Brown Pryor, who wrote a biography of General Lee as well as Mary's biography for *Encyclopedia Virginia*, gives the year as 1807, the same year that Mary's famous husband was born. One of the Custis family Bibles gives Mary's birth year as 1808, but the last 8 is smudged, as if a correction has been made. Some historians speculate that someone—perhaps Mary herself—changed the date in order to appear a year younger than her husband. In any case, writers of historical fiction must make choices, and I have chosen to accept Pryor's date of 1807 as Mary's birth year, making her just nine months younger than Robert.

General Lee's many biographers have had a field day with Mary; she has been variously described as selfish, spoiled, willful, slovenly, ugly, and dull. Typical of this type of characterization is Emory Thomas's description in *Robert E. Lee: A Biography*. He writes, "Mary Custis proved a liability [to Robert E. Lee]. She was spoiled and helpless and became even more so when confronted with the obligations of being spouse, adult, and parent." He goes on: "Mary was accustomed to having her own way. She tended to center attention upon herself . . . she was disorganized . . . and notoriously late, nor was she especially pretty, in sharp contrast to her husband, who was extremely handsome and seemed important when he entered a room."

From the glimpses of Mary in her husband's biographies, and from her own letters and journals, it is clear that she was not in fact always punctual, nor was she the most fastidious of housekeepers, though Robert noted, "She does try."

As the only Custis child to survive infancy, Mary was sole heiress to her father's extensive holdings and grew up surrounded by servants who saw to her every need. It is likely she was indulged and pampered, but in this she was no different from many other wealthy Virginia belles. She may not have been "especially pretty," but she had several suitors, including Robert E. Lee's brother Smith and Sam Houston, who would become president of the Texas Republic. Smith Lee took his loss in stride, serving as his brother's best man, but Mary's refusal stung Sam Houston; he questioned "the good taste and discernment of Mary Custis, who preferred to tie herself by long engagement to that shy underclassman at West Point when she might have been Houston's bride and the belle of Washington Society."

Far from dull, Mary was exceptionally well educated for the times, mastering French, Greek, and Latin and reading four newspapers every day. She was a gifted painter of the landscapes and people of Arlington, eclipsing her father's talent. One of her watercolors, a 4 x 5-inch study called *Enslaved Girl*, painted in 1830, sold in 2007 to Colonial Williamsburg for its museum collection.

At her father's death she took over the organization of his papers and completed a project he had begun some years before of gathering all of his "recollections" of his stepgrandfather, General Washington—pieces he had published in the paper—into a single volume. Mary added her own memoir of her father, writing with wit and elegance about his early ancestors. She selected an editor, negotiated through him with various publishers, and in 1860 published *Recollections and Private Memoirs of Washington by His Adopted Son, George Washington Parke Custis, with a Memoir of the Author by His Daughter.*

Mary and her mother were active in the American Colonization Society (ACS) and sold flowers from their Arlington gardens to support the cause. They were committed to the emancipation of all the Custis slaves and gave up their claim to the Fitzhugh slaves in exchange for a written promise that the children of those slaves would be free. She and her mother taught those at Arlington to read and write (including, presumably, Selina Norris, who was fifteen years Mary's junior).

Organized by Richard Bland Lee (one of Robert E. Lee's uncles), Henry Clay, and Daniel Webster, and supported by President James Monroe, the ACS sometimes purchased the freedom of slaves and outfitted them for immigration to Liberia. Their stated belief was that freed slaves were subjected to such deep racism that they could never succeed in America, and that a new start in Liberia was their best chance at a decent life. In the early 1850s, the state of Virginia appropriated $30,000 a year for five years to support the work of the society. A few other states followed suit.

The famous abolitionist William Lloyd Garrison, who originally supported the ACS, in time became its most vocal critic, accusing the members of more selfish motives. But by 1867, some thirteen thousand freed slaves had resettled in Liberia, the capital of which, Monrovia, was named for President Monroe. Among those thirteen thousand were Custis slaves William Custis Burke, his wife, Rosabella, and their children, who sailed for Liberia in November of 1853 aboard the ship *Banshee*, just as I have described it in the novel. Mrs. Lee continued corresponding with the Burkes at least until the late 1860s. Mrs. Lee's funding method for their trip as described in the novel, however, is entirely fictional.

Mary and Robert were married in June of 1831. Between 1832 and 1846, she gave birth to seven children, all of whom lived to adulthood. In addition to her support of the ACS and her work teaching the Custis slaves to read, Mary taught each of her own children to read and write and prepared them for entry into boarding school. She made all their clothes by hand in the days before the invention of the sewing machine. Despite her own worsening health, she nursed the children through a series of serious illnesses and injuries (one of her sons sliced off the ends of two fingers with a straw cutter, and a daughter poked out her own eye with scissors) and oversaw their religious education.

Mary endured years-long separations from her husband while he served in the Mexican War, in Texas, and in the Civil War. In his absence she reared her seven boisterous children alone. During the Civil War she organized her Richmond neighbors into a sort of sock-knitting factory, turning out hundreds of pairs of socks, which she sent to the general for distribution to his soldiers. The incident in Richmond with the young Union soldier actually happened, another example of Mary's concern for others.

After the war, General Lee accepted the presidency of Washington College (now Washington and Lee University). By this time severe arthritis had confined Mary to her "rolling chair," and she was unable to take part in the many events going on at the college. However, as she had done when her husband was superintendent at West Point, Mary opened her home to groups of students, continued work for her numerous charities, and answered the hundreds of letters that arrived at the president's residence in Lexington seeking some memento of the general.

Knowing all of this about Mary, I found it unfathomable that anyone could charge her with being a "liability" to her husband. And indeed, one of her husband's most famous biographers, Douglas Southall Freeman, paints a very different picture of her. He writes, "Rarely was a woman more fully a part of her husband's life. This fundamentally was because of his simplicity and her fineness of spirit . . . She did not hesitate to voice a fiery opinion in plainspoken terms. She loved wild flowers and old gardens and evening skies . . . A quick and understanding sympathy was shown in her kindly eye and ready smile . . . Loving her, he saw her best qualities and not her worst."

General Lee died in October of 1870 and was laid to rest in the Lee Chapel at Washington College. Their daughter Agnes died three years later, in October of 1873, and was interred beside her beloved papa. Mary never recovered from the loss and died just weeks later, on November 5, 1873.

On November 11, the *Tri Weekly Courier* in Rome, Georgia, printed an obituary of Mrs. Lee:

Intelligence has been received of the death of Mrs. Lee on Wednesday the 5th inst . . . Mrs. Lee was a lady of exemplary conduct and unassuming and gentle character. Her funeral was held on November 7th in the Lee Memorial Chapel. WHF Lee, Custis Lee, and Robert E. Lee, Jr. and her daughter were present besides a large concourse of friends . . . Business was entirely suspended in Lexington yesterday, many places being draped in mourning and the obsequicies [sic] were very imposing.

We know much less about Selina Gray. She was born a second-generation slave at Arlington around 1823 to Sally and Leonard Norris, believed to be among the favorites of the Custis family. The Norrises had at least three other children—Wesley, Mary, and Sallie. At some point Selina was brought into Arlington house and trained as a housekeeper. Later she began looking after Mary, probably as Mary's arthritis worsened.

In 1843, Selina married Thornton Gray, another Arlington slave who is thought to have worked in the stables or carriage house. Born in 1824 he is said to have been part Indian. The Gray family lore has it that Selina and Thornton were married in the same parlor at Arlington where Mary and Robert were married. General Lee's biographer Elizabeth Brown Pryor characterizes this story as wishful thinking on the part of the Gray family, "an idealized tale of warm bonds and powerful connections" between the two families.

There is evidence that Mary and her mother sponsored the wedding of another of the Arlington slaves, providing her with a new dress and bonnet for the occasion. If it's true that the Norrises were favorites of the Custis women, it seems likely that they would have given Selina a wedding too. And since Mary left Selina—and not anyone else—in charge of Arlington when she fled her home in 1861 ahead of the advancing Union Army, it seems that the "powerful connection" between the two women did in fact exist. I have chosen to accept the family's wedding story as true, for the powerful connection between Mary and Selina is the foundation upon which this story rests.

After the death of Mary's father in 1857, abolitionists targeted Arlington and often visited the slaves there to incite them to insurrection. In 1859, Selina's brother, Wesley, and sister Mary joined their cousin George Parks in an escape to Maryland. There they were apprehended and returned to Arlington, where General Lee had them punished quite severely, according to an account Wesley gave to a Northern newspaper some years after the event.

Yet when Mary left Arlington at the start of the war, Selina, who would not be freed until the following year, accepted the keys to Arlington and took charge of the Washington china, paintings, and furnishings Mary had not been able to send ahead to Robert for safekeeping. It was Selina who complained to General McDowell that his men were "stealing Miss Mary's things" and caused him to have those belongings removed to the US Patent Office. Many of "Miss Mary's things" were never recovered, but we have Selina Gray to thank for those belongings of General Washington's that were saved. Reading the account of her confrontation with the Union soldiers, I found it incredibly brave that an enslaved woman would confront a general of the United States Army with the demand that he stop his men from looting.

In December of 1862, as executor of his late father-in-law's will, General Lee freed all of the slaves at Arlington and at the other Custis properties across Virginia. His handwritten manumission letter names all of the Norris family, plus Selina and Thornton Gray and their children, among those being freed. Selina and Thornton had more children after they were freed, and eventu-ally bought ten acres of land near Alexandria where they grew vegetables to sell and where they lived for the rest of their lives. The cupboard and the blue-and-white pitcher Mary gave Selina upon her departure from Arlington remained in the Gray family until a restoration project at Arlington in the 1920s, when Selina's daughters returned them to the house. Selina died in 1907. Thornton Gray is thought to have died around the same time.

Because the cemetery was moved to make way for development, the current location of Selina's final resting place is unclear. However, one of her grandsons, Thornton H. Gray, who served with the US Army in World War I and died in 1943, now lies in Arlington Cemetery, just a stone's throw from the cabin where his grand-mother was born a slave.

Except for the reunion scene near the end of the novel, which is based upon the 1872 letter from Selina to Mary, the scenes between Mary and Selina and between Selina and her family throughout this novel are of necessity wholly imaginary. Otherwise, I have taken care to recount events mostly as they happened. One exception is Mary's discovery of her father's paternity of one of the Arlington slaves whom he freed when Mary was around eighteen years old. It is widely accepted that George Washington Parke Custis acknowledged Maria Carter Syphax as his daughter, freed her, and gave her seventeen acres of land on the Arlington estate, where she reared ten children and lived for the rest of her life. I found no direct evidence that Mary ever knew this about her father, thus the "discovery scene" in the novel is fiction. At his death she described him as "kind and indulgent," and I could well imagine her feelings of disappointment and betrayal had she learned of his shortcomings.

The best clues to one's character and thoughts are those that remain in one's own handwriting. Wherever possible I have used Mary's letters and journals, letters from her family, and Robert's numerous letters to her to tell her story. Mary's writings reveal a woman who could be sharp-tongued when her family was threatened, and critical of the behavior and character of her servants, but who was tenderhearted, committed to her faith and to her husband and children, and single-minded in her support of freedom for those in bondage.

Deeply attached to Arlington, she longed for it whenever she was away and managed to return home so that six of her seven children could be born there. After the war she saw Arlington only once more—in June of 1873. Just five months later she died without having regained ownership of her "dear old house." After her death the courts agreed with her son Custis that her home had been taken from her illegally, and it was returned to him. Unable to pay for its upkeep, Custis sold it back to the government and divided the proceeds with his four remaining siblings.

Reading Mary's words, I was moved by her sense of loyalty, her resilience, and her faith in the face of prolonged and profound loss. And indeed, as Freeman writes, "They [Mary and Robert] needed all the love and all the faith and all the self-mastery they could develop, for they were to endure more tragedy than is measured out to most mortals."

During the research for this novel, I visited Arlington. I was deeply moved to see Mary's gardens, the family parlor where she was married and where Robert announced his fateful decision to stand with Virginia when the war came, and the upstairs rooms where their children grew up. I saw the bedroom Mary and Robert shared and the small attached dressing room where her children were born. I stood on the porch that overlooks Washington and the Potomac River, the scene of so many of Robert's departures and homecomings, imagining Mary's sadness as he rode away and her joy at seeing the top of his carriage once again rising into view.

Behind the house, just steps away from Arlington's back door, stands Selina's cabin. I couldn't help wondering what she thought each day as she took those fifteen steps from her house to Mary's. History does not record what she thought about her situation, but I imagined her as her knowledge expanded, feeling loyalty to Mary and yet reaching toward freedom.

With *Mrs. Lee and Mrs. Gray*, I hope to illuminate the lives of these two remarkable women and to honor the fifty-year friendship they shared.

SELECTED BIBLIOGRAPHY

In addition to numerous magazine articles and scholarly papers, here are a few of the many books I consulted in writing this novel:

Dowdy, Clifford, and Louis H. Manarin, eds. *The Wartime Papers of Robert E. Lee.*

Flood, Charles B. *Lee: The Last Years.*

Haley, James L. *Sam Houston.*

Korda, Michael. *Clouds of Glory: The Life and Legend of Robert E. Lee.*

Lee, Eleanor Agnes. *Growing Up in the 1850s: The Journal of Agnes Lee.* Foreword by Mary Custis Lee deButts.

Lee, General Fitzhugh. *General Lee: A Biography of Robert E. Lee.*

McGuire, Judith W. *Diary of a Southern Refugee during the War by a Lady of Virginia.*

Pember, Phoebe Yates. *A Southern Woman's Story.* Introduction by George Rable.

Pryor, Elizabeth Brown. *Reading the Man: A Portrait of Robert E. Lee through His Private Letters.*

Thomas, Emory. *Robert E. Lee: A Biography.*

Winik, Jay. *April 1865: The Month That Saved America.*

Zimmer, Anne Carter. *The Robert E. Lee Family Cooking and Housekeeping Book.*

DISCUSSION QUESTIONS

1. Which aspects of the friendship between Mary and Selina did you find most interesting or surprising?

2. What role does Arlington house itself play in the story?

3. Both Mary and Selina are bound by family ties, conventions, and expectations. How does this help or hinder their friendship?

4. Selina remains loyal to Mary despite harsh treatment of her family members. What might account for this?

5. How do Mary and Selina help each other cope with loss and tragedy? What individual strengths do they bring to the relationship?

6. Mary's courtship and engagement to Robert was conducted mainly through letters and supervised social calls. How did this help or hinder their ability to adjust to marriage?

7. Mary comments that Robert's life was a response to the call of duty. In what ways do Mary and Selina respond to duty?

8. Robert's biographer Douglas Freeman writes that by loving Mary, Robert saw her best qualities and not her worst. What do you think were Mary's best qualities? Her worst?

9. Selina earned her place in history for her courageous actions to save General Washington's belongings. What surprised you most about her story?

ACKNOWLEDGMENTS

I am indebted to the Virginia Historical Society, owner of the Lee family papers, which were invaluable in writing this novel. I'm especially grateful to Frances Pollard, who helped me navigate the archives and pointed me to just the right resources. Thanks also to Lee Shepard for answering my questions about permissions and to Graham Dozier, editor of the *Virginia Magazine of History and Biography*, for his gracious permission to quote from an article detailing Robert Lee's courtship letters to Mary.

The Jackson-Lee papers collected at the Museum of the Confederacy contain General Lee's original letter of manumission of the Custis slaves. I'm grateful that such an important document has been preserved and is available to scholars and researchers.

Sincere thanks to my publisher, Daisy Hutton, who championed this project from the beginning; to my talented editors, Becky Philpott and LB Norton; and to my brilliant agent, Natasha Kern, all of whom provided essential editorial guidance as I worked to shape and reshape the story.

My friend and colleague Catherine Richmond connected me with resources that deepened my understanding of the experience of the Arlington slaves. Thank you, Cathy.

Mrs. Lee and Mrs. Gray is my twentieth fiction project and, like those that came before, owes no small measure of its existence to the encouragement and support of family, colleagues, and friends. I love you all.

ABOUT THE AUTHOR

A native of west Tennessee, Dorothy Love makes her home in the Texas hill country with her husband and their golden retriever. An award-winning author of numerous young adult novels, Dorothy made her adult debut with the Hickory Ridge novels.

Center Point Large Print
600 Brooks Road / PO Box 1
Thorndike, ME 04986-0001 USA

(207) 568-3717

US & Canada:
1 800 929-9108
www.centerpointlargeprint.com